MYSTIC

A BOOK OF UNDERREALM

GARRETT
ROBINSON

MYSTIC

Garrett Robinson

The author greatly appreciates you taking the time to read his work. Please leave a review wherever you bought the book or on Goodreads.com.

Interior Design: Legacy Books, Inc.
Publisher: Legacy Books, Inc.
Editors: Karen Conlin, Cassie Dean
Cover Artist: Miguel Mercado

1. Fantasy - Epic 2. Fantasy - Dark 3. Fantasy - New Adult

Second Edition

Published by Legacy Books

To my wife
Who gave me this idea

To my children
Who just make life better

To Johnny, Sean and Dave
Who told me to write

And to my Rebels
Don't forget why you left the woods

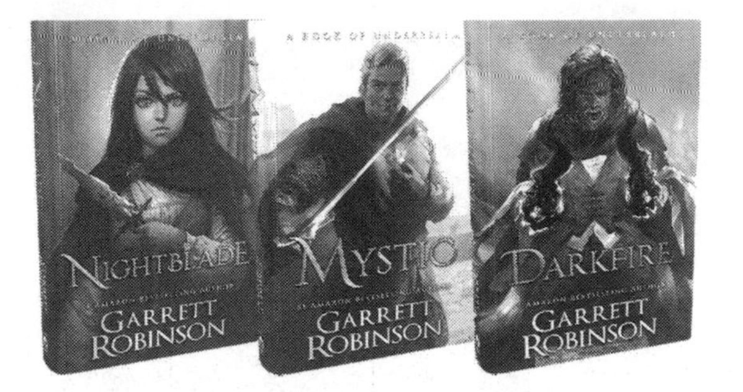

GET MORE

Legacy Books is home to the very best that fantasy has to offer.

Join our email alerts list, and we'll send word whenever we release a new book. You'll receive exclusive updates and see behind the scenes as we create them.

(You'll also learn the secrets that make great fantasy books, *great.*)

Interested? Visit this link:

Underrealm.net/Join

For maps of the locations in this book, visit:

Underrealm.net/maps

MYSTIC

A BOOK OF UNDERREALM

GARRETT
ROBINSON

ONE

The sun broke the horizon east of the King's road, spilling fallow rays across leagues of empty landscape that ran down from the mountains far, far away. Amber light wrapped around the boughs of the forests to the west, painting them a heady mix of green and yellow. A summer sunrise, a golden dawn that promised a warm day with little wind for relief.

Loren greeted the sun with a raised water skin as if in a toast and then placed the skin to her lips to drink.

She had slept little the night before, too wrapped up in thoughts of her dagger and Jordel and, above all, Xain and Annis. The wizard and the merchant's daughter could be anywhere by now, far ahead on the King's road, or lying in wait around the next bend.

Such thoughts spun behind her eyes in endless circles, and in the grey hours before sunrise they had pitched Loren from a restless slumber. So after creeping from camp to relieve herself, she had settled down against a carriage wheel to await the dawn.

From the other side of the carriage she heard Gem's snores, loud and insistent like a saw with rusted teeth. Though thin and wasted, the orphan boy slept, snored, and ate enough for two grown men. Now his noises brought a small smirk to the corner of Loren's mouth—but it could not last long before her face grew solemn once more.

"Thoughts of depth are all the more troubling when dealt with alone."

Jordel's voice, smooth and soothing, shook her from her reverie. She shifted against the carriage wheel, ill at ease. The Mystic sat beside her, folding his legs and pulling his dark red cloak aside to avoid crushing it on the grass. Once settled, he placed his hands upon his knees, staring with Loren into the east. For some moments they sat that way, bathed in sunlight and in silence.

"Not all thoughts bear mention," said Loren at last, uncomfortable with the quiet.

"You alone would know. But rest assured that if they burden you too greatly, I bear a ready ear to share them."

"I am assured of little, and rest comes hard."

Jordel nodded, and again in silence they sat. Normally Loren did not mind quiet, but she was used to the particular hush of a forest, a stillness filled with the murmur of life. She did not have much experience with the silence of another person—other than Chet, with whom no words had been necessary.

Thinking of Chet brought his face into sharp, sudden focus in her mind, and Loren felt a hollow ache in her gut. How long had it been since she saw him last? More than a week. More than two, in fact, but not yet a month. It felt like five lifetimes. The Loren who lounged now against the carriage wheel bore little resemblance to the one who had fled the Birchwood on the heels of a wizard.

Her thoughts went from Chet to Xain, pulling her to the present and to Jordel beside her. In her discomfort she had forgotten his promise, but now it returned to mind. "You said you would tell me of the badge you carry. What is a Mystic? Are you a sort of wizard?"

"No, not that, though we have many wizards within our ranks," said Jordel. "In fact they are prized among our number, and so highly sought after that many think we accept no others. But if that were the case, I would not wear this red cloak."

"It is a . . . Mystic cloak, then?" Loren tried to muster nonchalance, as though she did not burn with curiosity.

Jordel smiled. "We have nothing so uniform as that. I must confess again my surprise that you know nothing of our order. Though we are fewer than we were in past years, we are not uncommon across the nine lands."

"You are rare enough in the Birchwood," said Loren. "Never did I see such a badge of office, or hear of it in any tale."

"Our work sends us among the simpler folk more rarely than I might wish. Still, there might have been tales."

"There were not."

Jordel shrugged, as if that were answer enough.

"What, then, is your purpose? What sends you seeking after Xain?"

Jordel tilted his head, his mouth twisting. "It is . . . difficult to explain, and not all words are mine to speak freely. In the most general of terms, you might say we keep order."

"Like the constables."

"Not unlike the constables. Our dress bears common origin with the red of their leather armor. Some of us might wear a red tunic, mayhap, or breeches. But rarely do we travel in our full regalia. Not all look upon us kindly. And many of our deeds must be done in secret."

"They do not sound like honorable deeds, then," said Loren.

Jordel smiled. "So says the would-be thief."

Loren felt a flush creep into her cheeks. "Tell me of my dagger, that turns your face so grim. What danger does it bring?"

Jordel shifted where he sat. "It is a rare weapon. Well-made, as you have no doubt realized. You would find it difficult to dull the edge, and it will not break without great effort. Only a very few of them were made, crafted by gifted and magical smiths long ago, when Underrealm was but a young place."

"And what have they to do with the Mystics?"

"Your blade is . . . of special significance to our order. Any Mystic would recognize it at once. And if some of our highest members were to espy it, you would be in grave danger. As would any who accompanied you."

"I seek no trouble," said Loren. "I wish no one any harm, and I am no fighter besides."

"I am aware," said Jordel. "And it is something I admire in you. All of us must draw our lines in this world, and the one who will not take a life is not as weak as many would say. But you will find that not all agree with such a course, nor will everyone treat your own life with the same reverence."

"Am I in danger from you, then? Do you, too, see more in my dagger than steel and leather?"

Jordel cocked his head. "I am someone strange among my order. I hold certain of our laws less dear, while some laws I value above all else. I would not kill you for holding the blade, nor would I readily reveal to my brothers that you hold it."

"Nor would you take it from me," said Loren. "You could have done so easily while I slept in Cabrus. Why did you refrain, if it is so terrible?"

Jordel shrugged. "As I said. Some laws, however revered, must accommodate the time we live in. You bear the Mystics no harm; indeed, you did not even know of us until I told you. And while I hope you will cast the dagger aside for your own sake, that decision is yours to make."

"I will not abandon it. It is mine, taken as token of payment for many years of wrongdoing against me."

"By your parents, you mean."

Loren looked at him, surprised.

"You still bear some marks," said Jordel, pointing to her eye. "And if such has been the lot of one so young for many years, those who raised you must have had a hand."

Loren touched the skin around her eye. She had seen it reflected in the water; its nasty blue had faded, but a dull brown remained. "You make a good guess. And for repayment, I have only this dagger and the arrow I planted in my father's leg. But I cannot carry that arrow with me, nor clutch it at night when I remember their cruelty."

Jordel thought upon that. The air rang with Gem's snores. "Very well," he said at last. "Though I pray you will see reason to change your mind while you still can. I warn you again: let as few people see it as you may, and none from my order. If word were to reach them, and they learned where you came from, your parents would feel the full brunt of their justice."

Curiously, Loren's stomach clenched, and she thought of Damaris. The merchant had feigned ignorance about the dagger, but Loren knew better than to believe a word from her mouth. For some reason she could not place, it bothered Loren to think of her parents dragged from their ramshackle hut and put to the question, cruel and stupid though they were. But she said only, "Such justice would be well-placed."

Jordel nodded. "If you say so. Now let us break our fast. Leagues beckon still."

"Wait," said Loren. "Where shall we go now? We do not know where Xain might be, nor Annis. How will we find them?"

"I have thought on that much of the night, when I did not sleep as deeply as you. I think that if the wizard and the girl did not wait, or were forced to move on, then they would have made for Redbrook. It is a riverside town well south of here, where the King's road bends west along the border of Dorsea. In their place, I would make for Redbrook and wait for our arrival, for there are precious few other destinations along the road south from Cabrus."

They rose and made their way to the fire, where Loren roused Gem with a hard shake. The urchin woke bleary-eyed and blinking, and he cursed mightily at the sun as it fell into his eyes.

"In the city we never saw the daylight until we were ready," he groused. "No wonder country folk are half-mad."

They had a quick breakfast of hardtack and bacon, both supplied by Jordel, along with sweet, fresh water from the river that followed the road.

Seth, Jordel's driver, was a crafty man with a criminal look; he had a sharp smile and a cruel laugh that came too easily. Many scars criss-crossed his shaved head from crown to jaw. Loren viewed the man with some apprehension, but Jordel seemed easy in his company.

"I have seen nothing but birds this morn, sir," Seth told Jordel in the middle of their meal. "I have had my bow ready just in case."

"Do you think the constables follow us?" said Loren.

"The constables? No," said Jordel. "But they are not the only ones who seem to bear a grudge against you. The reach of the family Yerrin is long, and their fingers never stop grasping."

"I will cut those fingers off, they poke around us," said Seth.

Gem laughed, but Loren only felt her appetite wane.

TWO

THE ROAD REMAINED CLEAR FOR MANY DAYS, ROLLING down before them as the stream plunged close and then far again. Hours passed dull and slow, broken only by the occasional scampering rush of a startled animal by the side of the road.

At first Gem spent much time marveling at the sights, remarking often on how he had never seen such things within the walls of Cabrus. Every so often he would take in a deep breath for no reason, letting it out in a long, slow *whoosh.* He walked beside the carriage when they moved slowly, laughing as grass tickled his bare feet. He yelped with delight when they saw a quail and her chicks walking nearby, and he would chase butterflies whenever they passed a patch of flowers.

His delight did not last long. Well into the second day they passed an inn, and Gem brightened considerably. But Jordel bade Seth to pass without stopping. "No one must remember our faces," he said.

"What if Xain and Annis stopped at the inn?" said Loren.

"Look at it," said Jordel. "Do you see their carriage? And if I am cautious of letting others see our faces, consider Xain's fear of being recognized."

After that Gem grew quiet, only sitting and looking at everything without comment. Then, early on the third day, he began to complain.

"Loren, I am *bored,*" he proclaimed. "An intellect such as mine was meant for greater feats than sitting quiet in a carriage all day."

"Scholarly pursuits, you mean?" said Loren, hiding a smile.

"Yes, exactly!" said Gem, missing the gibe in her tone. "Soon the grass all looks the same, and the birdsong merely annoys. I may have known every building in Cabrus, but I could at least count on the people to hold my interest. Now there is nothing and no one, only an endless expanse of open ground and a sky that stretches forever. And that *sun!*"

"If you wish, I have a book you could read," said Jordel.

Gem brightened. "Ah! Something at last to stimulate the mind!"

Jordel bade Seth stop the carriage and went into his bags, from which he pulled a heavy leather tome. This he threw into Gem's lap, causing the boy to grunt and rub his stomach where the corner had poked him. But one glance at the title turned Gem's face sour like bad milk.

"A Treatise on the Great Families of the Nine Lands, Their Origins and Lineage," read Gem. He shoved the book away with disgust. "I thought you had something *exciting.*"

"The history of the nine lands has seldom been dull," said Jordel. "There you will find war and death, heroes and villains, and the rise and fall of a great many houses."

Gem looked at the tome distrustfully and pulled it open. Loren tried to peek over his shoulder, but the squiggles on the page might as well have been chicken-scratchings in the dirt. She had never learned to read.

After they had rolled forwards for a little while more, Gem gave a frustrated growl and shoved the book aside. "Oh, certainly there are great men and women aplenty in here. Described with all the vim and vigor of grave markings. *King Learen the Third of Dulmun. He begat three sons and met his end in a hurri-*

cane off the coast of Hedgemond." He snorted and stuck his head out the window to watch the grass roll by.

His complaints continued through the day, occupied most of the next, and then worsened when the forest vanished to the east, leaving only open grassland running to the high mountains far away.

At last Loren wearied beyond tolerance of Gem's nagging, and she did not like the way Seth glowered at the boy, fingering the knife at his belt. She cuffed Gem's head and threw the book full into his chest. "Be silent!" she snapped. "Read the book Jordel was kind enough to give you, and if we hear another peep of complaint, I will tie you to a wagon wheel."

Gem read, with much grumbling and many dark looks from beneath hooded lids. But at least he stopped complaining out loud.

At midday meal, Loren thought of something else to keep him entertained. She went to where he sat on the ground, sullen and staring.

"I need something of you."

He looked up in a pout. "What?"

"You were one of Auntie's best pickpockets, were you not?"

His eyes flashed. "Certainly. She always said so."

"Then teach me."

A slow smile crept across his lips, and he leapt to his feet. "That is something I can do. I warn you, of course, that you should not expect to become so expert as I without many years of practice."

Loren nodded, careful not to smile. "Of course."

"And you must call me master while I train you."

Loren cuffed the back of his head, but gently. "Just teach me."

From then on, Gem became a bearable traveling companion. They could do nothing physical while they rode, of course, but during those times he would tell her tips and tricks he had learned in the years he had spent on the streets of Cabrus. And whenever they stopped, he would have Loren practice. Jordel even volunteered to act as a mark, his back turned while Loren tried to remove a purse from his belt or from a pocket within his cloak.

Loren learned many things she had never considered. "The art," as Gem called it, required more than clever handwork. Often it was best to find a mark who seemed distracted, or whose valuables lay within easy reach. A merchant might have a fat purse, but it would be guarded jealously. The merchant's escort, however, had eyes only for her master, and might have a jeweled brooch or bracelet that could be lifted more easily.

Even Seth grew interested in the lessons after a time, and when he spoke Loren could tell he was no stranger to snatching purses. "Teamwork is best," he growled. "Girl. Tell our urchin what a big, strong man he is. Flutter your eyelids a bit."

Loren stared at him, her mouth hanging open, while Gem grinned at her. "What?" stammered Loren.

"Try, girl," said Seth. "Do your best. Pretend you are a professional."

Loren gulped and looked at Gem. The boy smiled back, clearly enjoying her discomfort. "Er . . . I have rarely seen such large . . . muscles . . . on such a small boy."

Gem scowled. "Is that your idea of a compliment? Calling me small?"

"And there we have it," said Seth, raising his hands. Within them Loren saw Gem's small knife, as well as a purse she never knew the boy carried.

"What?" cried Gem, feeling around his belt and the now-empty scabbard. "How did you . . ."

"Distraction," said Seth. He held the purse and knife just above Gem's grasping hands. "It is better when your partner knows what they are doing, of course, but almost anyone with pretty eyes will do."

Loren flushed and rubbed her arms. She did not much care for Seth's compliments, not with his cruel smile.

One day, when a week had passed, Seth stopped the carriage. Jordel frowned and stuck his head out the window. "What is it?"

Seth's voice came lower than even its usual growl. "Something you ought to see."

"Stay here," Jordel murmured, and climbed out. Loren and Gem gave each other barely a glance before slipping out after him.

Jordel and Seth stood by the lead horse, staring ahead. Loren went to the Mystic's side, Gem lurking just behind and beside her. Many paces ahead of the carriage, the ground lay trampled as though by many feet. The trail cut straight across the road, the grass squashed as far as Loren could see in either direction.

"What did that?" said Loren. "It looks like the passing of an army."

"And a sizable one," agreed Jordel. "Though I told you to stay in the carriage."

"Moving west, if I am not mistaken," said Seth.

"You are not. Pull the carriage off the road. I would know what such a force is doing here in the south of Selvan."

In a short while it was done. Seth found a small thicket of trees surrounded by low shrubs, drew the carriage within them, and hobbled the horses. Jordel discarded his cloak and the longsword he sometimes wore at his belt, pulling from his luggage a shorter blade as well as a long dirk. The short sword he strapped to his belt, while the dirk went into his boot.

"Stay here and wait for my return," he said, cinching the weapons tight. "I will not be long. That I promise."

"I will not sit here and wait for you," said Loren. "I want to come as well."

Jordel smiled. "I spoke to Seth, not to you. In fact, I rather hoped you would come."

Loren started, taken aback. "You did? Why?"

"I have told you many times how our fates seem intertwined, Loren of the family Nelda. You have proven yourself no simple young woman, and useful in situations when most would discount you. Besides, you have said already that you mean to do great things in the nine kingdoms. I would help you learn something of them first. Mighty deeds may be the stuff of songs, but oftentimes a small action is better, if it is guided by wisdom."

Loren flushed and turned to hide her face. "I hope not to disappoint," she said, trying to sound flippant.

"I am sure you will not."

"Very well," said Gem. "If we must be off, let us be off."

Loren and Jordel turned to him at the same time. "I am sorry, master pickpocket," said Jordel gently. "I did not mean for you to come as well. Someone must help Seth guard our carriage."

Gem glared at him. "I am young, but not a fool," he said. "If Loren goes, so will I. Her safety lies in my hands."

"And in mine," said Jordel. "And I will take no risk with it. My decision is final. We shall return swiftly."

He turned away as Gem's expression fell. Loren sidled up to the boy and put a comforting hand on his shoulder. "I am sure it will be boring."

"Do not mock me." Gem's voice was sullen. "It is the first bit of excitement we have had in many days, and you are both leaving me out of it."

"Jordel does not know that you are a mighty warrior," said Loren, nudging his chin with her hand. "And a brilliant scholar."

"And a wise advisor," said Gem, somewhat mollified.

"Give him time."

"He has had almost as much time with me as with you, yet I am excluded."

Loren shrugged. She did not understand much better than Gem, but she thought she might have an inkling of why Jordel requested her presence. The Mystic was most interested in her dagger, and likely he would be loath to let her out of his sight while it stayed on her belt.

But that explanation required too much time, and they had to be off. Jordel beckoned, and Loren left Gem with a final ruffle of his hair. They slipped out through the trees towards the trampled grass, turning to follow it west. Soon the road vanished behind them as they crept between low hills.

"We must stay silent and hidden," murmured Jordel. "You seem to have some knack for stealth. Use it now. I am not looking for a fight, only for information."

"I have never looked for a fight," said Loren. "Though that has not always mattered."

Jordel nodded and led her on. Soon they came to the bank of the river they had been following. There they found signs that a temporary bridge had been constructed for passage, but it had already been torn down. They had to walk a short distance south before they could find a place shallow enough to ford. The bank was silty and loose, and Jordel stumbled once or twice as they slid down. Loren felt no small blush of pride at her own sure footing.

Just after they reached the far bank, they heard a splash behind them.

Jordel whirled and drew his sword. Loren's dagger was in her hand before she could think to draw it. But when she saw the source of the noise, she rolled her eyes and quickly returned the blade to its sheath.

"Sky above, Gem, what are you doing?"

The urchin sat on his rear in the river's shallows. Somehow he looked sheepish and proud all at once. At Loren's hissed words, he raised his chin. "I told you. Where you go, so go I. I waited until Seth stepped away from the carriage and then came after you."

"Go back," said Loren. "We do not know what awaits us."

"Then you do not know that it is dangerous," said Gem. He got to his feet and waded towards them. He was much shorter than Loren and seemed barely half Jordel's height, so the water came nearly to his chest. "I will be invisible, a shadow at your back and quieter than a mouse."

"A large mouse, to make a splash like you just did," said Loren.

She looked at Jordel, expecting to see him looking angry. Instead she found a small smile tugging at his lips.

"It seems mine is not the only fate you have drawn into your own, Loren. And if the boy cannot be kept away, then let him come. But hear this." The Mystic grew solemn again and pointed his sword at Gem. "If you give us away, I will flay you myself. Do you understand?"

Gem placed a hand on the flat of Jordel's blade and pushed it away. "I have been flayed by worse than you. Or I am nearly sure I have." He looked at Loren. "What exactly is flaying?"

"It means he will peel the skin from your body while you watch. I will likely help him hold you down."

Gem swallowed. "You will find me a slippery mouse to catch, if you try." Most of the bravado had fled his voice.

"As long as we all understand each other," said Jordel. "Come. Our quarry awaits."

He set off at once, and Gem splashed out of the shallows to trot along at Loren's heels. They crested one rise after another, following the wide swath of trampled land, so obvious that even Gem could see it easily. But the end of the trail came suddenly, and took them all unawares. Loren led the way up a final hill, and suddenly an army of hundreds stretched out before them.

THREE

Jordel snatched Loren's shoulder and threw her to the ground. She heard the small *thud* of Gem's tiny frame hitting the grass a moment later.

"Hold perfectly still," said Jordel, falling beside her. "Do not move a muscle."

But already Loren could tell they had nothing to fear. The nearest tents lay far away, and even the sentries stood too distant to be easily seen.

She studied the force. Loren knew herself to be terrible at numbers, but she thought there must be several hundreds of foot soldiers, and a hundred or more of horses. These were on the far side of the army, though Loren knew she and her friends would be ridden down in no time if the alarm were raised.

The army did not look like Loren thought an army ought to. When old Bracken had told her stories of great battles, he had spoken of men all in their king's colors—blue and white for Selvan, red and yellow for Dorsea, and every other kingdom with its scheme. But now she saw men wearing every color under the sky—from bright and vivid hues to dull browns and greys. She saw many gathered with bows, and many in another part of the camp with spears, but none of the organization she would have expected.

"What kingdom do they hail from?" she murmured.

"No kingdom," said Jordel with a firm set to his jaw. "These are mercenaries."

"Well, that is good. I feared for a moment that some foe had crossed into Selvan." Loren did not know much of the machinations between the nine lands, but even children knew that Dorsea often launched raids on the kingdoms that lay upon its borders—which was all of them, if you counted the oceans.

"They may have yet," said Jordel. "We do not know whom these men serve, and I would wager that like as not, they do not owe allegiance to Selvan."

"What is it?" said Gem. He tried to wriggle up between them to the hill's crown. Loren shoved him back.

"I must get closer," murmured Jordel. "If I could but speak with one of them . . ."

Gem was undaunted, and had moved to Loren's other side. Now he sidled up behind her like a worm. He gave a low whistle between his teeth. "An army proper, and no mistake," he whispered. "One more sight I never saw in Cabrus."

"We could approach a sentry," Loren suggested.

"Approach a sentry without identifying yourself, and you ask for the arrow they will plant in your brain." Jordel shook his head. "No, I must enter the camp."

"Enter the camp?" squeaked Gem. "Filled with soldiers? Who may want to kill you?"

"I have faced greater dangers before," said Jordel mildly. "Men do not often look for danger among their own comrades."

"And I look for danger not at all," said Gem. "I will see you back at the carriage." He turned to scamper away down the hillside.

Loren whirled on him. "Do not run off by yourself, you fool!"

"I run alone towards safety," he called back. "You go accompanied towards peril. Who is the fool?"

He did not slow his pace, and soon he had disappeared behind the crest of the next hill. Loren gave a low growl.

"Let him be," said Jordel. "He is right, and will be safer at Seth's side."

"Not when I get hold of him," muttered Loren. "He needs a stern lesson in following orders."

Jordel chuckled. "I shall leave such lessons to you. Now, let us approach the camp."

Loren drew back. "You mean for me to come with you?"

"Unless you would wait here. But you have a witty tongue, and quick words might serve well to lower their guard."

Loren felt tiny pinpricks of pleasure, and was not humble enough to be ashamed of them. "Very well. It is a relief to deal with one who prefers a ready word to a ready sword."

"Come, then. Walk as I do, and try to look as though you belong. And whatever you do, do not reveal your dagger. I wish now that you had left it at the carriage. Come!"

Many small bushes and trees lay between them and the sentries, a line of men clearly visible halfway to the army. Each soldier was tall and grim, and carried a longbow of yew. Jordel led her from cover to cover, but still Loren felt exposed before those mighty bows, which were as nearly as tall as the sentries themselves.

She was surprised to see how easily the Mystic moved. His feet fell soft and quiet as her own, and he melted into the terrain like a woodsman. Loren realized suddenly that she knew little about this man, the lands of his birth, or how he was raised. Mayhap he, too, had grown up in a forest. The thought held a curious appeal, and she resolved to ask him once they were safely back at camp.

Soon they had neared the sentry line, and there Jordel stopped. They hid behind a cleft in two hills, where a tumble of rocks let them hide while still peeking out to see. But the sentries ranged across a line of unbroken ground, with no chance to slip by undetected. Always they kept their eyes turned outwards. Jordel studied them for a long time, while Loren tried to imagine what he was looking at.

"They are most watchful," said Loren.

"They are. What do you think that means?"

Loren thought about it, surprised by the question. It sounded like a test.

"If they are watchful, they fear an attack." Her thoughts moved slowly, but they gained speed as the pieces assembled. "And here in Selvan, the most likely attack they could expect would come from the king's army. But if they fear a strike from Selvan, then Selvan did not hire them."

"Good, good," murmured Jordel. "Who, then?"

"If they came from the east, as it would seem from their march, they could be from Wadeland. But this far south, I would wager they swear to Dorsea."

"And what else? Which direction do they travel? And why?"

Loren's smile turned to a frown. "West, and somewhat south. They do not move for the capital or the great cities, then. What lies west of here?"

"Precious little until one finds Wellmont at the southern foot of the Greatrocks. But if they were to turn south now, they would come upon Redbrook where the King's road meets the Dragon's Tail River. That would be my guess, though it is an ill thought."

Loren's head spun at the names of so many unfamiliar things. "I do not understand. I have never heard of these places. Are they important?"

"Yes, for many reasons, but now is not the time for a lesson in politics, or in history. Suffice to say that it is now more urgent than ever that we find this army's purpose."

"But how can we slip between them?" said Loren. "We will not become invisible just because we know their allegiance."

"Agreed." Jordel sighed. "What I would not give for a wizard to distract them. I had hoped to walk among them without bloodshed."

Loren felt a chill and turned to Jordel with a frown. "Bloodshed? You do not mean to kill them."

He turned to meet her with a steady gaze, and Loren felt suddenly uncomfortable before his light blue eyes. But he spoke in a voice of deep calm and not of wrath. "I would not take a life except at great need."

"At *utmost* need, and mayhap not even then," said Loren. "I thought you preferred a sharp tongue to a blade."

"Always. And I would that we lived in a world where no blood need ever be spilt. But—"

"No!" barked Loren, louder than she meant to. They both ducked on reflex, peering out at the sentries again. But her shout had gone unheard. "No," she repeated in a murmur. "I have heard honeyed words before, coaxing me to admit that murder was needed. I did not listen then, nor will I now. If you mean to kill anyone, leave me free from it. Do these sentries threaten your life?"

"Not yet, but one small army in the wrong place could spell the doom of many."

"That man," Loren insisted, pointing at the sentry straight ahead of them. "What has he done? Is he a villain? Does he plot the overthrow of Selvan? What is his crime that you would lop off his head?"

Jordel looked at the sentry and then turned to study Loren. He stayed silent so long, she feared he was gathering his anger to lash out at her, either with words or with his hands. She braced herself to run.

Instead his breath came out in a long, whispering sigh before he spoke. "You are right."

Loren blinked. "I am?"

"You are. Many claim to spill blood only when they must. Few who say so can live up to their words. I forgot myself for a moment, but you have reminded me. I am sorry."

Loren could find no reply. No one, not her father, not Damaris nor Auntie, had ever taken her side. Most took her for a fool child, unwise in the ways of the world—even Gem and Annis, who were younger than she was.

Before she could answer, or Jordel could speak further, they heard a shout and the clamor of hooves. They ducked behind the rocks, Jordel's hand flying to his sword hilt. Together they peeked through a gap in the rocks.

From over the hills came flying two mercenaries on horseback, outriders for the army. They carried long lances and had small bucklers on their arms. But Loren spent little time studying the riders after she spied the bundle slung across the back of one of their saddles. It was a small figure tied up and strapped to the horse, and that figure was Gem.

FOUR

THE HEAD OF ONE OF THE SENTRIES SNAPPED UP, AND he nocked an arrow as he stepped forwards. But one of the riders called out "Twin lights!" and the sentry lowered his bow. The riders pulled to a stop not far from the rocks where Jordel and Loren lay, and the sentry came forwards to meet them.

"Well met," said the sentry. "What have you there?"

"A small creature scuttling through these hills," said one of the riders. "He has a shifty look to him, and his eyes are wide enough to see too much."

The sentry came to Gem and grabbed the boy's hair, jerking his head up to look at his face. Gem winced with pain, but a gag muffled his cry. Loren winced and went to move forwards, but Jordel restrained her with a hand on her arm.

"We must help him!" whispered Loren.

"Hold a moment," said Jordel. "I am thinking."

"He is more than a decade from being a man," declared the sentry.

"You never can tell with spies," said the rider. "I have heard the king of Selvan recruits them this young, so that you would never look at them twice. And spy or not, one set of prying eyes is as bad as the next."

"True enough," grunted the sentry. "Off with him, then. They have put the cages in the—"

"Hail!" said Jordel, jumping to his feet and dragging Loren with him. They stepped out from the rocks as the sentry and outriders turned in astonishment. Once again, the sentry's bow leapt up, but Jordel raised both hands and cried, "Twin lights!" The bow lowered, but slowly, and the sentry's frown remained. On the horse's back Gem's eyes grew wide, and he ceased his struggling against the bonds that held him.

"I do not know your face," said the sentry. "What are you doing out here?"

"I do not know most of the faces here," said Jordel, shrugging amiably. "I am Brickand's man, a new face picked up on the road."

One of the outriders looked at the other, frowning. "Brickand? I do not know a Brickand."

"I know three," replied the other. "Brickands run rampant in this land. An odd name, but common as weeds."

Loren studied them curiously. The outriders spoke in strange voices, and had brown skin darker than most in Selvan. Black hair spilled to their shoulders, and they stood shorter than those who dwelt in the Birchwood. She wondered where they hailed from.

But she had looked long, and had finally drawn their notice. The sentry nodded at her. "Who is that one?" he growled. "Not one of ours, I know, for she is far too young."

"No indeed," said Jordel. "I have traveled through these parts before, and I knew of a farmhouse not far away. I went to visit, and the girl wished to see the army."

The outriders looked slyly at each other, and even the sentry's face seemed to lighten. Loren's cheeks burned as she understood their thoughts, but the lie was told, and she had little choice but to play along. So she let her blush deepen, and ducked her head under her cowl as she giggled.

"I never thought to find so many of you here," she said, letting her voice quiver. "It is like seeing the great warhosts of old, something from Father's stories."

Gem rolled his eyes at her words, she noticed with annoyance. She wanted to cuff him.

The riders guffawed, but the sentry scowled at Loren and turned to Jordel. "This is no place for sightseeing. She shall remember our numbers as well as any enemy's spy."

Jordel waved a hand airily. "She has no wish to return home just yet, nor if she did so would any think to ask her about us. Mayhap she will travel with me for a while."

Loren tittered again and turned away as if bashful. "If I would be no burden."

Again the outriders laughed. One of them used the butt of his lance to jostle the sentry on foot. "No burden she would be indeed, eh? I say good for the man."

"Yes, leave them be, friend," said the other rider. "She looks a pretty thing. Mayhap she would like to lighten the load of some others?" He grinned at Loren and kissed the air twice. She blushed deeper.

Jordel's hand moved to his side, where his sword hung ready. The air went chill, as though from a sudden wind, and the Mystic's voice came sharp as steel. "Surely no warrior of Dulmun would think to press himself unwelcome, even in this faraway land? A sellsword should have more honor."

The rider shook his head quickly. "You mistake me, friend. I give an offer, not an obligation. I am not fool enough to invite the King's harshest law."

Jordel relaxed. "I am glad to hear tales of Dulmun gallantry are no exaggeration. But what of your own passenger? That is no quail strung across your saddle, though he looks small enough to be."

"This one?" The rider reached back and thumped Gem's back hard enough to draw a groan. "Mayhap a spy. Or simply a small child on his own, far from home. It hardly matters. He will get the question all the same, and like as not a swift end. You know the captain. 'Silent and swift,' he says again and again."

"Until I think my ears might fall off," said Jordel with a nod. "But this one hardly looks to be a spy. Not even Selvan gets them this young."

"He moved like one, and he squealed like one when we caught him," said the rider. "And now I think we had best be getting him on, for I have been too long without a meal."

Loren's gut clenched. Struck by an idea, she wandered forwards, her eyes wonderstruck. She came to Gem, who stared at her with pleading eyes.

"But this is only the little boy from the next farm over." Her voice was singsong, airy and vacant, like a girl somewhat overwhelmed by the world. "I have known him since he was born, and a ripe little squealer he has always been." She raised her eyes to the rider, all innocence and curiosity.

Everything fell dead silent, and both outriders glared at Loren in sudden suspicion. Their gaze drifted to Jordel behind her, and she felt a sinking hole grow in her stomach. Gem winced as though in pain. What had she done?

"He told us he was a riverman's son," said one of the riders. "Wandering off from his father's boat while it rested on the bank."

Loren's mouth fell open, but she could find no words. She had grown suddenly very aware of the size of the men on horseback, and of the sentry standing unseen somewhere behind her.

"So, riverboy or farmer's son?" growled the other rider. "Which lie to believe? Mayhap we have laid hands on two spies instead of one."

"Or mayhap three of—" the other began, turning towards Jordel. But he never finished, for the Mystic leapt forwards with drawn sword and hacked the front legs from beneath the man's mount. The warrior pitched to the ground with a cry, and Gem tumbled from the saddle into the grass with a sharp groan. Loren seized the boy by his bonds and dragged him away from the horse's flailing rear hooves as the creature screamed on the ground in agony.

Loren stood just in time to see Jordel strike again. This time his blade plunged into the chest of the second rider, and the man fell dumbstruck from the saddle. Jordel gripped the reins with his sword hand as he spun, shoving them into Loren's grip. She took them without thinking.

Jordel jumped forwards, for the other rider had regained his feet. The taller man dropped his lance in favor of a curved blade at his waist, but in three quick strokes Jordel had struck the weapon away. His blade flashed in the sunlight once more, and the rider sank to his knees. His head rolled away through the grass, spurting blood.

Loren wanted to scream, but she was struck dumb. Her eyes darted to the last man, the sentry on foot, and she saw him with an arrow nocked and at full draw. He stood well out of reach of Jordel's sword, and finally Loren raised her voice in a shout, trying to warn the Mystic, even though it was surely too late.

The sentry let fly. The bowstring *twanged.* But just as it did, Jordel threw his knife from his belt. It was a wild throw, and the blade missed the sentry by more than a pace, but it threw off his aim. The arrow flew wide and sank deep into the ground paces behind him, buried up to the fletching.

Loren joined the sentry in a disbelieving gape, even as Jordel lunged, even as his sword took first the archer's hand, and then lay open his chest, and finally split the man's head nearly in half down the middle. Red spurted across Jordel's body, spattering his face, his silvery hair, his light tunic. But Loren had grown numb to the blood, to the fighting and killing she had wanted so badly to avoid. She could only see the arrow missing him by a handbreadth.

He turned and came to her quickly. Loren shied away, but he dropped to his knee beside Gem and drew the dirk from his boot. In a moment the boy's bonds were cut, and the gag removed from his mouth.

"Thank . . . thank you," gasped Gem.

"Up," said Jordel, but he did not wait before raising the boy by the shoulders. He took the reins from Loren and leapt into the saddle, seizing Gem's wrist and dragging the boy up to sit before him.

"Come, Loren. Quickly." Jordel held out a hand, ready to pull her up behind him.

Loren could only stare, unable to move.

A horn blast split the air. A ways off she saw a sentry looking at them, horn raised to his lips. Another blast cut the air, and the sellsword army erupted like a hill of ants. Loren saw many men leaping to horseback throughout the camp.

"Loren!" barked Jordel. "If we do not leave at once, our corpses will join theirs. Come!"

Loren hated it, but she could see the truth in his words. She raised her hand and let Jordel pull her up, sliding into the saddle behind him. She wrapped her arms around his wide chest, linking her hands so she did not have to press her palms against him. Gem bounced back against her wrists as the Mystic spurred the horse in a circle, climbing over the rise behind them and down the other side, riding east as fast as they could while the mercenaries roiled behind them.

FIVE

They came upon the camp in a clatter of hoofbeats to find Seth standing by the carriage, a naked sword in one hand and a dagger in the other. The driver's blades dipped as he saw them, but his face did not relax.

"We are pursued," said Jordel quickly. "Leave the carriage. Load the horses with whatever we cannot do without."

Without a word Seth went to do as he was asked. Loren slid from the horse, anxious to be away from Jordel. The Mystic dismounted next, and finally Gem jumped from the saddle. To Loren's horror, he wore a wide grin.

"You were like a great warrior from the old tales!" cried Gem. "You went through them like they were only children!"

Jordel did not acknowledge the words. He did not even look at the boy. Instead he fixed Loren with a pointed gaze, one it took her a moment to return.

"I did not wish it," he said.

"I have heard that said before," said Loren.

"Do you think I am like the merchant? Have I given you cause to fear for your life? Poisoned you? Sent the constables to hunt you down like a dog, to lock you up like a murderer?"

"Not yet. But Damaris, too, killed others long before she turned her wrath on me."

Seth appeared before Jordel could reply. The driver had cut the carriage horses free, and both bore saddlebags packed with supplies. In one hand he held Jordel's red cloak.

"Ready we are, and the sooner gone the better, I say," said Seth.

Jordel took the cloak and fastened it about his throat. "I shall ride with the boy."

"You are heaviest. I will take him." Seth put one set of reins in Jordel's hand and went to Loren with another.

Loren took a hasty step back. "I do not have enough skill in the saddle."

"Can you keep from falling off, at least?" growled Seth. "Any horse that bears you and one of us will be caught. You will ride alone or doom us all."

"I will ride beside you and keep a ready hand on your horse's reins," said Jordel. "We must travel with speed, but you need not fear."

Loren bit her tongue before telling him that her greater fear did not stem from the horse. She swung herself up into the saddle.

Jordel took her reins, and together they led their horses out of the trees and onto the road. There the Mystic spurred to a gallop, and Loren's horse leapt to life beneath her. She flung herself down and seized the beast's neck, clinging for dear life as its muscles bunched and thrust beneath her. Every jostle threatened to pitch her from the saddle, but somehow she held on.

They rode and rode, slowing to a trot once every hour to keep the horses from collapse. Loren turned to look back every time they slowed, but she never caught a glimpse of the sellswords. As the sun neared the horizon to their right, she felt herself relax somewhat. It seemed they would not be pursued, or that they had left their pursuers behind. By sunset, Jordel allowed the horses to slow to a walk. Once he did, he turned to Loren.

"They do not pursue us. Why?"

Loren was surprised by the question, and not entirely pleased. "I am in no mood for your riddle-games, Mystic."

Jordel gave a heavy sigh. "Loren, I understand your concern. But if I had not struck when I did, they might have alerted the others. If they had, we should not have rescued Gem so easily."

"Easily? Three bodies lay soaked in blood behind us. Their bones will go to rest far from their homes, untended by their families. Mayhap they had wives, brothers, sons, who will never know how they died."

"It is not an easy truth to face," said Jordel. "And yet that is the lot of a sellsword, and no man signs the company bill without knowing that truth."

"A fine excuse from the man who laid them to waste," spat Loren.

"I make no excuse," said Jordel quietly. "I have killed fewer men than I could in my life, and yet over many years the number has grown too high. I excuse none of it. There is always a way to avoid it. Yet I am like any man, and prone to error."

"It was not error that drove your blade, but terrible fury," said Loren. "And no words of yours will tell me otherwise."

Jordel left her alone after that, though she often caught him looking at her afterwards. Soon Seth found a clearing not far off the road, close to the river and hidden by a rocky rise. There they made a camp with no fire, for Jordel still feared detection. Seth chose to erect a tent, but Jordel went without, as did Loren. Gem still felt drawn to lie and look at the stars.

The air hung thick and silent with tension, broken only by occasional, meaningless words from the Mystic and the driver. Gone were any thoughts of asking Jordel about his childhood. Loren tried not to even look upon him. After a quick and bland meal, she stood. "I shall be back."

"Where are you going?" said Seth, looking at her with suspicion.

"That is not your business," snapped Loren.

"To make water, then?"

"Let her be, Seth," said Jordel. He studied Loren for a long moment. "Will you return?"

Loren's nostrils flared. "I said I would."

"Good." The Mystic nodded, and that was that. Loren headed for the river, following it south until she could no longer hear Seth and Jordel's conversation.

She found a log that jutted out into the river and sat upon it, pulling off her boots and dipping her bare feet in the water. Tilting her head back, she stared up at the stars. But they seemed to glow red, as if doused in the blood of the men Jordel had slain that morning. That image was slow to leave her mind.

"He had no choice, you know."

Gem's quiet voice startled her, and for a moment Loren thought she might slip from the log. But she regained her balance with a quiet curse as the boy sidled out to sit beside her.

"There is always a choice," said Loren. "Always. Even choosing to die, rather than kill, is a choice."

"Not one I would ever make," snorted Gem. "I am not too proud to say I value my own neck above any other's. Even yours, you will forgive my saying."

"I do forgive your saying," said Loren. Then, with a sharp shove, she pitched Gem into the river.

He sank beneath the current with a yelp, and Loren laughed. His head broke the surface a moment later, arms thrashing. She heard him cry *"Help!"* before he sank again.

She realized her mistake immediately. Gem had grown up in the city, and Cabrus' filthy sewers were not fit for swimming. He had likely never learned.

Loren shot up and pitched herself into the water. Almost immediately, she found a thrashing form in the darkness. She seized it before swimming for the riverbank. A few strokes brought her to standing depth, and she only caught Gem's elbow in her ear once or twice before she had him safe on the dirt, sputtering and coughing.

"You crazy witch!" cried the boy. "Were you trying to kill me?"

"Oh, leave off," said Loren, giving him another shove. He fell into the sand of the riverbank, and as he rose it stuck to his soaked clothes. "How was I to know you could not swim? Besides, the river is practically shallow enough to stand all the way across."

"For you, mayhap, you great tree," Gem grumbled. He ducked into the shallows again to get the sand off. "My body was built for wisdom and cleverness, not for height."

Loren laughed at that. Soon Gem had wrung himself as dry as he was going to get. Together, they climbed to the top of the bank where the grass formed a cushion for them to sit. Loren cast her hair out in the warm summer night's breeze, thankful the air had not cooled overmuch since daylight.

Gem spoke first. "In any case, what do you mean to do about it? If you would sooner take a blade than use one, that is your way. It is not Jordel's, nor most people's. Will you abandon anyone who dares fight for a living or for their own life? You will soon find yourself more lonely than you might wish."

"I will not bandy about with a killer," said Loren firmly. "And I will not excuse those who take another's life when they could spare it. You saw the way he fought. He could have struck them all unconscious without spilling their blood. He moved fast enough."

"He acted quickly, out of fear. Fear for our lives, not for his own, unless I miss my guess. And he acted on instinct, without knowing half what he was doing. As you did when you threw me into the drink. I might have died then, but would you have spent your whole life moping?"

Loren looked at him in shock. "Of course. Do you think you mean so little to me that I would not mourn your death? I mean to see you live to old age, Gem, a rich and lazy scholar who spends his days reading books."

Gem scoffed and turned away.

She placed a hand on his shoulder and turned him back towards her. "I mean it, Gem. I would have done anything to save you—from the water just now, or from the riders today. I only think it could have been done without murdering soldiers whose names we did not know, and who did us no harm."

The boy pursed his lips. He slowly looked up into Loren's eyes while his own glinted with starlight.

"I will tell you something now, Loren, and I will speak to you truly. No one has stuck themselves out for me before, certainly never so far as you. It takes getting used to. But those men today would have killed me, and not quick or honorable. Given a choice, I will take the man who spills blood for me in an instant over the girl who takes an hour figuring out a way to not hurt anyone."

Loren's heart felt suddenly frozen. Slowly she withdrew her hand. "Well, mayhap next time I will let them carry you off to die, then."

"I meant no offense. Only . . ."

"Only nothing. Come, we should be getting back."

Though he followed, Loren could see the misery in his expression and gait. Yet she could not find it within her to care. Was she mad for holding that each life was sacred? That no one, man or woman, held the right to kill with ease?

If I am the only one, then curse them all. I would rather stand alone on the side of right than stand on the side of wrong with an army at my back.

But that did not calm her churning doubts, nor did it help her sleep. She lay awake for a long, long time, staring up at the moons before slumber finally claimed her.

She came awake with a start, a rough and dirty hand covering her mouth. In an instant she was alert, and she tried to pry the hand away so that she could scream. But in the next instant her eyes met the face above her, and her body fell to sudden stillness. Dark locks swung from the man's head, and a quiet smirk painted his lips.

"Greetings, Loren of the family Nelda," whispered Xain. "Now come quick and quiet, before the Mystic awakens."

SIX

LOREN HAD TO WAIT A MOMENT BEFORE SHE FELT FIT to reply. When her nerves calmed and her heart regained its pace, she reached up and pried the wizard's fingers away from her mouth.

"What are you doing here?" she whispered.

"Not now," said Xain. "Come."

He slipped away, and Loren heard his heavy footfalls fading into the night's ink. A flash of starlight glimmered off his long brown locks as he crested a rise to the camp's south, and then he was gone.

Loren gained her feet without a sound, glancing at Gem for a moment. The urchin's snores ripped through the calm night air, the only sound apart from the gurgling of the nearby river.

Gem would keep. If need be, she could return for him. But the boy always woke with a clamor, and he might rouse Jordel or Seth if she tried to bring him now.

She crept away, far more quietly than Xain had. As she neared the rise, she saw Seth lying prone in the grass. For a moment she feared him dead. Then she heard his heavy breath wheezing out against the turf under his face. Xain had subdued him, then, but had not struck to kill. That comforted her. She wished for no more dealings with murderers.

Just over the rise, Xain waited with an expectant look. He motioned her forwards with a furtive wave as soon as she came into view. Together they moved on, drawing nearer to the river, where the running water's whisper would mask their voices.

At last Xain stopped and turned to speak, but Loren burst out talking before he uttered a word.

"Where have you been? We have ridden many days upon the road and found you nowhere."

Xain smirked. "I, too, am glad to find you safe and whole."

Loren rolled her eyes, though she realized he might not see it in the dark. "I am glad you are safe. But where is Annis?"

"Which question shall I answer first, girl? Or may I make everything clearer in my own time?"

Loren folded her arms and stamped her foot, glaring at him. But she spoke no further.

Xain nodded, taking her silence for assent. "Annis waits nearby, along with our horses. We left behind our carriage long ago, as you did today. We have been waiting for the right time to rescue you, and I am not yet sure it has arrived. But with an army at your back, a better time might never come. And mayhap the mercenaries' pursuit will distract the Mystic enough to make good our escape."

"What do you mean, rescue? We were in no danger before today, and I think we have left our pursuers far behind."

"Do not be so sure," said Xain grimly. "For while their main force cannot cover ground as quickly as you four, they may yet send outriders after you. I say 'may,' but it is more than likely. Such a fighting force will not like four wandering mouths and wagging tongues to be free in the world. We would do well to be away before they find the Mystic."

"You know with whom I travel, then. Have you met before?"

Xain's eyes grew hooded, and he looked away. "You might say I know the man less than the cloak he bears upon his shoulders. None should trifle with Mystics, for they are fey and quick to turn from friend to foe. Had I been there when you encountered him, I would have warned you against him. But tell me, why does he travel with you in the first place?"

Loren thought hard upon her answer, looking over her shoulder towards Jordel's camp.

I owe the Mystic nothing.

"He seeks you," said Loren. "He heard from the constables that you traveled with a girl—that is, me—and soon guessed that I could help him find you. I might have ignored his offer, except that without him I might never have escaped the walls of Cabrus."

Xain's face paled in the moonslight. "Why does he seek me? Has he told you? What is his name?"

Loren smirked at him. "Which question shall I answer first, wizard? Or may I make everything clearer in my own time?"

Xain grabbed her shoulders and shook her. "I play no games, girl. What is his name?"

But Loren had well earned her reputation as the best wrestler in her village. She seized his forearms and spun, twisting the wizard's arms until he yelped. Then she gave him a gentle shove while placing her foot behind his, sending him crashing to the ground. Again she folded her arms as she looked down upon him.

"You may command the elements, but you are a poor fighter. As for your question, his name is Jordel. Does that mean anything to you?"

Xain looked more frightened than angry. Slowly he rose, and ran fingers through his hair as he paced back and forth. "Jordel. The face behind the name. I thought I had left him back at the High King's Seat. He must have followed me all the way to Cabrus. Our escape was far more fortunate than I knew. We must put as much distance between ourselves and that man as we are able, and as quickly as possible."

"I wish for the Mystic's company no longer," said Loren. "I will go with you. But I would know: what brought you back? You have left me twice already, and you have tried to leave more often than that. You could have been halfway to one of the outland kingdoms by now."

Xain's jaw twitched twice in quick succession, and he scowled. "I have told you often enough that I have no interest in watching over a young girl. Yet I suppose when I saw you in the company of a redcloak, I could not leave you to your fate without at least trying to help."

"Annis had nothing to do with this decision, then?"

The lines in his face deepened. "It is true that for such a young child, the girl can be most persuasive. Indeed I would not have left her alone even now, except that she cannot seem to stop talking for so much as a moment."

Loren smiled and stepped forwards, patting Xain gently atop his long curls. "Oh, dear wizard, when it comes to it, are you nothing more than a soft-hearted old man?"

Xain swatted her hand away angrily, and his eyes glowed white in the darkness as flames sparked from his fingers. “Remember to whom you speak, girl, lest I roast you for supper.”

Loren chuckled. “Very well, then. Let us away, but not until I fetch Gem.”

“The boy? He is nothing to the Mystic, and will be safe in his company. You risk detection if you return. If the Mystic finds out about me, I will not hesitate to leave you behind.”

Loren waved an airy hand. “You are the one who forgets to whom you speak. They will no more hear me than they would a breath of wind in the night.”

She turned and walked away without waiting for Xain’s reply. The river’s murmur faded behind her as she crept towards the camp without a sound.

Her eyes had grown used to the starlight now, and she saw clearly where Jordel lay wrapped in a bedroll mere paces from the horses. Gem lay nearby, but not too close. Their escape would be easier than she had feared.

She measured each footfall. Her every breath came slow and careful, gently nudged through slightly parted lips. Once Jordel shifted in his sleep, and Loren froze for a heart-stopping instant. But the Mystic only rolled on his side, facing away from Gem. After a moment, Loren pressed on.

In moments she reached Gem’s side. As Xain had done with her, she placed a hand over the boy’s mouth to stifle any cry as he woke. His eyes shot wide, almost glowing as they caught the reflection of the moons.

Loren waited for him to still before she leaned in, close enough that her lips almost brushed his ear.

"We are leaving," she breathed. "Xain has returned, and I wish to travel with the Mystic no longer."

Gently she drew her fingers away, but rather than move to rise, Gem whispered back far too loudly. "I do not want to go. Why would we?"

Loren clapped her hand back over his mouth. "Be silent. You will wake him. Come with me beyond the bounds of the camp. I will explain everything there, but you must trust me for now. Xain says that Jordel is dangerous. After today, I am inclined to believe him."

Gem rolled his eyes at that. But he remained silent when she removed her hand, and once she drew back, he rose to follow. He quietly scooped his pack from the ground and padded away after her. Loren was glad to find his steps far softer than Xain's. She collected her own pack, slinging it over her shoulder under her cloak, and together they stole away south.

They had nearly reached the camp's edge when Seth snorted above them, and half rose on his forearms.

Heart in her throat, Loren grabbed Gem's arm to lead him away. She dragged him west around the rise. The driver started, his head lolling as though he were drunk. In moments he would realize they were gone.

"Hurry," Loren dared to whisper.

They slipped far enough away that Seth vanished from sight, and then she broke into a run. Gem struggled to keep up with her on his much shorter legs, his silent feet darting over the grass like a rabbit's.

"Attack!"

Seth's voice behind her made Loren jump. She doubled her pace as she landed. Now she very nearly dragged Gem, and the boy struggled to stay upright.

"Jordel!" cried Seth. "There has been an attack! Wake up!"

Loren felt a moment's relief—he had not spotted them. But Jordel would search for them in the darkness, and it would not take much guesswork to see that south seemed their most likely course.

"Faster!" hissed Loren.

She led Gem slightly west until they came near the bank of the river. There they sped along until at last she saw Xain lurking in the darkness not far ahead.

"The driver woke," she gasped as they reached the wizard. "It will be only moments before they are upon us."

"To the horses!" said Xain. "Be quick, but be silent."

He ran on ahead, and Gem groaned as Loren pulled him along. They climbed up and down the rolling hills that marched beside the river, until at last Loren crested one to spy a pair of horses below them.

"Can you ride?" said Xain.

"Poorly," said Loren.

"I will take the boy, then. Come!"

Xain vaulted into the saddle and reached down for Gem's outstretched hand. Loren's legs shook from fear and exertion, but somehow she managed to gain the saddle. The wizard seized her horse's reins before spurring his own mount forwards, and together they galloped into the night. And though Loren looked often over her shoulder, she saw no sign of pursuit.

From danger into the unknown, she thought, and wondered if she might ever know peace again.

SEVEN

AFTER A WHILE HAD PASSED AND STILL THEY SAW NO sign of pursuit, Loren took a moment to study the sky. She had failed to note the time since Xain found her, but now she saw the moons hung almost straight above. It would not be more than an hour before the first greys arrived to herald the dawn. She felt a bristle of fear at the thought of riding these wide, open lands in daylight, when Jordel and Seth would be able to see for many leagues.

Xain, too, must have noted the hour. He shouted at her over the galloping hooves. "We must be well fled before the sun rises."

"We could find a place to hide," Loren called back.

"There are no caves or woods, and if they find us we will be trapped."

She saw the truth in his words. Nothing but low hills sprawled in every direction, and to hide in their dells would be to play a game of chance where they were as likely as not to be found.

So on they rode. Loren wondered how far they would have to go before reaching Annis. But soon Xain guided his horse to the right, swinging south to a small dip in the land between a matching set of hills. They descended together as the sky lightened above.

There stood Annis at last, in the ridiculous patchwork cloak she had acquired in Cabrus, looking up at them in trepidation and hope. Loren dropped from her saddle nearly before Xain had brought the horse to a stop, and the girls crashed into each other's arms with whoops of delight.

"You are here!" said Annis. Loren thought the girl might never release her, so tight was her grip. "I feared I would never see you again!"

Loren wrapped her arms around Annis' torso and heaved her into the air. "You would need to try much harder than that to be rid of me."

"Enough of this," snapped Xain from horseback. "Ready our things. We must be away, and quickly."

Loren sobered, releasing Annis and turning back to her horse. "He is right. Jordel and his driver seek us even now."

"Who is Jordel?" said Annis, cocking her head.

"The Mystic we followed," said Xain. "And a greater danger to us now than ever the weremage was. Ready your horse, quickly!"

Annis turned and scurried off, and now Loren saw that a third horse waited nearby—a grey palfrey splotched with white. The girl threw her bags across the creature's back and moved her hands to the straps and stirrups, checking each of them. Loren turned to Xain, now looking dark and grim atop his horse. Gem had not moved, and indeed appeared only half-awake.

"What danger is the Mystic to us?" said Loren. "You have not explained that. Does he wish to harm you?"

Xain turned from her. "Not in the manner you mean. But still, I would no sooner find myself in his hands than upon the headsman's block. I will say no more, not yet at any rate."

Loren frowned, but her attention flew away as Annis rode back up to them. The sky had edged from grey to pink, and Loren felt a sudden pressing urge to move on. She got herself into the saddle once more, albeit with much more trouble than Annis. As Loren mounted, Annis skillfully guided her steed alongside Xain's and reached over to pull Gem into a warm hug.

"You, too, I feared I might never see again. I am glad I was wrong." Annis pulled back slightly to give him a peck on the cheek.

Gem grimaced and swiped at his face. "Sky above, girl, remove yourself. I am a scholar, not some stable boy you found behind the barn."

Annis giggled and nudged her palfrey away. Loren settled in her saddle, and Xain flapped his reins. Together their horses walked carefully up the side of the dell until they reached the wide plain above.

A quick scan told Loren nothing. No figures were visible across the landscape, but the sky had only barely grown bright enough to see by. She felt exposed, as though hungry eyes watched her from shadows unseen.

"We ride south," said Xain, "as fast as we can, and mayhap we can leave the Mystic behind."

"Not due south," said Loren. "We should move west and make for the river."

"That is a fool's path," said Xain. "It brings us too close to his course."

Loren was unsurprised to find herself already annoyed by the wizard. "We must do more to evade him than simply ride and hope. They are one to each horse, and better riders than I am. Jordel will follow the signs we leave on the land with our passing, as soon as the sky grows light enough. Only masking our trail in the river will save us."

"If we ride west, we ride straight into his arms," said Xain. "If he is upon our trail already, he will come east to meet us."

"He cannot be. Not yet. He will wait until sunrise before trying to follow us. He knows that if he tried in the dark, he would almost certainly head in the wrong direction." Loren remembered Jordel's walk while stalking the sellswords, his footsteps like a woodsman, eyes wary and searching, so much like her own.

Xain's jaw clenched twice, and he gave a curt nod. Loren returned it in thanks, and then led her horse to the fore.

They rode hard, and once again her world turned to the thunder of hooves and the rush of wind in her ears. She led them south and west, at an angle from the path they had taken to find Annis in the dell. Ever she caught herself looking upwards to see the growing light in the sky, and twice she turned to see the sun's ruddy glow painting the mountain peaks far behind them. Whenever her gaze turned to the lands around them, she half expected to see a mounted figure in a crimson cloak. But they rode unmolested, and before long they crossed the King's road to find themselves back among low hills east of the river.

A sigh escaped Loren, and she let the horses slow to a trot. They reached the riverbank and paused. Xain still searched for signs of pursuit, but Loren felt calm for the first time since she had seen the wizard's face.

"Now we ride south in the shallows of the river, as fast as ever we can," she said.

"The water will slow the horses," said Gem.

Loren tilted her chin at him ever so slightly. "A bit, yes. But Jordel will find our trail and see that we entered the water. He will not know whether we mean to ride east or west once we leave it, and so he will proceed with care, so as not to miss our marks. We will move slowly, but he will move more slowly still."

"Clever," said Xain, his voice doing little to conceal a grudging respect. "Mayhap I am too quick to forget your woodcraft, Loren of the family Nelda."

Loren thrilled at the compliment, but she gave him only a brisk nod. "I have few enough skills in this world and must make do with what I can."

"Mayhap not as few as you believe."

"Shall we ride on?" said Gem. "Or would the two of you prefer a moment alone?"

Xain cuffed the boy on his ear. Loren reached across and punched him gently just under the ribs. Gem gasped for air.

They rode forwards with Loren in the lead, heading into the shallows. Xain and Annis guided their mounts into line behind her. She kept them at a brisk trot, and soon water moistened their boots where their horses' hooves kicked up a spray.

On and on they rode, and at long last they felt the kiss of true dawn as the sun broke above the low hills to the east. By now Loren knew Jordel must have been following their trail for a while—the sky had been light enough for near to an hour. But tracking required a slow pace, and he would not find their entry to the river for some time yet.

Or at least, so she hoped.

Their horses devoured the distance in silence. Eventually the sun passed straight overhead, and their mounts flagged beneath them. Xain ordered them to leave the river for a brief rest. When Loren protested, he fixed her with a stern glare.

"You know your woodcraft, but you are a novice when it comes to horses. Our mounts will die beneath us if we do not care for them, and then the Mystic will have no trouble catching us. Though I do not doubt his steeds are worthier than ours, still they too must rest, and that will make up for the time we spend."

Loren grudgingly acknowledged her ignorance. No villager in the Birchwood had ever hoped to afford a riding horse. The thought of suddenly losing their steeds here in this wide foreign land chilled her.

"Will they not see our marks here?" said Gem. He pointed to the ground, where the sopping hoofprints of their horses stood clear on the loose grey sand of the riverbank.

"They will, but it will hardly matter," said Loren. "They will see only that we rested and then returned to the water. It will reassure them that they are on the right path, but there is little we can do about that, unless you wish to lunch within the river."

"No, thank you. I am soaked through already." Loren saw it was true, for without boots Gem's legs were well doused.

They hobbled the horses and ate a cold meal there on the riverbank. Loren took the opportunity to speak with Annis again. After another brief hug, they sat on the water's edge, heedless of the damp sand that clung to them.

"I feel I am learning everything in bits and pieces," said Loren. "What happened to the carriage? Or rather its driver, for you and Xain did not leave Cabrus alone."

Annis' face grew dark. "The driver proved himself less than staunch in his loyalty. He chose to flee once we saw you with the Mystic. Or rather, once he saw that Xain seemed set upon stalking the two of you. It seemed that he did not like the idea of crossing a redcloak, and after seeing Xain's dark mood I cannot say I blame him. I know little of what the Mystics do, but I do know that even my mother must pay them respect. In any case, we came to an inn upon the road. There the driver abandoned us, calling our purpose a folly he wanted no further part in. He made us buy horses of our own, though to his credit, he gave us some coin for the purpose. A pittance compared to his payment for our transport, but still it allowed us to mount and ride on after you."

Loren let herself smile. After all the terror of her last days in Cabrus, it seemed an eternity since she and

Annis had spoken. She had almost forgotten the girl's manner of speaking: a tumble of words that nearly overran each other, flowing from her lips like a waterfall.

But a more serious matter tugged at her attention, and she glanced over her shoulder at Xain. The wizard sat well apart, tearing with almost vindictive fury at bread and meat from his saddlebag. He seemed preoccupied, but still Loren leaned in before she answered. "You had a package when last we spoke—something you claimed from your mother before we left her company. Do you have it still?"

Annis' look grew furtive. She too stole a glance at Xain, and then Gem. "Indeed." She drew back her cloak to show a pocket within, and from it poked the edge of a brown cloth packet.

"Xain does not know you have it?"

"I have spoken no word of it until now. Do you know anything more of its purpose? It has been a great weight upon me these last many days, and more than once I have had the urge to fling it aside upon the road."

"I know nothing more than the last time we spoke. Only the name *magestone,* and that such things sit well outside the King's law."

"Magestones? If they are a wizard's tool, then mayhap we should tell Xain. He may know their purpose, or at least what we should do with them."

But Loren remembered the shock and hatred on the constables' faces when the magestones had scattered on the ground outside Cabrus. She still shuddered to think of that moment, when she and Annis had fled from Damaris and earned themselves enemies beyond comprehension.

"Of things concerning wizards, I would sooner learn from those who have no spark of magic within them," said Loren. "Any matter of great power seems to attract only intrigue and ill will, and those I would avoid where I can."

Annis nodded solemnly. "Very well. When again we reach a city, let us see what we can learn. Until then, I will guard the stones with my life."

"Not that," said Loren vehemently. "They are not worth that."

Loren heard Xain moving to rise behind her, and hastily she shoved Annis' hand back beneath the cloak. Together they rose and turned to the wizard, who looked at them with blank eyes. If he had heard their words, he gave no sign.

"We have rested long enough," said Xain. "Let us ride on."

EIGHT

THE DAY PASSED, AND THE HORSES PICKED THEIR CAREFUL way through moonslight. Though the travelers looked often over their shoulders, they never saw any sign of Jordel or Seth behind them. Xain made them press on through the night, though he did let the horses slow to a walk. When dawn came they increased their pace once again, and so passed another long, tense day of riding. Still they saw no sign of pursuit, neither from the Mystic nor the army at their backs.

"Mayhap the army found them, and they are embattled," said Gem as they paused for lunch on the second day.

"Mayhap," said Loren. She hoped not. Though she had no wish to ride beside the Mystic, neither did she wish him harm.

Xain said nothing.

By the second day's end, Loren nearly slept in her saddle, and she had to jostle Annis again and again to keep the girl mounted. Xain kept one arm wrapped tight around Gem as they rode, for the boy's head lolled back and forth as the horse slowed and sped. He looked like a puppet dangling on a limp string. But Xain himself looked exhausted, and more than once he almost let Gem spill to the ground.

As the sun neared the horizon, Loren pulled her mount to a stop, letting the river flow idly around the horse's hocks. "We must rest, for the children's sake. They cannot go on like this forever, nor can you, nor can I."

Xain blinked hard as he looked at her, and his lids rose slower than normal. "The Mystic will not stop. Not if I know his kind."

"He has ridden slower than us, I tell you. He had to, or risk passing our trail when we left the river."

Xain blinked again and looked down, confused. "We are still in the river."

"That settles it," she said, rolling her eyes. "Find your way to land, wizard. Your wits are addled." She put action to words by seizing the reins of his horse and spurring her own forwards until they reached dry land.

"Only for a few hours," insisted Xain.

"Agreed," said Loren. "I am tired, not eager to be found."

Gem only woke enough to keep from tumbling from the saddle, and as soon as Xain lowered him to the ground, he lay upon the grass and slept. Annis dismounted more demurely, taking the time to hobble her horse and fasten its reins to the branches of a willow that stooped over the water. Then she, too, lay upon the ground and fell to slumber without unpacking her bedroll. She curled herself next to Gem, her head resting against his shoulder. The boy slept on, heedless.

Loren saw Xain sway on his feet and sighed. "You are nearly dead with weariness," she said. "I will take the first watch and wake you after two hours have passed."

"There is no need," said Xain.

He raised his eyes. They glowed fire-white in the darkness. Loren saw nothing else, but she heard it—a faint whispering in the wind. And she felt it—a brush against her cheek, a murmur running along her skin. The glow left Xain's eyes slowly, dimming to nothing. After a moment, the sound and feeling passed. Loren suppressed a hard shiver.

"What sorcery was that?"

Xain grunted. "A spell of warding. A wall of air now stands around us. It will not bar a determined attack, but a blow upon it will pull me from even the deepest sleep. None will come upon us without warning."

"A firemage has more uses than simple flame, it seems." Awe made Loren forget her weariness for a moment. "If you have such tricks, why do you fear the Mystic? What harm could he offer you?"

Xain scowled. "I told you he does not mean to kill me, nor to maim. The Mystics may yet be terrible when they go to war, but greater still is the danger of their velvet tongues. They spin lies as a weaver does cloth, and their schemes stretch beyond the most ambitious plots of kings and merchants. If you find yourself within their web of intrigue, you are not likely to escape it."

Loren gulped as her throat grew dry, and her fingers strayed to her dagger. Xain followed the movement, and his gaze grew hard as it met hers. But he spoke no word, instead turning to pull his bedroll from the saddle.

She thought she might sleep uneasily, but the moment Loren's head hit the ground her world faded to blackness. When next her eyes opened, it was to a bright blue sky and an urgent hand on her shoulder.

"Wake up!" said Gem. "We have all of us overslept, it seems, though I hold the wizard most to blame. A mind such as mine needs its rest."

Loren stood, sleep banished from her head in an instant. She found Xain furiously throwing his bedroll into his saddlebag, every movement sharp, angry.

"Your barrier," said Loren. "Is it breached?"

"It stands undisturbed," said Xain. "They have not yet found us. But they could be upon our very heels. Dawn has long since passed."

Loren looked up to see the sun several fingers above the hill tops. She could not believe she had slept so long, and yet they had gone a long while without enough rest. Now there was nothing for it; they must ride on and hope for the best.

In moments they had mounted, and now Xain pushed their steeds to the limit. Even running in the cool river water, soon Loren's horse burned beneath her, and a thick lather formed on its flanks. Its breath came harsh and gasping from flared nostrils.

"How long can the horses run like this?" she called out. "You said yourself they are no good if they die beneath us."

"Long enough, I hope," said Xain. "Today we should reach the water town of Redbrook. There we will trade horse for boat."

Loren took some heart in that. She was used to the open road, a wide country and a clear sky above. But when fleeing from pursuit, she thought she would rather be within the walls of a city, where there were buildings and rooftops aplenty on which to hide.

Xain had guessed well. Long before Loren thought to ask for lunch, they spotted a black streak crouching on the horizon. As they rode ever southward, the streak became a long stretch of squat buildings, peeking above a derelict wall made here of stone, there of wooden spikes. The wall and the buildings both had the look of an afterthought, as though the ramshackle constructions had been erected in some curious blend of haste and laziness by whoever happened to wander by them each day. As they got closer still, Loren saw the river they had followed join with a much larger one, which ran on until it passed through the center of the town that lay before them.

Xain let the horses slow to a trot as they finally left the river and made for the road. As they drew nearer to the walls, the horses slowed to a walk, and Xain spoke as if making a proclamation.

"The town of Redbrook. An outpost of Selvan in name, but peopled by a lazy and unambitious folk. Still, they have their charm, and they do not ask many questions of travelers, for they see them aplenty. Nor are they overly fond of Mystics—a quality I often admire, and never more so than now."

Loren studied the town, so much smaller and quainter than Cabrus, grander than her own village in the Birchwood, and utterly unlike either place in appearance or manner. They approached the walls and stopped before a single wooden gate that swung open instead of drawing up. Its bottom rested deep in the mud, and looked as though it had not moved in months. A single old guard sat watch, leaning heavily on a pike. Loren saw a wineskin resting beneath his chair.

"Who goes there?" called the guard as they approached.

Xain spoke for them. "Travelers from Cabrus, seeking passage east along the river for Wavemount."

"A pretty young family, if you do not mind my saying so," said the guard. Loren blushed as she realized he took her for Xain's wife. But did he think her the mother of Gem and Annis, with Loren's young age and the dark skin of both children? Loren looked again at the wineskin beneath the guard, and she wondered how many others the man had had today.

Xain, meanwhile, proved the picture of courtesy. "My thanks. May the sun warm your brow, and the river cool your toes."

They rode through the gates with no further word, the guard giving a single bleary nod as they passed. Loren felt a twinge of guilt as she remembered the army of sellswords to the north. Jordel had thought it likely that they made for Wellmont or one of the other western cities, but he mentioned they might march on Redbrook. What if that were true? From what she could see of this town, they would be utterly unprepared for war at their doorstep. Every building seemed to lean. It did not make them seem weak or rickety, so much as relaxed and waiting for some moment of excitement. She imagined each building, every house and inn, as a farmer resting his forearms upon a fencepost while watching the sun's march through the sky.

The people matched their homes, most sitting or standing in positions of lazy rest. Their clothing varied in tone only between the dark brown of dyed wool and the lighter shade of dry burlap, and many wore hats woven of river reeds. Those walking the streets moved without hurry, and often Loren had to slow her horse to keep from trampling them underfoot. Outsiders within the town were easy to spot—they moved more quickly, their faces bearing signs of purpose as they wove their way between the uncaring locals.

"What in the world is wrong with them?" wondered Gem out loud. "Even the children move like old men."

"This town has not seen battle for many generations," said Xain. "No other kingdom has made true war upon Selvan in centuries, and Redbrook has no wealth to make itself the target of a border skirmish with Dorsea. Even Selvan scarcely remembers they are here. Day in and day out these people fish, farm the lands around, and spend their days with their families. After a time, it is easy to forget that any troubles plague the outside world."

The wizard seemed to hold some contempt for the simple folk, and Gem looked horrified. But Loren felt a calm settle upon her as she walked the streets, and she found it hard to mind very much that Jordel and Seth still pursued them. She caught herself nodding and smiling at each passerby as they did the same, and soon felt at peace in their company.

A thought came in a flash. Aside from her parents, Loren's own village in the Birchwood felt very much the same as this town. Nothing moved too quickly, nor did anyone speak too loud. Life simply went on, as it always had and always would. And here, her father's meaty fists did not threaten her. For just a moment, Loren thought that she could have stayed for a while in Redbrook, and might even have been happy.

But such thoughts were madness. A Mystic haunted her footsteps, and behind him an army.

"We must make for the river," said Xain. "There we will find a boat to take us east along the Dragon's Tail until it meets the sea. There a ship can take us to Wavemount in the east, to wait for a while until our heads are less sought after by . . ." He looked around, as though suddenly cautious of being overheard. "Well, less sought after in general."

The river did not lie far away, and the street carried them straight towards it. Soon Loren heard the gurgling of water again. This time it came stronger, swelling on the air like a choir, and when they reached the water she saw why. This river stretched far, far wider than the one they had followed south, wider even than the Melnar by the Birchwood back home. Loren had never seen so much water all in one place, and suddenly she looked with distrust upon the stone bridges that spanned its width.

But even as she stood in awe at the river's great size, Annis yelped with fright and seized Loren's reins. The girl kicked her horse hard, guiding both mounts down a side street. Xain cried out and followed, swerving when Annis ducked between an inn and a smithy, where their horses came to a sudden stop in the deep mud that lined all the streets of the town.

"Stay out of sight," said Annis. "It is an agent of my family. My cousin, I think, though distant. His name is something ridiculous, like Fortinbras."

In a flash Loren dismounted and moved to the mouth of the alley, leaning around the edge to look back at the main thoroughfare. From the bridge stepped a small procession of horses and men on foot. At their head rode a tall man, his skin as dark as Annis', hair close-cropped and flecked with grey. Unlike Annis or Damaris, or any member of the family Yerrin that Loren had yet seen, this man was fat, and wore it poorly. He draped himself in garish silks and fine clothes that looked more ostentatious than fancy, and he laughed too loud and too long.

But it was not the merchant that drew Loren's eye, nor the warriors riding before and behind him who were clearly bodyguards. Nor did she look upon the small train of followers behind the man, tittering at his every laugh and looking furtively at him from behind long eyelashes. Instead, Loren looked upon the woman who rode at the merchant's side.

The woman sat short and slender in her saddle, and her horse was sized to match. Fortinbras' charger towered above the smaller horse, and the merchant must have stood two heads taller than the woman. But beside him, the woman was like a dagger of pure steel next to an ornamental greatsword; the greatsword, though bedecked in gold and jewels, had little purpose beyond display, while the dagger was meant for swift and deadly deeds in the night. So seemed the woman. Her eyes and hair were dark, her skin fair enough to seem ghostly. She reminded Loren of Bracken's tales of Elves, ethereal creatures who lived beyond the ken of men. And about her shoulders hung a deep red cloak, its hood thrown back, clasped at her throat with a silver pin. Loren could not see its design from so far away, but she would have wagered everything she owned that it was the badge of a Mystic.

Even as Loren took all of this in, and began to sweat along the back of her neck at the knowledge, the Mystic woman turned to look at her. It was as though she knew Loren lurked in the shadows and watched her, and knew what dwelt in Loren's mind besides. Their eyes met across the long distance, and Loren blanched under the Mystic's gaze.

Then the procession moved on, and the Mystic vanished from sight. Loren, freed from the stare, stepped back into the alley with a long sigh of relief and leaned against the smithy's wall.

"What?" said Xain. "What did you see?"

"You will not like the sound of it. I saw Annis' kinsman, and I do not think we need fear him much. But at his side rides a Mystic, and I would rather not guess at her purpose here. She saw me."

Xain sucked a sharp breath between his teeth. "Did she recognize you? Did she know your face?"

"Of course not," said Loren, scoffing. "How could she? Word could not have come from Jordel so quickly, nor do I think he would have sent any."

"It is not Jordel who worries me, but the merchant Damaris," said Xain.

"That is a wiser worry," said Annis. "My mother would have sent word to all our clan as quickly as riders could carry it. They may well know of your look and be wary to spot you, thinking we travel together."

"They would be right to think so," Loren pointed out. "But I said already, the merchant was not the one who saw me. Would your family work in league with the Mystics, and tell them to look for me as well?"

Annis thought hard. "I do not know for certain, but it seems unlikely. We have dealings with the Mystics, but they are generally far too nosy for my family's liking."

"Then I doubt the Mystic knows to look for me, or for you. In any case, she took little notice of me—

though even so little seemed too much." Loren shivered despite her cloak and the day's ample heat.

"At last it seems you learn wisdom in dealing with their kind," said Xain. "We would do well to move on. I have no wish to work against the agents of your family and the Mystics at once. A clever foe is hard enough to outwit, and two may be impossible."

After checking once more to ensure the merchant's retinue had passed, he led them out of the alley and back to the main street. They turned left and rode their horses slowly across the bridge.

The crossing allowed Loren to forget her momentary fright at the sight of the Mystic, and she marveled to see the high arches of the bridge, which rose so high above the river. When she first left the Birchwood and chased Xain south towards Cabrus, she had crossed a simple stone bridge that spanned the Melnar. She remembered marveling at its size and construction then, but the bridge she rode on now was many times greater. It made her curious as to what wondrous sights there were to see across Underrealm, and when she might see them. A sudden wanderlust gripped her feet, and she felt an urge to spur her horse to a gallop, to lead it south out of Redbrook and west along the King's road until she passed through each of the nine lands in turn, seeing all the strange sights and people they had to offer.

Then the moment passed, and she remembered Gem and Annis beside her, and Xain riding ahead with his shoulders hunched over his saddle horn. Wild thoughts and unmet goals were all well and good for daydreams, but now she must keep her wits about her, or she risked everything.

On the other side of the river, Xain led them down a row of low, flat riverboats. Loren saw how the river had been rimmed with great stone walls, and wooden stairs and platforms built all along them so that smaller boats could be lashed for embarkation.

Xain rode swift and sure to a small bucket of a vessel at one of the docks. The thing did not look as though it could carry more than five people. Loren wondered how the four of them would fit upon it along with the crew. Xain dismounted and bade them tie their horses to a nearby post. Then he took them down the steps to the platform where the boat rested, and without asking permission he stepped on board.

No sooner did his boot strike the deck than Loren heard a stirring from below. Moments later, a man burst out onto the deck. He stood far shorter than Loren, scarcely a head taller than Annis, but his ample girth made him seem taller. Two days of beard clung to his chin, and his heavy eyebrows seemed all the more severe as they drew together in a scowl. But that scowl lasted only a moment as he cast eyes upon Xain, and then wide brown lips cracked in a smile to reveal yellowed and bent teeth.

"Sky above, what is that face doing in this pisspot of a town?" he barked. "Xain, what in the nine lands has brought you here? I cannot imagine it is good, or you would have found a prettier face to rest your eyes upon."

And Xain—dour Xain, solemn Xain who had rarely shown Loren anything more than a glare, a frown, an exasperated roll of his eyes—Xain laughed heartily and loud and leapt forwards to meet the captain, throwing his arms around the shorter man and hoisting his heels off the ground in greeting.

"Brimlad, I would have feared I might not find you here, had you ever shown a spark of talent that might have brought you anywhere else."

The captain laughed and slammed his hands against Xain's back, and then held the wizard at arms' length to look up at his face. "Redbrook is good enough for this old man. But you? I thought you were holed up in some noble's mansion on the High King's Seat."

Xain cleared his throat sudden and loud, throwing a quick glance over his shoulder at Loren, Gem, and Annis. Brimlad closed his mouth with a *clack* of teeth and looked at them.

"You have brought friends, I see. And I would guess that means you are not here to visit."

"You guess aright," said Xain. "But that is a story for when we are on the open water, and well away from prying eyes and ears. We need transport, and an hour from now would not seem too soon."

Brimlad scoffed, drawing back and folding his arms. "An hour? How much trouble are you in, boy?

Even a salt dog has a reputation to uphold, and I am no such scoundrel. I could not leave my clients and expect to find any more when I come back. I have thirty weights sitting in my pocket that will keep me here until tomorrow evening. Can you match them?"

Xain's face fell, and he turned to the others behind him. "No, not unless at utmost need."

"As I thought," said Brimlad. "And in that case, you will have to hole up somewhere until then. I would offer you a bunk below, but I fear I cannot take all four of you."

"I hope you can take one more upon the morrow, Captain."

The voice behind them almost made Loren leap overboard with fright. She whirled to the wooden dock along the stone river wall to find the slender Mystic standing beside the merchant from the family Yerrin.

NINE

LOREN TOOK A STEP TO BLOCK ANNIS, TRYING TO HIDE her from view of the merchant, Fortinbras. The Mystic's eyes darted towards her, and in them Loren saw an understanding. But she made no comment. The merchant, meanwhile, said nothing, and did not seem to be paying attention. His eyes wandered across the river to the far shore.

Xain tensed beside Loren, his hands forming to fists. She feared for a moment that he might unleash his magic, and then she knew they would be hard beset by the city's constables. But before disaster struck,

Brimlad stepped between the two groups, standing at the foot of the gangway leading down to his little skiff. He folded his arms and looked up at the Mystic without expression.

"My boat is full enough already, my lady. These four mean to secure passage as my crew, and I will be overmanned. Besides, my little bucket is hardly the fastest passage you could find. You would be better off on one of these worthy vessels." He gestured at the boats to either side of him, both looming more than twice the height of the little skiff.

The Mystic shook her head firmly. "I am afraid that only this ship will do," she insisted. "After all, who could bear to travel without such interesting company?"

At that her eyes went to Xain. Loren had the uncomfortable feeling the Mystic knew exactly who they were and where they had come from. Jordel's many warnings rang loud in her mind, and she drew her black cloak tighter to ensure the dagger remained concealed at her waist.

But if the Mystic knew anything about them, the merchant Fortinbras did not seem to share that knowledge. Still he stared idly about, looking as if he sought some entertaining distraction. Loren wondered where his retinue had gone, but she was grateful for their absence. The more eyes upon them, the more likely they would be recognized.

Fortinbras shrugged and turned to the Mystic. "Please, my lady, you cannot travel on this floating sieve. Let me provide you one of my own ships. I have a schooner whose captain has sailed for twenty years. Let him carry you to Wavemount, for your own safety. It would cause me endless shame if you were lost upon this pauper's raft when I could have prevented it."

Brimlad scowled beside Loren, but he held his tongue. Clearly the captain was no more eager than Loren and her friends to share a vessel with the Mystic.

The woman ignored Fortinbras, looking past Loren to where Annis stood. Her eyes lingered a moment before they returned to Xain. "An odd-looking party the four of you make. What purpose carries you to Wavemount? The girl behind you might be a jester, but you wear clothing fit for a noble. The boy has the look of a city urchin, but this young woman carries herself like a wildlander. Whatever am I to make of you?"

"We are companions of chance." The scowl had not left Xain's face, nor had the anger and anxiety gone from his voice.

He will have us discovered, thought Loren. The wizard had no gift for bluffing, and he lacked Jordel's silver tongue. Loren would have to control the conversation, or they were lost.

She stepped forwards, further obscuring Annis behind her. "Truly, we wish we could offer a grand tale of our meeting. Alas, there is little to tell. I came here to fetch my little cousin—" she patted Gem's head "—for his parents have not returned from a voyage, and we fear them lost. I found him thrown out of his home and abandoned on the streets. I mean to bring him to relations in Wavemount. This man I met fresh from his contract in a sellsword company." She gestured at Xain. "Battles here are few, and he means to sail to other lands where fighting men are worth more coin. As we travel in the same direction, his services as a bodyguard came cheaply."

For the first time, the Mystic's veil of calm shifted, and she gave a humorless smile. "One of you, at least, speaks with courtesy. You I would have taken for a poor man's daughter, and not one given to easy words. How did you come by such a fine cloak?"

Loren flushed, and her fingers picked at the edge of the black cloth. Fear shortened her breath as Fortinbras' wandering gaze finally found her, and his eyes narrowed as if searching for a memory. She let a flush bloom in her cheeks but held her head high, as if she were hiding embarrassment under false pride.

"I am a barmaid in a tavern in Wavemount," she said. "The gentlefolk who go there are of high breeding, and some lords enjoy a girl with a quick tongue. The cloak was a present from one such."

Understanding flashed in the merchant's eyes, followed swiftly by dismissal. His gaze floated away. But the Mystic's look changed not one whit, and her cold smile only widened.

"Such a story would explain it, indeed," she said. Loren realized the statement could have two meanings, and it seemed clear which the Mystic had intended. "But you have given three accounts, not four. What of the mute behind you? Why does she hide behind her cloak of many colors?"

Loren glanced behind her, as though she had forgotten Annis' presence. "Ah, the beggar girl. I saw her being beaten in the street, by some stuck-up landsman from Dorsea. When I paid him off to leave her alone, she took to following me. She has spoken no word since we met. I think she may be . . . well . . ." Loren put both hands to her temples and tilted her head in the universal sign for the mad.

She turned to Annis, and the Mystic's gaze followed. A moment of silence passed. Then Annis burst into a mad giggle and skipped back and forth on the balls of her feet, hands flapping like wings beneath her cloak.

The Mystic's look grew less hungry, and she frowned at Loren. "It is sad to see a soul so broken. I think I would like the girl much better with a quick tongue and a fine blue dress." Once again Loren shuddered inwardly at the meaning hidden in the words, down to the description of what Annis had been wearing before she went into hiding. "You claimed you had no great tales of how you all met, and yet you have spun nothing but pretty words. You could have been a bard, girl. Mayhap you still can be."

Loren made herself blush again and tried to curtsey with her cloak—though she made sure the dagger remained covered. "My lady is too kind."

"I speak selfishly. For I could wish for no better companions for my journey to Wavemount. Tomorrow evening did you say, Captain? I shall meet you here then."

The woman spun on her heel, and Fortinbras went to gallantly take her hand, helping her up the steps. But Brimlad took a quick step towards her. "My boat is full already, woman! I can scarce hold these four, but they will not part from each other. I cannot take one more."

The Mystic stopped. Slowly she turned, moving her deep red cloak back and off her shoulders. Beneath it she wore no armor, and Loren saw no blade or other weapon hanging at her belt. But in each movement came a deliberate threat, as though she had parted her folds to reveal an assassin, waiting with a poisoned dagger ready to pierce—and the motion fully exposed her brooch, the mark of her position as a Mystic.

"Do you see this badge, Captain?"

Brimlad hesitated. Loren had no doubt the captain had noticed the badge from the moment the Mystic appeared on the dock. "I see it."

"Then you know that by the King's law, I can compel your vessel to carry me whether you will it or not, so long as I provide compensation. Which, of course, I will do happily. Therefore you have two choices: bring me to Wavemount along with your other passengers, or leave them here and take me alone. What is your choice?"

Brimlad scowled, and Loren saw his fingers twitch at his side as though itching to form fists. "I will see you here tomorrow evening, then, my lady. May I know the name of my new passenger, or do I presume too much to ask it?"

"Of course not, Captain. I am Vivien, and I am most grateful for your service." With that the Mystic turned and took Fortinbras' hand. He led her up the steps, and together they vanished over the edge of the stone wall beside the river.

Xain waited a moment for the Mystic to drift from earshot, and then he turned to Brimlad. "The woman cannot sail with us."

"Well I know it," grumbled Brimlad. "We shall sail in the morning, and without her. I would curse you for bringing this trouble to my deck, Xain, but I suppose you would not have come here in the first place if you had another choice."

"We must sail west," said Loren.

Both wizard and captain turned to her, blinking.

"Say again, girl?" said Brimlad.

"The woman means to sail east. She knows we mean to sail east. She seems no fool, and she will expect us to try and evade her. I would guess that she will have her merchant friend post guards at the city's east watergate, or bribe the guards posted there already. If we try to leave without her, we will be caught and put to the King's justice."

Both men blanched at her words. Xain gave a slow nod. "Once again, you prove yourself more than a simple forester's daughter."

"It is what I would do," grumbled Brimlad. "At least, if I were a thin wisp of a woman with a butcher's heart and a face of ice."

"But what lies west of here?" said Gem. "Where will we go?"

"Few towns along the river that way," said Brimlad thoughtfully. "And none where I know friends who might help you lot. Not until we sail all the way to Selvan's western border, and reach the city of—"

"Wellmont." Loren said the word along with the captain and felt her heart sink.

"Yes," said Brimlad, cocking his head in surprise. "What is it, girl? You look as though you just lost your favorite dog."

Loren remembered spying upon the sellsword company beside Jordel. *Precious little until one finds Wellmont at the southern foot of the Greatrocks,* the Mystic had said, as they studied the tracks leading west. "I do not know if Wellmont is a safe place to hide."

"Why not?" said Xain.

Loren shook her head. "It is too long a tale, and not every word of it should be spoken in the open air. Besides, it seems our only choice at present. We will go to Wellmont, and if we find danger there, we will find another place to run."

Xain nodded slowly. "Still, I would hear the story you fear to repeat. But for now we should find ourselves a place to sleep for the night. Brimlad, can you point us to an inn with few curious eyes, and without fleas, if it can be helped?"

"The Dog's Dinner if the second is more important, and the Moonslight Inn if you care more for secrecy," said Brimlad. "Though like as not every place in the city is infested, for summer is not yet gone."

"The Moonslight Inn, then," said Xain. "And thank you. You save us from greater peril than you know."

"And more than I would like to guess, I imagine," Brimlad said gruffly. "Be here come dawn's first light, or I will leave this city without you."

"You have my word," said Xain.

"Very well," said Brimlad. "Four streets south and three east, you will find the inn. Rest well. Do not be late!"

His words were gruff, but he looked up at Xain with worry plain in his eyes. They gave each other a final grasp of the wrists, and then Xain led Loren and the children up the dock and into the city. And where they had at first seemed lazy and relaxed to Loren, now she felt the buildings loomed over them with menace and evil intent.

TEN

XAIN LED THEM THROUGH THE TOWN TO FOLLOW Brimlad's directions. They soon came to the inn. Over its door hung a sign painted in faded blue, with a dirty white moon looming above a farmhouse on a green field.

"Here we are, and not too soon," said Xain. "I shall sleep uneasy tonight, but certainly better than we have upon the road."

"Hold a moment," said Gem, stopping short.

Loren heard something wary in his tone, and she stepped to his side. "What is it, Gem?"

His lips pressed tight in worry. "Two others follow us. It might be chance that puts them upon our path, but chance has carried them with us too long for my liking."

Xain looked over Gem's shoulder, but the boy shoved him. "Do not look for them," said Loren, careful to keep her gaze on Gem. "Keep your eyes upon us."

"They must work for the Mystic woman," said Annis. "If they worked for my family, they would have taken us already."

"I will deal with them, if you point them out," said Xain.

Loren looked at him aghast, but the wizard met her eyes without hesitation. "Calm yourself, girl. I would not kill them. But if they were to find themselves tied up in some shop basement, then they could not tell their masters where to find us."

Gem sniffed at him. "I have a better, and less brutish, idea. Now that I know where the inn stands, follow me."

He set off without waiting for agreement, and Loren had to half run a few steps to catch up. Suddenly Gem swerved left down the side of the inn, and once within the alley he broke into a jog. The others did the same once they were out of view. Gem turned left at the end of the alley, leading them farther from the inn, and broke into a run.

Soon they were tearing at full speed in between and around buildings. Gem would lead them back to a street, and they would stroll casually across it as though nothing were amiss. Then, out of sight in another alley, they would run once more.

Loren found herself turned around and utterly unsure of where they had ended up. Xain, too, must have become lost, for he growled in frustration. "All of this is well and good, boy, but now we have no idea where we are."

"He means to ask," Loren said hastily, glaring at Xain, "how do you know where you are going?"

Gem sneered back at them. "A boy from Cabrus knows how to keep his head among buildings, even if the wandering girl and the wise wizard with him do not. Observe."

He burst out of the alley and into the street, and Loren looked up with shock to find them standing below the sign of the Moonslight Inn. Annis squeaked beside her, and even Xain looked impressed.

Brows raised, Gem polished his nails on the breast of his filthy tunic. "Remember this the next time you question my guidance."

"I will, little master," said Xain, which made Gem's chest puff still more.

"If the little lordlings will cease complimenting each other, mayhap we could move inside before we are found," said Loren. She heeded her own words, stepping inside the inn's tall front door, and the others filed in behind her.

The common room held only a few drunkards wasting away their afternoon in the darkness of the corners well away from the wide fireplace. A large, swarthy woman stood behind the bar, using a dirty rag to polish a dirtier glass. Loren remarked upon the glass with some surprise. It was an unexpected show of wealth in such a mean little place.

Annis saw her expression. "The sand of the Dragon's Tail is the best in the nine lands for glassmaking, they say, and so glassware is common along the river's shores."

"Common as dirt, you might say," said Loren. Gem snickered.

Xain took Annis to the woman, and Annis pulled some coins from the purse at her belt. A small boy led them upstairs to a room with a large pallet, but there was hardly enough room on the floor for two to lie down.

"You girls may have the straw," said Xain. "The boy and I will sleep upon the floor."

"I want the bed!" said Gem. "Do you know how rarely I have been granted such a luxury? I was meant for a gentler life than I have been given." He flung himself down on the pallet and turned to look at them, spreading his arms wide as though guarding the thing.

"A soft scholar's life, to be sure." Loren looked skeptically at the pallet—only Gem could have called it a luxury. "You may have it, then, Gem, and share it with Annis. I have slept on far worse than an inn's wooden floor."

Xain frowned and rubbed at the back of his neck with a dirty palm. "I did not . . . I would rather you have the pallet."

Loren understood his meaning and rolled her eyes. "Sky above, wizard, this is not a house of lovers. Do you think a maiden cannot sleep on the floor with a man and remain a maiden?"

Xain's face turned beet red. "You are being ridiculous. I meant only a simple courtesy, not a . . . I will fetch us some dinner."

He retreated through the door as quickly as his feet could carry him. Annis giggled and flung herself on the pallet beside Gem, reaching over to poke his ribs. Gem yelped and rolled away, batting at her grasping hands.

Loren could not share in their light mood. Xain had made her think of Chet, and how when they were younger they would sleep beside each other on the forest floor when hunting. Her parents had put an end to those trips almost as soon as they had begun. They were some of Loren's most treasured memories, and more valuable because of their rarity. That had only been a year ago, but seemed a lifetime away.

She wondered what Chet was doing now, and how his parents fared. The bump she had put on his father's head would be gone, she hoped. A desire to see him again almost overcame her, and she felt the need for distraction. Sitting upon on the pallet's edge, she turned to Annis. "We must think of what we wish to do once we reach Wellmont. Wavemount would have been a shorter journey, I know, but from Wellmont I think we can travel to one of the northern outlander kingdoms. Mayhap even as far as Calentin, where they would never find us, though that would take us many months."

Annis sobered as she spoke. "That may be the only road left. I fear my mother may never stop hunting. And she would not seek you at all were it not for me."

Loren shook her head quickly. "No. I earned my ire from Damaris on my own. She stands at fault, not you."

Annis nodded, but she did not look as if she believed the words. Even Gem grew solemn as they spoke.

"But to make such a long journey, we will need more coin than you have in that purse," said Loren. "And I know a few ways to earn some, but all of them take too long. Do you think we could find one who would trade coin for the magestones?"

Annis reached into her cloak for the brown cloth packet. Quickly she untied the string that held it shut, and the cloth unfolded to reveal the glistening black crystals.

Loren studied them for a moment. She had had precious little chance to look at the magestones so close. When she had seen them first, they had been far away and scattered upon the ground. Later, when she shattered them in Damaris' dwelling, she had been near-delirious with snake venom. Now she could see each glistening facet, the smooth and glasslike sheen of every carefully carved surface. Each was hardly longer than her smallest finger, and they were carved in such a way that they stacked perfectly in neat little rows. When laid flat in two lines, side by side and stacked four high, they formed a neat little package only slightly bigger than a large man's hand.

Annis thought deeply. "I am unsure. The only person I could ask for advice is my mother, and I do not think she would give it willingly." That drew a snort from Gem. "It may be that my family are the only ones who traffic in such stones. It does not seem the sort of business we would willingly share with others. If only I knew their purpose, we might more easily find a buyer. Can we not ask Xain?"

Loren's brow furrowed, and she opened her mouth to answer. But then the door crashed open, and she looked up to see the wizard standing with a wooden tray full of food. With both hands occupied, he had opened the door with a kick.

Before Loren could think of covering the magestones, Xain's eyes fell upon them. The tray slipped from his hands, food spilling across the floorboards. He darted into the room, slamming the door shut behind him, and then he threw the deadbolt.

Loren blanched as terror seized her gut—not at Xain's urgent speed, but at the raw, animalistic hunger burning deep within his eyes.

ELEVEN

"Where did you get those?" Xain's voice came harsh, insistent, merciless as the look in his eyes.

Loren stepped forwards between the wizard and the magestones upon the bed. "They are hers. Where she got them is none of your concern."

"You must know what they are," said Xain. "Of course they are my concern. Give them to me, at once."

"No," said Loren, putting steel in the word. "They are hers."

Annis sat quivering upon the bed, her eyes wide on Xain's face. Gem stood uneasily at the back of the room, his hands twitching as though he longed to move but did not know which way to go.

"You could have no possible use for them," said Xain. "And you do not know the danger you place yourself in, carrying them upon you. At least in my hands they could be used to good purpose. With those stones, I could return to the High King's Seat and . . ."

He stopped suddenly, as though he feared to say more. Loren turned back to Annis. "Wrap them back up. Put them in your cloak. Do it!" Annis jerked as though woken from a dream, and she hastened to comply.

The magestones vanished beneath the brown cloth. Xain took a step towards them. Loren stepped to meet him, and her hand went to the dagger beneath her cloak.

"Foolish girl!" said Xain, his voice rising. Loren hoped it would not carry into the inn's other rooms. "You know not what you trifle with. In your hands you hold the power to conquer a city."

"And the wealth, I imagine, to travel anywhere in the nine lands we might wish," said Loren. "With the profits from those stones we mean to make good our escape and keep ourselves hidden from the long and grasping arms of the family Yerrin. I will not lose that chance to you, wizard, not for any price beneath the sky."

Xain's hands rose, and he whispered a word. A white glow grew in his eyes, and soon it eclipsed the meager candlelight flickering upon the room's only side table. Sparks danced above his fingertips.

Loren drew and brandished her dagger. The movement was instinctive, unthinking, and she balked at once. What would she do to protect Annis and the magestones? Not kill Xain, that was certain. But if not that, then what? What could she do to stay the wizard if he decided to take the magestones by force? She could take him in a fight, she knew, but his gift of magic would not make any fight fair. Only words could save them all now.

"Tell us what they are to you," she said quickly, as Xain's sparks danced higher. "What do you mean to do with them? What do the magestones do?"

Xain blinked, and the light in his eyes dimmed somewhat. "You do not know their purpose?"

"We know only that they are of a mighty value, and they lie well outside the King's law."

He stared at her for a moment. Then, to her surprise, he laughed. After thinking a moment, he closed his fist to stop the sparks. The light left his eyes, and Loren could feel the tension leak from his frame. He raised his closed fist to his lips, pursing them as he studied her. She could see thoughts brewing behind his eyes, and she was not entirely sure that she liked it.

"Tell me everything you *do* know. Have you seen others deal with them? And where did you procure so many?"

Loren considered her answer. She feared to tell Xain the whole truth, knowing as little as she did about the stones. But neither did she know what lie to spin, for the wrong one could turn the situation from bad to worse. It seemed her best choice was to feed the wizard one truth at a time, and feel her way forwards from his reaction.

"Annis' mother, Damaris, gave us the stones," said Loren. "Well, 'gave' might be the wrong word. We stole them when we fled from her. Annis thought they might be valuable to the right buyer, and could grant us the coin we need to secure passage far away."

Xain grunted. "You are right and wrong all at once, and in different ways. Magestones can earn one wealth, but they are more likely to land one in a constable's cell, soon to be killed slow. Take them into a trinket shop, and you will soon find yourself hard pursued by the King's law."

"What are they, then?" said Loren. "What makes them so dangerous?"

Xain's eyes glittered as he studied Annis. The girl's hand still lurked beneath her cloak. "Though they look like hard black glass, the stones will break without too much effort. When placed upon the tongue, they melt like ice on a frying pan. Consuming them so increases a wizard's power manyfold. Weak wizards become strong, and powerful wizards—well, a powerful enough wizard may cast down a mighty castle. Long ago, Wizard Kings would use magestones as a weapon of war, and with such power they were unstoppable. It is just that power which led to the High King outlawing both Wizard Kings and magestones."

Loren felt that there was more to the explanation, but she did not know where to begin asking. "What do you want them for, then?" she said. "You seem mighty enough without their help."

Xain studied Annis, as though waiting for her to produce the magestones once again. When she did not, he sighed and slumped back against the door, slowly sliding down to sit against it. His rear came down in the stew he had dropped upon the floor, but he took no notice. "It is true that I am uncommonly strong among my kind. Less than one born in a hundred is a wizard, and less than one wizard in a hundred is as mighty as I am."

Gem snickered. "The wizard has a high opinion of himself."

Xain's dark eyes flashed. "I give no idle boast, boy. I have heard as much my whole life, and have seen more than enough to convince me it is true. I bear no responsibility for my own power. It was a gift of my birth and nothing more. But it would do neither of us any good to deny it."

Loren gave Gem a hard glare to keep him silent. The urchin snorted and turned away in dismissal, staring out the window. Loren looked back to Xain. Now that he was talking, it seemed prudent to keep him going. "I say again: if you are so strong, what need have you of the magestones?"

Xain's look grew darker still. "Strong I said I was, and yet upon the High King's Seat one may find many comparable wizards. We cannot rule, and yet we hold our own sort of power. Rulers enjoy collecting us, like trinkets or furniture, to use as they see fit. Nowhere is this truer than at the court of the High King. One wizard there—a mindmage—was mighty in his gifts, and yet not so strong as I. And I, in turn, was mayhap more boastful than would have been prudent. In any case he grew jealous, and when his envy festered into hate, he tried to murder my son."

Loren heard the word like a slap. "Son? You made no mention that you had a son."

"And why should I?" said Xain, eyes flashing. "What concern is he of yours?"

Loren shook her head. "It . . . paints you in a different light. I had not pictured you as a father."

"A poorer one than I fear I should be," said Xain, his voice growing quieter again. In his gaze Loren saw a deep sadness, made the more poignant for the helpless tone of his words. "Now he lives at the court of the High King, guarded and safe, but without his father. I fear fate may keep us apart many years yet. How, then, can I claim any part in his upbringing? He is yet a boy, and unless I right the wrongs done to me, he will grow to a man far away from the only parent he has left."

His voice twisted, turned to something broken, and Loren averted her eyes in embarrassment. She had received precious little comfort when she cried as a child and was unfamiliar with giving it.

"Why did your rival try to harm him instead of you?" she asked, hoping to turn the wizard's mind to anger and keep him from the darker pit of grief.

It worked. Xain's voice grew in strength as he continued. "The wizard's name is Drystan, and as I said, he could not best me in magic no matter how he tried. I have known him a craven since first we met. Striking out at a child suits him far better than a fair fight against another man. Cowardice and deep pockets have long been ill friends, and Drystan is of the family Drayden."

Annis and Gem both sucked in a sharp breath between their teeth. Loren looked at them in confusion. "What is it? I do not know that name."

"The Draydens are a family of merchants, like mine," said Annis. "But where my family has been comfortable a long time, the Draydens have had wealth unimaginable since before history began. Where many fear to anger my family, most would slit their own throats before crossing the Draydens. And where my family has a reputation for walking outside the King's law, the Draydens are known as the darkest and most fell of criminals, whose black deeds in shadow and silence would send the hardest soldier's heart skipping."

"Even Auntie feared the Draydens," put in Gem. "And she was mad enough to taunt constables when the mood caught her. She would accept any mark, target and steal from anyone who took her fancy, or even kill them. But she gave the Draydens a wide berth on the rare occasions they showed their haughty faces within Cabrus' walls."

Loren shuddered. Gem's and Annis' words frightened her less than the tones of their voices. They sounded like old Bracken telling her a tale of some frightening ogre, a vicious monster that appeared in the night to drag children from their beds and swallow them whole.

Xain nodded at Gem. "Every word you speak is true, and yet not the half of it. And Drystan is a festering sore of a man even upon the blight-ridden face of that family."

"What did you do, then, when he attacked your son?" said Loren. "From all your words, it would not seem wise to trifle with such a man."

Xain stiffened as he scowled at her. "You think I should have let him get away? Bear a child of your own, and then speak to me of prudence. If a man brandishes a knife at your flesh and blood and you do not act to turn the knife back on the wielder, I will call you a shameful kinsman and no one I wish to walk beside."

Loren's cheeks burned. "I meant no offense. But whatever action you took, you ended up fleeing the

King's law far from your family. How did that come to be?"

Some of the fight left Xain. "When I heard what had happened, I sought Drystan out and confronted him. He was no match for me, of course, and I bested him quickly. I do not know if I would have killed him. Certainly I wanted to, but some part of me wants to think I would have stopped at the end, extracting a confession only to have him banished by the High King. But before I could, the Grand Magister arrived."

"Who is the Grand Magister?"

"Be *silent,* Gem."

Gem folded his arms in a huff. Loren turned back to Xain.

"I have told you I am powerful, even among wizards. Yet I have met others more powerful still, and the Grand Magister is such a one. He would not have received his placement at the court of the High King if he were a lesser wizard. He found me in Drystan's chambers and swiftly broke through my defenses, though I managed to make good my escape before Drystan could kill me. After the battle, any return seemed hopeless. The Grand Magister has long been in Drystan's pocket, and those pockets stretch to the bottom of the earth and out the other side into the great night. The little worm would certainly have kept the Magister nearby at all times, ready for any attempt I might make. Without the power to defeat them both . . ."

His eyes strayed back to Annis, and to her hand where it rested beneath her cloak.

"I understand at last," said Loren, her voice growing cool. "You think that with the magestones you could best the Grand Magister and overpower Drystan all at once. And what then? Would you kill him? How would the King's law view such an act, especially if you used magestones to do it? Would you flee with your son and give him the same life you now live?"

"If not that, then what do you suggest?" said Xain. "Do I let Drystan run free? Would you, if it were your child? I find that hard to believe. Anyone, wizard or no, may do what they like with me. Threats and violence I have faced before and will face again. But my son? Do you know what it is like to have your boy living in the court with the man who tried to kill him, and know you can do nothing?"

His voice grew almost pleading, and Loren felt herself waver. Though she could never see herself wishing the death of another, still she could not imagine the mind of one who would kill a child. Especially not for such a petty motive as envy. Almost she could see Xain's mind, and almost she felt herself agreeing with him.

Suddenly Gem blurted a curse from the window. "They have found us."

"What? Who?" said Loren.

"Come see for yourself."

Loren leapt up and went to his side, and Xain came quickly to join her. Looking out into the dimming daylight, Loren saw two dark-skinned men dressed all in green, their eyes upon the front door of the inn.

TWELVE

"Those men are from my family," said Annis, her voice quaking.

"Are you certain?" said Loren.

"I would wager much on it. They wear our colors. That Mystic woman must have told Fortinbras about us after all."

Loren saw something she had missed before—a small girl standing beside the men. Wasted and thin, with a large belly and giant eyes, she raised a finger to point at the window where they all stood. Loren dropped to the ground a half-moment before Xain,

Gem, and Annis did the same, but not before they saw the Yerrin men approaching the building.

"Cursed beggar rat!" said Gem. "Some children should learn when to keep their mouths shut."

Loren avoided the obvious retort. "We have to leave, now."

"Out the back," said Xain. "We shall have to leave the horses."

"I thought you meant to sell them to purchase supplies for our journey," said Annis. "How will we pay for food and lodging?"

"Would you like to stay behind and barter with your relatives?" said Xain. "We must leave them or be caught. Come!"

He rose to a crouch and slunk to the doorway. Loren hastened to follow, keeping Gem and Annis on either side of her. Together they slipped through the door, feet squishing in the discarded food with a meaty *slurp*.

"Is there a back staircase?" asked Loren. "The front will take us into the common room, and they will find us."

"There is," said Xain. "I found it when I went to fetch our dinner."

Gem's stomach rumbled at the word, and kept going as they ran down the hallway behind Xain. Loren thought darkly of the meal they had missed. Poorly had they eaten upon the road, and their supplies had run low. She did not know how long the voyage to

Wellmont might take, and she feared they would run out of food as they sailed. But there was nothing for it now.

Xain led them down the corridor, which turned left twice before ending in a steep staircase. Loren offered Annis a helping hand to keep her from tripping over her skirts as they descended to the stone floor of the inn's kitchen. A cook and two servants barely looked up as they walked hastily to a back door and stepped outside.

"We could run blind, but I think it would be wiser to spend a few moments discouraging our pursuers," said Xain. He turned to Gem. "Little master, can you ape your trick from today and abandon them in the alleys?"

"Of course," said Gem. "Only take care to keep up. I cannot lead effectively if I am looking behind me at every corner."

Gem ran ahead, and they followed. The alley behind the inn was scarcely wide enough for two to walk abreast, and did not split before it reached the street. Gem burst out into the wide open space, and there ran straight into another man in a green waistcoat and trousers, who cried out in surprise. Gem stared up at the man in horror.

Loren took in the man's clothes in an instant—surely another agent of Yerrin. She lunged forwards as he gawked in confusion. One foot darted behind the man's heel, and she gave his chest a great shove with both hands. The man tripped over her leg with a shout and crashed to the ground. His head hit the cobblestones hard, and he rolled, stunned, onto his side. But his shouts had roused others, and Loren saw them emerge into the moonslight from side streets in every direction.

"Run!" she screamed. Gem needed no further urging, and Loren seized Annis' hand to yank the girl after them. Gem found another gap between buildings, and they slipped inside.

"Does Yerrin pursue us with an army?" growled Xain. "Where did they all come from?"

"I knew we had a strong presence in Redbrook, but I do not think there were this many." Annis's voice came quick between deep gasps for air. "I would wager my cousin has hired more men to pursue us."

Loren turned to Gem. "Why do we not take to the rooftops? Could we lose them more quickly from above?"

"Look at them!" cried Gem. "Thatch!"

Loren saw his point: Cabrus had had roofs of wood, shingle, tile, or stone. Some roofs here might hold them, but their feet might sink through others, and they could not know which would be safe.

"Then our only hope lies in reaching the docks," said Loren. "Do not try to confuse them, Gem. If they know who we are, they know we visited Brimlad today. Get us there quickly."

Gem swerved left without answer. From alley to street, narrow winding roads to gaps in wood fences, he ran with the scuttling pace of a mouse, never charging at full speed but never slowing. Then, sudden as a thunderclap, they came to a dead end in a long alley. At the end was a wooden fence four paces high.

"Turn around!" cried Loren.

But as she followed her own advice, she saw it was too late. Four men skidded to a stop at the alley's mouth. Only one of them wore green and had Annis' dark skin, but all of them carried naked broadswords that glittered in the moonslight. Loren thrust Gem and Annis behind her.

"Stop!" said the man in green. "You are fugitives from the King's justice and will come with us!"

Loren looked around. They must have stopped near a brewery, for all around them stood tall stacks of empty wooden barrels with spigot holes punched in each.

"Xain, your fire!" Loren seized the bottom barrel of one stack and heaved as hard as she could. The stack wobbled, but did not topple. Gem, seeing her intent, squeezed between the stack beside it, and together they heaved again.

Barrels crashed to the ground, some shattering and sending their staves to scatter across the stones. Xain guessed at her aim and cried a word. His eyes glowed, fire flashed from his hands, and the line of fallen barrels burst into flame before them. The Yerrin men cried out and shielded their eyes with their hands, backing away from the fearful heat.

"Up!" cried Loren. "Quickly!"

"I said the roofs are no good," said Gem.

"We must risk them, or we are lost."

"There is another way," said Xain. Again he spoke words of magic, and his hands flashed with fire. A great ball of flame slammed into the fence with a crushing blow. Splinters flew as the fence burst. The blast nearly threw Loren from her feet. Annis and Gem were cast to the ground. Xain seized Gem while Loren took Annis, and together they fled through the burning hole while the Yerrin men shouted and cursed behind them.

Loren heard a familiar murmur and looked ahead to see they were now very close to the river. But there at the docks stood another four men in Yerrin colors, all of them armed and two wearing armor besides. The men looked up at their approach, and the air rang with the hiss of drawn steel.

"It looks like a fight." Though her stomach twisted, Loren heard a strange calm in her own voice. "Annis and Gem, stay back, and board Brimlad's boat at the first chance. If we are bested, sail away with him."

"Spare us your paltry heroics, girl," said Xain with a growl. For a third time he spoke words Loren could not understand, but no sparks blazed in his palms. Instead he spread his arms wide, fingers splayed like a child stroking water on a riverboat.

For a moment nothing happened, and Loren thought his magic had failed him. Then a breeze kicked up, and dust and discarded straw swirled all around them. The breeze turned to a wind, and then a gale. Loren pulled Gem and Annis to her side for fear they would blow away.

But though the wind buffeted the children with terrible strength, the men on the docks got it far worse. The wind slammed into them like a battering ram, flinging them screaming into the water. Xain closed his fingers, and the glow died in his eyes. The wind faded to nothing.

Loren could feel herself shaking. Everything she had seen from Xain seemed like parlor tricks next to the gale, and yet he had called forth the power in moments. What else was the wizard capable of? But even as she watched, Xain faltered as he tried to take a step forwards. Loren took her arms from Gem and Annis and went to support him, lifting him up by one arm and helping him stand.

"I am all right," said Xain. "A moment's weakness only. Let us hurry, before they surface and find their way back to the docks."

Together they stumbled and staggered their way to the docks, where they saw a line of boats still swaying in the swelling waters of the river, stirred by Xain's mighty storm. No sooner had they descended the steps and found Brimlad's skiff than the captain himself emerged from belowdecks, cursing mightily and squinting at them all in the meager light of a candle.

"What in the nine lands was that?" he barked. "It felt like a sea gale come from nowhere. I thought I would capsize."

"A little distraction for the imps who plague us, nothing more," said Xain. "But I am afraid circumstances have changed somewhat dramatically. We must leave, Brimlad, and now. Certain parties seek an uncomfortable conversation we would rather avoid."

Brimlad scowled, and Loren feared he might refuse them. But the captain's hesitation lasted only a moment, and then he ran to the boat's rear.

"You! Boy! Are your arms as weak as they look?"

Gem started as he realized Brimlad was talking to him. His chest puffed up, and he stood straighter. "I am strong enough to be a warrior, even if my mind is sharp as—"

"Be silent! Run to the bow and cast off the lines when I tell you to. You will find a pole there—use it to keep us from hitting the dock as we leave."

Gem looked back and forth, taking a step in either direction. "I . . . er . . . where is the bow?"

"The front of the ship, you imbecile," roared Brimlad. "Scholar indeed. Girl, get yourself belowdecks. I have no use for one as slim as you."

Loren threw her shoulders back. "I can help. I am as tall as Xain, and mayhap stronger."

"I meant the little one," said Brimlad, pointing to Annis and causing Loren's cheeks to burn. "You I need. Join the boy at the bow, and use the oar you will find there to keep our nose pointed the way I tell you. Have you ever rowed before?"

Loren balked. "No. We had no boats—"

"We have no time for a speech!" Brimlad bellowed. "Do as I say. You will learn the way of it soon, or we shall all be dead. Xain, can I count on your witchery?"

Loren saw the wizard sag a bit. "I am weary, but I will do what I can."

"We should not need much," said Brimlad. "Just enough to get us free and clear in the open water. Blow when I tell you to."

Xain nodded and went to stand beside the captain. Brimlad turned his sharp eyes on Loren again and growled, "What are you still doing here, girl? I sent you to the bow."

Loren leapt to comply. Once she reached the front of the boat, Brimlad shouted for Gem to cast them off. Another breeze began to gather, and when Loren glanced back she could see the glow of Xain's eyes in the night.

Behind them as they floated away from the dock, a party of men reached the stone wall that bordered the river. One slight, foolish man thought the distance not too great. He leapt at them, but missed the boat by two paces to land in the water.

"Girl!" cried Brimlad. "Steer us to port! That means row on the right side."

Loren had forgotten about the oar. She quickly found it lying on the deck and seized it, thrusting it into the water on the right side of the boat with a splash. She pulled until her arms burned, and to her surprise saw the skiff's nose turning easily beneath her. When Brimlad called at her to stop she did, and the boat coasted gently upriver. When they drifted too near the dock and the other boats, Gem pushed them away with his pole. And as the shouts of the Yerrin men faded behind them, they slipped out upon the water and through Redbrook's western rivergate with hardly a sound.

A true wind rose as they sailed into the darkness, and Xain ceased his magic with a relieved sigh. The wizard slumped against the boat's railing. Brimlad lashed the tiller and went to unfurl another sail. Loren watched as the shore passed with gathering speed.

"You are done, girl," said Brimlad. "If I need your help steering now, I am no fit captain for even a rusted barrel."

Loren dropped the oar and went to sit facing Xain. Annis poked her head out from belowdecks, and then emerged when she saw the danger had passed.

"Well, I do not know what we were worried about," said Loren. "I have had closer calls than that."

"Long waters stretch between us and Wellmont," said Xain. "And closer calls we may yet have before they end. Do not tempt fate, for she can be wily."

"She has been wily enough for a lifetime recently," said Gem.

"Yet we have been wilier still," said Loren. "And will remain so."

Xain snorted, but said nothing.

THIRTEEN

So began their voyage to Wellmont, which Loren swiftly decided was the most miserable time she had spent since leaving the Birchwood.

It began pleasantly enough. The river remained calm and peaceful, and a gentle wind remained ever at their backs. For the first few days, Brimlad would trade his duty at the tiller with Xain, and the wizard took to the work with the ease of long familiarity. Loren wondered why he seemed so acquainted with watercraft, and how he knew Brimlad. Yet she feared to delve too deeply into the wizard's past. He had little patience for such things, and she did not wish to breach another sensitive topic as she had done with his son.

But the pleasant calm of the voyage soon turned to monotony. And with little activity to occupy their attention, their thoughts turned to dark wonderings about their pursuers. Little did Loren think that the family Yerrin would simply let them escape without incident. Surely there would be ships after them even now. Brimlad assured them that, with Xain's wind to help them, few vessels in Redbrook could catch his boat on the open water. Still, Loren often found herself looking warily behind them.

Xain cast his winds whenever the natural wind died, while Loren and Gem took to the oars often. But their efforts only worsened another problem: they were desperately low on food. Brimlad had stored enough provisions for himself and more, certainly, but held his passengers responsible for providing their own foodstuffs. There had been no chance for that in their escape, so they rationed carefully and slept hungry each night.

"How long will it take us to reach Wellmont?" Loren asked Xain on the first day of their journey, shortly after dawn rose pink behind them.

"Almost three weeks." Xain had turned away from the sun, and deep shadows filled every pocket of his face. Loren thought he looked more gaunt than he had before, but it could have been her imagination.

"And how much food do you think we have?"

"If we barely keep ourselves from starving? Mayhap two weeks." Xain said it without emotion. Loren shivered.

On the third day, they stopped at a small fishing village nestled against the river. There they spent the last of Annis' coin on food, but in their haste they did not bargain as well as they might have, and barely bought enough to fill their bellies for three weeks. Still, this improved their mood—until two days after their purchase, when they woke to find the fish spoiled and rotten.

"Curse those fishermen and their families for six generations," spat Brimlad. "When I return this way, I will crack their skulls open."

"I am sure you shall," said Xain. "But we cannot do so now, and I find the rest of our voyage more pressing."

"I have some fishing line, but it is ill-used and not likely to do us much good. Still, we can try."

Loren knew something of fishing, which she had done often with Chet beneath the boughs of the Birchwood, so the duty fell to her. All day she would sit at the boat's rear, dangling a bone hook in the water behind them with some scrap of meat upon it. But the first day she caught only one fish, and on the second none at all.

As day after day passed, and all on the boat grew hungrier and hungrier, they turned to conversation to distract themselves. In particular Xain held intense, whispered councils with Loren, in which he again spoke of the magestones and urged Loren to join him in his mission.

"Surely you cannot deny my need for justice. If nothing else, help me rescue my son. I would need little to do it. A few of the stones would suffice."

"I have told you, they are not mine to give," said Loren.

"But Annis listens to you," the wizard insisted, frustration growing in his voice. "And if you will not help me, neither will she."

Loren thought hard. "How can I know, wizard, that if we give you the magestones you will not use them to strike down your foes? I hear the anger and pain in your voice when you speak of Drystan and the Grand Magister. Can you swear an oath that you will bring them to no fatal harm?"

Xain glared at her. "What are they to you? I have told you how they wronged me, and even the children have told you of the ill repute of that clan."

"All of you have told me this, yes," said Loren. "And yet what have I seen for myself?"

"Do you trust nothing but your eyes?"

"Why should I believe anything else? And even if I did, why should I raise my hand against them when to avoid them altogether is easier, and does not require any bloodshed?"

Xain surrendered with a frustrated growl, as he always did, and left Loren alone on the boat for two whole days. He avoided her eyes whenever they found themselves sharing the deck.

Loren did not know whether the wizard talked to Gem, but soon the boy came to speak to her as well. He tried to make it seem natural, sitting beside her in silence a long while before he broached conversation. But Loren could feel the tension in him, and she saw him fidget with his hands and feet as together they watched the distant riverbank coasting by. From somewhere far ahead, they heard shouts from a trading vessel sailing downstream.

"I have meant to ask you something ever since we found that force of sellswords with the Mystic," he said at last.

Loren felt a qualm of anxiety. The mercenaries, Jordel had said, most likely made for Wellmont—the very city that was now their destination. With any luck, she hoped they could reach Wellmont and leave it again before the mercenaries reached it, but still it made her uneasy.

But she said none of this to Gem, and only showed him an open hand. "Ask me, then. But know that if your question angers me, I will not hesitate to pitch you into the water."

Gem scooted away from her. "You know I cannot swim!"

She snickered and gave him a playful shove. "I jest, little master. What do you want to know?"

"You cannot think to go through your whole life without harming another."

Loren glanced at him, unsure what to say. "That is not a question."

"Mayhap not, but you avoid an answer. You know what I mean to say."

"I have not failed to defend myself, or others, when necessary. Even Xain forgets that I planted an arrow in my father's leg to save his life. But that does not mean, either, that I will kill anyone. Killing is a judgment, and not one for me to make."

"But why?" said Gem. "Can you not see that you are the only one holding to your rules, and with them you place yourself at unfair advantage?"

Loren shrugged. "What of it? Whence stems this insistence of yours that I play by the rules *you* deem fit? If I have made a poor choice, it is mine to make."

Gem's brow furrowed. "I do not ask for some idle debate. Do you mean to end up dead by some stranger's blade? Because that is the only outcome I see for you, as foolishly as you have comported yourself since we met."

Before Loren could reply, soft footsteps approached. Annis came to sit beside them, settling on Loren's left while Gem remained on her right. A quick glance told Loren that Xain sat at the ship's other end, and though he did not face them she saw he kept an ear cocked towards the conversation. Mayhap she was right to suspect the question did not come from Gem.

Well, Loren would not play his game. "Have you given much thought to your course after Wellmont?" she asked Gem, rather than answer his last words.

"I had not finished my question," said Gem.

"I have, for I said all I mean to. Now, where will you go once we leave the city?"

"Somewhere with an endless supply of food I never have to pay for," quipped Annis. Loren laughed, and even Gem smirked, but their humor was dampened as their stomachs gurgled in concert like a choir of minstrels.

"Casting aside all jest," said Loren, turning to Annis, "what will you do after Wellmont? Have you even decided?"

Annis shrugged. "I mean to go to Calentin."

"As you said. But what then?"

Annis looked perplexed. "There I will hide, until I am but a distant memory to my mother and all my family. What else could I do?"

Loren stared at her. "You mean to just . . . remain there? And do what?"

"Well . . . live, I suppose. I still hold hope that we can fetch a good price for our . . . cargo." She gave a meaningful look and patted her cloak, beneath which Loren knew she still had the magestones. "If we can, I would purchase a simple house far from prying eyes. I could raise my own food, or buy enough to stay comfortable. Mayhap even find some handsome young man and marry him." Her eyes darted to Gem, and she giggled.

The boy still stared out at the river, oblivious. "Marriage," he scoffed. "The useless binding of oneself to another for all your life, when you have known them for but a sliver of it. If I made it rich, I would buy a house, certainly, and I am sure I would keep many lovers there. But to promise myself to just one?" He grunted a laugh.

Annis' cheeks grew darker. "You speak very plainly of such things, for such a young child," she said, and Loren could hear the irritation in her voice.

Gem's face darkened. Loren remembered what he had told her beneath the streets of Cabrus, about Auntie and the way she treated the children who worked for her. The boy knew more than Annis might guess. Loren interrupted the conversation with a sigh, leaning back on her hands.

"I cannot envision myself in a life of idle luxury. Not yet, at any rate. I would go mad sitting about a house all day. There is too much I wish to do, too much in the world waiting to be seen."

Gem snorted. "Of course. You want the life of an infamous thief, for reasons I shall never understand. But how do you mean to reach it?"

Loren looked at him in confusion. "Why, what do you mean? Just that."

"He *means,*" Annis said, her voice ringing with authority, "how do you mean to get there? Will you simply stroll into the next great city you see and try to liberate the wealthy of their gold? Do you really believe that would work? You have seen less of the nine lands than even me. Do you think a great thief springs full-formed into the world, without years of training and many brushes with danger?"

"Well, they must start somewhere," said Loren, annoyed.

"Yes, and that is the point," said Gem. "Where will you start? Let me ask this: where will *you* go next? I do not mean so simple an answer as fleeing from Annis' mother, or escaping the grasp of Jordel. *Where* will you go?"

Loren's annoyance grew still further. "Anywhere I please. I am bound to no one."

Gem only sighed and shook his head. Annis rose and primly dusted her filthy skirts, seemingly unaware of the gesture's futility. "It is as I thought. You have no more direction than a wandering chick fresh from the nest. You would be better off following me to Calentin, at least to start."

Annis strode towards the ship's bow, and when Loren turned to Gem she found the boy had risen to follow. She sat alone, leaning with her elbows on her knees, staring out at the water. And at last she caught a glimpse of the truth: she had no idea in the world where she wanted to go—nor how to find out.

The river whispered to itself below her, giving no answer.

FOURTEEN

Two weeks into their voyage, everyone on board had grown irritable with hunger. Loren spent much of her days curled up on a coil of rope Brimlad kept near the ship's bow, trying to avoid speaking to anyone to keep herself from growing angry. The captain yelled as often as he spoke in a normal voice. Gem and Annis' bickering was simply insufferable. Xain stayed silent for the most part, and rarely could he muster the strength to bolster the ship's small sails with a gust of wind. Loren feared to dip her fishing line in the water, for the disappointment of an empty day made the occasional reward of a finger-long fish seem less than worth it.

And then on the sixteenth day, they spotted the sail approaching behind them.

It was Gem who saw it first. Loren noticed the boat had grown curiously quiet, and looking up she saw the boy standing at the boat's rear rail, unmoving as his gaze remained fixed behind them. She almost looked away again, relieved at the silence, but there was something in his posture—a tense, fearful sense of anticipation—that captured her attention.

"Gem," she called out. "What is it?"

"A cloud pursues us. Only I do not think it is a cloud."

Brimlad whirled on the spot, shoving the tiller into Xain's hand and going to Gem. Loren rose from the deck to join them. Annis remained where she was by the railing, barely raising her head to see.

"Who cares if there is a cloud?" she said. "I would welcome a little rain, if only to relieve this unbearable heat."

"Remove your cloak, then," snapped Gem.

Loren slapped him lightly on the back of his head. She searched the horizon behind them, towards which the river curled and twisted like a long, shimmering snake. They had sailed around a long bend in its course, so that three leagues of river were now only a league east of them as the crow flew, and the land around which the river turned was low and wet. There at the start of that wide bend, Loren spied what Gem had seen. A small white shape hovered above the horizon, tilting slightly back and forth. It was fuzzy and indistinct to Loren's eye, and indeed looked quite like a cloud, as the boy had said.

But Brimlad sucked in a sharp breath, and in a grim voice he said, "That is no cloud. It is a sail. And by the looks of it, the sail of some mighty ship indeed." He spat over the railing, and a gob of thick brown phlegm vanished into the water.

A thrill of fear ran through Loren. "Whose ship? Have we anything to fear?"

"I would wager so," said Brimlad. "No port we have passed has held any ship like that one. That means they are from Redbrook, and they have been sailing day and night to catch us, just as we have been sailing day and night to flee."

"But I do not understand. How have they caught up?" Loren was annoyed to hear a high edge of panic in her own voice. Spots danced at the edge of her vision. She was nearly starved—they all were. "No matter how fast they sailed, we had a strong lead. And you said that with Xain's magic, no ship in Redbrook could catch us."

Brimlad's look was grim. "I would wager they have themselves some kind of witchery aboard, same as us."

That roused Xain's attention. With his hand on the tiller he rose and looked towards the sail. "Will they catch us before we reach Wellmont?"

"Yes," said Brimlad flatly. "Their wizard is better fed than you are. The gap will only narrow, and now that they have caught sight of us, they will expend every effort to speed that narrowing. I think we have a day, mayhap two, before they are close enough to take us."

"And what will happen then?" said Gem.

Xain looked at him with hooded eyes. "Then they will capture the girl and kill the rest of us. If we are lucky, they will be quick about it."

Annis rose slowly and walked towards them with leaden feet. "Not if I commanded them to leave you. I have angered my mother, certainly, but as her daughter, my words must still have weight."

"Even a young lass like you cannot be fool enough to believe that," growled Brimlad.

Annis raised her chin, nostrils flared and lips quivering. "Very well, then," she said, and her voice almost broke. "Put me ashore. I will wait for them here. They will not pursue you once they have claimed me, and you will be safe."

Brimlad's lips twisted, and he looked to Xain with a shrug. "She might have something there. I think it means our skins if we do anything different."

"We cannot!" cried Loren. "You would abandon this girl back to the clutches of her mother? Captain, you do not know the fate you consign her to."

"Then offer a better idea," said Brimlad, and again he spat off the side. "For if we do not do as she says, they will catch and kill us all, and then they will have the girl regardless. Her way, at least we get to live."

"He is right, Loren," said Annis. "It was always a fool's hope that I could escape. You all should go. You can still make it to Calentin, or anywhere else you choose."

Loren's mind leapt ahead of Annis even as she spoke, and she cut the girl off with a sharp wave. "We will make good our escape, and with you besides. Xain, a moment."

The wizard gave Loren a curious look, but he gave the tiller back to Brimlad and followed her to the bow. There Loren huddled close and kept her voice low.

"The magestones. Do you know where we can sell them?"

He arched an eyebrow. "I know a place. It is far to the north of here, in Dorsea to the west of the Greatrock Mountains. A city known as Bertram, where a friend could assist me."

"And for how much? I imagine they must be valuable."

Xain shook his head. "Beyond your reckoning, but I cannot see how this will help. The Dragon's Tail does not lead to Bertram, nor could we hope to reach it before we were caught, and even then gold would do us no good against—"

Hunger stoked Loren's temper, and she interrupted with a frustrated growl. "I am not a fool, wizard! I am trying to strike you a deal. With the value of half the magestones, could Annis and Gem buy passage to Calentin and make lives for themselves there?"

Xain looked irritated in his turn, but he shrugged. "Of course. They could live like royalty, for a long while at least."

"And would half the magestones be enough for you to reclaim your son from the High King's Seat?"

Xain's eyes flashed, and his face frightened her for a moment. "With half, I could conquer a kingdom," he said, and his voice was terrible.

Loren felt a qualm at that, but she pressed on. "Then we will keep our course for Wellmont. Mayhap Brimlad overestimates our pursuers, and we will reach the city without incident. But if they catch us, we will give you one of the crystals. With its power, do you think you could stave off the ship that pursues us?"

Excitement sparked in his eyes, and he gave a quick nod. "I could rend it into kindling and sink the splinters to the river's bed." He grew solemn again. "But I would rather not. Not unless our plight was desperate indeed."

"Then do not destroy the ship," said Loren impatiently. "Only damage it enough that they cannot make good their chase."

"I mean that I would rather not use the magestones unless I must. As for why . . . it is a matter for wizards."

"Tell me," said Loren. "For without this plan, we are lost. But if it works, and we reach Wellmont in safety, there we can finish the deal. We will procure passage to Bertram and give you half of the magestones. The other half we will sell to your friend, and with the coin, Annis and Gem can travel to Calentin. But if this will not work, you must tell me now."

Again she saw hunger grow in the wizard's eyes. "Half of them? You would do this for me?"

"Not for you," said Loren, sniffing and raising her chin. "For both of us. A mutually beneficial transaction. Two people, walking outside the King's law together, doing what is best for both of them."

Xain grunted. "Call it what you will. Still, to use the stones now . . ." He turned from Loren and looked back towards the sail on the horizon. To Loren, it looked to have grown bigger even in the short time they had spoken.

"What? You look like a man who spies a coming danger."

Xain opened his mouth, and then closed it again. Something changed in his face. It became a mask, firm and stony, as though behind his eyes some arrangement had been made.

"It will be as you say," said Xain. "We will keep the girl with us, and I will try to best the ship without use of the stones. I have told you that few wizards can match my power."

"Yet you are half-starved and weakened because of it," said Loren. "You must promise me that you will use the stones if you must, or else we are all lost."

"As I said. At utmost need. And one more thing, girl. You must not tell Brimlad of this. Even in the heat of it, when I fight their wizard. If I must take the magestone, I must do it in secret, so that the captain never sees."

Loren did not like his tone, the sudden resolution that had filled him. She felt that he held something back, some secret he feared for her to learn. But she saw little choice other than to place her trust in him. In the back of her mind a voice whispered, *He left you upon the King's road.* She did not listen.

"Your word," she said, and offered her hand.

"My word." The wizard took Loren's wrist in a firm grip, though hers was firmer still.

FIFTEEN

WITH THEIR PLAN LAID, THEY COULD ONLY SAIL ON and wait for their pursuers to catch them. The day passed in uneasy silence, and though they all pretended not to, each of them looked back often at the white canvas on the horizon. Loren threw her line over the ship's stern and was pleasantly surprised to hook a fish almost immediately. Gem and Annis cheered as she pulled it aboard, but she snatched it away from them with a glare.

"Upon Xain's shoulders rests our doom," she said. "Half of this is for him."

They both grumbled, but Loren ignored it. The boat had a small brazier fixed near its mast, and after gutting the fish Loren fried it. Xain devoured the white flesh in moments, scorching his fingers in his impatience. The rest of them took more time, savoring their few bites each. Loren threw the line again, hoping for another success, but the day passed without a nibble.

Night came, and Brimlad retired belowdecks after telling Xain to rouse him at any sign of trouble. Loren tried staying awake to help the wizard watch. But hunger and weariness claimed her before the second moon had peeked above the northern horizon.

She roused herself just before dawn to find Xain swaying at the tiller. She went to his side and looked off the boat's stern. The white sail had grown closer still. Now Loren could see the vague black shape of a ship skimming across the water.

"They are closer than I thought they would be," she said.

"Closer than Brimlad guessed, as well." The wizard's words slurred with weariness.

"You should rest. Our safety depends upon you today."

"Brimlad has been asleep a few scant hours," said Xain.

"Brimlad will be as useful as a knothole if the ship holds a wizard, as he guesses it does. I will rouse him."

She stepped away, ignoring Xain's halfhearted protest. The captain came awake the moment she stepped belowdecks, and he went swiftly to replace Xain. The wizard stumbled down the boat's few steps and flung himself on a pile of blankets he had built into a sort of bed in the corner.

Another day wore on, and now they could see the ship growing closer by the hour. Half a dozen times, Loren thought she had better go below and rouse Xain, but each time she stopped herself. He would need every bit of his strength.

Then, as the sun hung above them at full noon, Loren saw something that froze her blood.

All of them had given up any pretense of ignoring the ship behind them, and most of the time they kept their eyes fixed to its sails. It stood over six paces above the water without the mast, and the top of its sail stretched higher than the towers on the walls of Cabrus. From its prow sprouted a figurehead of a beautiful maiden whose legs turned into a fishtail, and she held one arm stretched forwards as she sped above the waters.

Staring at the figurehead, Loren saw a slim, slight woman upon the forecastle. Her hands were on the rail, and she leaned out as though trying to capture the prow's spray in her billowing hair. And around her shoulders was draped a cloak of deepest red, its hood thrown back.

"Is that . . ." muttered Gem.

"Vivien," breathed Loren. "The Mystic. She sails with Yerrin."

And Vivien was not merely watching their boat. Her eyes glowed with a pale white light, a glimmer that Loren could see even from so far away.

"A wizard," said Annis. "The Mystic is a wizard. She is the one who let them sail so fast, who brought them down upon us."

The time had come, Loren was certain. She spun and ran belowdecks, seizing Xain's shoulder and shaking him awake. "They are almost here! And the Mystic is with them. Xain—she is a wizard."

Xain blinked furiously as he woke, trying to understand her words. "What? Who, the woman upon the dock?"

"Come and see for yourself."

Xain followed her and studied the ship for a long moment. "Worse and worse," he muttered at last. "I feel no stirring in the air. She is a mentalist."

"A mindmage?" Annis shuddered. "What can we do?"

"I can stop her, though I would rather she were an elementalist," said Xain. "Mentalism and elementalism are two sides of a coin, the same as transmutation and therianthropy. But I will have to watch for what she is doing, rather than feeling it with my own gift. It makes things . . . less predictable."

"Then do not give her the chance to attack," said Gem. "Strike first, so that she must defend against you instead."

"I cannot know how strong the woman is," said Xain, "but she is at least strong enough to speed the progress of a large vessel, and I am weakened. I cannot hope to maintain a constant assault against her, but only to stave off her attacks as long as I can. Brimlad, how long before we reach the rivergates of Wellmont?"

"Two days at least. Mayhap three."

Loren seized Xain's arm, but she remembered what he had said about the captain. "Xain, you cannot hope to fight her for that long." She put extra effort into each syllable, hoping the wizard would catch her meaning. He had to use the magestones, or they would be caught.

Their eyes met, and Loren could see he understood. But he reached up to remove her fingers, and not gently. "I will fight her as long as I can, and if I need help I will ask for it."

Loren wanted to say more, but she saw Brimlad give them a suspicious look. So she held her tongue as Xain went to the rear railing, ignoring them all to look upon the Yerrin ship.

With nothing else to do, Loren sent Gem and Annis belowdecks. Both complained mightily, but Loren would accept no argument.

"You will do us no good up here. I do not know if they have archers upon that vessel, nor if they would risk Annis' safety with arrows. But I, at least, will not take a chance."

"You are no good up here either," said Annis. "Why not come down with us?"

"*I* am in charge. Or that, at least, is the way you seem to treat me. Do not always ask me what to do and then refuse to do it when I tell you."

Annis scowled, but Gem ducked his head. He had pledged himself to her in Cabrus when he had left Auntie's employ. Loren worried often about keeping him safe, but at least she knew herself for a better caretaker than that woman had been.

With the two of them safely stowed below, Loren took her place at the ship's rear with Xain and Brimlad. The captain struggled to keep his eyes fixed to the front, steering the boat down the river's center. But ever his eyes returned to the ship, and to Vivien on its bow. She was close enough now that Loren could see her white-knuckled grip on the railing.

"Does she really move the whole ship with her mind?" said Loren. It seemed to her a mighty feat, and for a moment she feared the Mystic might be a more powerful wizard than Xain after all.

But Xain only scoffed. "If she tries, she is foolish. One need only push a ship's sail in order to move it. That is no easy task, but it is certainly easier than trying to grip the whole vessel in one's mind. Just as I pushed this boat with the wind, a mentalist can do the same with her thoughts."

"Still, it is a great ship," said Loren. "She must be very powerful."

"I do not think she is as powerful as we might fear," said Xain, and he sounded calm. "If she were, they should have caught us many days ago."

That was somewhat comforting—so long as Xain was not putting on a false show of confidence to reassure her.

Then again, Xain has never been one to offer reassurance, false or otherwise, she thought.

Loren expected that there would be some signal, some clear sign of when the battle would begin. But in the end, there was nothing. One moment Vivien's eyes glowed, her hands still gripping the railing. The next, Brimlad's boat shuddered, and Loren nearly fell to the deck. Above them the boat's meager sail strained against its lashings, and the lines groaned in protest.

"What was that?" said Brimlad.

"She has gripped us." Xain spoke through gritted teeth. "A moment, and I will . . ."

The boat shook again, but this time it lurched forwards through the water rather than slowing. Loren fell to the deck, and Brimlad stuck out a boot to keep her from sliding towards the stern.

"I broke her hold, but she will try again," said Xain. He spoke in grunts, as though he was in pain. "Hold on to something, and I will try to slow them down."

The glow of his eyes intensified, and he pushed his hands forwards with a smooth, flowing motion. The boat bucked and kicked underfoot, and Loren leapt desperately for the nearest railing. Just as she wrapped her arms around it, a great swell of water rushed up and soaked her through. Her fine black cloak clung to her body.

As she gasped and sputtered for air, a wave went swelling down the river towards the Yerrin ship. Vivien scrambled to keep her feet as it struck, her hands gripping the rail ever tighter. But the ship was too large, and after tilting back and forth, it settled back out. It looked nearer than ever.

"They draw too close!" said Loren. "They will ram us!"

"I see it," said Brimlad through gritted teeth, jerking the tiller to the left. Their boat drifted closer to the river's northern shore. But they moved slowly, for little wind filled their sails, and Loren knew Xain could not spare a moment's effort to summon more.

Hand over hand, she forced her way up the railing towards the front of the ship. If she could only get the pole Gem had used during their escape from Redbrook, mayhap she could prevent the ship from striking them. It might be a foolish plan, but she could do nothing else.

The wind snapped and tugged at her cloak, whipping some of the water out of it. She looked back towards Xain. Now it seemed the wizard was pushing back at the ship with air. Loren wondered if he could possibly summon enough to stop it in his weakened state, until she saw that he did not target the vessel at all. Instead a blast of concentrated air slammed into Vivien. The Mystic fell on her back and slid across the deck, vanishing from sight. But a moment later the gale subsided, and Vivien clawed her way back to the rail.

"You almost had her! Keep going!" cried Loren.

"She can halt my magic, just as I can halt hers," said Xain. He sounded wearier than Loren had ever heard him, even when they rode without sleep to escape from Jordel. The magestones flashed into her mind, but she dared not suggest them to Xain in the open, where Brimlad would surely hear.

With one hand firmly on the rail, Xain reached the other forwards and plucked at the air. A stream of water erupted from the river's surface, and when the wizard lifted his arm the stream rose ever higher. It faltered as Vivien made a gesture, but Xain swept upwards again and the stream resumed. With a hiss it crashed upon the Yerrin ship's two great sails, soaking them straight through.

"Heavy sails will not slow them enough," cried Brimlad. "That ship is made for the sea."

"Heavy sails, no." Xain's clutching fingers tightened into a fist, which he dragged to his waist. Water in the sails coalesced, forming something almost solid, like ice but warm. Where it descended, it tore great rents in the canvas. Soon both sails hung limp and listless in the air. Slowly the ship fell back as Brimlad's boat sailed on.

The captain and Loren shouted in victory, but their elation died quickly. From the sides of the ship sprang a dozen wooden spars, like the arms of a spider sprouting from its carapace. They plunged into the river and swept backwards, and Loren realized they were oars. As the glow in Vivien's eyes brightened, Loren looked up to see a hole appear in their own sail. It was the width of only a few fingers, but as she watched it began to spread downwards.

"No!" Xain thrust his left hand at the sail and cried a foreign word. The hole stopped moving. With his right hand he swept at the Mystic and spoke again. A blast of water and air nearly threw her from the foredeck.

The Yerrin ship drew closer still, now powered by its oars. While Vivien fought Xain's hurricane, he summoned forth a beam of flame. It slammed into the hull of the Yerrin vessel just above the water, but then it vanished, leaving only a blackened smudge of charred wood. Xain tried again, but once more Vivien thwarted him. Worse, Loren could see him swaying. The wizard was nearly dead on his feet.

The time for caution was past. "Xain!" she cried. "You need Annis!"

He risked a glance over his shoulder, but she could read nothing in the white glow of his eyes. "Very well," he said, his voice hoarse.

Loren dove for the hatch leading into the ship's gut. There she found Gem and Annis cowering in the corner. Gem had his head buried in Annis' shoulder, and his front was covered in vomit. Annis held him tightly, trying to reassure him, but the terror in her eyes seemed no less than the boy's.

"A magestone," Loren gasped. "Give it to me. Only one."

Annis stared with vacant eyes.

"Now, Annis! Or we are all dead!"

The shout threw Annis into motion. She dug in her pocket. The cloth packet spilled as she opened it, and black crystals scattered on the floor. Thankfully none broke. Annis snatched one up and held it out.

Without a word Loren took it and ran to Xain's side. He summoned no magic now, but only held his hands out in warding. Loren could see no result, but she imagined he must be holding off the Mystic. Yet the ship was almost upon them now, spurred by the oars.

She gripped the rail with one hand and offered the magestone with the other, careful to hold it where Brimlad could not see. "Here," she said, quiet and urgent.

"Break it in half and put one piece between my lips," he said through gritted teeth.

Loren gripped the magestone and bent. To her surprise, it broke as easily as a sliver of carrot. She lifted one piece and put it into his mouth, where he crushed it in his jaws.

The glow in Xain's eyes turned black. Loren jumped in surprise. His body shuddered, shoulders trembling under his brown coat. Then he went still, the look on his face almost serene. He swept his arms together in a calm, even gesture.

Every sound died. Vivien was too far away for Loren to see her face, but the Mystic's arms jerked back as if she had been shoved in the chest.

Xain's hands curled, and from each sprang a white-hot beam of light. Only the way it licked at the air told Loren it was fire, for it was not orange, but glowed as white as the sun. The beams ate straight through the ship's hull, and with a great sweep of his arms Xain tore a rent seven paces long just at the ship's waterline. Steam plumed where flame met water, and Loren saw many crewmen on the ship recoil from the insufferable heat.

But Xain had not finished. With another sweep of his hands, he sent long tendrils of water shooting up. They wrapped about Vivien's legs and hauled her over the rail, dragging her beneath the river's surface. Her scream vanished with a splash.

"Xain!" Loren seized his shoulder and spun him around.

Though she could see no emotion in the black glow of his eyes, the twist of fury in his mouth made her shrink back. But then the glow vanished, and Xain's face returned to normal.

"She lives," said Xain. "See?"

He pointed, and Loren saw Vivien's red hood erupt from the water. The Mystic sputtered and cried out, and a crewman threw her a rope. But the ship listed to the side, drifting towards the shore—or mayhap the captain steered it there, for it seemed clear the thing would sink soon, after the damage Xain had done.

Loren breathed a sigh of relief. "Good. The last thing we need is to stir even greater wrath from the Mystics. The family Yerrin seems intent enough on catching us already."

"And of course, we would have broken your precious *rule,*" said Xain, and his voice twisted on the word. Loren looked at him again, but he seemed calm. Mayhap she had imagined his scorn.

Brimlad looked over his shoulder at the two of them, and at the ship slowly sinking into the water. "Good work indeed, lad. How on earth did you manage it? I knew you were something special among your kind, but this . . ."

Xain met Loren's eyes, and she knew his mind: *Do not speak of it.* "The Mystic is uncommonly strong," he said. "But not as strong as I. We were fortunate."

"Fortunate indeed," said Loren.

Soon the river twisted, and Loren lost sight of the Yerrin vessel just before it reached land. Brimlad pushed the tiller to bring them to the river's center, and under a hot sun they sailed on for Wellmont.

SIXTEEN

They saw no other ships behind them after they left Vivien's ship stranded upon the riverbank. Nor did they see any ship ahead for the next two days. It made for eerily quiet sailing, and all the more unsettling for the violence that had preceded it.

They were still without food, and no effort of Loren's could produce any fish from the river's flowing waters. Late in the afternoon the day of the battle, Xain managed to snatch one from the water with his magic, but the effort left him so weak he could hardly stand. Under Brimlad's strict orders, he retired below-decks and remained there all that day and the next.

Just after dawn, on the second day following the wizards' duel, they at last drew near to Wellmont. Loren woke with the sun, too famished to go back to sleep. Hunger and fatigue had worked her hard. When she cupped water in her hands and looked upon her reflection, she was shocked at the hollows in her cheeks. She had just begun to prepare herself for another day spent lying on the deck, trying not to move or think any thought about food, when she heard Brimlad's gruff voice.

"What under the sky . . ."

Something in his tone pulled Loren's attention from her growling stomach, and she wandered listlessly to his side. The captain looked to the horizon ahead. As she followed his gaze she saw a black cloud sitting low in the sky. Long tendrils stretched down from it, like fingers sinking into the land.

"A storm?" Loren could do little more than mumble.

"I would wager not," said Brimlad. "Not the right season, and it moves up."

"What, then?"

"Smoke," said Brimlad, "from many fires, or one of great size."

Loren remembered the mercenary army she had seen with Jordel, and fear clutched her heart.

Gem and Annis rose shortly. Xain remained below; he hardly roused from slumber now. Together they all stood upon the deck, watching the cloud slowly swallow the sky.

"Mayhap it is only from the city's fires," said Gem. "Surely they must have smiths and chimneys."

"I have sailed this river most of my life, boy," said Brimlad. "For Wellmont to make that much smoke, you would have to set the whole city ablaze. And look—it is too far south."

Loren could not see more than a few leagues upriver, but it seemed the captain spoke true; they were heading quite a ways north of where the smoke cloud sat upon the horizon. That, at least, heartened her. The city was not burning.

But her heart sank again when they drew at last within sight of Wellmont's great rivergate, and saw the army that waited upon the city's doorstep.

Loren had thought the mercenaries a mighty force. They were many hundreds strong—more people than she had ever seen in one place, more than on any street in Cabrus. But the army that now stretched before her dwarfed the force of sellswords. Men and horses were clustered so tightly that they ceased to appear as individuals—instead they moved like swarms of insects across the land. They stood well beyond the range of bowshot from the city walls, waiting for something. But they were not idle. Up and down the lines, soldiers strode left and right, the army arranging itself as it prepared to march forth into battle.

"A siege," said Brimlad, though it hardly needed saying.

"Who are they?" said Gem, his voice quivering.

"Dorseans," said Annis. "See? They wear red and yellow."

Loren saw it now. Neither bright nor proud, these men wore colors smeared with mud, and mayhap more sinister things. Only their banners still hung high and clean, whipping in the air as wind battered them about.

"Some border skirmish, then?" said Loren. "I have heard that Dorsea enjoys making war upon Selvan's southern cities and towns, trying to reclaim land they have long considered their own. The people here have grown used to it, they say."

"Open your eyes, girl," said Brimlad. "That is no border raiding party. It is a force of conquest. They mean to take the city, and when they do they will march north into Selvan."

"But . . . but they cannot do that," said Loren. "The High King would never allow it."

"The High King is countless leagues away, and like as not has heard nothing of this yet." Annis' face was uncharacteristically grim, and Loren saw steel in the girl's eyes. It made her look very like her mother. "The Dorseans will take care that no word of this escapes the city. The High King will hear nothing until the campaign is all but over and the time for response of arms is past."

"And then what?" said Loren.

"Then it will be easier to do nothing," said Annis with a sigh. "The High King will censure the Dorseans, to be sure, but what more can she do? She would not muster the other kingdoms against them. Some king's minor conquests are hardly worth civil war."

Gem looked at her with wide eyes, his lips parted in wonder. "How do you know this?"

"I have lived upon the Seat all my life," said Annis. "Most merchant children learn only numbers and roads, but my mother was Damaris, and she was no mere merchant. I learned these games before most children learn dice. There are always kings hungry for power, and families such as mine must learn to use that hunger for our own ends."

"My respect for you grows, girl," Gem muttered.

"And mine, but respect will not gain us the rivergate, nor a bite to eat," said Brimlad. "If the city is besieged, they will have sealed the gates. What is more, if the Dorseans have half an bit of sense, they will have placed a blockade on the river. We cannot reach Wellmont."

"What?" said Loren. "Then what do you propose? We are close to starving."

"You think I do not know it, girl?" growled Brimlad. "I have more belly to lose than all three of you together. We will put up on the shore and see if we can enter the city from the north. Mayhap we can wait within while the kings sort out their differences."

"No!" said Loren. "We cannot stay within the city, not any longer than we must."

"Are you afraid it will be sacked? Worry not," said Brimlad. "The Dorseans will march through the gates, take Wellmont's food and water, and move on. So goes warfare in the nine lands, girl."

"They do not mean only to sack the city," said Loren.

"And what makes you so sure of that?"

Xain's voice startled her. She turned to see him standing at the hatch that led belowdecks. He leaned heavily upon the jamb, and dark bags hung beneath his eyes. He looked worse than Loren, if that were possible.

Brimlad's face turned grim. "You are not fit to be walking, Xain. Get back to bed. You have done enough."

"I am fine," said Xain, and to Loren's surprise she believed him. Though his body was weak, there was strength in his voice. His eyes held much pain, but they pierced her like a hawk's. "I say again, girl: what do you know of Wellmont?"

Loren cleared her throat. "It is something I saw with Jordel."

"Who?" said Brimlad.

"Another Mystic," said Xain. "The girl is simply thick with them. Let her speak."

But the captain erupted into a sputtering shout. "More Mystics? Sky above and sea below, I have had enough of this madness, Xain. All my life I have never found cause to tangle with their kind, and now you have brought me two in a week."

"Only one," said Xain. "Jordel is long behind us. We are fortunate in that, for he is more dangerous than the mentalist I vanquished. But I say again, let Loren speak."

"As we rode south in search of you, we saw an army near the road. Sellswords they were, though Jordel seemed to think most hailed from Dulmun. We found them north of Redbrook, but they marched west, and Jordel thought they made for Wellmont."

"I see," said Xain. "So you fear they may approach even now?"

"Yes, and I believe they mean to catch Wellmont unawares while it fights this foe from the south. I think they mean to raze it."

That threw a grim mood upon them, but Brimlad scoffed again. "Or they might mean to force the city's surrender. Surrounding a foe does not mean you wish to slaughter them all."

"Jordel thought—"

"Mystics again!" snapped Brimlad. "Let them rot, I say. For if we do not make the city, that is just what will happen to us."

Loren scowled and turned to Xain, hoping the wizard would believe her. He stood deep in thought, his eyes boring holes in the deck. All fell quiet as they watched him, until at last he noticed and looked up.

"Whether they mean to raze the city or not, we would not be wise to remain within," said Xain. "For whether their archers mean to kill us or not, still they will fire arrows. A stray shaft is deadly, no matter its intent. We must gain the city or perish, but we will leave it quickly."

"Agreed," said Loren. "Thank you."

"You lot may do what you wish once inside," said Brimlad. "But the city comes first."

At that, they were stuck again. Brimlad steered the boat to the riverbank, where they disembarked and traveled a little ways west. Before much walking they saw the blockade, a small flotilla of four ships that lay at anchor across the river, each lashed to the next and flying the red-and-yellow banner of Dorsea.

"It is well we did not sail into their jaws," said Brimlad. He spoke in a murmur, although the ships were a league away yet. "They would not likely have asked questions before they made pincushions of us."

"Fortunate indeed," said Xain. "Though I would call us luckier if we were not starving."

"If we go farther west, we shall find Wellmont's northern gate," said Brimlad. "There they may let us in."

"Or shoot us," said Xain. "They will be no more trusting than the Dorsean blockade."

"We could sneak in," said Loren. "Under cover of darkness, slipping over the walls."

Gem scoffed at her. "So says the Nightblade. But have you a grappling hook? Have you even a rope? Mayhap you and I could scale the walls with just our hands and feet, but not the wizard or the girl. Certainly not while guards will no doubt be watching."

"The boy speaks truth," said Xain. "I doubt I could climb a staircase just now, much less a city wall both tall and strong."

"What if I present myself to the guards?" said Annis. "They are not likely to shoot a girl on sight, and if I give them my family's name they may grant us entry."

"The family of Yerrin has never been well-liked in Wellmont, and will be less so now, considering the trade your kin ply within Dorsea," said Brimlad.

"We are merchants, not warriors," said Annis.

"A coin carefully spent is twice as deadly as a sword skillfully wielded."

"Mayhap we could ask him," said Gem.

Loren turned to ask what he meant, and then she saw it. A small creature, crouched on all fours down by the bank. Its eyes were huge and bulbous, and close to white. Pale and clammy was its skin, and thin webbing stretched between its fingers. It wore a close-fitting jerkin of what looked like snakeskin, but with scales much larger than any serpent Loren had ever seen; its breeches were of the same material.

Brimlad sucked in a sharp breath between his teeth. "A wurt! Be off, you little creature!"

The wurt scuttled back a bit, but it did not run away. It stopped a pace into the water, its eyes still on them. Quickly it blinked—a thin film of transparent skin slid over the eyes, then vanished again.

Loren stared at the creature in wonder. "A wurt? I have heard of them only in children's tales."

"They are real, and slimy as any water snake," said Brimlad.

"It has a fish!" said Annis.

It was true, Loren could see—in its webbed fingers, the thing clutched a fish the size of Gem's arm. The fish lay still, dead or stunned. Loren's mouth became a sea of saliva.

"Hello there!" said Gem. He skipped lightly towards the wurt, hands outstretched. "Never a more beautiful creature have I seen in all my life, O fair wurt, or whatever you call yourself!"

The wurt turned and disappeared underwater. Gem skidded to a halt on the riverbank, shoulders slumped in defeat.

"It is for the best, boy," growled Brimlad. "You do not want to trust those creatures. Slimy, untrustworthy thieves, the lot of them."

"How can you be so cruel to the poor thing?" Annis' voice climbed in register as she glared up at Brimlad. "It came here to help us."

"Oh it did, eh? It told you that?" Brimlad folded his arms over his chest. "Mayhap I shall trust my own experience, whelp. Wurts find boats plying good, honest trade and make off with whatever they can. Nasty little insects, and you would do well—"

He fell silent as a splash sounded on the surface of the river. Something silver sparkled in the air for a moment, and then the fish flopped upon the ground at Gem's feet. The boy snatched it up like a prize and waved it in the air.

"A fish! He brought me a fish!" Gem crowed.

Annis turned back to Brimlad, eyes alight. "You had words, I believe, Captain?"

Brimlad glared at her.

"Look," said Loren. "He is watching us." She pointed to the river, and the others turned to see. The wurt's head poked slightly out of the water, his large eyes peering at them unblinking.

"Be off!" cried Brimlad, waving his hands. "You have left us your fish, though I am sure it is poisoned. Be on your way!"

"Brimlad," barked Xain. "Leave the thing be. It does us no harm."

"Not yet," muttered Brimlad.

Loren walked slowly down to the river's edge to stand beside Gem. She knelt by the water, holding her hands where the wurt could see them clearly. She had enough experience approaching animals in the forest to know how to comport herself: no sudden motions, no loud noises.

"Hello," she said softly. "Can you understand us?"

The wurt's head rose farther from the water. Loren could see that it kept itself in place by paddling against the current with its webbed fingers. Slowly it nodded, and then its lips parted to reveal a wide row of sharp teeth. "Yes. Bubble speaks well to men."

Loren blinked and looked back at Brimlad. The captain scoffed.

Turning back, Loren kept her eyes on the wurt. "Bubble? Is that your name?"

"It is what men can call me," said the wurt.

"Well, Bubble, we thank you for the fish. What can we do to repay you?"

The wurt's head turned slightly to the side, an eye trained on her. "Bubble does not know this word: repay."

Loren thought for a moment. "You have done something for us. Can we do something for you? That is fair."

"Bubble also does not know this word. But you cannot do anything for Bubble. Bubble does not need anything. He is not hungry."

As he spoke, the wurt paddled gently through the water to the shore. Once he reached the shallows he stood, and the sunlight gleamed off the scales of his clothing. Now so close, Loren could see that the wurt stood hands shorter than she was, barely any taller than Gem. Quickly Bubble's eyes darted to the boy, who still clutched the fish.

"You are hungry," said Bubble. "Why do you not eat?"

Loren looked at Gem and thought she understood. "We are very hungry, Bubble. Do you have more fish? We will trade for them, if we have anything you find valuable."

"Do not bother," growled Brimlad. "He probably stole the fish in the first place."

The wurt's eyes turned to Brimlad. "Bubble did not take from men. Bubble is quick in the water. Watch him."

He turned and leapt into the current, vanishing with hardly a splash. Loren straightened, fearing the wurt had run off, but in no time at all he leapt back out. In his hands he clutched a thrashing fish only slightly smaller than the one Gem held. With a flick of his arm, Bubble slammed its head into a rock on the riverbank. Cautiously the wurt stepped forwards and placed it in Loren's outstretched hand.

"See. Bubble can catch fish. He does not take them from men."

"Thank you, Bubble, again." Loren turned and gave the second fish to Gem, who stared at his prizes as if they were gold.

She paused, expecting Bubble to say something else. He merely stared at her, thin film sliding across his eyes every so often in a blink. Soon the silence became awkward.

Loren cleared her throat. "Well, Bubble, if we cannot offer you anything in return, mayhap we could ask you a question. Do you know the city that lies just up this river?"

Bubble nodded. "Humans call it Wellmont. We have another name for it, but your tongues cannot say it."

"Wellmont, yes," said Loren, nodding. "We need to enter the city. Do you know a way in?"

"What would he know?" said Brimlad. "The city never lets the wurts in, not with their reputation."

Loren rounded on him. "A captain you may be on your own vessel, but we stand upon it no longer," she snapped. "Unless you have a better idea, remain silent, and stop insulting the one who just brought us our first food in days."

Brimlad's brows drew closer together, and his lips turned down. But he said nothing, and Loren turned back—only to find that Bubble had vanished. Far out into the water, she saw his eyes poking out.

"Come back," she said. "I am sorry. I will not grow angry again."

Slowly the wurt swam back. When he had emerged from the water, he nodded at her. "Bubble knows a way into the city. Their large water door. Bubble can swim beneath it. You cannot without his help, but he will help you. Come."

"Right now?" said Loren in surprise.

"Not now. Bubble must make things ready. You will wait, but not here. Here, the men in their ships will see you. Bubble will take you somewhere safe."

"Thank you, Bubble," said Loren. "My name is Loren, of the family Nelda."

"Loren," said Bubble, tasting the word. "I like my name better."

SEVENTEEN

BEFORE THEY COULD FOLLOW BUBBLE, BRIMLAD TOLD them he meant to depart. They all protested—Xain, mayhap, more ardently than Annis or Loren—but the captain was adamant.

"I have no use for wurts, and I think you are fools to trifle with them," he declared. "Though times are strange, and who knows? Mayhap the little beast can get you into the city after all. But my journey is over. I will not let my boat sit and rot here on the shore, and I would have precious little to do within the city besides. I must return to my trade."

"How will you return to Redbrook?" said Xain. "The Mystic and her ship lie along the way."

"Yes, but marooned," said Brimlad. "What will they do if I pass them by? The river is more than wide enough to keep me safe from arrows. Besides, they have likely moved on by now. The Mystic girl does not seem the sort to give up a chase easily."

"What will you do for food?" said Xain. "At least come with us to get provisions."

"I will take those two fish the wurt gave you, for starters," said Brimlad gruffly. "And I shall consider it cheap fare for this journey, which has been fraught with far more peril than you told me."

Xain gave him the fish without hesitation, and Loren gently asked Bubble if he would mind fetching some more. In less than an hour, the wurt had caught more than a dozen. They cooked one on the spot to sate the strongest pangs of their hunger, kept another for later, and gave the rest to Brimlad.

Just as noon passed, they sent the captain off and wished him safe voyage down the river. Gem waved hardest and did not stop until the captain had nearly vanished from sight. Annis seemed less sorry to see him go.

"I think he was mean," she said, glancing over at Bubble. "And I am glad he is gone."

"He risked his life for us, and his ship, which he values even more highly," said Xain in a voice of quiet steel. "If he did not laugh and sing bawdy songs all the while, remember that he was a simple tradesman before he met us. And if he has no love for wurts, remember that you have not lived his life."

Annis folded her arms. "Still, Bubble brought us food. Brimlad had no call to be so rude, and I think he is wrong about wurts. Just look at the creature. He could offer no real harm, even if he did lighten a fisherman's load every so often."

Loren saw Xain's nostrils flare, and she spoke before disagreement became argument. "In any case, it is over and done. I am sure we are all grateful to the captain for helping us reach Wellmont. Now we must look to our next step."

Bubble had waited for them to see Brimlad off, lurking in the shallows upstream. Now as they approached, the wurt stood and pointed. Half a league upriver, Loren saw another waterway split off. The smaller stream poured down from the faraway mountains, lending its strength to the Dragon's Tail.

"That way is Bubble's home," said the wurt. "There live Bubble's people. We will not go to them—they are afraid of men. But we will come close, and there you will wait while Bubble makes ready to take you into the city of men."

They began their slow trek along the riverbank, Bubble swimming effortlessly through the water beside them. The wurt moved without leaving a ripple. Often he would swim far ahead of them, only to double back like a dog leading its master. Sometimes he would swim on his back, letting the scales of his clothing glisten in the sun. Other times he would swim face down, and then Loren saw that the back of his shirt and breeches were not scales, but a brown material that looked like leather.

When she remarked upon it to Xain, the wizard looked as though she had distracted him from a distant dream. When she repeated herself, he nodded.

"The scales gleam even in very little light. When fish see the wurt from below, they think his scales are part of the sky. The leather upon his back, however, looks like dirt from above. In this way the wurts hide themselves from both hunters and prey."

"You know of these creatures, then?" said Gem in surprise.

"They are not *creatures,*" said Annis.

Gem gave a contemptuous shrug. "We are all creatures."

"I have heard only stories," said Xain. "Some from Brimlad—those are less than pleasant. But many others have I heard from sailors and rivermen, and not all view the wurts with such distrust. It is true, though, that the creatures are not allowed within cities. Not in Selvan, at least."

"Do they live in all the nine lands?" said Annis.

"Many, but not all," said Xain. "Hedgemond lies too far south, and many of its rivers are covered in ice. But in the north the wurts are plentiful, for the water is warm and the air is warmer. They do not love the cold, apart from the cool of deep waters near the riverbed. Nor do they love the ocean, for they cannot breathe the saltwater."

"Breathe . . . water?" said Gem. "I do not understand. Is this some kind of magic?"

"If so, it has been a part of them for years beyond counting. They do not enchant themselves, for they do not have wizards among their number."

Soon they reached the place where the tributary joined the river, and Bubble led them up it. The land grew quiet and wooded, and behind the trees they lost sight of the smoky cloud that darkened the southern horizon. That made their steps lighter and their hearts less heavy. Soon, Annis and Gem began to speak animatedly, asking Xain one question after another, all about the wurts. The wizard did not have many more answers, and he swiftly grew irritated. Loren watched him with unease. Xain had begun to use his right hand to pick at his opposite elbow—a nervous tic she had never seen in him before. His cheeks were gaunt as ever, and his eyes seemed to grow more sunken every day.

He will recover with rest and food, Loren told herself. But a shadow covered her heart, and she could not banish it.

After a time, Bubble emerged from the stream and bade them to stop. "You will wait here. Bubble will fetch one to help make things ready. Wait."

He returned to the water and vanished from sight. The day was pleasant in the shade beneath the trees, and they stood on a soft, grassy knoll, so they cast themselves upon the ground to await the wurt's return. Loren cleaned their second fish. They had suffered many long days of starvation, and the first had been eaten in little more than a blink.

"I hope Bubble will keep fetching us fish." Gem crossed his legs at the ankles and folded his hands beneath his head, looking at ease for the first time in days.

"He is not your trained hound," said Loren. "Treat him with respect. Without his help we will never enter the city's gate, and we might well starve."

"Why do you suppose he wishes to help us, in any case?" he said, ignoring Loren. "He could have left us sitting on that riverbank and spared himself Brimlad's ire."

"Kind hearts and willing hands may be found in all the nine lands," said Xain, almost to himself. "And often in the unlikeliest of places."

It had the sound of a saying, and Loren looked at him with interest. But Xain stared off into the darkness beneath the trees. His right hand plucked at the other elbow—pick, pick.

Loren thought they might have to wait a while for Bubble to return, but it was not long before a slight splash marked his presence. He was not alone. From the water beside him emerged a second wurt. This one looked almost the same as Bubble, but half a hand shorter. The new wurt stared at them with eyes unblinking, and he did not follow Bubble up the riverbank towards them.

"Bubble has brought his brother, Stream," said Bubble. "Stream does not speak with men or know your words."

"Hello," said Loren, inclining her head towards the wurt. "Can you tell him we are thankful for his help?"

Bubble turned, and from his mouth issued a series of high, melodic whines. They hung on the air, haunting and beautiful, with slight sibilance scattered among the sounds. Stream blinked his curious wurt blink, and then turned to look at Loren. He did not say anything in reply.

"What is your plan, then, wurt?" said Xain, standing to come beside Loren. But at the wizard's motion, Bubble crouched on all fours and leapt back, looking like nothing so much as a frog. Stream flung himself back into the river, where in a moment his eyes popped above the surface to observe.

"It is all right," said Loren, her voice a soothing murmur. "He means you no harm. Please do not be frightened."

"This one is large," said Bubble.

In fact Loren was as tall as the wizard, though Xain had more bulk. "What is our plan?" she asked, hoping to bring the wurt's mind back to the matter at hand.

Once he seemed convinced Xain would come no closer, Bubble straightened. Stream's head emerged from the water, but he did not approach.

"Bubble will go to the rivergate. You will need air to pass beneath it. Bubble can give it to you. He can build a . . ." The wurt thought for a moment, film flashing across his eyes as he blinked. "I do not know your word. But it will let you swim far in the water."

"Can we help?" said Loren. "I have some skill with handcrafts."

Bubble shook his head. "You do not know this making. Bubble will take Stream there to show him, and then return to watch you. It would not be well for other wurts to find you without Bubble here."

"I understand," said Loren, though she did not see the danger in meeting more wurts. They seemed a harmless folk. "Again, we thank you."

"Indeed, you are more than kind," said Gem, jumping to his feet. "Do you often swim up and down the river, searching for wandering strangers to aid?"

Rather than answer, Bubble blinked at the boy. Then the wurt sidled up to Gem and placed a wide, webbed hand on his belly. "You have not eaten the fish?"

"He has had his share, and more besides," said Annis. "I do not know where it all goes, for he is still skinny as a spar."

Bubble looked at her with interest. "But you are not. Why is this?"

Annis looked at Loren, confused. Loren said, "Annis has never wanted for food. Her family has the wealth to eat as much as they wish. Gem was raised in hardship and often went hungry."

"His . . . family does not feed him?" Bubble said the words slowly, as though piecing each together in his mind.

"I have no family," said Gem. "My parents are dead, or lost to me."

"Family . . . clan . . . others," said Bubble. "The others who see you. These ones." He pointed at Loren and Xain. "Why do they not feed you?"

Loren felt perilously close to offense, as though they had broken some wurt law they knew nothing of. "We only just met the boy. We have done the best we could since our paths crossed."

"Before you, then," said Bubble, and now his voice was insistent. "Why did others not feed him?"

Loren looked at Xain, who seemed to know more about the wurts than any of them. But the wizard only shrugged.

"He has no kin," she said helplessly. "Few would take in an orphan boy."

"But he was hungry?" said Bubble.

"Often, yes," said Gem cheerily.

"But they did not feed him." Bubble pondered this, looking back to his brother. "This is a great evil. I did not know men were so cruel."

Annis sniffed and folded her arms. "It is not cruelty. Only one cannot go around feeding every poor and starving orphan in the nine lands. There is not enough food, for one thing."

"There are always fish. Bubble will go now and build your air. Feed the sick child."

He turned and leapt into the river. Stream slipped into the current beside him. Gem stared after them, flabbergasted.

"I am not sick!"

"You could be," said Loren. "Look at you. You are more bone than meat."

"And it has brought us the wurts' help when our journey seemed hopeless," said Xain. "Be thankful for that. Sometimes a frail look can be a distinct advantage."

His eyes stayed on Annis for a moment, and his right hand stole to his elbow. Pick, pick.

EIGHTEEN

THEY WAITED UPON THAT RIVERBANK THE REST OF THE day, with Bubble vanishing and reappearing every so often. An hour would pass with no sign of the wurt, and then he would spring from the shallows clutching yet another fish.

"You are still hungry," said Bubble, pointing at Gem. "Eat."

After the second or third time, Gem threw up his hands and scowled. "I have eaten fish until I never wish to taste it again! I am not hungry!"

Bubble indicated the boy's belly, still thin enough to see the ribs. "You have not eaten enough. You are sick."

"I am *not* sick!"

Loren was more than happy to keep eating, for they had been hungry many days, and she did not know how they would acquire provisions in Wellmont. Xain and Annis had spent the last of their coin. Loren would have to steal something, she supposed, and the prospect thrilled her less than she thought it might. But when she put a fish upon the fire, Bubble interrupted her.

"Bubble saw you do this before," he said. "Why?"

"Do what?" said Loren. "We are eating the fish you brought us."

"You are burning it. Ruining it with fire."

"She is only cooking it," said Annis.

Bubble blinked. "Bubble does not know this word."

"Cooking!" said Gem, exasperated. "Putting the fish on the fire until it browns, so you can eat it. Do you think we would eat the foul things raw?"

"Bubble does not know this word."

"Bubble does not know *any* words!" said Gem. "How do you eat fish?"

The wurt vanished into the river and reappeared with another fish. Then, to Loren's disgust, he tore into it with his sharp teeth, swallowing the meat without chewing.

"Ugh," said Gem. "I was full before. Now I will not eat for a week."

Bubble also seemed fascinated, if terrified, by Xain. The wurt would sit a few paces away, staring at the wizard while Xain pretended to take no notice. If ever he glanced in Bubble's direction, the wurt would scuttle away. After Bubble had studied him for almost a half-hour, the wizard finally pounded his hand on the ground.

"What? What are you staring at, creature?"

Bubble vanished into the river and did not reappear for more than an hour, while Xain pointedly ignored the disapproving stares of Loren and Annis. Gem, however, seemed to enjoy the reprieve, and took a nap upon the grass in the afternoon sun.

When Bubble finally surfaced, Loren headed him off before he could approach Xain. "You must forgive our friend. He is spent, as are we all. Do you require anything from him? Mayhap if you asked . . ."

"His face," said Bubble. "It is covered with weeds, like your heads. But only his face bears them, and not yours."

Loren looked at Xain for a moment before she understood. "His beard?" In truth it was a poor thing, merely a few days' growth the wizard had not had time to shave. "All men have such. Well, almost all," she amended, thinking of Chet's laughable attempts to grow a beard back in the Birchwood.

"It is . . . a sickness?"

Xain's scowl deepened, and Loren fought not to laugh. "No, not a sickness. It is natural. The same as growing teeth."

Bubble blinked at her. "Bubble has seen it before, but has never understood. Thank you for this lore."

Loren shrugged. "Of course. Such knowledge is commonplace among us, and would hardly be considered lore."

"Bubble knows more of man-lore than any other in his clan," said the wurt, and Loren thought she heard pride in his voice. "One day the leaders will come to him to learn everything about men, the way they once came to Bubble's father."

"Is your father very wise?" said Loren.

"The wisest," said Bubble. "He was loremaster of our clan, and all of our knowledge swam in his mind. But he is gone now." The wurt's gaze dropped to the ground.

"I am sorry," said Loren quietly. "I have often wished for a father I would miss, and you do him a great honor."

Bubble peered up at her, and his already-watery eyes gave him the appearance of weeping. "It is well. Bubble is proud to have had him for a father." He sprang up suddenly. "Bubble must go see what Stream has done."

Finally, just as the sun finished its long descent beyond the far horizon, Bubble and Stream emerged from the river together. As before, Stream hung back while Bubble came forwards to speak.

"Your air is ready. You must follow Bubble now, and we must all of us stay silent. You cannot go in the water, so you must hide yourselves upon the land."

"We can go unseen when we wish," said Loren. "Show us the way."

First they had to cross the stream. Loren wished Bubble had told them this earlier, for they had to do it in the dimming glow of twilight. They could not swim across with their cloaks and packs; Gem could not swim at all. By the time they came upon a shallow place to ford, the sun's rays had nearly gone. Gem slipped once upon the rocks as they crossed, and thrashed wildly in the water until Stream sprang forwards to rescue him. Loren thanked the sky above that the boy did not have any food in his pack, for it would have been soaked through.

They walked south down the river until it rejoined the Dragon's Tail, and then slipped along the shore towards Wellmont. They passed the Dorsean blockade that stretched across the river; the decks were alight with the glow of torches and lanterns. But the light did not reach the shore, and there were many low bushes and trees to hide them. They passed the ships after a moment, and Loren sighed with relief.

"The worst is over," said Annis. "At least, I hope so. I do not know how the wurts mean to get us under the rivergate, and I only hope we do not have to—"

"Cease your prattling," said Xain, and Loren thought his voice far too harsh. She tried to glare at him in the moonslight, but either he did not see it or he avoided her gaze.

More torches dusted the tall walls of Wellmont, rising higher and higher as they approached. These walls were far greater than those of Cabrus, which had been the largest she had ever seen. Some ten paces high they must have stood, and seemed several paces thick. They stretched out far in both directions, promising a sprawling city within, and Loren felt overawed at the sight of them.

"What army could hope to breach these walls?" she whispered, hardly aware she had spoken aloud.

"Enough men can destroy a mountain if they take a pebble at a time," said Xain. "And there are more ways to conquer a city than flinging your arrows and swords at it."

Though no one gave a command, they all fell silent as they came still closer to the walls. They could see the guards pacing far above, and they knew an alarm could mean their death. No doubt every man bore a longbow and would fill the air with shafts at the slightest provocation.

It was a harrowing experience, but soon they reached the rivergate. Wide and strong, the gates were formed of steel. They met in the river's middle, and Loren could see a great spar across the top that held them closed. Where they met the water they became grates, with holes so narrow that Loren doubted even Gem could slip his hand inside. The grates tore and tugged at the flowing water, creating dozens of streaming whirlpools that gurgled loud in the night. The grates sank into the river, and in the darkness Loren could barely imagine how far they descended.

"How do they mean to get us under that?" whispered Gem. "It must go down to the river's bottom."

Loren thought of telling the boy to be silent, but she realized that the swirling water would mask all but a shout. "They seem to know their business. Let us wait and see."

Bubble emerged from the river. Stream followed a moment later. Behind him, Bubble dragged something in his webbed fingers. It looked to Loren like a bowl, only much larger than any she had ever seen. It stretched almost as wide as her arm span, and it was as deep as half her body. It looked to be formed of some combination of branches, reeds, and mud.

"Here is your air," said Bubble. "Beneath it you can breathe long enough to swim under the gate."

"What?" said Gem. "How will an oversized dinner bowl help us?"

"Come," said Bubble, motioning to Loren. "Bubble will show you."

Loren hesitated, but they had come too far to turn back now. She removed her cloak and folded it into her pack, while Xain and Annis did likewise. Slowly she waded out into the river. Summer had warmed the waters from spring's chill, but still the cold almost took her breath. She waved her arms back and forth, trying to work her blood up.

"Now we will give you air," said Bubble.

Together, he and Stream lifted the bowl and placed it over Loren's head. In another moment, she heard a splash as Bubble's head came out of the water below her. It was pitch-black in the bowl, so dark that she could not see his face.

"Go farther into the water," he said. "Your air will come with you."

Loren swallowed hard. She forced herself to take a step deeper into the river. Then another. The water stayed at her chest, leaving her head and shoulders in open air within the bowl. A thrill shot through her, and she took yet another step. The water must have been over the top of the bowl, though not so much as a drop fell upon her head. She was shrouded in utter darkness, and could not see an finger's length in front of her nose.

She heard Bubble splash into the water. "You see? Now turn around and go back to the others."

Loren turned—it was hard to keep a sense of direction when she could see nothing—and retraced her steps. Soon the bowl rose up and over her head, and she found herself in the open air upon the shore. She shivered as the night's breeze struck her soaked breeches.

"It works!" she cried out, before remembering to whisper. "The air stays inside, and you can breathe. It is like magic."

"Not magic," said Bubble. "Bubble only knows the way to craft things water cannot enter. Many wurts know the skill." The wurt's modesty was only slightly less charming coming from his pointed teeth and white, lidless eyes.

"You expect me to climb into that thing?" said Annis. Her voice had grown shrill and raspy, and she clutched her arms in a panic.

Loren's face fell. She had forgotten. Annis feared any dark and closed space. In the sewers of Cabrus she had been nearly useless, unable to move without constant goading and guidance.

"I will come with you," said Loren. "We will do it together."

"No!" cried Annis, and now she had forgotten herself completely. Loren started and looked up at the top of the wall, but no watchful faces emerged. "I will not climb willingly into that death trap!"

Before Loren could respond, Gem came between them and put his hands on Annis' shoulders. He sought to catch her gaze, waiting until finally she looked into his eyes. "Let me accompany you, then. You remember what I taught you beneath Cabrus? Breathing. Everything is in your breath. I will teach you again, reminding you as we pass beneath the gate together."

"I . . . I cannot . . ." said Annis.

"You can," said Gem. "Slow. In. And out. Come—do it for me now, as practice."

Annis took one long, slow breath in, and then released it in a heavy sigh. In and out. Once more, and Loren saw some of the fear drain from her, like water from a twisted rag.

"Good," said Gem. "You can do that a few more times, can you not? While we take a night's stroll on the riverbed?"

Annis shook her head, but the conviction had left her. "I am still frightened."

"We live our lives frightened. But still we must go on," said Gem.

Annis did not answer. Loren could see her shoulders shaking beneath Gem's fingers. But finally the girl nodded, a quick, furtive movement.

"Good," said Loren. "I will go first to show you it is safe. Gem, bring Annis after me. Xain, you will come last."

The wizard nodded. Loren gave Annis a quick hug and a reassuring smile before stepping back into the shallows.

"Remember, come as quickly as you can," she told Annis. "And close your eyes if that will help."

"It certainly will not," said Annis. "Just go, so that we may get this over with."

Bubble and Stream raised the bowl and placed it over Loren's head. She walked forwards, and soon the water passed over the top. Darkness enveloped her, a darkness as complete as any she had ever experienced.

The ground grew slicker the farther she went, until she sank up to her ankles with every step. But the bowl kept the water around her thighs, and she could place her hands on either side to hold her footing. It swirled as it passed, but there was not enough of it to matter. After many steps, the bowl moved to Loren's right. *Bubble is guiding me,* she thought. So she turned with the motion, and now her steps carried her to where she knew the rivergate waited.

Her breath began to come hard, and she felt lightheaded without knowing why. Each step grew difficult, and she put her hands on the bowl to keep from falling. When it suddenly stopped, she nearly bumped her head.

She heard a splash as Bubble's head poked out of the water by her legs. "Bubble has made a mistake. The bowl is too large to pass under the gate. You will have to swim from here."

"Swim?" Something about that bothered her, though she could not remember what. Her mind spun, and she could scarcely consider Bubble's words. Spots of light danced before her eyes, and she thought they were stars, until she realized the stars were high above and hidden from her. Her lungs burned.

"Go into the water and swim forwards. You will feel the gate. Pass beneath it and swim up."

"Which way is up?" said Loren, but Bubble had vanished already. Then, without warning, the bowl began to rise around her.

She almost panicked, but then she felt Bubble's hand on her arm. The wurt pushed her forwards, and as she thrust her hands out they encountered the iron of the rivergate. She used it to pull herself under. Her lungs screamed at her now, and she pushed from the river floor as hard as she could. Up and up she rose, bouncing off the gate in her ascent as the flowing waters threw her against it.

The world grew lighter. *More spots in my eyes,* she thought, until she realized the stars had returned. Then her head broke the surface, and she sucked in a deep gasp of air. The river hurled her against the gate, and she did not resist. She sat in the current, sucking in the sweetest air of her life.

After a moment Loren came to herself and opened her eyes. Thankfully, no one stood anywhere close by. Like Redbrook, Wellmont had built stone walls along the river's edge, with docks for small boats. But no one patrolled those docks, and the only fires came from torches and lanterns mounted on walls. No one in Wellmont feared entry through the river—the gate was too strong.

Loren paddled towards the closest dock, keeping her movements slow and soft to avoid a splash that might alert the guards. She had crossed half the distance to the dock when she remembered something—

the thought that her mind had struggled with when Bubble told her she must swim: *Gem.*

She froze in a panic. The boy could barely tread water.

But Bubble would tell them all the bowl was too large, and then he and Gem would work out a plan, would they not?

What if he failed to warn them? What if Gem chanced it anyway, and died below the rivergate, his body sinking to the bottom?

Lorch looked at the water. She did not know how deep the river was, but she had to try to swim beneath it, or Gem might perish.

She took a breath and readied herself to dive, but lost her nerve at the last moment. She gasped again, steeling herself. Then at last she plunged into the blackness of the water.

Struck by a thought, she seized the iron grating of the rivergate and used it to pull herself down. That, combined with her swift kicking, propelled her at a good speed. Down and down she dove, hoping she kept the right direction and that Bubble did not bring Gem to some other part of the gate. But the river seemed bottomless. With each outstretched hand she expected to touch its silty bed, but there was only more water.

For a moment she thought of surfacing to breathe and trying again. But the thought of Gem drowning propelled her. Again she felt dizzy, her head light, the darkness around her impenetrable.

Her hand reached for the next rung and found nothing. She had found the rivergate bottom.

She pulled herself underneath it. Whether Gem was near or no, she could not wait for him. If she did not surface, she would drown. But just as she seized the gate and prepared to launch upwards, Loren felt something strike her leg. A fish? She reached towards it. It struck her again—a limb, certainly.

It slipped from her grip when she tried to seize it. With one hand she pulled herself along the rivergate, reaching again. This time she found it—a wildly flailing arm. It must be Gem. She seized him and pulled, trying to drag him under the gate. She could feel the panic in his thrashing.

The figure fought her, but somehow she managed to push them both beneath the rivergate. It took nearly every bit of strength she had.

The spots in her eyes became a milky white film. Everything grew white, a faint glow of peace and tranquility. She tried swimming for air, but her limbs could not move. Why should they? It was so peaceful to float. Each limb drifted of its own accord, bouncing against the rivergate in a beautiful dance.

White turned to black, and Loren knew no more.

NINETEEN

LOREN AWOKE AND FOUND ONLY PAIN.

It burned in her chest, and it attacked her throat as a fountain of water spouted forth. She hacked and coughed, but the water flowed of its own accord whether she tried to breathe in or out.

Why did it keep flowing? She needed to *breathe.*

The last drops finally slipped out, and Loren sucked sweet life from the air. It still burned, but now she did not mind. She rolled onto her stomach, coughing until she thought her heart might stop. Saliva spattered the wood beneath her, and then bile as she vomited.

A sour, brackish taste washed across her tongue as the day's fish fled her stomach in a rush.

"Steady on!" cried Gem. "You nearly got my feet."

"Be silent, boy!" growled Xain.

Loren felt strong hands roll her over and pull her into a sitting position. Someone struck her back again and again, pounding her until the vomit halted and she could breathe. Loren tried to tell them to stop, but only a croak came out. Desperately she tried to push the person away, but her hands flailed uselessly against them. The effort nearly made her faint again, and she collapsed into the person's arms, feeling her vomit-soaked lips soil their clothes. She found it impossible to care.

"You are all right. You are alive. Can you sit up?"

She did not know the answer at first, did not even understand the words. Slowly they became clear in her mind. Almost she fell over again, but by placing a hand on the ground to either side she managed to keep upright.

"I am all right." Her voice sounded awful, like some vile creature from a dark tale.

"Hardly," said Xain.

Loren looked up at him and saw the last remnants of light fading from his eyes. Magic. "You saved me?"

"Something I learned upon the Seat," said Xain. "Moving the water from a person's lungs is not so difficult, once you know how."

"I . . ." She dissolved into a fit of coughing. "Thank you."

"I think I had little to do with it," he said gruffly. "Death seems to avoid you like a leper, though the same cannot be said for peril."

As her head cleared and she looked up to see Gem, Loren slowly remembered what had happened. The darkness of the river. The rushing waters. A flailing, grasping hand.

Gem stood there, soaked but safe, a curious look in his eyes. Bubble crouched not far away, at the edge of the stone wall that rimmed the river. But Annis . . .

"Where is Annis?" cried Loren.

"She is alive," said Xain. "Though hardly unscathed."

He pointed, and Loren followed his gaze. They were several paces from the city wall. Against it, sitting in shadows cast by nearby torches, she saw Annis. The girl seemed slight and shrunken. Her cheeks were wet from the river, and were made wetter still by the tears that poured from her eyes.

"Annis! Are you all right?" Loren tried to stand, but her limbs betrayed her, and she collapsed to the cobblestones. She had to move in a sort of sliding crawl, slithering along the ground like a snake.

"Stop!" said Annis. She got up and ran to Loren's side, helping her sit up again. "I am fine, I am unhurt. Only, what I did . . . you almost . . ." She could not speak more, and bent her head to hide her face.

"This one grew frightened beneath the rivergate." Bubble had not spoken since Loren awoke, but now he hobbled closer on all fours. "Both children went mad, screaming at Bubble and Stream in the water. Bubble decided to push them under the gate, and chose the smaller child to bring up. Stream was supposed to move this one, but when she struck at him in fear Stream ran away."

The wurt hung his head, clearly ashamed.

"I was surrounded by blackness," said Annis through her tears. "I thought I would drown there, and I could not find anything to save me. Then I felt your arm—though of course I did not *know* it was your arm, I thought it was some *thing* come to seize me in the darkness. So I fought until I felt the gate, and I swam for the top, but you . . ."

"I am all right," said Loren. She reached out and dragged Annis into an embrace. The girl's clothing was clammy against her skin, but Loren did not care. "I am alive. And you are, too."

"I would have died were it not for you," said Annis. "I will never forget that."

"All quite silly, if you ask me," said Gem. "I did not think it so bad when Bubble carried me."

"Stream has done a great evil," said Bubble, head still bowed. "Bubble is sorry. Bubble will ensure the masters know what Stream has done. They will punish him."

"As well they should," said Annis, some of her tears turning to anger. "He nearly got me killed!"

Bubble flinched, shrinking like a wilting flower. Loren put a hand on Annis' shoulder and spoke calmly. "What is done is done, Bubble. You must forgive him. He was probably as frightened as Annis when she attacked him. And without you, we would be starving beyond the walls of Wellmont. Please, speak nothing of this to your people, and tell Stream that we are all right."

Bubble's head lifted slightly. "You . . . Bubble does not know the word."

"We forgive him," said Loren. "You have both helped us beyond measure. Do not punish him for that."

Bubble blinked twice, slowly, the thin film of his eyelids glistening in the torchlight. "This is a good thing that you do. A grand thing. Bubble thanks you."

Loren felt herself blushing, warm against the chill of her wet clothes. "Anyone would do the same."

Above them, Xain looked back and forth warily. "We need to move on, and quickly," he said. "If anyone were to see four soaked strangers sitting by the rivergate, it would not take long to work out how we entered the city, and they would think we were invaders."

Loren nodded to him and turned back to Bubble. "You have our gratitude, Bubble. If ever you require my help, consider me at your service."

"And that is no idle promise," said Gem. "That is the promise of the Nightblade."

Bubble blinked. "Bubble does not know this word."

"Hush, Gem," said Loren hastily.

"Nightblade is her," said Gem, pointing at Loren. "And she is the greatest thief in the nine lands, or soon will be. She is cloaked in darkness, and no lock can keep her from coin or treasure."

"Gem! Enough!" barked Loren. All of them flinched and looked around for guards. She went on in a whisper. "That is enough. Bubble, we must leave. If ever I pass by your lands, I will try to visit you again and bring a token of my thanks. Until then, fare well. And do not forget to tell Stream that Annis is all right."

Bubble nodded slowly. "Bubble will do this. Fare well, Nightblade."

He turned and leapt into the water, vanishing with hardly a splash.

Loren turned on Gem. "Just what was all that about? I am cloaked in soaking, filthy clothes, not darkness."

"Words of your deeds have already spread throughout Cabrus," said Gem, shrugging. "Why should they not spread farther?"

"You are being ridiculous," Loren growled. "Bubble has seen us do no deeds except nearly drown in a river."

"Some have grown famous for less," said Gem.

They slipped into the city's dim torchlight, searching for an inn where they could dry themselves and sleep. Fortunately it did not take long to find one, and the innkeeper greeted them joyously. They soon learned that the city had nearly emptied, as all in Wellmont grew fearful of the army at their gates. Thinking quickly, Loren lied and said they planned to stay for some time, and at the prospect of such business the innkeeper offered them a free dinner.

Loren had wondered how they would pay for their room, but Xain produced a coin from a hidden pocket in his cloak. Loren raised an eyebrow, for she had thought the wizard spent all his money on provisions after they left Redbrook.

Xain shrugged. "I learned long ago never to spend my last coin unless I had no other choice."

And that seemed to be the truth of it. The free meal was fortunate, for they had no money with which to buy food. Loren did not know how they would pay for a second night if they stayed in the city. They huddled near the common room's fire to dry off, for they had no clothing to change into except in their packs, which had gone beneath the rivergate with them. They devoured their fare and traded glances from hooded eyes.

It was Annis who finally broke the silence. "What will we do tomorrow?"

"Live in an alley, I suppose," said Gem. "It is not so bad as you might think, though I understand a merchant's daughter like yourself may disagree."

"We will have to find somewhere to work for coin," said Xain. "At least enough to pay for passage from the city."

"How?" said Annis. "Bubble told us they are not letting anyone in or out."

"Not through the river," said Xain. "But mayhap we can leave by the northern road. No army besieges the city there, so they may let some pass through it."

"We cannot afford to wait long enough to earn coin," said Loren. "We must leave tomorrow, and no later. We can trade work for passage."

"Work?" said Xain, scowling. "What work can we four offer?"

"Guard work?" Even as the words left Loren's lips she heard how ridiculous they sounded. She had only her dagger, and Xain his knife. A wizard he might be, but surely a caravan driver would prefer steel and armor to words of power.

Xain snorted. "We will have to work for the coin, and there is nothing for it," he said.

"We could always steal it," said Annis. "I have it on good authority that we dine with the greatest thief in all of Underrealm."

Gem smiled. Loren frowned and kept her eyes on her food.

TWENTY

ONCE THEY HAD DRIED THEMSELVES ENOUGH THEY went to bed, laying their clothing all across the room to let the water drain from it. But though the summer night was warm, it did not prove warm enough. They woke to find their things still damp and smelling faintly of mildew.

"Ugh," said Gem, curling his nose. "This will only get worse as we travel on, I do not doubt."

"If mold is our worst problem in the days to come, I shall count us lucky," said Xain.

"Do you know where you mean to look for work today?" said Loren. "You know this city, do you not?"

"I do, but not as well as some others. We might try the inns, but if their guests have fled Wellmont they will not need more mouths to feed. The smiths, no doubt, are busy making weapons and armor. Can you pull a bellows?"

"I can learn," said Loren. "Annis, you should remain here today and keep an eye on our clothing. You can take it down to the fire a few pieces at a time to help it dry faster."

"I wish you fortune plying honest trade," said Gem. "As for me, I will gather coin in the manner to which I am accustomed."

"Meaning steal it," said Annis, sniffing slightly.

"You are yourself a thief, do not forget." Loren pushed Annis gently on the shoulder. The girl had not quite recovered from her fright the night before, and Loren wanted to bring her out of it. Those who lived in fear were often unpredictable, and hard to count on at need. Annis gave her a wan smile in return.

They asked the innkeeper, who did not know any smiths looking for hands but recommended they try the craftsman's quarter in the city's northwest corner. So as Annis began laying out their clothing, they set out upon the city's streets.

Gem decided to tag along, saying, "Where there are crafts and trade, there is coin." Certainly it seemed the marketplace would have purses to lift.

Loren wore her black cloak again, and she enjoyed the looks it attracted as they walked in the early morning light. With a plain-clothed man at her side and an urchin boy at her heels, she probably looked like some lesser noblewoman with a valet and footman.

But the city's mood soon dampened her enthusiasm. Everyone seemed on edge, and looked at one another with wariness if not outright fear. It was a solemn reminder that these people were besieged. Mayhap some had lost friends or family. That sobered Loren, and it seemed less amusing to play the little noblewoman.

In the craftsman's quarter they found many smiths hard at work, but none in need of assistants. One of them took a look at Loren's black cloak and another look at Xain's arms, and laughed as he sent them away. Smithies were busy, and so smithies were paid, and so smithy assistants were plentiful. In each they saw strong young men pounding at anvils and pulling hard on bellows. It was the same at the fletchers, where men sat at benches by the dozens nailing arrowheads and feathering shafts. One fletcher was willing to take on more, but when they asked for a gold weight a day he grew angry.

"You see these workers? I pay them two silver pennies, and they already know what they are doing. Do you wish to get rich off the war? Become a soldier, and hope you do not take an arrow in the eye. And that the mayor does not forget to pay you."

Gem, on the other hand, did quite well for himself. By midday he had already gathered several pennies. It bought them lunch, at least, when they rejoined Annis at the inn.

"The fletcher is right, you know," said Loren. "These people do not work only for coin. They labor to save their city. We look like grave robbers if we ask for enough money to get beyond the walls."

"What, then, do you suggest?" Xain said. "It is easier to see a plan's flaws than to think up your own."

"I had thought of a plan, in fact, but it is not . . . respectable," said Loren.

Xain's eyes narrowed. "Tell us. We have all of us passed beyond the bounds of respectability some time ago."

Annis shifted in her seat and looked about nervously, while Gem leaned in to listen. Loren drew a breath.

"They cannot have closed the gates entirely," said Loren. "Still some wagons must be let through. To bring in and sell supplies at least, else the city will starve. And if those wagons come in, some must leave."

"Guard work again?" said Xain. "They will take one look at the children and throw us out. And neither you nor I have arms or armor, nor the skill to wield them."

"I know something of swordplay." In truth Loren had only had the one dance with Gregor when she rode with the merchant caravan, so it was an idle boast—but Xain did not know that. "Guard work is not what I plan, however. Supplies from outside Wellmont will be few, and so they will be precious. Any merchant who plies his trade here will gain a purse fat from coin."

Gem's eyes lit up. "And a fat purse could buy our way out."

"Just so," said Loren with a nod. "If we could liberate even one wallet, that might be enough. We could buy our way onto a wagon—or at least get supplies and bribe a guard to let us out the gate."

"The Nightblade you are indeed," said Gem as he laughed. Loren frowned at him.

But Xain still looked dour, and his nervous twitching increased. "I think you view the task too lightly. It would not do you well to believe all the stories you tell others about yourself. Are you a master thief in truth, or only in aspiration? For no merchant will simply leave a purse hanging idle, its strings awaiting the kiss of your dagger. They will keep their coin hidden, and they will have guards."

Loren shrugged. "Then ignore the merchants. Seek the craftsmen who come here from their farms and villages. They will have thinner purses, but a thin purse unguarded is better than a fat one under lock and key."

Xain looked at her in surprise. "These are not wealthy folk you mean to rob. I had not thought you so ruthless."

"It is not ruthlessness," said Loren angrily. "It is necessity. Do you think I jest when I say another army marches upon this place? I know what I mean to do. I grew up in a village of simple craftsmen. Losing the sale of a single cartload will cause no one to starve, only to tighten their belts for a few months. If we do not escape Wellmont, and soon, we invite our own doom."

The party fell silent at that. Xain looked away, Annis stared at the table, and Gem gazed upon Loren with awe. She saw a respect in the boy's eyes that had not been there before, something beyond his usual affection. She was not sure whether to be pleased.

Xain picked at his elbow, and his eyes drifted to Annis. "I should come. In case you are discovered, and more powerful measures are required to aid your flight. Annis, too."

"Why Annis?" said Loren.

"She has the stones. I might need their aid again."

Something came over Xain as he spoke, and Loren did not like it. His eyes gleamed with a curious light, akin to and yet unlike their glow when he used his magic. His lips drew back from his teeth, and the hunger in his face was unmistakable. Loren felt the desire to move away.

"We mean to prey on peasants, not wizards," she said. "You should come, yes, but Annis should remain to guard our gear, paltry though it may be."

Xain's mood soured. "If you do not respect my counsel, then you may excuse yourself from my help. I will stay too, and help Annis tend to our things."

Loren felt a pit form in her gut. She did not know what this was about, but she did not like it, and she knew with certainty that she had no wish to leave the wizard alone with Annis, not even for a moment.

"You will come with us, or we will not go at all," she said. "You spoke truly in the first place: if we are hard beset, we shall need you. I will not risk both our lives on this errand without your help."

Xain's jaw clenched once, twice, a third time. The fingers of his right hand ceased their endless picking and formed into a fist. Loren readied herself to spring back from the table, dragging Annis with her. But then the wizard sighed, and Loren saw some of his frustration leave him.

"Very well," he said, his voice hollow and quiet. "We shall do as you say—Nightblade."

"Good." Loren tried to sound as though she had noticed nothing amiss. "We should be off at once, then."

"But I am not finished!" said Gem, speaking through a mouthful of stew-soaked bread.

"Get up, Gem."

She dragged him from the table, his fingers grasping at the last scraps on his plate, and they left the inn. As Xain readied himself, Loren stepped aside and whispered to Annis.

"Where are the stones?"

"Within my cloak, as they have always been," said Annis.

"Find another place to keep them. Off your person, if you can manage it. They are too important to risk, and I do not trust Xain not to steal them."

"Steal them?" said Annis. "But I thought we meant to deal with him after all this—to give him half our store."

"We did. That is, we do," said Loren, correcting herself hastily. "But he may mean to claim his share early, leaving us with nothing."

"Is he dangerous?" Annis looked over Loren's shoulder to where Xain had stooped to lace his boots.

"He is a wizard," said Loren. "They always are."

"Are you ready, girl?" came Xain's voice behind her.

Loren turned with a smile. "Ready and eager. The Nightblade prepares to strike again."

Xain snorted, and for a moment he seemed his old self. "You are far too taken with that name, as well as the dreams behind it." Then his face grew hungry again as his eyes fell upon Annis.

Loren swallowed hard. "All great tales start with a name. Let us be off."

TWENTY-ONE

THEY RETURNED TO THE CRAFTSMAN'S QUARTER. DESPITE what Loren had said at the inn, it pained her to think of robbing such simple folk. But she consoled herself that such craftsmen would be living fat now, fed by the desperation of a fearful city, and might do so for many days to come.

They reached the great square at the center of the quarter. Hundreds of paces wide it was, and with a great statue of an armored man in the center. His head was bare, and he held a sword aloft. Just at the statue's feet, a wagon sagged to the side. Moving through the press of people, she saw why: the wagon had lost a wheel, and now the horses could not pull it. The owner, a large beast of a man with hair all over his face and arms, tried to lift the wagon where the wheel had come loose, while a boy tried to fit the wheel back to its housing. The wagon held scraps of lumber, but they were only dregs—its cargo had been sold already. The woodsman's cries of anger went unheeded by the crowd swirling round.

"This looks promising," said Loren. "Come, let us see more."

They drew closer still. And just as they approached, the woodsman dropped the wagon and straightened with a cry of anger, turning on the boy beside him.

"You useless whelp! If you do not get that wheel on, you will regret it."

"The cart is not high enough, Da," said the boy. He was skinny and pale, and hardly looked to be the son of a woodsman. "I cannot get it on unless it is higher."

"Talk back, will you?" And the woodsman lashed out with a punishing slap across the boy's face.

Her qualms fled. With boiling blood, Loren murmured to Xain and Gem, "Yes, this will do wonderfully."

"What do you mean to do?" said Xain.

"Never you mind," said Loren. "Only remain silent. Your tongue is as smooth as a sandy riverbank. Gem, watch for the purse, and take it as soon as you may."

"I will," said Gem. From the tone of his voice, Loren did not imagine he held any more love for the woodsman than she.

"Ho, friend!" said Loren amiably. "You look to be in a fix."

The lumberjack turned to her, scowling. "What is it to you? Be off, beggar."

Loren gave her cloak a little flourish, and she saw the lumberjack's eyes flick to its fine black cloth. "No beggars here, friend. Only a passing maiden who sees a stranded carpenter."

She saw the woodsman's chest puff out slightly. As a woodsman's daughter, Loren knew well that carpenters were highly regarded by the laborers who supplied them. "Only a simple woodsman, my lady," said the man with a leer. "Though bless your sweet tongue."

"A woodsman? Truly?" said Loren, feigning delight, though she wanted to slap him. "I was a woodsman's daughter until my father came into fortune. He fought for the king and earned himself a title."

"He is a fool who got lucky, then." The woodsman grinned. "Fighting wars is no business for a man who likes living, though I am pleased to hear a fellow workman profited from it."

Loren kept her smile bright. "Indeed. But I cannot let a fellow craftsman suffer so. Come, cousins. Let us help with their wagon."

"Not that one," said the woodsman, pointing at Gem. "I will not have him getting hurt on my account. Look at the little waif. He cannot have eaten in days."

"He is of that age," said Loren. "Three lunches have filled those legs today, with room to spare."

"That is a sign of health," said the woodsman. "I wish my son were the same." He cuffed the boy beside him once more, eliciting a yelp.

Loren's heart broke. The boy could not be a year older than Gem. "There is time yet," she said. "Come, then, cousin."

Xain looked at her with a blank expression until Loren seized his arm and pulled him to the wagon. Gem stood back, eyes darting everywhere, waiting. Together they lifted, and as the wagon rose, the woodsman's son fitted the wheel to the spoke. Then the woodsman cut himself a new spar to stick through the hole in the hub, and the wheel was fixed.

"Many thanks," said the woodsman. "I hope you expect no pay from a simple man such as myself."

"I would never dream of it," said Loren. "Payment spoils the virtue of the deed."

"As I have always said. Though that does not stop us from taking a good coin or two from those who need our wares, eh?" He laughed loud and long, as though sharing a secret joke.

Loren joined the laugh, hating the man more with every moment. "Right you are. I imagine things must be quite well for you here, with the city worried about the Dorseans."

"Arrows, fortifications, even stocks for deserters." The woodsman glanced around and, seeing no one else near, reached into a hidden compartment in his wagon. When his hand reemerged, it held a purse bigger than his fist, filled almost to bursting. "Just look at the measure of their need. Mayhap I can buy myself a title like your father, and never need wield a sword to earn it."

Over the man's shoulder, Loren saw Gem perk up. "My wishes are with you, my friend," she said. "But hide that quickly. They say this city has more thieves than cobblestones, and never more so than now."

"I do not doubt it," said the woodsman, stowing the purse again. "Hoy! Gillam! Get yourself on the wagon quick. We are off." His son scrambled to obey.

"I wish you safe travels under the sky," said Loren.

"Yourself as well, and may your road soon take you away from this place." The woodsman extended a hand. "If ever you travel along the Greatrocks, look for my village. It is two days' ride north of here. Gillam is my name, as it is my son's. We shall put you up and feed you well, though I am sure you would find our fare meager."

Loren was taken aback for a moment, but she swiftly recovered and took his wrist. "Thank you, Gillam. I am . . . I am Damaris. May we meet again."

Gillam gave her wrist a firm shake and went to the back of his wagon to ready it for travel. From the corner of her eye, Loren saw Gem wave the coin purse behind the man's back. But she had one thing to do before they could leave. Quick and silent as a fox, she stole to the front of the cart. The boy Gillam looked down at her as she approached, still nursing a welt on his face.

"Boy," she whispered. "Come with us."

He blinked. "What?"

Xain had followed Loren, and now he seized her shoulder. "What are you doing?" he whispered.

She shook him off. "There is no need to stay with a father who beats you. I ran from home. You can, too. Come with us, but quick! Now!"

"You are a fool, girl," said Xain, trying to pull her away.

Little Gillam drew back from her in fear. "Who are you? Get away from me!"

Loren balked. "I saw him hit you. No parent should treat a child so. Come with me, and you can find a better life." She took the boy's hand, but he yanked it from her grasp.

"Da!" cried the boy, sliding away on the wagon's seat. "Da! Help!"

The woodsman appeared like a ghost, his face an ugly scowl. "Stop yammering, boy. We are ready."

"Da, she wants to take me away!" cried the boy Gillam, thrusting an accusing finger at Loren.

The woodsman paused a moment in confusion and then rounded on her. "What is this?" he said, his voice suddenly low and dangerous.

Loren gulped. "The boy is mad," she said. "I know not what he speaks of."

"She said she would take me away," said little Gillam. "I do not want to go, Da."

It seemed the right time to escape, but before she could move Loren found Gillam's iron grip upon her. "What is this, then? You try to take my son away from me?"

His other hand swept up to strike her, but Xain caught his arm. "That would be a mistake, friend."

Gillam released Loren and gave Xain a great shove with one hand, at the same time catching his wrist. Xain fell to the ground, and the woodsman twisted his arm cruelly, drawing a cry of pain.

"Constables!" roared Gillam. *"Constables!"*

They must have been close, for a man and a woman in red leather appeared in an instant. "Who calls for the King's law?" said the woman.

"These ones tried to take my boy." Gillam pointed a meaty finger at Loren. "Them and their little . . . where is the child?"

Gillam spun, searching for Gem. Meanwhile the constables looked at Loren and Xain, brows raised in confusion.

"This man is spinning a tale," Loren said. "I am Damaris, of the family Yerrin, and I can assure you I . . ."

"She tried to take me away!" cried little Gillam from the wagon.

"There was a third one," said Gillam loudly. "He must have . . . wait . . ." His eyes squinted like a pig's. Releasing Xain, he ran to the wagon's side and stooped beside it. A moment later he rose with a roar of pure hatred.

"My coin! They have taken all my coin! Everything I had!"

He stomped around the wagon, approaching Loren with his fists raised high. But one of the constables stepped forwards to cut him off while the other constable stepped up to seize Loren's arm.

"Where is that little whelp of yours?" cried Gillam, trying to push past the constable. But even he was not so foolish as to strike the King's law. "More thieves than cobblestones, indeed! Where is my purse?"

"We do not know what he is saying," said Xain, finding his feet. "He attacked us in madness after we helped him with his wagon wheel."

"Woodsmen may be coarse, but they are not often mad," said the constable who held Loren's arm. She looked searchingly into Loren's green eyes. "You say you are of the family Yerrin? I have seen more than a few of them, and you do not share their look."

"She is a thief!" spat Gillam. "She has my coin!"

"I have nothing," said Loren. "You may search me if you wish."

"We will, and more besides," said the constable. "This mess needs sorting."

"There is nothing to sort! She has robbed me!"

"We shall have the truth of it soon," said the constable. "You will come with us. Bring the boy."

Xain stepped up, and Loren saw a terrible look in his eyes. But before he could whisper a word of power, Loren cried out "No!"

The wizard stopped, a hand held out before him.

"No, Xain," Loren said, more quietly. "It is all right. We will go with them. This shall all be sorted out. After all, we hold no stolen goods, do we?" She looked at him, trying to impart her meaning. Gem was gone. Without the urchin and the coins he carried, Gillam had no case against them.

Xain may have taken the point, or else he merely trusted her. In any case he relaxed, giving Loren a slow nod.

"This is madness!" bellowed Gillam. "I have been robbed, and you lot mean to ask *me* questions?"

"You will come to answer them, or spend the night in a cell," said the constable. "Which shall it be, woodsman?"

Gillam fumed. He grimaced and growled and ground his teeth. But he had little choice. His boy climbed down off the cart, and the constables led them all out of the market, pushing through the curious crowd that had formed around them.

"Let it be known, girl," said Gillam beside her. "I will see you face the King's justice for this. They take a finger for every stolen penny in Wellmont. Then they pull teeth. You will be a cripple by the time they are done with you."

"That is enough," said one of the constables, pushing Gillam along—and not gently.

Loren's mind raced. Without Gem, the woodsman seemed to have little claim upon them. But what if someone recognized Loren and Xain from their earlier search for work? What if it was discovered which inn they stayed at? The constables would go there, and they would find Gem—presumably with all of Gillam's coin. She knew she must think of something, and quickly.

They came to a tall, wide building with a yard bordered by a wooden fence. Within the gate, Loren saw constables at drill with blunted swords. Their cries rang out in the muggy afternoon, and each clash of steel on steel made her flinch. Behind them, a wooden gate closed with an ominous click.

"Well, this bodes excellently," said Xain.

The station's front door opened, and the constables led them inside. The lower floor held a large common room like the constables' station in Cabrus, with a desk where a clerk waited to record their names. But there, too, were many wide tables for officers to eat at and talk around. At one of those tables sat a constable with gold trim on his armor. He sat in counsel with many figures in red cloaks and hoods.

One of the figures looked up at them and froze. Then he stood, casting off his hood to reveal silvery hair and piercing, pale blue eyes.

Jordel.

Loren felt Xain stiffen beside her at the same time her own blood ran cold. And then beside Jordel, another figure stood—smaller, slighter, with pale skin and dark eyes. And next to Jordel's expression of perplexed wonder, Vivien's hungry smile turned Loren's heart to ice.

TWENTY-TWO

"LOREN OF THE FAMILY NELDA," SAID JORDEL. "I AM surprised to find you here, though not surprised to find you in the hands of the King's law."

Xain had frozen beside her. Loren risked a glance at the wizard, hoping he had enough wisdom to remain silent and still. Though the fear was plain on his face, she saw no light in his eyes, and his hands did not move.

Jordel came around the table with Vivien at his side. The other Mystics turned to watch. The constables who had captured Loren and Xain clearly did not know what to make of this, for they stood still in confusion. Gillam, too, looked puzzled, though still angry and suspicious.

"What offense brings them to the King's law?" said Jordel, addressing the constables. "Wait, I have a guess: thievery."

"That is right enough, my lord," said the constable. "Suspicion, anyway, though if you know them for the thieving kind it makes our job easier."

"I am afraid you will have to grant them a pardon and release them into my care," said Jordel, sighing as he looked at Loren. "Though they may not wish to come, I think they will prefer it to a cell."

"Hold a moment!" said Gillam. "These two have stolen a purse of my coin, and I will not leave here without my justice."

Jordel studied him. "I have no doubt they wronged you, though if I know this girl, it was not without some cause. Still, never let it be said the Mystics did not uphold the King's law. Vivien, see to it."

Vivien's smile broadened. Loren might have taken that for a good sign, an indication that the Mystic woman bore them no ill will for the battle of magicks upon the Dragon's Tail. But in Vivien's eyes was a hunger, and a promise Loren could not identify.

From her cloak Vivien withdrew a purse of coins. This she threw to Gillam, who caught it in a clumsy hand and opened it. The purse looked twice as fat as the one Gem had taken, and within it Loren saw the gleam not of silver, but gold. Gillam stared, his jaw so slack it nearly struck his chest.

"That is far more than his purse held," said Xain, fuming.

"I thought you said the woodsman was spinning tales," said the constable who held his arm.

Xain's face flushed, and Loren glared at him. "You call me a foolish girl," she said, "yet you speak with the grace and skill of a horse. One with no legs, at that."

"It is no great shame to be a poor liar," said Xain, but he would not meet her gaze.

"Enough of this," said Jordel. "We require haste—more than you know. Constable, leave them in my care."

"I am not partial to thieves," said the one who held Xain's arm, and her grip tightened.

"All folk have their uses, if the cause is great enough," said Jordel, with a look at Loren. "I will invoke my rights under the King's law if I must, but I would rather you gave them to me with trust than by duty."

"Take them, then," said the constable, pushing Xain forwards. "But take care that their grasping fingers do not stray again, lest they lose them."

"You have my word," said Jordel, and he bowed. "Thank you. Now come."

He waved them out. Loren needed no second urging and made for the door, but Xain hesitated. She gave him a look and gripped his arm, her hand replacing the constable's.

"Come, Xain," she said. "You cannot tell me you prefer even a constable's cell to Jordel's company."

"Yet I do, and I would prefer many worse things," said Xain. "Though mayhap we can still escape the cell and his company both."

At last he followed Jordel and Vivien outside, where Gillam scuttled off into the streets after a final wrathful look. But once they had left the constables' training yard, Xain stopped.

"I will not withhold gratitude for your help, Mystic, but I wonder at its cost," he said. "You have pursued me since first I left the High King's Seat, or so I have heard. Now you have found me, but I must disappoint you. I wish no business with you or your kind, now or ever, and I would take my leave."

"Mayhap you would take it, but I do not yet grant it," said Jordel. "I know not what you have feared from me these past months, but I do not mean to bring the King's justice upon you. We do not trouble ourselves with such things."

"No, you trouble yourselves with things much darker," said Xain. "Things I know little of, and have little wish to learn about."

"Darker than you might imagine," said Jordel, "though not dishonorable, for the most part. But come. Let us speak of these things over wine, where

I may explain my cause. I have earned that much, at least."

Still Xain was reluctant, and for a moment Loren thought he would refuse. But with a wary look, he nodded and let Jordel lead them on.

They did not go far; soon Jordel opened the door to a small tavern with a cold hearth. The place felt close and stuffy, and though it was mostly empty their voices did not carry far. It was as though the air, which was even soggier than outside, formed a thick cloud that stilled the voice. It felt like a place for discussing dark deeds and terrible secrets, and Loren immediately wished to leave.

Jordel led them to a table in the corner and ordered a bottle of wine with four cups. While the innkeeper bustled to bring the drink, Loren studied Vivien. The woman had remained silent ever since they left the constable's station, though her eyes rarely left Xain's face, and she held herself taut as a bowstring. She caught Loren staring at her once or twice, but her predator's smile only widened. At last the wine appeared, and the innkeeper vanished. Loren leaned forwards to speak before Jordel could begin.

"I do not relish the thought of speaking with this one present," said Loren, pointing at Vivien. "She has pursued us since Redbrook, and nearly killed us upon the river."

"Yes, I have heard the tale," said Jordel. "But Vivien is a loyal member of my order and has been of great service. Though our paths have rarely crossed, I have heard only the highest praise."

Vivien folded her arms on the table and spoke in a voice of silk. "You misunderstand me if you think I bore you animosity—or indeed, if you thought I pursued either of you. It was only the Yerrin girl I recognized, or thought I did. Her family and I have many dealings, and I thought it prudent to return their wayward child. Where is she, by the by?"

"Never you mind," spat Xain. "If you bore us no ill will, you had a queer way of showing it. You almost sank our vessel upon the Dragon's Tail."

"You *did* sink *my* vessel," said Vivien. "A curious thing, for I had thought you would be weak when I caught you. Yet you withstood me at my full strength. How was that done, may I ask?"

"I was born with a powerful gift," muttered Xain. "Though it has seemed more and more like a curse of late."

"It must be *very* powerful to have beaten me so thoroughly." Vivien tapped a fingernail against her teeth, studying him.

Xain's nostrils flared, and Loren thought of the magestones. The family Yerrin had dealt in the things for many years. If Vivien had befriended that family, she might know of their smuggling. Did the Mystic suspect Xain of using the stones? Would she even care? Loren still knew far too little about the things to guess.

"Enough of this," said Jordel. Vivien and Xain broke off from staring at each other and looked down at their cups. "You continue your swordplay of words, Xain, but I tell you again that I mean you no harm. Already I have commanded Vivien to withhold her hand from you, as well as any who travel with you. She will tell the family Yerrin nothing of the girl Annis—nothing more than she has already, I should say. Does that satisfy you?"

He looked from Xain to Loren. The wizard would not answer, but Loren nodded. "It satisfies me. If she holds to her word."

"I will obey my commander," said Vivien, but Loren thought she heard annoyance in the woman's words.

"Then let us return to the matter at hand," said Loren. "You have found me again, Jordel, and Xain into the bargain. I want to know what you mean to do with us. And how did you find us, in any case? The nine lands are wide."

Jordel shook his head slowly. "Still you ignore what I told you often in Cabrus. In the fabric of this world, some strings are woven close and some far apart. Some are intertwined, bound together, and find it hard to break free."

"You blame fate, then," said Loren. "You will pardon me if I think there is more to it."

"I am not blameless, it is true," said Jordel. "When you left me, I tried to follow your tracks. But once they met the river, I knew it for a fool's errand. You could have gone anywhere. I sent Seth to Redbrook to search there, and took a horse southwest here to Wellmont. Though it seemed an unlikely destination after you and I had discovered the mercenaries, still I felt a pressing need to see the city. For one thing, I hoped to warn them before the sellswords came. My road took me along the north bank of the Dragon's Tail, and that is how I chanced upon Vivien's ship. I found her the day after her battle with Xain, and she told me what had happened. I recognized you from her description of the riverboat's passengers, and knew I had taken the right course. Then I hastened my steps, trying to reach Wellmont before you could leave it for some other place. I have only arrived today, and no sooner had I instructed the constables to search for you than you walked in the front door."

"A pretty tale, if it is true," growled Xain.

"What of the other Mystics in the constables' station?" said Loren. "Who are they, and how did they come to be here?"

"The Mystics have long had a presence in Wellmont," said Vivien, "though we have no stronghold as we do in many other cities. They were assigned to help us find you."

"But while you may think my journey the more important part of the story, it is not," said Jordel. "An army marches towards Wellmont still, and I think it will grow larger the closer it gets, as Dorsea finds more sellswords to join the host. I have warned the city, but that is the most we can do. I fear Dorsea means to level Wellmont for good."

Loren looked at Xain, and he gave her a slow nod. "I told him as much, though he did not believe me," she said. "We mean to leave the city as soon as we can."

"Yet you found the gates barred, and had no way to attempt the journey," said Jordel, nodding. "I thought that might be the case. But under my badge, we may yet leave the city without incident."

"I cannot imagine that is the end of your plan," said Xain. "I do not doubt you have further schemes for us, Mystic, and I would sooner march myself back to the constables and sleep in their cells until I rot."

Before Jordel could answer, Vivien turned to him with disbelief. "You mean to flee? We should aid the city. With such a *powerful* wizard in its defense"—and here she looked at Xain—"the Dorseans cannot hope to breach the walls."

"I have no interest in the wars of the nine lands," said Xain, "and less in fighting by the side of a woman who tried to kill me only a few days past."

"I will not say I share Xain's sentiment," Jordel told her. "All conflicts bear some import in the work of our order. But we cannot lend our strength in this battle, for we would risk losing a far greater war. I am sorry, Vivien, for I know you once called this city your home. If you wish to stay and aid it, I will raise no hand to stop you."

"What good would I do on my own?" said Vivien. Her frigid mask slipped away as an angry fire burned in her eyes. "We are meant to maintain order. The fall of Wellmont would throw the whole south of Selvan into chaos. How can you turn away?"

His jaw clenched. "We forsake all ties when we don our cloaks. I have permitted you to remain if you wish. Do not ask for more, lest I revoke that privilege."

Vivien turned from him, and her gaze drifted far away. Loren saw the woman's mask slide gradually back into place, and soon it was as if there had never been any emotion there at all—only a smug indifference.

"As for us, we will leave at our earliest convenience," said Jordel. "Do you still have the urchin and the Yerrin girl with you?"

"Yes," said Loren. "They remain at the inn where we stayed the night."

"Good," said Jordel. "They, too, should come. The Yerrin girl may be of quite some use, and neither of them deserves to stay here while the city is at war."

"No one is more eager than I to leave this place," said Xain, "but I will not go with you, Mystic."

"Xain, I implore you," said Jordel earnestly. "There are great forces at work in Selvan and across all lands. Ones such as you may be our only hope of thwarting them. A darkness gathers."

"What do I care for that?" said Xain. "Only one thing concerns me—a boy who waits for me upon the High King's Seat."

Loren saw him pick at his elbow, and noticed he had almost worn through the fabric of his sleeve.

"You mean your son," said Jordel. "I know what happened to you on the Seat. If that is your only worry, I can ensure he is returned to you."

That stunned Xain to silence. Even Loren was taken aback, for she had not known Jordel knew of the wizard's child. The Mystic had never mentioned it before.

But Xain recovered swiftly. "So you say, and yet if it means entering into dealings with you and your order, I will not risk it. It would only bring greater sorrow upon him in the end. I will retrieve him by my own devices, or not at all."

Jordel's hands clenched, and Loren saw a flash in his eyes that frightened her. "Wizards are supposed to be men of learning, but your blind prejudice may be the doom of us all. Will you give me no measure of faith?"

"None willingly. You ask for trust, yet you tell me of whispered secrets and gathering darkness. You have given no faith yourself."

Jordel studied him for a little while, and then spoke in a heavy tone. "Very well. You leave me little choice."

Xain's hand leapt up, and with an arcane word his eyes began to glow. But in an instant, Jordel jumped across the table and seized his wrist, twisting it until Xain cried out. Vivien gestured, and Xain's arms slammed to his sides, his body cavorting like a marionette.

"Stay your hand, wizard!" cried Jordel. "I did not mean that I would bring you harm, and your suspicion suits you ill. Hear my words, nothing more."

Xain glared at him with hatred plain in his eyes, but he could do nothing. At last he gave a curt nod, and Jordel released his wrist. The tavern's keeper and some of the other patrons had stopped to give them odd looks, but at a glance from Jordel they returned to their drinks.

"You ask for faith," said Jordel. "I will give it to you. Let us speak privately. I will tell you all that I know—which is too much, as many in my order would be quick to remind me. And when I am done, you will wish I had held my tongue. But if that is the only way to earn your trust, let it be so. Will you agree?"

Xain studied him silently for a long moment, and his fingers drummed on the table. Vivien's eyes sparkled with interest.

"Why would you do this?" Xain said at last. "All of this. The pursuit, and this counsel. And do not tell me again how important I am. I do not trust the flattery of Mystics."

"I never flatter," said Jordel. "And when I tell you that your gifts are needed, it is only because I have never believed anything more. Tell me now: will you hear me?"

More drumming, and then Xain reached over to pick at his elbow. Loren noticed again how gaunt his cheeks had become—worse since they entered Wellmont, not better.

"Very well, Mystic," said Xain with a heavy sigh. "Let us speak and lay all our knowledge before each other. Then I may refuse you with a clear mind and both eyes open."

Jordel shook his head slowly. "If you refuse me when I have told you all, then you are not the man I thought you were."

TWENTY-THREE

THEY FINISHED THEIR CUPS IN HASTE. THE DAY HAD worn on, and so they returned to the inn where Gem and Annis waited. Vivien accompanied them, much to the displeasure of Loren and Xain. The children leapt up in joy when Loren entered the room, but recoiled in fear at the sight of the Mystics.

"Be still," said Loren, raising a hand to calm them. "Vivien is under Jordel's thrall, and has pledged to do us no harm. Annis, your family will learn nothing of you from her."

"Do you believe her promises?" said Annis. "She has the smile of a jackal and serpent's eyes."

"Such charming words from a child of the family Yerrin," said Vivien. "Your breeding shows well."

Loren decided to ignore that. "I do not believe her," she said. "But I have decided to believe Jordel, at least in this."

Gem, for his part, seemed pleased to see the Mystic again, and reached out to grip wrists. Jordel returned the boy's grasp with a grave nod before Gem turned back to Loren. "What happened when the constables took you?"

"They took us to Jordel," said Loren. "That is, they took us to their station, and Jordel was there. It was sheer happenstance."

"I was curious about that," said Vivien. "They brought you in for petty thievery. Tell me, why did you take that purse from the woodsman?"

Loren looked her in the eye. "As I said before, he spun a tale. We stole nothing, and were apprehended without cause." From the corner of her eye, she saw Gem slide something out of sight with his foot. It looked very much like a purse of coins.

Vivien met her gaze a long moment, and then turned to Jordel. "This one is too skilled a liar," she said lightly, as though praising the green in Loren's eyes. "The wizard admitted the theft, and yet I can see no falsehood in her expression."

"What makes you think I am lying? Mayhap the wizard was mistaken." If this was the only victory she could win against Vivien, Loren would take it.

"Oh, I think nothing," said Vivien, and there was sudden venom in her voice. "I *know* you are lying. Everything about you stinks of a liar." Then she smiled, and the venom disappeared. "I suppose I am able to tell because we are so much alike."

Loren shuddered.

Jordel had watched all this passively, though Loren noted that he looked at Vivien with something like disapproval. Now he turned to Xain. "You would do well to rest tonight before we speak on the morrow. It looks as though your road here was unkind, and many sleepless nights await you."

"Mayhap the road was unkind, or mayhap fellow travelers upon it," said Xain, glaring at Vivien. "But I feel as well as can be expected. My strength has never been greater."

"As you say," said Jordel, nodding. "We shall meet in the morning. And though I believe you will keep your word and remain here, I hope you do not blame me if I have two men stand guard downstairs to ensure it."

"If I blame you, will it change your mind?" said Xain.

"It will not."

"Then I will not."

"Where shall we meet you?" said Loren.

Jordel gave her a stern look. "I am sorry, but it seems you have misunderstood. I mean to speak only to Xain."

"What?" said Loren, putting her hands on her hips. "I traveled with you across half of Selvan, and with him across the other half. I deserve to hear your words as much as anyone else."

"What you deserve has little to do with it. My words for him are of dire importance, and many would think they should not be shared at all. I am only fortunate that I outrank most of those who believe so." Loren saw Vivien's eyes flash again.

"You mean to leave me waiting on your doorstep while the two of you discuss matters of great importance?" said Loren. "I will not be left out in the cold."

"It is the midst of summer, and you may wait wherever you wish," said Jordel. "But still my words are for Xain's ears alone. You seem to have regained some of your faith since you abandoned me on the King's road. If that is so, trust me in this."

Loren wanted to shout at him, to give him a thousand reasons he was wrong—but she could think of none, for she knew nothing of the dark news he withheld. She folded her arms and turned away from him in a sullen silence.

Jordel seemed to take that for an answer, for he spoke again to Xain. "You will find me at the constables' station where we met today. I will see you in the morning."

"No doubt you will," grumbled the wizard.

"I can trust your word in this?" said Jordel. "Remember, Xain, I have no darker motive than your own good—and you will regain your son, upon my honor."

"Yes, yes," said Xain, waving a hand. "I have heard this before. Leave, or you will press me too hard and I shall change my mind. Go!"

Jordel gave a nod and left. After giving them a final, uncomfortably familiar look, Vivien followed.

Loren waited long enough for them to move out of earshot, and then checked the hallway to ensure they had left before she spoke to Xain. "I assume you do not mean to attend the meeting he has offered?"

But to her surprise, Xain heaved a sigh. "I suppose that I shall, actually. I have only a half-formed idea of using magestones to blast my son's way to freedom. Who knows what Jordel may accomplish? Hearing his words cannot do my cause any greater harm than it has suffered already. And besides, his plan for leaving the city seems safer than our own. If he must be betrayed, we can do it once he has secured our escape."

"I am only glad he is back," said Gem. At Loren's frown, the boy shrugged. "I bore him none of the ill will you felt. He saved my life, after all."

"And ended many others," said Loren. "And now Vivien stands at his side."

"Where did she come from, anyway?" Annis shivered under her patchwork cloak. "I do not like the way she looked at me, nor do I have your faith in this Jordel. Xain told me plenty of tales about the Mystics when we traveled the King's road in pursuit of you."

"Even if Vivien seeks to betray you, she could bring no word to your family until long after we have left this place," said Loren. "And I think she means to stay here, to aid Wellmont in its siege against Dorsea."

"I hope that is true," said Annis. "I would not spend one moment longer at her side than I needed to. Did you hear how she spoke of my family and breeding? She is a serpent in human form."

"That I doubt," said Xain, "for she is a mentalist and not a therianthrope."

He smiled, but Loren, Gem, and Annis looked at him blankly. As he caught their looks, his smile soured, and he rubbed his arms as though cold.

"A jest for mages, I suppose. Some therianthropes—weremages, you call them—can take the form of a serpent. It was . . . it was only a jest."

Gem gave him a gentle pat on the arm and a condescending smile. "Leave the jests to those with quicker tongues, wizard. Stick to your magic—you seem skilled enough at that."

Xain shoved his arm away and left the room.

Both children had many questions about what had happened after Loren and Xain were captured, and Loren gave them the whole account. They also wanted to know about Jordel and Vivien, but for the most part Loren had no answers.

When they had exhausted themselves with asking, and Loren had told them what she could, she went downstairs to find Xain in the common room. With her she brought a coin from Gem's stolen purse to pay for another night's stay and food for them all.

Downstairs, she noticed two figures in red cloaks by the front door. Their cowls were thrown forwards so that Loren could not see their faces. She guessed these were the Mystics Jordel had left to guard against Xain's escape. She gave each a long look, and one by one they turned away.

Loren found the wizard deep into a bowl of questionable stew and halfway through a mug of dark ale. Another empty mug sat beside the first, and an empty bowl beside the one he ate from. Loren motioned to the innkeeper for a cup of wine and sat in silence before the wizard. He ate busily for a while as if oblivious to her presence. Soon his bowl was empty, and he drained the rest of his ale in a single long pull. Only then did he look up at her, wiping the foam from his scrub of beard.

"You seem ravenous," she said.

"We ate poorly on the river." It was true, but they had all sated their hunger long since, and Loren well knew it. "What do you want from me, girl? I cannot move the Mystic's mind, and it seems he will hold council with none but myself."

He had cut to the heart of the matter, to Loren's surprise. But she took it in stride, placing both elbows on the table as she leaned forwards. "But you could tell me after," she said. "I want to know of these great matters he means to hold as a secret."

"It could be nothing," said Xain. "Some conspiracy by lesser nobles to seize a throne in the outland kingdoms. Mystics are known to place greater importance in things than they deserve."

Loren thought of Jordel's icy blue eyes, of his stern mouth, so often smirking and so rarely frowning. "Jordel does not seem the kind of man who would call a thing important unless it truly was."

"Oh? And what do you know of him?" A serving woman came with Loren's wine, and Xain motioned for another mug of ale. "You have known him less time than you have known me, and still you know precious little about my past."

"It takes me hardly any time to take the measure of a man. But you avoid the point. Whatever Jordel says to you tomorrow, be it of high import or low, I want you to tell me."

She took a sip of the wine. Loren had never drunk in the Birchwood, and compared every cup to the first she had had with Damaris in Cabrus. That had been fine stuff, sweet and heady. What she drank now was base swill by comparison, but still it brought a lightness to her thoughts that she rather enjoyed.

Xain shrugged. "I will tell you whatever secrets the Mystic imparts upon me, then. Though I fear you will be disappointed."

"Do not be so sure," said Loren, taking another sip. "Even small bits of knowledge can be useful, if one can gather enough of them. Mennet once brought down a mighty king with the strength of a single whispered word."

Xain burst into laughter. His ale arrived, and he kept laughing as he drank deep, sending splashes of it to darken his coat. "Mennet? Now you talk of stories and legends."

"Not all legends are pure fancy," said Loren.

"Mennet's are. Do not tell me you believe his tales to be true? It is likely no one named Mennet ever lived at all."

Loren's ears burned, and she glared at the wizard. "Of course he did. There are a thousand tales of him. How could they all be false?"

"How could they all be true? You have lived a life of adventure for months now. Have you done even one great deed worthy of a story? Have you had the chance? How could you have a thousand such chances in a lifetime?"

"I am young yet." The wizard's words angered her, but she did not know why. Of course some of Mennet's stories must be flights of fancy, but to doubt his very existence? She had never considered that, and she did not like it. Then she remembered how she had escaped from her cell in Cabrus. "And besides, some of his tales are certainly true. I have already used one to escape my prison."

Xain ignored that. He had grown silent and intent, studying her face as though seeing her for the first time. Loren found his gaze uncomfortable. His cheeks seemed even more hollow in the dim glow of the fireplace, and his hair had grown thin and stringy. She thought suddenly that he looked like a skull with its skin stretched too tight, a scrap of wig desperately clinging to the top. But as sallow as his face seemed, his eyes had lost none of their vigor. In fact they gleamed brighter than ever, and bore some hint of a glow even though he used no magic. It was a frightening visage, and Loren found herself wishing he would look away.

"I feel I understand you at last," he said quietly. "That day I found you in the woods, you did not only seek to escape your home. You meant to find for yourself a life of adventure, some mighty quest that would lead you across the nine lands in search of fame and glory. You meant to become Mennet."

Loren scowled and took another sip of wine. "Do not be ridiculous. Mennet had a cloak of shadows and the blessings of the darkness itself. How could I hope to become that?"

Xain laughed again, and this time it came harsh and scornful. "You prove yourself out. You have already gained for yourself a cloak of deep black, and you call yourself the Nightblade. Oh, this is rich. You seek to live the Elf-tale life of a man who never even lived at all."

Loren wanted to strike him and flee from the table all at the same time. "Because they tell tales of him does not mean he did not live! People tell tales of the Wizard Kings, too. Do you think they were only a flight of fancy?"

That sobered him. "You compare the sun to the moons. We still feel the echoes of the Wizard Kings' power today. Laws exist, written in ancient texts from the days of their dark rule."

"And a story of Mennet helped me bend bars of iron using only cloth," said Loren triumphantly.

Xain's mood darkened further, but he waved a hand in dismissal. "Very well. Believe what you wish, only stop trying to pull me down your mad path of fancy. I would discuss with you another matter."

It was a poor victory, but a victory nonetheless, and Loren let it go. "Very well. What plagues you, wizard?"

Xain leaned forwards, and his eyes grew hungry. "After I speak to Jordel, I do not mean to go along with his plan. This you know."

"Of course," said Loren, nodding. "Though he may convince you."

"He will not," Xain insisted. "I may pledge myself to him anyway—we must escape the city, after all. But he may suspect a trick, and so refuse my service."

Loren knew that for the truth. Xain's tongue was as clumsy as a drunk merchant. "And if he does? What then?"

"I have another plan for escape," said Xain, speaking quickly now. "But for it to work, I will need another magestone."

Loren felt her heart skip, and she did not know why. "Tell me your plan," she said, not sure how to refuse him outright.

"With the power of a single stone, I could blast a hole in the city wall. Nothing dangerous—just large enough for one to slip through at a time—but enough for the four of us to flee. It would be over in a moment, before the guards could react."

Loren stared at him. "And then the armies of Dorsea would widen that crack, and come pouring through to kill everyone here."

Xain blinked. "I had not thought of that. But no, we could do it on the wall's northern side. The Dorseans would have to cross the river to reach it, and could not do so before Wellmont sealed the wall behind us."

"Leaving it weak, and ripe for sapping. And you have forgotten that a second army approaches from the north even now. Besides, the guards could easily shoot us with arrows."

"Very well," said Xain quickly. "I could use wind to lift us over the wall, flying away like birds."

"And they would shoot us down, just the same," said Loren, shaking her head. "No, Xain, our best and safest route of escape is still to purchase our way upon a wagon. What we stole yesterday should be enough."

Xain slammed a hand on the table. "I am telling you, we must use another—"

He caught himself at the last moment, and looking around, Loren saw that all eyes in the common room had turned to him—including those of the Mystics by the door. He glared at them until they looked away, and then leaned in to whisper.

"A magestone," he said. "It is the only way to be sure."

Loren steeled herself. "No, Xain. I will not. We agreed that you would receive your half when we reached your contact in Dorsea."

"But it is my share, is it not?" said Xain angrily. "Or do you mean to cheat me out of what is mine?"

"Of course not. But I will not have you squander it all before we arrive. You must save some for your son's rescue. Or have you forgotten him?"

She had pushed him too far, and she knew it before the words left her mouth. Xain snarled, and his hand clenched on the table. But suddenly he winced and lifted his hand, and Loren saw that the motion had driven a splinter deep into his flesh. Xain stared at it for a moment as though woken from a dream.

His eyes rose to her. "I . . . you are right. We shall escape with Jordel. That is safest."

Something had changed in his eyes, and for a moment he looked as he had when Loren first spied him in the Birchwood.

"Xain?" Loren said quietly. "Are you all right?"

"I am . . . I will be fine. I should go. It seems I have much to learn tomorrow."

He stood and left the table, making for the rooms. Loren watched him go, and somehow she was more frightened than before.

TWENTY-FOUR

Loren rose before dawn the next morning to find that Xain had already left. Annis rose soon after, but Gem snored on and on as if he might never stop.

"Xain is gone?" said Annis. "Do you think he will try to run?"

"I do not know," said Loren, "but I would wager not. Jordel posted guards downstairs, and Xain could not have escaped them without some commotion—enough to wake us here, I think."

Together they decided to enter the city. If they were to leave with Jordel, they would need supplies and provisions. Loren would rather not be beholden to the Mystic, since she planned to leave his company the moment she could, and they had enough coin now from their stolen purse to pay for what they needed.

Loren led Annis downstairs, where to her surprise she still saw one figure in a red cloak seated by the common room's front door. She had not thought Jordel meant to guard them as well, since it seemed clear that he was only after Xain. But then the figure rose and approached, casting back its cowl—and Loren saw that it was Vivien, her dark hair drawn back in careful braids that looped about each other. Despite what Loren knew of the woman, she looked beautiful, and her smile caught both girls off guard.

"Risen at last, little songbirds," said Vivien smoothly. "The morning wears on."

"It is scarcely past dawn," said Loren, irritated. "Jordel has assigned you to watch us, I suppose?"

She meant it as an insult, if a weak one—Loren had gathered that Vivien did not agree with Jordel in everything, and that serving him grated on her. But Vivien only smiled and spread her hands.

"I am here by my own will. Since Jordel seems in such a rush to leave this city, I gathered that you would need to fetch some supplies. I grew to womanhood upon this city's streets, and can take you to all of the best shops. My cloak will provide a better barter than you could gain with even the most silvered tongue."

Annis bristled beside her, but Loren spoke first and kept her tone as civil as Vivien's. "We thank you, but we would sooner go alone. So much of the nine lands are still unknown to us, and they say a stranger may see more of a new city than the tired old eyes of one long accustomed to its sights."

Another barb, but again Vivien only smiled. "My eyes are nearly as fresh as yours, for I have not been home in years. And it sounds as though you have had many thrilling adventures on the long road here. I would have you tell me all about them."

"We would not speak of them," said Annis angrily.

Vivien shrugged. "Then I will walk beside you regardless, and mayhap you will find my tales entertaining instead."

That piqued Loren's interest. If indeed Vivien would only talk and not try to pry for information, who knew what they might learn? "Very well," she said. "We shall need fresh bedrolls for a start—ours have grown musty. And salted beef and hardtack, if they can be found."

"In plenty, and many finer things to eat besides," said Vivien. "Come. I will take you to the clothiers first. Bedrolls are not in high demand, and they shall likely have to make yours on the spot."

"Lead the way." Loren quieted Annis with a look; the girl was fuming. "It will not be so bad," she whispered as Vivien turned. "Mayhap we can learn something of value."

Annis did not look pleased, but neither did she speak against going with the Mystic. So the three of them set out upon the city, Vivien swiftly taking them north and west to the craftsman's quarter. The streets were quiet, and what few people they saw walking did not let their gaze linger anywhere for long. Loren had felt a pall upon the city yesterday, and it seemed to have worsened since.

"They await the next attack," said Vivien. "It wears heavily on every nerve, though they do their best to hide it."

"The city has seen many wars, has it not?" said Loren.

"Many, yes, though 'war' might be a strong word," said Vivien. "Often do the Dorsean hounds yap at our heels, seeking to avenge some imagined slight. Most times they come and bray at the walls for a day or two before slinking back to their homes, often without a drop of spilled blood. Other times a few lives are lost on either side, victims of stray arrows. Never in my life have swords clashed upon the southern wall—not until now, at any rate."

"How bad was it?" said Loren.

"They managed to scale the wall in three places, but each time they were thrown back quickly. Some of our guards were wounded, but none killed—the Dorseans lost a score of men."

She seemed to grow more earnest with each word, her mask slipping away as it had in the tavern the day before. Her voice took on more life than Loren had heard in it—proud when she spoke of Wellmont, livid when she mentioned the Dorseans. If Loren could only keep her talking, she might reveal much indeed.

"That sounds like a victory," said Loren. "What, then, worries these people so?"

"Jordel is to blame for that, though I bear him no grudge. The city felt it had nothing to fear, for though the Dorsean host is great, they had no way to pressure our northern wall. Supplies would have no trouble reaching us—or so we believed. Now Jordel has told them of the sellsword army, which even now marches upon us from the northeast. When they arrive we will be hard pressed—but our walls are strong yet. We will best them. More than that—we will destroy them. While Selvan does not lightly put forth its strength in war, neither does that mean that Wellmont has grown weak."

Vivien spat the last with fury, and Loren fell silent. The quiet lasted too long, for Loren saw Vivien's mask return again, all calm and without a single angry line upon her brow.

"You must forgive me for going on so long. As I am a child of this city, its fate weighs heavy on my mind. But I have heard nothing of you, Loren of the family Nelda. I do not know that name. Where is it from? Do you hail from here, in Selvan, or some other kingdom?"

"I come from a nameless village in a forest you would never have heard of," said Loren. "It is a place of little interest, to me or to anyone else."

"Surely each of us holds our homes to be important, at least in a small way," Vivien pressed.

Only one person in the Birchwood was important, and I am not likely to see him again, thought Loren. But she would no sooner have told Vivien about Chet than she would have revealed her dagger.

"Such words come easily when you hail from a great city," she said.

"You flatter me," said Vivien with a small bow, hardly more than a nod of the head. "If you will not tell me whence you come, then mayhap the little one will tell me where she means to go? You must know that your family seeks you eagerly, and if I will not tell them of your whereabouts, that does not mean others will be as restrained. Where will you hide from their watchful eyes?"

"Do you think me a fool?" snapped Annis. "If I tell you, I may as well whisper it into my mother's ears."

"I have given my word, and I am sorry that means so little to you," said Vivien, giving a sorrowful shake of her head that Loren knew for farce. "But here. We have reached our first destination."

It was a small clothier's shop with a green sign hanging above the door. The Mystic gestured them in, where a buxom woman greeted them warmly. Vivien she received with particular grace, bowing low and remarking upon the lovely state of her cloak. True enough, the cloth looked lustrous, vivid as if it were brand new—a stark contrast to Jordel's faded and threadbare garment.

"Only half as fine as the poorest item in your shop, I am afraid," said Vivien. The clothier blushed.

In no time, the woman had cut them four new bedrolls of a sturdy green cloth, thick and durable yet soft and comforting. Loren had never seen such fine fabric used for so mean a purpose. When she asked after the price, the clothier said she would take only a few silver pennies.

"Come now," said Vivien quickly. "A gold weight would be a shrewd price. You cannot give away your wares."

"I will not take a spot of gold from friends of the Mystics," insisted the clothier. "Not when rumor has it you have come here to save us from those Dorsean dogs."

There was a moment's silence, and Loren felt her chest grow uncomfortably tight. Vivien's face froze in its gentle smile, and for a moment she seemed unable to speak.

"Will you take twelve silver pennies, good lady?" said Loren, hoping to break the awkward pause.

The clothier looked at her, seeming lost. But she recovered in a moment, smiling brightly and nodding. Loren reached beneath her cloak for the purse of coins she had taken from beneath Gem's bed and pulled out a fistful of silver. She counted out sixteen coins and dropped them into the woman's hand, and then she left before the shopkeeper could realize the mistake.

"Do the people of Wellmont really believe the Mystics will save them?" said Loren.

"I had not heard that before," said Vivien stiffly. "Imagine their disappointment when Jordel rides out tomorrow and takes all his men with him."

"But they will still have you. A mighty mindmage." The thought of the Dorseans razing this city troubled her greatly. Loren might never have played a part in great matters of the nine lands, but still she was Selvan born, and like anyone in her village had been raised to know the Dorseans as warmongering thieves. Even old Bracken had not held a high opinion of the kingdom to the south, and he had been one of the kindest people Loren had ever known.

Vivien gave a small smile, but it had grown cold again, like her demeanor upon the docks in Redbrook. "Not so mighty as your friend Xain. You must tell me—how often have you seen him wield such power? I could scarcely believe it."

"I had witnessed nothing like it from him before," Loren admitted. "But neither have I ever seen a duel of mages. Before that, small bursts of flame and gusts of wind were the extent of what I had observed."

"It seems he found some inner well of strength," said Vivien. "I only hope he is in control of himself. He might have killed me."

"He would not," said Loren quickly. Vivien's words had made her think uncomfortably of the magestones. "He holds life more dearly than that. It is one thing we hold in common."

"Yes, Jordel mentioned something of the kind," said Vivien. "I must say I admire your conviction. It would be a better world if all lived with such stringent morality."

Loren looked at her askance. "I suppose you mean to say I am a fool."

"Not a bit. We were all young once."

Loren did not like that at all, and felt certain Vivien meant to anger her. So she held her silence, and indeed they spoke of nothing important the rest of the day. After a while they had gathered all the provisions they could need, and so as the sun began to set they turned their steps towards the Inn. No matter how Vivien tried to pry more information out of Loren, she received no answer, and Annis too walked in stony silence.

When they returned, they did not find Gem alone. He sat in the room waiting for them with wide eyes, and beside him sat Xain and Jordel. It seemed Loren was not the only one who had gone shopping, for Xain's ragged brown coat was gone, and in its place was a blue one, very much like the one he had been wearing when he and Loren first met.

"You have returned," said Jordel. "That is good, for we have much to plan."

"We were preparing to leave the city," said Loren. "I hope you have not waited long." She looked at Xain, hoping for some sign of what had transpired, but the wizard would not meet her gaze.

"We only just arrived here," said Jordel. "We spoke of much and more besides through the day. My voice is weak from it."

"And?" said Loren, still looking at Xain. "What came of it?"

Xain finally looked up at her, and she nearly took a step back. The wizard's skin was ghostly white, and while his eyes burned with the same hunger as they always did recently, now they bore heavy clouds of something else: fear.

"I will go with Jordel," said Xain. "He says he means to travel to Feldemar. But wherever he may lead me, I will follow."

Loren could sense no trace of duplicity in his voice. Shock seized her as she realized the wizard meant what he had said.

"You will," she said. She meant it to be a question, but her voice failed her. "Very well, then. Your path is your own to choose."

"As is yours," said Jordel. "But it is my strong hope you will join us."

Loren blinked. "Me?"

"Who else?"

"What do you want me for?" said Loren. "You know I do not share your purpose."

"I do not seek blood and death, as you have decided," said Jordel. Though the words were harsh, he spoke them gently. "You have considerable talents that seem born to you. I would have those talents nurtured and grown, for they will be invaluable in the coming months. Not every fight takes place on the battlefield, nor is every blow struck with a fist."

"You do mean for me to fight, then," said Loren. "I will not, nor will I leave Annis and Gem to their fate. Or have you forgotten them in pursuit of your quest?"

"Of course we will not abandon them," said Jordel. "As I said before, they do not deserve to be left here in the midst of a war, and the Yerrin girl may be of great use."

"You speak of use, but not of safety." Loren saw Vivien from the corner of her eye. The woman studied her with grim amusement, and that only stoked her temper further. "I cannot hope to guess at the grand purpose you serve, but you seem to look upon the rest of us as pieces to play against some opponent. That is not an enticing prospect."

"I know you have plans of your own, and mighty dreams," said Jordel. "Come with me but a little while, and you will find them closer than ever—almost within your grasp. And I pledge to you this—I will never ask you to do violence. Please, Loren. This is the best chance for you, Annis, and Gem. I do not doubt your resilience nor your resourcefulness, but it cannot hurt to have powerful allies."

Loren felt torn. Jordel seemed a mighty friend indeed, and if he could promise care for Annis and Gem, how could she refuse? But then in her mind she saw him plunge his sword into the mercenary's chest, saw the cold light in his eyes as he killed three men in a blink.

"What do you think of all this?" she asked Xain. The wizard had turned his gaze towards the corner, as though he had forgotten the rest of them were there. "You seem willing enough to join the Mystic. Would you have me do the same?"

Xain stared at her blankly, and again she saw that nameless fear drifting in the wizard's eyes. "You must keep your own counsel," he said, his voice a bleak shadow of its former strength. "I would not force any other to step upon this road—not though it might be the only road we have left."

Loren did not like any of this. Neither Jordel's mysterious hints at great danger, nor Vivien's gloating smirk. She did not like the way Gem and Annis stared at her as though waiting for an answer, as though both their fates rested on her next words. Even less did she like the way Xain had turned into this dead thing on the bed before her.

She tried to speak, but her words were drowned out in a sudden, clanging peal of sound. A deep, reverberating clash of brass, soon joined by a choir of others throughout the city.

Loren spun towards the door. “What under the sky is that?”

“Bells,” said Vivien, her voice hushed and furious. “Dorsea is at the gates.”

TWENTY-FIVE

JORDEL STOOD. "IT IS TOO SOON," HE MUTTERED. "I thought they would not attack for another day at least. The northern force must have been closer than our scouts reported."

"We do not know that the sellswords have reached us," said Vivien. "Mayhap the Dorseans are making another feint. But regardless, they will need me on the wall."

"Go, then," said Jordel. Vivien gave Loren a final look and left. "And you, Loren of the family Nelda.

What say you? If you would go with me, you must go now, or else fall with this city."

Loren tried to answer, but her voice seemed to have fled. On and on the bells pealed, and she could feel each thundering strike deep within her chest. What must she do? What if Jordel led them beyond the gate only to find the flying arrows of the sellswords before them? What if she stayed, and the city fell to rubble around her?

"You—you cannot expect me to decide this now!" she said. "Not when a host of foes is on our doorstep and these *accursed* bells will not be silent!" She looked up at the roof as though she could spot the bells and somehow pull them from their mountings.

"I would not, but I have no other choice," said Jordel. "What is your answer?"

"Get us out," said Loren desperately. "Get us beyond the city's walls, and then let me answer. You owe me that much, Mystic. I did not ask to find myself in this war, caught between two armies while the world falls around me. Nor did Annis and Gem. Let us escape this city, and then we will each answer in our own time."

It was not a fair thing to say, mayhap. Jordel had done no more to bring them here than had Annis' mother or Xain. Yet the Mystic looked thoughtful at her words, and after a moment he nodded.

"If that is all you can promise me, I will take it," he said. "Only let us leave now. A wagon waits beyond the northern wall. Make ready!"

Loren gave Gem and Xain their new bedrolls, and the four of them packed their meager things. With their supplies slung across their backs, they let Jordel lead them from the inn and into the streets.

Where before all had been quiet with the calm of uneasy waiting, now chaos raged around them. Men and women ran back and forth, some carrying empty buckets, others lugging bags and sacks the contents of which Loren could not guess at. Through the masses moved guards and constables, islands of calm in an ocean of fear. In rank and file they marched, on many streets but always south.

As they paused to let a column pass through an intersection before them, Loren turned her gaze to the southern wall. Her breath caught in her throat. In the dimming daylight, the sky glowed red with the light of raging fires. Smoke rose from many places, and under each column of it she imagined a home burning. She had a sudden, mad urge to run towards the fighting and see the battle for herself, but Jordel commanded them to move forwards, and she shook the thought away.

They reached the north gates to find them closed and barred. At Jordel's mighty shout, a pair of guards appeared at the parapet above, scowling down under their helmets of bronze and steel.

"Let us out!" bellowed Jordel. "We must leave the city at once!"

"These gates open for no one," said the guard. "Under command of the mayor."

"I am of the order of Mystics." Jordel's voice rang with an authority and command that Loren had never heard in it before. His hand rose to his breast, and when it came away he brandished his silver badge of office—the three winged rods bound by a circle. "By this badge and the authority of the High King herself, I command you to open the gate."

"The High King is a thousand leagues away, and cares little for us!" said the other guard. "But the mayor is close, and his constables all around, and he has promised to hang any man who opens this gate, however just the reason."

"Do your duty to the High King, or I will come up there and open it myself!"

They all jumped at his shout, and the guards paused before replying. "You shall have to, then, but I beg that you do not, my lord. For it is no idle threat—we will hang, and our families starve. You do as your duty commands you, and we must do the same."

Loren put a hand on Jordel's arm. "Do not do it," she said. "We can leave once the battle is done."

"Not if the sellswords strike from the north, as I believe they will," said Jordel. But some of the fire had gone from him, and Loren could sense it. "Still, we could evade them, at least long enough to escape. And

I would not see men come to harm for doing their duty."

"Nor should they," said Loren.

Jordel looked at her, and she wondered if he was thinking of his promise—that he would never command her to violence. "Very well. We shall return to the inn, there to wait until this is over. Even if the mercenaries arrive, they cannot bring down the walls in an hour. At least I hope not."

They turned and retraced their steps, and this time they found the going easier. Many had left the northern part of the city, and those few who remained were shut indoors. Indeed, Loren would have thought the place abandoned if she had not been able to hear a distant roar in the south, like thunder ripping through the hills. The noise gave haste to her steps and made her heart hammer.

They reached the inn, but before they could enter, the front door burst open to reveal Vivien. She was covered in ash and soot, and where her hair had been carefully arranged before, it was now tousled and hung about her head in a mess of fraying strands. Her eyes fell upon Xain and washed through with stark relief. She went to him and seized his sleeve. Xain was too startled to draw away.

"There you are," she said. "The city needs you for its defense. Come with me."

Jordel stepped between them and pushed Vivien's hand roughly away. "He is not meant to fight in this war of yours, Vivien. I have told you as much already. He must leave the city, and the sooner the better."

"Yet they will not open the gate to you, will they?" cried Vivien. "How will he help you in your great purpose if this city is toppled stone by stone, and him inside it? The Dorsean dogs throw their full strength at us. If the mercenaries have not already reached the northern wall, it is only a matter of time. If we do not hold them back now, at once, they will kill every soul inside these walls."

"I granted you leave to stay and fight," said Jordel in a voice of steel. "No more will I grant you, and certainly not the lives of these here before you."

"And are our lives yours, to bandy about and barter with?" said Loren.

That gave Jordel pause, and the Mystics both turned to her. She fought the urge to quail before Jordel's hard look and Vivien's smug one.

"A moment ago you begged me to help you escape," said Jordel.

"Yet that is now impossible, and so we have a new choice," said Loren. "I . . . I have no wish for fighting. But if our hands can keep the city walls standing, then I, for one, would pledge mine."

"The city will *not* fall," said Jordel. "Not yet, at least."

"They have brought wizards, Jordel," said Vivien quietly. "Wizards of great power. I fear they may be abominations. Eaters of the black crystal."

Jordel fell silent, his face suddenly grave. Loren saw Xain behind them, and his eyes had taken on their hungry glint once more.

"They overpowered me on the southern wall," Vivien went on. "Barely, for neither alone was mightier than I, but together they were too strong. But he could beat them." She pointed to Xain. "If he can fight as he fought upon the Dragon's Tail, the walls will stand."

Xain studied her, his face betraying nothing. Jordel heaved a great sigh, running a hand over his eyes as though weary. Then he turned not to Xain, but to Loren. "You would help this city? Of which you know nothing, and have been in scarcely more than a day?"

"It is a city of Selvan. I will not fight, but I will help where I may. And if Vivien speaks truth, then no help will be unwelcome."

"Certainly not. We would all be in your debt," said Vivien, and in her voice Loren heard the same earnest passion she had shown that afternoon in the craftsmen's quarter.

"Then I cannot stop you," said Jordel. "And I should have expected as much, I suppose. I will come, then, and try to ensure your safety. But each of you must decide this for yourselves, and do not pledge lightly. For you are all strangers to battle, and may find it unpleasant to your taste afterwards, if you come through it at all."

Loren turned to Gem and Annis. "You should stay here," she said. "You will be safe here at the inn. It is like the riverboat—our hopes rest with Xain."

"You mean to go," said Gem, standing as tall as he could, "and I will not have you go alone. But I would fight upon the wall. Where may I find a sword my size?"

"Do not be an idiot," said Loren, giving him a small shove. "You will stay by my side."

Annis looked at them both helplessly and threw her hands in the air. "You are *both* idiots. This is a fool's errand, as anyone with sense can see. But if you can promise we will not be in the fighting, I suppose I cannot let you run off by yourselves—though no doubt you deserve it."

"And you, Xain?" said Vivien. "I mean no insult to the others, but Loren speaks true. Your help, not theirs, will sway the battle. What say you?"

Xain looked to be deep in thought, his eyes unblinking. But Loren noticed that he stared at Annis. Again she heard a voice crying out a warning in her mind, but she pushed it away.

"I will go," said Xain. "And they shall not stand against me."

TWENTY-SIX

THEY LEFT IN HASTE, ABANDONING THEIR THINGS AT the inn. On the street, Loren tugged on Xain's arm to draw him back, letting the others drift ahead. Once out of earshot, she leaned in close to whisper.

"Are you well enough for this fight, wizard? Vivien thinks the other wizards have magestones."

"And yet they are not as strong as she," said Xain. "I took her measure upon the river. Had I been well, there would have been no contest to our match. And even now, some remnant of the magestones courses in my veins. I think it will prove more than enough."

"You think?"

"Do not fear for me," Xain said scornfully. "Only keep your head from becoming too friendly with an arrow."

The roar Loren had heard in the south grew louder the closer they approached. And as they drew near to the wall, she saw its source at last: thousands of Wellmont's citizens, crying in unison with hate and fear and pain and death. The sky was streaked with spears of flame; burning arrows raining upon Wellmont, sending the buildings into a blaze.

"You will help with the fires," Vivien commanded, pointing to Loren, Gem, and Annis. "The arrows have caught many buildings alight. When buckets are brought from the river, you will carry them wherever they are needed."

"Very well," said Loren.

"Xain, with me," said Vivien. "We will be needed on the wall."

Jordel seized her arm. "See to his safety, Vivien. I will hold you accountable if any harm should befall him."

"I have seen his power," said Vivien. "You need not fear for him, and I will have little part to play."

"Regardless, do not forget my words." Jordel released her, and together Vivien and Xain vanished into the streets, enshrouded by the black smoke that seemed to pour from everywhere.

"You will not join them?" Loren asked Jordel. "A wizard you might not be, but a sturdy sword will no doubt be of use in the fighting."

"Not as much as a wary eye keeping watch on the three of you. If Xain is as powerful as Vivien claims—and as powerful as I have been led to believe—the battle will be a short matter once he takes the field. I would sooner see you through this in safety."

They joined the bucket lines and ran from building to building, throwing water upon any flame that reared its golden head. It was the most draining experience of Loren's life, taxing both her body and her mind. In no time she panted from exertion as she lugged impossibly heavy buckets through the streets. Every few moments, another flaming arrow overhead would force them all to duck. The shafts were spread so far apart that there seemed little danger of being hit. Yet Jordel directed them to hide within doorways and behind walls often, and whenever he did a whistling would fill the air—a fresh volley to pepper the city.

There was no mistaking the moment Xain joined the fight. Amidst the chaos, an even greater clamor arose—a tremendous swelling crackle that drowned the shouts and screams around them. Looking up, Loren saw a small figure crowned in a corona of light. Fire and lightning spit from Xain's hands, flying over the wall to strike amidst the host on the other side. Sometimes his flames were dashed away, and sometimes magic vaulted the wall to strike at him, but always Xain cast it back. She could not watch him long, however, for fire had spread through many of the city's buildings and required all their efforts to put out.

No matter how many blazes they doused, ever more were born. Arrows never ceased, and though sparse, they were still many. A constable would seize her shoulder without warning and point her to some building. Loren would follow their finger and find a blaze licking the roof, or somewhere inside, and splash water upon it until her bucket was empty. Then she would return to the line to find another bucket waiting.

She had a thought in the midst of it all, as she took shelter from another flight of arrows: not once in all this had she seen any Dorseans. The chaos atop the wall was too far and too frantic to see much of anything, and no men had yet breached the southern gate. Here she was, fighting as hard as anyone in Wellmont to save their city, and she could not even see the foe. In her weariness the thought struck her as uncommonly funny, and she gave a quick bark of laughter.

"What?" said Gem, wheezing as he leaned on his knees beside her. "What could possibly make you laugh in the middle of all this madness?"

"We cannot even see them," said Loren. "The Dorseans. Where are they?"

Gem stared at her, his large eyes brilliant white in the middle of a soot-blackened face. "They are on the other side of the wall, you imbecile."

"Never mind. Another bucket. Annis?"

A silence followed, and her heart stopped. Frantically she looked around, but the girl was nowhere in sight.

"Annis!" she screamed. Her fingers grasped at Gem's threadbare shirt and pulled him close. "Where is she? Which way did she go?"

"I do not know!" said Gem. "Let go of me!"

"Annis!" she screamed, stepping heedless into the street. *"Annis!"*

"Loren!" cried a voice, and she found herself thrown to the ground as a small form tackled her. She raised her arms to strike it, until she spotted Annis' face.

"Annis? What are you . . . ?"

"Down!" she shouted, and pushed Loren into the cobblestones.

A whistling filled the air, and fire-arrows passed over and around them, striking cobblestones and ricocheting with a sharp *tang.* But none found their mark.

"Thank you," said Loren. "I thought we had lost you. I was searching—"

"I thought I had lost *you.* Let us try to find—"

The rest of Annis' words were lost in a roar of flame and snapping timbers. A building farther down the street had collapsed, and from its ruins bloomed a shower of sparks that singed the air around them.

"Put it out!" screamed a voice nearby. "Get that building before it catches the others!"

"Come on," said Loren, rising and tugging Annis to her feet. Gem joined the girls, and together the three of them ran towards the collapsed building. It was either a shop or a house; Loren could not tell. She paused as she realized Jordel was not there—in her panic to find Annis, Loren had almost forgotten the Mystic.

As they came to the wreckage, Loren heard a bloodcurdling scream from within. Poking from between two timbers, a hand grasped at the air. Inside she could see the licking tongues of flames.

"There is someone inside!" said Annis, but Loren had already seized one of the beams and was trying to move it. Annis went to her side, and in a moment two men appeared. Together they heaved the debris away from the body, and Loren reached for the hand that clutched for her.

She pulled as hard as she could. A woman slid out among the dirt and the filth, screaming still louder as she came to rest on the cobblestones. Flames had roasted her flesh like meat on a spit, and the stench made Loren gag. The woman had been rendered sightless, with deep burns across her eyes, and every limb flailed as she screamed in agony.

"Calm down, calm down," said Loren, though she herself wanted to run crying. "Help me get her to a healer."

Together with Annis she heaved the woman up, and slowly made their way to the bucket line.

"This woman needs a healer," said Loren, but no one paid any attention. "A healer! Where can I find a healer?"

Finally her calls caught the attention of a constable, one of the men directing those who carried buckets. He took one look at the woman and turned away. "Leave her. Those burns will kill her, and no medicine can prevent it."

"We must try," said Loren, angry.

"Put your efforts towards saving the buildings. Else many more will die from the fires." The constable walked away, and Loren was left standing with the woman's arm slung across her shoulders.

"Come," said Annis gently. "He is right. We must do as he says."

Loren wanted to argue, but as Annis lowered the woman to the ground she had little choice but to do the same. The screams had redoubled, and she clutched hard at the black cloak. Loren tried to pry her fingers away, but the woman had a grip of iron.

"I am sorry," said Loren, voice shaking. "I am sorry, I am sorry. I must go."

At last she freed herself from the woman's grip and stumbled away, but not towards the bucket line. She did not know if it was the smoke or the red glow of the fires, or merely the shock of it all, but Loren felt blind. A wall reared up before her and she crashed into it, her shoulder smarting from the impact as the ground swam up to meet her. Her throat seemed to constrict, burning as it sucked in the smoky air. The smell of the woman still lingered in her nostrils—then all at once it overwhelmed her, and she lost her food to the cobblestones.

When she was done she sat up and leaned against the wall. Where was Annis? She looked around, searching, and spotted the girl on the other side of the street. Annis sat beside Gem, holding the boy in her arms while he shook uncontrollably with tears. Gently Annis rocked him back and forth, while Gem scrubbed at his eyes.

Though her limbs still felt weak, Loren forced herself to rise and go to them. She was struck by the calm on Annis' face. The girl could have been riding a carriage on a country road for all the distress she showed. Gently she stroked Gem's hair, rocking him back and forth as the boy fought for control.

As Loren approached, Annis looked up at her. "Are you well?"

"I am not," said Loren. "But I shall have to pretend. And you? This madness does not seem to trouble you as much as I would have thought."

"I have seen death before." Annis shrugged. "Sometimes much worse than this."

Loren wondered at that, for the image of the burned woman would not leave her mind. But then she thought of Damaris, and what Annis had said when they escaped—how she had seen her mother kill before, in many terrible ways. Loren shuddered.

"Can you go on, Gem?" she said. "No one will think worse of you if you wish to return to the inn."

"I will not leave you here in this madness." Gem's voice was brave even as his tears continued to flow. "I only . . . it is only that I have never seen such things before. This is no battle like they tell of in stories."

"Battles rarely are," said Annis, still holding him tight. "Send your mind from here. Think of a day in the future, when we have left this place far behind and live in Calentin as wealthy nobles. It will come true if you keep thinking of it."

Gem shook his head, but he did not shrug her arms away. "I am not a child. I do not play such games. Only give me a moment to collect myself."

"In the darkness under the river, you told me to do the same thing," said Annis. "Send your mind somewhere more pleasant, and keep breathing."

That calmed him. Gem sucked in a deep gulp of air and slowly released it. A few more times, and at last he scrubbed at his eyes with the back of his hand. Then, with Loren's help, he rose.

"Very well," he said. "If we mean to return to this chaos, let us do it now. Before one of you loses your nerve."

Loren gave him a gentle smile, and he returned it. Then she led them back to the bucket line, and soon they plunged back into a world of roaring flames and pain-soaked screams.

All the while, Loren found herself looking anew at Gem and Annis beside her. She wondered if she would have been as strong at their age, or if she would have run in terror from the flames. In the Birchwood, under the sway of cruel parents, it had been easy to envision herself as the brave girl at the center of a great tale waiting to be told. But now she had met two others whose courage might have eclipsed her own. Were they exceptional, as she had imagined herself? Or did they only answer the call of circumstance?

The thought weighed heavily on her mind as they kept running, dousing, and running again. And then the bells pealed throughout the city once more, and a great shout rose up all along the southern wall. No more arrows hissed at them through the air.

The Dorseans were retreating. The battle was over.

TWENTY-SEVEN

Loren stumbled out of a building, her last fire doused. Steam rose all through the streets, lingering misty remnants of the small, inglorious fight the city's inhabitants had fought against the unrelenting flames. Gem lay on his back in the middle of the street, chest heaving and eyes closed. Annis sat cross-legged nearby, head drooping as though asleep. Mayhap she was.

Moving listlessly, Loren went to lean against the building's wall, her head bumping against the bricks. They were still warm with the heat of the fire she had just put out. Every part of her wanted to lie down as

Gem had, and sleep in the street for days, only waking after the siege was over and the Dorseans had left. But now that the battle was done, Jordel would want to flee Wellmont. And Loren wanted that even more than rest.

Somewhere in the chaos and the burning, she had reached her decision. If this was war, she wanted no part of it. And if Jordel meant to stave off a war, she would help him. She did not doubt it would come to killing in the end—the Mystic seemed prone to such—but he had promised her she would have no part in violence. If he would teach her the ways of shadow and secrecy, and could guarantee the safety of Gem and Annis, then she would help him, if it gave even a small hope of stopping more battles like this one.

She heard hasty, urgent footsteps, a distinct cadence amidst the shuffling walk of all those around her. Her eyes snapped open, and she saw Xain walking towards them.

The wizard's clothes were a mess, and his hair stuck out in all directions. One of his eyebrows had burned off, and the top of one boot was tattered. But his eyes gleamed clear and bright, and his steps did not falter. He caught sight of Loren leaning against the wall, and his eyes darted nervously around.

"There you are. Where is the Mystic?"

"Vivien left with you, before the battle began," Loren mumbled. She could not find the strength to speak louder. "We have not seen her since."

"Not the woman," Xain said. "I left her behind. Jordel."

"I do not know. We lost him somewhere in the chaos. He must be nearby."

"Let us hope not," said Xain. "Come. It is time for us to go."

"Go?" Her hackles rose. "Go where? Jordel is our way out of the city."

"I do not need him." Xain spoke quick and harsh. He looked to Annis in the street. "Girl. Do you still carry the . . . cargo you had with you?"

Annis looked up at the wizard, her eyes blank and unseeing for a moment. When they focused, she gave a slow nod. "I have them."

"That is all we need," said Xain. "Come, quickly, before those meddlers can find us."

"You said you would leave with Jordel," said Loren. The wizard was worrying her, and that seemed to give her strength. She pushed off from the wall and stood facing him, feet spread, hands at her sides. "There was no lie in your voice this morning, wizard, and do not tell me there was. You have no skill for deception. You meant to follow Jordel, and now I have decided to do the same."

"Then you are a fool," snarled Xain. "Only one lost in madness would go with the Mystic or aid him in his plans. If you had heard half the things he told me, you would run screaming from this place and live forever terrified by the sight of a red cloak."

"What things?" said Loren. "You pledged to tell me what he said. Let me hear it now, then, if you are determined to run off and leave him."

"We all will," said Xain. "You have promised a half share of something, and I will have it."

"Not until we reach your contact," said Loren angrily. "As I have told you again and again."

"Foolish girl!" Xain shouted, making Loren jump. "Do you not think I could take them if I wanted? I pledged an agreement, but you have twisted the terms until they have nearly snapped. With a single word I could have what is mine. Mayhap I shall."

His eyes glowed white as he whispered. With a twist of his hand, a gust of wind slammed into Annis. She flew into the air with a cry, landing on her feet beside him, where the wizard seized her arm.

Loren rushed forwards but paused as the glow in his eyes increased and he raised a hand towards her.

"Stop this!" cried Loren. "We made a deal. Have you no honor?"

"You speak to me of honor, when you would deny me my due?" said Xain. "Now, will you come with me willingly, or must I take my share by force, and yours as well?"

Loren was nearly swaying on her feet from exhaustion. She knew not what to do. Already she had decided to go with Jordel, and even if she had not, she no longer had any wish to travel beside Xain. But what choice did she have? If she refused, she did not doubt he would take Annis and flee Wellmont alone, and then she might never find him and the magestones again.

And then, over Xain's shoulder and far down the street, Loren saw a pale figure in a red cloak. Her hair was a mess and her shoulders slumped, but still she walked with her head held high.

"Vivien!" cried Loren. "Help!"

The Mystic's gaze snapped towards her and took in Xain's grasp on Annis. Her eyes glowed white, and an invisible force propelled her through the air towards them. She landed between Loren and Xain, her eyes on the wizard.

"What are you doing, Xain?" said Vivien, in a voice of ice.

"I am leaving this place, and you and your master besides. Do you think you can stop me?"

"That was not the agreement," said Vivien. "And if you would break your word to Jordel, at least do it to stay here and help Wellmont live."

But Xain laughed at her even as he pushed Annis away. The girl stumbled and fell to the street, scrabbling away from Xain as he gave Vivien a cruel smile. "I care nothing if your precious home is reduced to rubble. Only one person in this world concerns me, and every moment I spend away increases his peril."

"Jordel is your best chance to see your son again," said Vivien. "You know it to be true. Do not risk his safety for your own pride."

"Has Jordel told you all he told me?" said Xain. "I think not, for then you would know him for a madman more dangerous than any serpent on the High King's Seat. Not even you would march behind him into his madness."

"Say what you wish, but you will not leave except by Jordel's side."

"You cannot stop me," said Xain, and attacked.

A blast of fire screamed for Vivien. Loren flung herself out of the way. But Vivien dashed the bolt aside, and it dissipated into the air high above. Then she responded, flinging Xain into the wall where Loren had leaned only a moment ago.

Xain broke her hold. His glowing eyes brightened, and with a snap of his fingers the hem of Vivien's cloak caught fire.

Her eyes lit with fear, but she quickly recovered, waving away the flames while she struck Xain with an invisible cudgel. Then, to Loren's surprise, Vivien leapt forwards and attacked him with her fists. Once, twice, three times she struck him, in the face and stomach.

Xain stumbled, nearly falling to the ground. Loren knew him for a poor fighter, and it seemed he had not expected the Mystic's assault.

But he was not finished. With a cry he seized Vivien's shoulders, and from his hands crackled fingers of lightning that danced across her body. Vivien screamed in pain as she convulsed. When Xain pushed her away, she fell senseless to the ground. Loren waited, expecting Vivien to rise again, or at least to try. But the Mystic did not move.

Xain stared at her prone form for a long, quiet moment. The street's activity had ceased, with all eyes on the mage-battle. But no one dared make a sound. Then, satisfied, Xain turned from Vivien and strode for Annis.

"No!" cried Loren, but she was too late.

Xain seized Annis' arm and hauled her up. Quickly he dragged her north. When Loren shouted again, he turned and wrapped an arm around Annis' throat, holding one hand to her face.

"Stop, girl!" said Xain. "You have tried to betray me once, and even set your Mystic sow upon me. I will tolerate no more. The girl comes with me to the High King's Seat, and there I will secure my son's freedom. Only then will she be free to go, to return to you with your share if she wishes. I am not cruel, after all."

"Let me go!" said Annis, but Xain tightened his arm around her throat and she fell still.

"You have gone mad, Xain," said Loren. "You would threaten the life of a child? Her parents love her no less than you love your own son."

"Her parents are serpents who kill without a second thought," said Xain. "How many others have they robbed of fathers and mothers, daughters and sons? Taking their child would be only fair play. But even so I will not do it—unless you force me. If I for a moment suspect your pursuit, the girl dies and I keep the stones for myself."

Loren stomped the ground hard enough to hurt her foot. A useless gesture, but she had had enough. "You will not leave again! You abandoned me on the King's road and tried to leave again in Cabrus. I will not let you disappear a third time. And I do not believe for a moment that you will kill her."

"You doubt my resolve?"

"I doubt you are heartless." Loren knew it was a risk, and yet she took a step closer. Xain tensed, but he did not move. "You are callous and a terrible liar and incredibly, stupidly stubborn, yes. But you would not harm a child. You are not a man who kills. I have seen it. I know it to be true. Please, Xain, end this madness."

Xain shook his head. "You know little, you believe easily, and you assume so very much. A dangerous combination. Did you take my tale for true when I told you what happened on the High King's Seat? I did not stir up some mage's duel. The constables hunted me for murder."

Loren felt her heart stop. "No. You said . . ."

"I told you a lie. And you believed it. And if you still doubt my conviction—"

His eyes glowed as he whispered a word. White flames erupted on his finger. He pressed the finger to the side of Annis' neck, and Loren heard the sizzle of flesh.

Annis screamed, her legs kicking. Still, Xain held her up with an arm wrapped around her throat.

"Stop!" screamed Loren. "Stop it, Xain!"

Xain withdrew his finger, and Annis fell to whimpering in his arms. "If you follow me, I will not hesitate. Fare well, Loren of the family Nelda, and may we never meet again."

He backed slowly away, and Loren could only watch him go. Together with Annis he vanished around the corner of a building. As soon as he was out of sight, Loren ran to it. The street beyond was empty. Xain was gone, and with him, Annis.

TWENTY-EIGHT

Loren turned back, wanting to ask Gem what to do, wanting someone, anyone, to give her instructions. Instead she saw Vivien struggling to her feet, shaking her head as she looked around. The Mystic's face was cloaked in the night's shadow, but Loren caught the reflection of torches in her eyes, so that they appeared to be aflame.

"What happened?" Vivien's words were slightly slurred. "Where did he go?"

"He is gone," said Loren, her voice shaking. "He took Annis and vanished."

Vivien strode to stand beside Loren, looking down the street where Xain had fled. "Nonsense. Even a firemage as powerful as Xain cannot disappear. That magic does not exist, and that means we can find him."

"But how? He holds Annis hostage. He said if he catches me following him, he will kill her."

Vivien's lips pursed slightly, unsure. "And do you believe him?"

Loren nodded. "He burned her with his flames. I thought that was beyond him, yet he did not even flinch."

"Still, we may take him unawares. Sky above, where is Jordel?"

"Loren!" Gem ran up to them, seizing Loren's arms and shaking her. Small as he was, it had little effect. "Loren, we must save her. The wizard has gone mad."

"We will," said Loren, resting a calming hand on his shoulder. "I promise. I will not rest until we do."

Gem's lip trembled, and for a moment she feared the boy might cry. She did not think she had the same gift for comfort that Annis did. But after a moment, he steeled himself and nodded.

"Yet we cannot find Xain on our own," said Vivien. "Answer me. Where is Jordel?"

"I do not know," said Loren. "We lost him in the battle."

"Then we should return to your inn. He will look for us there, now that the fighting is done. From there we may plan how to recover Xain. Jordel will know best how to find him again."

"And Annis as well," said Loren, glaring. "I doubt your friends in the family Yerrin would be pleased if she was harmed or remained in Xain's care."

"Do not lecture *me* on the family Yerrin," hissed Vivien. "We have enjoyed a long friendship, while you have only stirred their ire since first they met you. I heard of your deeds in Cabrus, girl. Your inn. Now."

She stalked off, leaving Loren little choice but to follow. She wanted Vivien's company even less than Xain's, but all their belongings remained at the inn. And without Jordel's help, how could she hope to find Annis? Gem hurried along at her side.

The city bustled with a hurried melancholy in the darkness, as workers bore torches from building to building, hoping to repair what damage they could. Many homes would have to be torn down and rebuilt, Loren was sure. She saw no faces but those covered with black soot, and everyone stepped wearily. But no one knew when the Dorseans would return, and so they kept going, in hopes of being better prepared the next time flaming arrows flew.

At last they reached the inn, where they found many people seated at tables all around the common room. The innkeeper bustled by, but she stopped when Vivien seized her arm.

"I will have a bath," Vivien snapped. "For while you cowered here in fear, I fought to defend your home. Make it fast, and if you think I will pay for it you are mistaken."

So venomous and yet so soft were her words, that the innkeeper ran red-faced to prepare a tub. Vivien turned and motioned to someone behind Loren. A figure in a red cloak appeared from nowhere—one of the other Mystics from Jordel's company.

"Find our captain. He may be in the south where the fires burned, or he may not. But he must come here as quickly as he can, for much has happened."

The Mystic's cloaked head bobbed in a nod, and he retreated through the front door. The innkeeper reappeared with several nervous nods to Vivien, who looked to Loren a final time.

"If Jordel comes, fetch me immediately. Wait here in the meantime, and do not eat. The shock will not have worn off yet, and you might lose anything you manage to put down. You may drink, if you wish."

With a whirl of her cloak she retreated into the back, leaving Loren and Gem in the common room.

"So much for her gratitude," Gem grumbled. "She was more courteous when she wanted Xain to help in the city's defense."

"Shush," said Loren. "Let us take a seat, or I will collapse."

They looked but could not easily find a seat; patrons sat at all the tables, each looking as weary and soot-blackened as Loren herself. It seemed as though everyone present only wanted to lose themselves in wine and ale until the next morning or the next Dorsean attack—whichever came first.

Loren approached one anyway, a table with six chairs but at which sat only two people. One, a well-muscled woman, had arms like thick oak branches covered with scars, and she wore a smudged blue vest. Around her forehead was tied a long blue cloth stained with sweat and something darker—blood or wine, Loren could not be sure. By her side sat a thin, sharp man in a trim purple coat, whose fingers were slim and dexterous and whose eyes glinted in the firelight.

"May we take a seat?" said Loren, too tired for proper manners.

"Always," said the thin man, "especially with eyes like those."

Another time Loren might have answered his flippant tone with her own, but she was too weary. She slumped onto a bench with Gem beside her. When a server came by, she ordered a flagon of wine and a cup.

"Two cups," said Gem. "I have earned one today, I think."

Loren gave him a long look, but she could find no heart to refuse him. "Two cups," she said, and reached for her coin.

"I will not hear of it," said the slim man. "You look as though you have been trampled by a horse." His hand flashed into his coat and out again, and he handed the server a few silver pennies.

Loren nodded her thanks. No words were spoken until the wine arrived and Loren and Gem had poured. She drank deep, and Gem tried to do the same, but his mouth twisted with the sour taste, and he decided to sip more slowly. All the while, the large woman in the blue vest seemed content to ignore them. Her slim companion, however, studied them with glittering eyes.

"City dwellers, are you?" Though he spoke to them both, his eyes remained on Loren. "And friends of a Mystic, or so I guess the woman in the red cloak to be."

"I would not use the word friend," said Loren.

"Smarter than you seem, then," said the man. "As smart as your eyes are entrancing."

"Leave off," said the woman. Her eyes flashed as she gave him a dirty look.

"Do not be silly," said the thin man with a laugh. "Words are harmless."

"Not with you." The woman turned to Loren. "Those are wisest who say the least to this one. His words hold a greater power than most."

Loren thought of Xain. She looked at the thin man with renewed interest. "Are you a . . ." She did not know how to ask—was it considered rude?

"A what, lovely?" The man's smile widened. "Only say the word."

"A firemage," whispered Loren.

He tilted his head forwards, looking at her from beneath his brows. "Not as far as anyone on the south wall knows." He snapped his fingers, and a few small sparks leapt forth. For just a moment Loren saw the glow of white in his eyes. "But then, things in the nine kingdoms are not always what they seem."

"Is that all you can do?" said Gem scornfully. "We know a firemage who could light the whole city ablaze if he wished."

The wizard's look soured as he glared at Gem. "Then we must count ourselves lucky the Dorseans have not hired him."

"You are sellswords, then?" said Loren. "I had not thought Wellmont hired its own company."

"We are mercenaries indeed, but we are between companies," said the wizard. "We happened to be here when the Dorseans arrived. The mayor's call to arms promised pay without contract to any man who would lift a sword on the wall. I have lifted many by now, and the coin is not half bad. The city's coffers have grown fat with many years of peace and plenty."

"But why not tell them of your gift?" said Gem. "I am sure they would pay better for a proper wizard."

The man's eyes hardened, and though the smile never left his lips it became something twisted. "Be not so hasty to call magic a gift, boy. Nor is it always wise for others to know you command it, for it raises a certain . . . expectation that many are unable to fulfill."

Loren thought again of Xain, of the look in his eyes as he dragged Annis away. Suddenly she did not feel so kindly towards the wizard before her, and she dropped her eyes to her cup.

"But I am a mercenary by trade, and there is no doubt it is a hard life," said the wizard, and again he turned to Loren. He leaned forwards earnestly to fold his hands on the table before her. "We grow lonely, marching back and forth across the nine lands. Who knows whence may come the bolt that will end our lives? Who knows which swordsman will at last plant his blade in my—"

His words cut off abruptly as the muscled woman seized his arm and hauled him up.

"That is quite enough," she said. "Let us find comforts more pricey, yet honestly bought."

"Who calls me dishonest?" said the wizard in mock protest. But he did not resist as his friend pulled him away. "Fare well, sweet maid! I will remember your eyes ever until I see them again! Fare well!"

Loren and Gem watched until they had vanished through the inn's front door, and then stared at the threshold for several long moments afterwards.

"What an imbecile," mumbled Gem, his words thick with wine.

Just then, Jordel stepped inside the inn. He saw Loren immediately, and his grave look said he knew something was wrong.

Swiftly he approached and sat opposite them. Loren snatched Gem's cup and shoved it towards Jordel, but the Mystic waved it off.

"What has happened? Vivien's messenger seemed to think it most urgent that I come here quickly. Where are the others?"

"Vivien is bathing," said Loren. "Gem, go and fetch her."

Gem paled. "But . . . but she is *bathing.*"

"Do not be a child," said Loren. "If it bothers you so, you need not open the door."

Still he hesitated, but she shoved him off his chair and prodded him towards the back of the room, where he soon disappeared.

"That is only one," said Jordel. "Tell me: where are Xain and Annis?"

Loren opened her mouth, but words would not come. She felt a hard stinging at the back of her eyes. All her shock at Xain's actions seemed to descend upon her at once, and she felt her throat constricting.

Jordel's eyes softened as he studied her face. "Speak, child. Hard words are yet better when spoken, and I will think no ill of you if you weep."

Loren's hesitation vanished, and she gave Jordel an evil look. "Do not call me child. I do not need your sympathy or your condescension, but your aid, if you spoke truly when you offered it."

With that she explained all that had transpired with Xain and Annis. She spoke of what had happened during the battle and after, though of course she did not tell Jordel all that Xain had said about the magestones. Vivien arrived in the middle of her story, hair braided and still dripping from her bath. Gem stood beside her, red-faced and staring at the floor. All listened silently until Loren had told the full tale, and were quiet many long moments afterwards.

"I see," Jordel said at last. "This is grievous news, yet not so terrible as I had feared. At least they are both alive."

"So far as we know," said Loren. "Xain may have killed her to rid himself of the inconvenience. He told me what happened upon the High King's Seat. That the King's law pursues him for murder."

Jordel's eyes narrowed. "He told you that?"

"I should have known better," said Loren. "I should have known he spun a tale before, for who would flee so ardently from constables only for some mage's duel? After all he has done to me, I should not have been so surprised to—"

"Be still," said Jordel. "Xain has deceived you indeed, but that does not mean you should be ashamed of your trust. For the lie was in his words today, when he named himself a killer. Xain took no life upon the Seat."

Loren stared at him, unable to find words. Gem said, "Why would he lie now? Who would willingly take the title of murderer? I have done wrong in my life, but I would fight anyone who accused me of that."

"One who wanted to escape, and quickly," said Vivien, her voice full of scorn. "You were fool enough to believe him."

"I had no reason not to," said Loren angrily. "You might have told me the truth, had you not slept through the ordeal."

Jordel raised a hand, and Vivien's angry response died on her lips. "It is done in any case, and arguments will not help us now. We must find Xain, and quickly, before he devises some way to escape the city."

Loren considered telling Jordel about the magestones, but Vivien's presence would not let her risk it. She had heard the Mystic woman when she told Jordel about the wizards over the wall; she had said they ate the black stones and had called them *abominations*. What, then, would she think if she knew Loren had provided Xain with the stones in the first place?

"We would do well to rescue the Yerrin girl whole, if we can," said Vivien. "Else I fear the family Yerrin will blame us for any harm that befalls her. Our presence here has not gone unremarked, and if her body is found in this city they will soon learn the truth."

"We should rescue her because she is blameless," said Jordel firmly. "And we will. I do not believe for a moment that Xain would harm her, whatever he may have done to convince you in the moment."

"Yet you do not know." Gem's words were angry, his cheeks and eyes dark. The wine might have been a mistake. “You are content to sit here and talk while the wizard gallivants around the city with her in tow.”

“We will find her, boy,” said Vivien. “More quickly without your help, I would guess. You look as though you need a nap.”

“You and yours may visit the darkness below for all I care,” said Gem, and there was no mistaking it now—the boy was drunk. “I will not leave Annis on her own with a wizard gone mad.”

“I promise you I will do all I can to recover her,” said Jordel.

“Not fast enough.” Gem stood, shaking off Loren’s hand when she tried to steady him. “I will find her myself, and sod the lot of you.”

“I wish you the best of luck, little master,” said Vivien, her voice sickly sweet. “Do come and tell us when you have done it.”

“Be silent,” snapped Jordel. “Gem, I think it would be best for you to stay.”

“I think I never asked you what you think,” said Gem. “Farewell.”

He bumped the table as he left, but he pressed on for the door. Loren ran after him. Just before he stepped outside, she seized his shoulder and spun him around.

“Do not be an idiot. You are in no state to look for her.”

“And what shall I do? Stay here and sit on my thumbs?”

"Stay and help us," said Loren.

Gem snorted. "You have no need of my help," he muttered. "The Mystics seem to have everything well in hand."

"You will *not* go out on those streets in this condition," said Loren. "I will not allow it."

Gem scowled, unmoving. But then Loren saw his angry mask crack, the pieces crumbling to reveal a frightened little boy.

"I must do something, Loren," he said. "I keep seeing the flames and the buildings, and that woman . . ."

Loren shuddered, hearing the woman's dying cries, the stench of burnt flesh returning to her nostrils.

"I see them too, Gem."

"And Annis helped me, in the middle of it. How can I sit here and wait, or tag along at your heels? Let me go. Let me try and find her, to help her as she helped me."

Loren could think of no way to refuse him, so she slowly drew aside. "Very well. But if you fall drunk into the river and drown, I will slap you. And if you *do* find them, do nothing. Merely come and tell me. Do not try and rescue Annis yourself. Will you promise me that?"

"Of course," he said with a smile. "A pickpocket's promise." Then he vanished through the inn's front door and into the black of night.

TWENTY-NINE

WHEN LOREN RETURNED TO THE TABLE, SHE FOUND Jordel had already devised a plan of action; together he and Loren would search the city for Annis and Xain. Jordel seemed to have many contacts in Wellmont, and he felt confident he could uncover the wizard without too much trouble.

"After all, I had already planned to comb the city for the two of you when first I arrived," he said. "Now the search will be narrower."

"Very well," said Loren. "When do you mean to start?"

"Now," said Jordel. "No time is too early, for if Xain escapes the city we may lose him entirely. Our only hope is to find him before he refines a plan of escape."

"Let us be off, then," said Vivien.

"You misunderstand me," said Jordel, looking at her coldly. "I mean to take Loren with me, while you return to the constables' station and coordinate their search."

Vivien stiffened, her gaze dropping to her hands, which lay clenched on the table. "Have I displeased you, my captain?"

"You have only made me displeased with myself. I should have known the lengths to which you would go to protect this city. It was not the mayor who threatened to hang the men at the north gate if they opened it, Vivien."

Her eyes grew hooded, but she did not respond.

"By your counsel alone did Xain fight upon the wall, and because of that we lost him. Were it not for you, we would be riding hard for the north in retreat to Feldemar where we could plan our next step. Now, all our plans may come to ruin."

"I did not mean for this to happen, Captain. Allow me to rectify my mistake."

"I shall," said Jordel. "But from the constables' station, and not at my side. Use all your wit and cunning in aid of the search, and I shall forgive you. But if I should find that you take any further steps to keep the wizard from me—"

He slammed his hand on the table. A terrible wrath flashed in his eyes, and then it was gone, and he was only Jordel again.

"I understand," whispered Vivien. "I will not betray your faith again, my captain."

"I believe you. Now come, Loren. Wellmont is a wide city, with many nooks and crannies in which our friend the wizard might be hiding."

Together they left the inn and set upon the streets. Nearly everyone had gone home, with only a few scattered passersby to give them curious looks. Jordel cut an impressive figure in his crimson cloak, and Loren felt small beside him in hers of midnight black.

"I may have made an error when I placed my faith in that one," said Jordel heavily. "If any great harm comes from it, I will not forgive myself."

"Vivien, you mean?" said Loren. "She seems . . . strange. It is as though she is a walking secret, with another mind behind whatever face she chooses to show you."

"And never is such a mind more dangerous. I can admire her single-mindedness, and her resourcefulness in pursuit of her goals. But her actions sit ill in my stomach. I wonder what it may portend for us, and especially for the Yerrin girl."

He stopped suddenly and turned to Loren, placing a hand on her shoulder and making her face him.

"Above all, I worry what it might mean for you." He glanced over his shoulder and leaned in to murmur. "I have warned you already not to reveal the dagger, not to anyone but me or your friends. You must be doubly sure not to let Vivien see any trace of it. That would spell not only your own doom, but the death of your friends. Even me, though I doubt you hold me as such."

Loren felt a thrill of fear at his words. "Why her?" she said. "What is it you fear?"

"It is not her, but those I suspect she is in thrall to. I have told you some within my order would wish your death simply for holding the dagger. Unless I miss my guess by a wide margin, Vivien would report you directly to them in exchange for their favor. It seems to be within her character."

"I will remember," said Loren. "And . . . I would not so hastily excuse yourself from the company of my friends."

Jordel cocked his head, and for the first time since they had met in Wellmont, his eyes softened and his mouth twisted in a smile. Then he turned with a whirl of his cloak, and Loren followed him towards the docks with her hand on the dagger's hilt.

"Often have I visited Wellmont, and its captains are well known to me. With Vivien's command, Xain will not leave the city by any gate—not, at least, without blasting it open, and then we shall hear of it quickly. He may think he can escape by the river, though, and so there we begin our search. Scant hours remain until dawn, and the captains will be awake."

Loren thought of the way they had passed beneath the rivergate, but she dismissed it. Xain would not have Bubble's skill at crafting a bowl of air. He would go by boat, or not at all.

"One thing has troubled me," said Loren. "What do you mean to do with Xain once we find him?"

"I will not kill him, if that is what you mean," said Jordel. "He has done nothing to earn such a punishment, and his powers are too valuable besides."

"That is not what I mean. His powers are exactly the problem. I gather you mean to subdue him. But how? He is a wizard, after all. Though I am glad for her absence, would it not be wiser to hunt Xain with Vivien by our side? She at least might stand a chance against him."

"Anyone is vulnerable when surprised, and a wizard may be knocked senseless like any other. But you strike upon an important truth. When first I joined the Mystics, I was one of the mage hunters. They are a special force, well trained and with a single purpose: to subdue wizards who threaten the nine lands, either through magic or lust for power."

"Are such services often required?" said Loren, surprised. "Wizards are few and far enough between, it seems. How often do they pose a danger?"

"Not often, and yet when they do it is awful indeed. Hence we must be ever at the ready, for *Only in Watchfulness Lies Safety*. Those are the words of our order, though many have forgotten them." His eyes looked troubled. "But as I say, I spent my early years in that company. And one of the first things we learn is how to subdue the four types of wizardry. You know of the branches, yes?"

"I have heard," said Loren carefully. "I know of firemages and mindmages. And weremages," she added, thinking of Auntie.

"You have forgotten alchemy—though of course any wizard would shake their head and grouse at our use of such common terms. Among the learned, they are called elementalism, mentalism, therianthropy and transmutation. But no matter. Each type of magic relies upon a certain something, and each type of wizard may be cut from the source of their power. You have seen Xain cast his spells?"

"I have," said Loren.

"What does he do?" said Jordel, his eyes careful upon her.

Loren felt it was a test, and she was determined to pass. "He speaks words, and his eyes glow white. Then he moves his hands, and his fingers twist in just such a way." She tried to imitate one of Xain's signs, but it was hard to remember. His fingers were always so quick.

"That is close to the symbol for wind. But yes, his words are the true source. Thus an elementalist—a firemage, you would call them—who is gagged is rendered powerless, at least until the gag is removed."

"You mean all you would need to do would be to tie a cloth in Xain's mouth, and he would be just like any other man?" said Loren, astounded.

"Just so. On the other hand, mindmages must envision their magic, and so a blindfold will do the trick. They cannot see the thing they wish to move or strike. Alchemists must touch the things they change, and so you may use gloves of silk to subdue them. Only the most powerful alchemists can shift silk, and when they do, the glow in their eyes gives you enough warning to stop them. Weremages are the most difficult. They can become whatever they imagine, within the limits of their power, and so it is their thoughts you must constrain. Keeping them unconscious will do it, as will some herbs that muddy the mind."

"But weremages seem the least dangerous. They cannot unleash bolts of flame or throw a man through the air. That, at least, is a blessing."

Jordel's eyes drifted far away. "Not always," he said quietly. "I know one more fearsome than Xain even at his mightiest, but that is a story for another time. Suffice it to say that each type of wizard bears their own danger, and none must be trifled with lightly."

"Nor do I wish to," said Loren. "Once Annis is rescued, I will be quite content if I never deal with a wizard again."

"I do not think that is your fate," said Jordel. "But come. We approach the docks, and have much to do."

The docks of Wellmont were no more than half-full; any captain able to leave had done so when word first came of the Dorsean attack, and no more had come since the river blockade went up. Jordel studied the boats, their lashings creaking as they strained in the current. He saw one he must have known, for he approached it quickly. A thin rat of a man looked up as Jordel's boots landed on his deck, and he rose to shake the Mystic's wrist.

"Jordel," said the captain. "Well met, though I would it were in happier times."

"And I as well. I have a favor to ask."

He described Xain and Annis and told the captain to keep a watch for them. The man swore his oath. Then Jordel pulled forth a gold weight and placed it in the man's palm. The captain tried to refuse, but Jordel waved him off and left the boat, rejoining Loren on the dock.

"He gave me passage down the Dragon's Tail towards Wavemount once," said Jordel, "and on the journey I saved his life from brigands who tried to rob him."

"His life? Surely that debt cannot be repaid. Why, then, did you need to bribe him to keep a lookout?"

"It was not a bribe," said Jordel solemnly. "It was a gift, one friend to another. My order has no shortage of wealth. If I may bestow it upon those who rarely have an extra coin to their name, it will do my masters no harm—and will earn that much more loyalty besides."

At the next boat, Jordel told Loren he had served as the captain's first mate for two months while hunting a rogue wizard. At the next, Jordel recounted how he had met the captain—a woman—as they drank together in a tavern on the docks of Redbrook. Jordel grew somewhat red in the face and spoke curtly of her, offering no further explanation.

"Do you know every riverboat captain in all the nine lands?" said Loren.

"Not quite, but enough to serve my purpose. In Selvan especially, riverboats are the lifelines of the kingdom. Rarely does word travel more swiftly than the water will carry it, and those who steer these craft have seen more of the world than most who dwell here in Wellmont. It pays to know such folk. Indeed, the more people one knows, the more one can learn about any land one might wish to travel in."

"I feel as though you are giving me a lesson," said Loren.

"And you should take it to heart. If you would travel from kingdom to kingdom, do favors wherever you may. One never knows when such friendship might be repaid, and the rewards may be great."

Loren thought of the men she had met in the bar that afternoon. "I made two friends today," she said quickly. "Sellswords who fought on the southern wall when the Dorseans struck."

"That is good," said Jordel, and he gave a nod of approval. "Mercenaries, too, often roam far and gather much knowledge. Though they are more prone to die than a riverboat captain."

They kept on their way down the docks, and Loren saw that Jordel would stop even at boats where he did not know the captain. But she saw still more vessels that gave him no pause, and when she looked closer they appeared to be empty.

"What of these ones?" she said, pointing. "Xain could be hiding in any one of these empty boats, holding Annis captive."

"He might," said Jordel, looking troubled. "But we cannot simply step aboard and search any boat we please. At least not yet."

"If it is time you need, I could start. You hardly need my assistance to speak with these fishermen."

"I would not do that," said Jordel quickly. "Not unless we can find them no other way. This is a river city. To many who live here, their boats are more precious than their lives. It is not meet for the law, whether it be the Mystics or constables, to step aboard their vessels without permission or cause."

"Do you think Xain will hold to the same rule?" said Loren, growing angry. "He could be sitting on the other side of that door, laughing as he hears you speak of propriety."

"If he is, we will find him. No doubt Vivien has already sent word to the mayor requesting his help.

Word will find every captain, and the constables and my men will search the boats stem to stern. But it will be properly done, and will spark no ire."

Loren growled in frustration. "But what if they hide here *now?* You have spoken to nearly every captain in the city, and Vivien has sent us no word that your men have found him elsewhere. It seems we have scant few places to search, other than the empty boats."

"And there you should have searched from the beginning," said a voice.

Gem slid out from the shadows of a nearby building. His nose was as red as when Loren had last seen him, and his speech still sounded thick. But his jaw was set, and his eyes burned with determination.

"I have found your wizard, Mystic, and his captive. Come and take him, before I decide to kill him myself."

THIRTY

"Gem," said Loren. "How did you . . ."

"I guessed from the first that the wizard might look to the boats," said Gem. "We arrived by the river, and it seems he means to leave the same way. There is an old and empty green vessel at the west end of the docks. There Xain waits, and with him Annis."

"You went aboard without leave?" said Jordel. "That was perilously done. You could have been brought to the constables."

"None saw me. Certainly not Xain."

"Is Annis alive?" said Loren. "Is she whole?"

"She is, or I would not stand before you. For if the steer had hurt her any more, I would have killed him and fled Wellmont a murderer. But Xain is . . . acting oddly."

"How?" said Loren. "What do you mean?"

"He moves and sounds like a man in great pain, though I can find no sympathy for him."

"You did well," said Jordel, though he looked troubled. "But now you must leave it in our hands. Show us to this boat."

Gem gestured off into the darkness and turned to walk. Loren saw a slight stumble in his step, but other than that he did not falter as he guided them towards Wellmont's west end.

She saw the boat before Gem pointed it out—she had spotted the thing's ugly, chipped green paint while passing the first time. They hung far back to keep their voices from being heard, and from the darkness of a narrow alley they surveyed the boat. Low and listing in the river it sat. It hardly seemed the thing could keep water out. Loren saw rot in many of the boards, and its mast was bare of sails.

"There he waits," said Gem. "If he has not fled."

"We must have him out," said Jordel. "This must be cautiously done. Loren, you should—"

"She *should* slit his throat," said Gem. "She has a dagger, after all, and can move without being heard when she so wishes."

"Gem!" said Loren.

"What?" he barked. "Is your precious rule more valuable than the life of a friend? She lies within that boat, unable to escape from the wizard who might kill her. You saw him press his flames into her neck. You heard her scream."

Loren had heard it, and the sight of Xain pressing his finger into Annis' flesh would not leave her mind's eye. Of its own accord, her hand snuck down to the dagger.

Were someone to place a blade at her throat and force Loren to choose Xain's life or Annis', she would have chosen the girl in an instant. The wizard had tried to leave her too many times; he had lied to her; and he had harmed Annis. And certainly if Xain was dead, Annis' safety would no longer be in question. They could all of them travel to the north of Dorsea, there to search for Xain's contact on their own, or find somewhere else to sell the magestones.

But then she imagined it; she saw herself crouched over Xain, his lifeblood seeping from a gash in his neck, her blood-covered dagger in hand. She saw his lifeless eyes staring up at her, and her mind recoiled. She shook her head and shivered, though the night was muggy and warm.

"We will not kill the wizard," said Jordel. "No more blood need be spilt today. Wellmont has seen quite enough of that."

"What do you know of *need?"* said Gem. "You said you came to protect us, but you were not there when the wizard took her. His eyes were mad, I tell you, and his face like a skeleton's. Kill him, I say, or he will murder us all and more besides."

"He has killed no one yet," said Jordel.

"And you need him for your precious war," sneered Gem.

"Jordel is right, Gem. We will not kill him. Certainly I will not. And you should be less quick to wish such a judgment, lest it finds you yourself."

"As you say then, Nightblade." Gem stood tall as he could and glared at her. "But know this. I meant to deal my own justice to Xain. If you fail to do the same, and Annis comes to harm because of it, that justice will fall upon you."

Loren almost laughed, but she realized how great a mistake that could be in his state. Instead she nodded solemnly. "I have heard you. And will keep your promise in mind. Annis shall not come to harm while I live."

She turned to Jordel. "I have an idea for how she might be recovered, but I will need your help."

"Let me hear your plan, and if it is a good one, you will have my help and more besides. I shall have my men brought."

"No, no others," said Loren. "There is no time. If he should try to escape before they arrive, then my plan is foiled—and I will need Gem as well. You said you used to hunt mages. Do you know more than how to restrain them? Can you fight them?"

"You saw me in the tavern," said Jordel.

When Xain had thought the Mystics were attacking, he had summoned his magic. Jordel had struck like a serpent, and had stopped Xain cold.

"Good enough," said Loren. "I will catch Xain's attention and draw him out, away from the boat. Once he is gone, the two of you can come aboard and rescue Annis. He will return to the boat once he loses me. Jordel will lie in ambush, waiting to take him captive."

"That is a dangerous course," said Gem. "For it pits you alone against the wizard."

"I can escape from Xain on the streets easily enough. A wizard he may be, but he has poor wisdom when it comes to chasing quarry. And besides, I do not think him a killer—not after what Jordel told us at the inn."

"I can save the girl myself," said Jordel. "Send Gem to gather the others from my order. They can help us if this plan of yours goes ill."

"Gem must go with you," said Loren. "Annis is no doubt terrified, and does not hold you in great esteem. She might fight you if she sees you, and so draw Xain back too early. Gem will calm her."

Jordel looked troubled and did not answer immediately. "Still you must be careful," he said at last. "And if it grows too perilous, you must withdraw. I would not have you come to harm on my account. Mayhap it would be better if I was the one to draw him away. He might pursue me more readily, and the two of you can save Annis as easily as I might."

"You will not," insisted Loren. "Annis found herself in this mess because of me. I shall take the risk."

Jordel sighed. "If you insist. But still you must promise me: if you think you might be harmed, you will withdraw so that we may summon the others. Xain cannot stand against Vivien if I am at her side."

"Very well," said Loren. "Now stay back, and let me lure this bear from his cave."

THIRTY-ONE

LOREN CREPT TOWARDS THE GREEN BOAT. GEM AND Jordel watched from the alley's mouth, and as she looked back over her shoulder she saw their eyes glinting in torchlight. She gave them a small smile of assurance, though she felt little for herself.

She only hoped this scheme would work. Nothing felt more important than saving Annis from Xain's clutches, and as quickly as possible. The girl had suffered too much already, standing all her life in her mother's shadow. Now Loren had brought her to this. If anything should happen to her . . .

Loren pushed that thought aside, for now she would need a clear mind. She reached the dock and snuck carefully down the steps towards the boat. She could not hear her own footfalls for the gurgling river and creaking boat lines. Step by step she slid along the wooden planks, searching for any sign of movement in the moonslight. There was nothing to see, nor could she hear any sound.

She reached the edge of the dock, and only one large step separated her from the boat's deck. Her feet grew leaden, and she paused. Then she thought of Annis captive within, and with a leap she gained the deck.

The boat swayed ever so slightly beneath her, and she froze. But no sound came from the cabin, and after a long moment she finally exhaled. The boat was like Brimlad's, with one hatch leading into a cabin that grew out of the main deck—but this cabin had small portholes that now hung open. Loren guessed that Gem had seen the wizard through one of them. Mayhap it would be wise to look inside before she tried to get Xain's attention.

Loren came forwards at a crouch until she stood directly beneath the porthole. She straightened slowly with her head tilted, so that only a single eye came into view. The cabin was dirty and unkempt. She supposed the boat had not been used in some time. Rubbish lay in the corners, and the walls were rotten. A single pallet of straw lay to one side, but its contents had been ripped out and spread across the room—probably by rats.

On the empty cloth lay Annis. Loren's heart quickened at the sight. But she could not see Xain anywhere within, and Annis did not see her. The girl had curled into a ball, her face against the wall. Where was the wizard? Had he stepped out since Gem left to fetch Loren?

It did not matter. With the room empty, she could save Annis. If she was quick, Loren would not need Gem or Jordel after all.

Like a ghost she made for the hatch. Only an old wooden lever held it shut, and the lever's hinge was rusted. After a glance around the deck to ensure Xain was not lurking in some dark corner, she drew her dagger and struck the hinge with the hilt. It fell to the planks at her feet, and she threw the door open to dash inside.

"Annis!" she hissed. "It is me! Quickly, we must—"

She jumped and cried out as the door slammed shut behind her.

Loren whirled to find Xain standing there, his eyes glowing as flame danced between his fingers.

"You forgot my walls of air, girl."

She *had* forgotten, but all thoughts of the wizard's magic vanished as she took in his appearance. Xain looked far worse than when she had last seen him. Skin clung to bone, which stuck out in jagged points. His shoulders were stooped and hunched, and his blue coat hung loose off his shoulders. His lips were frozen in a grimace of pain, and there were bare patches on his scalp where hair had fallen away from it.

All this she saw in a moment, before Xain spoke.

"Why are you here? I told you if you followed me . . . I told you . . ."

He faltered, and his arms folded in on themselves as the light died in his eyes. His flame guttered out, and he collapsed against the inside of the hatch, moaning in agony.

Loren ran to Annis' side and wrapped an arm about her shoulders to protect her. She thrust the dagger towards Xain. "You will not harm her, wizard. Jordel told me the truth of what happened at the High King's Seat. You are no murderer, and you will not . . ."

Words died on her tongue, for Xain paid them no heed. He merely kept rocking back and forth, hugging his arms about himself as he cried out again and again. From the sound, Loren would have imagined him pierced by arrows, with hooks digging into his flesh. She shot a quick glance at Annis, but the girl only stared at the wizard in terror, her eyes bright in the glow of moonslight.

"Xain?" said Loren. She wished her voice had not come so softly. "What is wrong?"

The wizard's wailing ceased. "Wrong? Nothing. Why should anything be wrong? The world is ending, and the Mystics wish for me to fling myself into its death throes."

"Do not excuse your actions by blaming them on others," said Loren fiercely. "Jordel did not set fire to Annis' flesh."

Xain looked up, and in his eyes she saw tears. "I am sorry. Sorry, so very sorry. I never wanted to hurt her. I only wanted . . . I had to get away. From him. From the woman. They are mad, all of them, Loren. Mad."

Loren thought of Jordel and Gem. Surely they would have seen her enter the boat and would wonder what had happened. It was only a matter of time before they followed. But she longed to hear what the wizard had to say, as she had longed since Jordel first mentioned it.

"You promised to tell me of the Mystic's words. Tell me now, if as you say they drove you to this madness."

"A war is coming," Xain mumbled. "A war, a war."

"The war is here. You fought in it yesterday. We all did, Xain, but that does not—"

"I do not speak of the petty squabblings of the nine lands," he spat. "The war that will end war. A darkness. A great evil like nothing we have seen in our lives. They mean to use me as a weapon—all of us, all the wizards, all with the gift. We are to be their arsenal, to be flung into the maw of . . . of the . . ."

His limbs seized up again, and he moaned with whatever dark pain plagued him. Loren saw that two of his fingernails had fallen away, and as she watched another lock of hair drifted from his scalp.

"What has happened to you, Xain? Have you been stricken by plague?" Loren shuddered and covered her mouth with her sleeve.

Xain shook his head. "No. This is . . . this must be the work of the Mystic woman. She did something to me upon the river. She must have, for I feel my mind slipping away from me. My body wilts like a flower held to flame."

"How does she have such power?" said Loren. "This is no mind magic."

"She must. What else could it be? Some of them can do more than lift rocks with their thoughts. Legends of Wizard Kings told of those who could strip flesh from bones with their minds. If only I . . . if only I could . . ."

His eyes shifted, and he saw Annis by Loren's side. He looked at the girl as if seeing her for the first time. His lips trembled, and tears slid down his cheeks to drip from his skeletal chin.

"I did not wish to hurt you," he said softly. "I only need . . . I need to . . ."

"To escape," Loren whispered.

She thought back to when she had met Xain in the Birchwood. How her parents had thought to use her as a game piece, to lure the eye of some old man who could pay for a young bride. In escaping that fate, Loren had knocked Chet's poor father unconscious—to say nothing of the arrow she had planted in her father's leg.

No one wanted to be used. No one wanted to live a life served up by others. And the desperation, the need to flee such a life, could drive one to acts they would never before have considered.

Did Loren's actions in the Birchwood make her a villain? Doubtless they would, in some tales. But her life was not about tales, and it never had been. If she had lived like a sweet maiden, she would have spent the rest of her days in her parents' shadow, wed to a man who cared for nothing but her youth and the children she might bear him.

Even Mennet had been a bandit once. And Loren saw now that she could cast no shadow on Xain without first allowing the light to burn her. Xain had helped her escape the Birchwood—her, a small slip of a girl with green eyes. She could do no less for him now, twisted wretch that he had become.

"All right then, wizard," said Loren. "Let us see about getting you out of this mess."

THIRTY-TWO

LOREN MOVED AWAY FROM ANNIS AND STOOD TALL, towering over Xain as he curled upon the floor. "If I help you leave Wellmont and escape Jordel forever, will you release Annis? If we give you your share of the magestones, will you leave us and never return?"

His eyes blazed with hunger, and he nodded vigorously. "Yes. Yes, the magestones. With them I could . . . I could cast off the Mystic woman's enchantment, mayhap. Mayhap it would strengthen the magic in me enough . . . yes. *Pleassse.*"

The word stretched out until a heavy cough racked his body. Xain drew his hand from his mouth, and Loren saw blood on his thumb.

"Loren . . ." said Annis.

"Shhh," Loren said quietly. "It will be all right. We will return for Gem, and all will be as it should."

Loren saw the brown cloth packet in the pocket of Annis' cloak and pulled it out. From within she drew the second half of the magestone they had used upon the river, which she brought to Xain.

The wizard snatched it from her grasp with clawed fingers and bit into it like a starving man into freshly baked bread. The stone vanished in an instant.

Xain swallowed and sank back against the bulkhead with a sigh. Before Loren's eyes his skin filled out, its color returning. His breath came more easily, and though his eyes glowed black for a moment, when the glow died away they were bright and full of vigor. Even the hair on his head sprouted slowly back, though it looked a tangled and uneven mess.

"It worked," said Loren.

"It did," said Xain, and his voice was smooth and powerful. It rebounded off the cabin walls, and Loren felt each word thrumming through her chest. "You may have saved my life, Loren of the family Nelda."

"Do not act as though it is the first time." Loren stuck out a hand.

Xain ignored it. Instead, with a wave of his fingers and a whisper, a gust of wind sprang from nowhere and lifted him to his feet. "I will not, though there is little time to repay you. If we mean to escape the city, we must move quickly."

"More quickly than you know," said Loren. "Gem and Jordel wait outside the boat even now, and I have been gone too long. We came to rescue Annis, and they will not let you leave without trouble."

"They cannot stop me," said Xain, and his eyes flashed black. "Not even with Jordel's whole order at their backs."

Loren quailed at that, but she threw back her shoulders and looked him in the eye. "There is no need for your bluster. Can you open the city's rivergate?"

"I can," said Xain with a nod. "Iron cannot stand against my fire now. But I thought you were concerned that the Dorseans might find a way inside if the wall were breached."

"Not on the upstream side. For Wellmont could move a boat outside, and the current will hold it fast against the breach. It will be just as good as the iron grating, and meanwhile we will have made our escape."

"Very clever," said Xain.

Loren gave a small bow. "I am not without my own talents. But we must move. Ready yourself to make this boat sail, and the sooner the better."

"Only say the word."

Loren nodded and gave a final reassuring look to Annis. The girl had not moved from her place in the corner, and she trembled in the moonslight. Loren hoped she would understand once this was all over.

The hatch creaked open, and she stepped back into the night. Not a moment too soon, for she saw Gem and Jordel just up the street. They froze as they caught sight of her, their expressions masks of anxiety.

"Loren!" whispered Gem. "What happened to you? Where is the wizard?"

She did not answer. Instead she looked at Jordel with sorrow as she walked to the boat's railing. He would be angry at losing Xain, Loren knew, but if he would still have her services, she would gladly give them to repay the debt.

Loren lifted her foot and placed it on the line that held them to the dock, and her hand stole under her cloak.

"Jordel, I am sorry," she called out. "Find me beyond the city walls."

The Mystic's eyes widened with understanding, and he leapt forwards with an outstretched hand. "Loren, *wait!*" he shouted.

"Now, Xain!" cried Loren, and from her belt she drew the dagger. With one quick slash she cut the line. A frothing gush of water slammed into the stern. It flung the boat forwards, and Loren barely kept her footing as they cut through the water. Jordel's angry cries died behind her as the vessel shot upstream. Xain used water to move them, for the sails had long rotted away.

Xain emerged from the cabin to stand with her as the northern rivergate approached. "Do you think the Mystic will forgive you?"

Loren thought she heard mockery in his tone, but she shrugged. "I do not know. I hope so, for I mean to help him fight whatever darkness is to come."

Xain looked at her in surprise. "You do? Even after my warning?"

"Even then. You do not wish to fight, for you have a home and a child waiting. I have nowhere to go and no one to expect me. What better use is there for my time? I will go with him at least until I learn the truth Jordel told you. Unless you will share it with me now?"

Xain studied her face, and she thought for a moment he might tell her. But then his black eyes grew hooded, and he turned away. "It is not my place to say. Not yet, at any rate. I know now why Jordel would not tell you—would not tell anyone. And though I gave you my word to reveal the secret, I must break that promise. Dark knowledge in the wrong hands may doom us all."

"Very well. I will find it out in my own time."

"I do not doubt it. But now we are at the rivergate, and you would do well to go into the cabin. This will not be a safe place to stand."

"Since when have I wished for safety?" said Loren. But she went to the creaking mast and wrapped her arms around it. "Do your worst, wizard. I was too far away to see you fight upon the southern wall. Let me witness your power now."

Xain nodded, and the black glow grew in his eyes as he whispered. Flame sprang to life—but not the ragged, wispy flames Loren had grown used to. This was a white-hot ball, like the one Xain had used to breach the hull of Vivien's ship. It swelled in size, roiling and twisting in the air until Loren could no longer look at it. It seemed brighter than the sun and nearly as hot. She feared it might set the boat ablaze.

Even with her eyes shut she could sense its light and feel its heat, and so she knew the moment Xain flung it. Then her eyes opened to see the fire speeding towards the rivergate. She braced herself, thinking there would be an explosion, some great impact to shake the air and send the river water gushing up in a torrent. But there was nothing. The river gate offered no resistance—the ball of fire passed straight through, leaving a great gaping hole with red-hot, glowing edges. The only sound was from the river erupting in a hissing roil of steam where the fireball touched it. That steam plumed towards the wall, and Loren heard men there cry out as it struck them. They ran away in both directions, shielding their faces with blistering hands.

"No archers will harry us, at least," said Xain. His words were nearly lost in the sound of the water slapping at the sides of the boat. In darkness and confusion they shot through the northern rivergate of Wellmont, and soon the torches on the wall faded to pinpricks of light behind them. Xain turned back to look at them just once. On his face Loren saw a smile of triumph more frightening than the rictus mask from Vivien's enchantment. She shivered and turned her gaze away.

THIRTY-THREE

LOREN LEFT THE DECK AND ENTERED THE CABIN. ANNIS still sat in the corner. She jerked in fright when Loren opened the hatch, and though she calmed at once, still she looked ready to flee at a moment's notice.

"We are free of the city," said Loren. "Soon we will return for Gem. This will all be over."

"Will it?" said Annis. "Too much has happened for me to believe that."

"Much of it has been Xain's fault. I cannot ask you to forgive him, but Vivien nearly drove him mad. You saw what she turned him into. I do not think he was in control of himself."

"And if he loses control again?" said Annis. "How can you be sure he—"

She stopped short and looked over Loren's shoulder. Loren turned to find Xain standing behind her. That was a surprise—the wizard had no gift for stealth, and she would have expected to hear him.

"We shall gain the shore soon. Then we strike north for the road." Xain's voice still rumbled deep, lingering in the air, strumming through Loren's body as though she were a bowstring. "But there is something ahead that I thought you should see."

Loren looked to Annis. "You should come. The air in here is dank, and a breath of something fresher might do you well."

Annis had dropped her eyes away from Xain, and she did not lift them now. But she nodded and rose, coming to Loren's side as they followed the wizard back out onto the deck.

The boat sat still and silent in the river. Xain no longer propelled it. Far ahead, Loren saw the glow of many torches and lanterns. They were spaced out in three lines, each separate from the others. Figures passed before them, making the lights blink and flutter.

"The Dorsean blockade," said Loren. "Three ships, the same as we saw east of the city. We should put ashore here, out of range of their arrows. They have not seen us yet."

"We could do so," said Xain. "But I had another idea. You hail from Selvan, do you not?"

"I do," said Loren, brow furrowing.

"As do I." She saw the flash of his teeth in the moonslight as he smiled. "And while our thoughts have been preoccupied with other things, still I am not blind to Wellmont's suffering. What say we play our part to alleviate this siege?"

"I know nothing of this war, and it does not concern me," said Loren. "I am no fighter."

"Nor I," said Xain. "Yet I have my talents. Watch."

He raised his hands, and his eyes turned to black. In the night, they became pits where Loren could see nothing, giving his face a skull-like appearance. It reminded her of how he had appeared in his madness, and she suppressed a shiver.

Her gaze was drawn to the Dorsean blockade against her will. She expected to see the ships burst into flame, white tongues lapping at the sails, or mayhap for a great gale to descend from the sky and dash them to kindling against the shore. But at first she saw nothing.

"What are you doing?" said Loren.

"Look closer," said Xain. "See the darkness within the night."

"What is that supposed to mean?" said Annis.

Loren clutched the girl's sleeve. "I see it."

A black . . . *something* swelled around the ships, whorling about the hulls where they met the water. Like flame it moved, but darker than the night that surrounded it. She could only see it by its absence of light—like a blot of ink on dark skin, like blood on a crimson cloak. Where the thing spread, the river water lost its glint, and the moons no longer shone on the wooden planks of the hull.

"What is it?" said Loren, her voice shaking.

"It is called darkfire," said Xain, his voice quivering with force. "It is like my flame, but made stronger by the magestones. The stones do not only empower a wizard's gift—they change it. Spellcasters of every branch become more powerful, each in their own way."

"It is only flame, then?" said Loren.

"It burns twice as hot, it gives off no light, and neither water nor wind will douse it. Darkfire will not die until it has consumed all it has touched. Our Dorsean friends must make for the shore, or they will be lost."

Loren turned on him angrily. "Put it out, wizard! You could kill everyone aboard those ships before they see what you have done."

"That is unlikely." He pointed. "See? Even now they are aware of it."

Loren heard a shout. The men on the ships erupted into a flurry of activity, like ants whose hill had been doused by rain. Some ran for barrels of water and dumped them over the side, but it had no more effect on the darkfire than the river did. The flames licked higher and higher up the hulls, and one of the ships began to sag in the water, its bow tilting up as the stern slipped slowly downwards. Shouts of anger turned to fear, and Loren saw some men fling themselves over the side of the ships. Thankfully they landed far from the flames—Loren did not want to imagine what would happen if the darkfire caught the sailors in its blaze.

"Put it out!" she commanded. "If they do not burn to death, they will drown!"

"The river is gentle," said Xain, his voice hard. "Any sailor can make the swim to shore. And if the captains are wise, they will set their sails for solid ground."

It seemed he was right. Even as some men scrambled for the water, others sprang into action at the shouts of the ships' officers. Slowly, achingly slowly, the sails rose. They caught the night's gentle breeze, and the ships drifted for the southern shore.

"We have watched long enough," said Xain. "They make for land, and we must do the same. There is much ground yet to cover before dawn."

Their boat lurched as Xain used his magic to push it through the water. In no time at all Loren felt a grinding beneath their feet as the hull scraped the riverbank.

She turned one last time to the southwest. Two of the ships had landed. The third almost made it, but its back half sagged, slowing it down. Water sloshed through the railings onto the deck. Abandoning all discipline, the crew flung themselves headlong into the river. The captain was the last to go. Loren could see him—a tall man in a yellow coat that fairly glowed in the torchlight. He bellowed at his men as they abandoned him, but in the end he had no one to scream at. Then he shucked his coat and joined the crew in their flight.

She turned her back and took Annis' hand, helping the girl over the riverboat's railing and onto the shore. Together they struck north as the ships burned behind them, consumed by flames darker than midnight.

Xain fell into step with them, bouncing a little with each stride. "I feel stronger with each passing moment. The Mystic's enchantment seems to be losing the last of its hold on me."

"I am glad," said Loren, though she was not. "Mayhap it is best if we part ways now. Annis and I can return to the city before the sun rises. It will be harder to sneak in during daylight."

"Though it sounds strange, you will have a quicker time of it if you carry on north for a while," said Xain. "The road out of Wellmont runs north, but soon it turns west into the foothills of the Greatrock Mountains. We are scarcely an hour's hard walk away, and from there your journey to the city will take you half the time. Fear not, for you will be parted from me soon."

"Not soon enough." Annis rubbed at her neck where the wizard had burned it. Xain only smiled.

"Very well," said Loren, though she wanted badly to part from the wizard's company. "North it is."

They placed the southern moon at their backs and hastened their steps. The land sloped gently upwards, and the moonslight was more than enough to reveal any uneven ground. But of this there was precious little, for they walked on green grass that bent pleasantly underfoot, and beneath the boughs of trees that soughed sweetly in the night's cool air. If their circumstances were different, Loren might have enjoyed herself. The ground, the trees, and the sky all joined together to remind her of the Birchwood. Not her parents or most of the villagers, but her best memories of home: the nights she had spent by Chet's side, exploring the forest.

They would walk together in the light of stars and moons, and most of the time they felt no need to speak. They would listen to the forest's nighttime song and watch the way the silver rays fell through the leaves above to paint patterns on the ground below, more elegant than the intricate designs of a merchants' silks. The song of the nightingale sounded like a bard's ballad, and the rustle of small beasts and birds in the underbrush was like the whispering of friends.

When they did talk it was in quiet murmurs, and their words were never of their troubles. They imagined brighter futures, good times yet to come, a thousand impossible ways to escape the dull and dreary fates they saw stretching before them. Though Loren knew such thoughts for dreams, still it was easier to imagine them there in the night, to see them stretching out, sylvan and wondrous as the starlight itself.

But she had never told Chet about her dreams of the Nightblade, nor her determination to see those dreams come true. He listened to her wildest imaginings and never questioned them, but still her dearest hope was something too personal. She wondered what he would think of her now. A poor excuse for a master thief, running penniless and hungry from one danger to the next, only making all her problems worse with each passing day and well-meant action.

"We are nearly there," said Xain, pulling Loren from her thoughts. He raised a hand and pointed at a low hill ahead. "We shall find the road just on the other side of this hill. Then our ways will part, well and truly."

"Good," said Annis, stepping a bit faster. "Let us hurry."

"You wound me," said Xain with a smirk, but he increased his pace to keep up with her. He was not tall, but still he did not have to strain to match Annis' short legs.

Halfway up the hill, something tickled the back of Loren's mind: a sense that something was wrong, though she could not place what. She looked around them, but there was no sign of danger. Then she heard it: a low murmur, growing louder the higher they climbed.

"What is that?" she said. "Do you hear it?"

"I do," said Xain, looking troubled. "Though I do not know what it is."

Annis gave an exasperated snort. "I do not hear anything, nor do I care. I only want this mad adventure finished so I may return to the city and things can go back to normal. Well, what passes for normal in our lives. Make haste, Loren."

She reached the top of the hill and stopped in her tracks. Loren caught up a moment later, and when she saw what Annis had seen, she froze.

An army lay below them, camped north of the road and stretching over the foothills on the other side. There were hundreds of soldiers, many hundreds more than there had been before. For Loren had seen this army already, and even in the darkness she knew who they were. At long last, after a march of many leagues, the Dorsean mercenaries had arrived at Wellmont.

THIRTY-FOUR

Loren fell to the ground, bringing Annis with her. She swept her feet at Xain's legs, and he crashed to the ground with an angry grunt. But when he rose to his elbows and glared at her, Loren put a finger to her lips.

"Be silent and still," she whispered. "They will have sentries posted, and you will not see them in the dark."

The anger did not leave Xain's eyes, but he remained silent as he turned to the army before them.

No campfires burned among the host, but the moonslight was more than enough to illuminate hundreds of canvas tents. A few torches shone, held by night watchmen who walked among the tents.

"Why are there no fires?" whispered Annis.

"They are trying not to be seen," said Loren. "But they must know they cannot hide so large a force for long. I would wager they mean to attack tomorrow. And if they meant to march at dawn, the camp would be roused already. They are letting the soldiers rest so that they can attack at midday, or mayhap at sundown." She nodded to herself. "That is when they struck yesterday, so that the darkness would hide them from the city's archers. They think that if they are careful, Wellmont will not see them until their first volley."

"But the city knows they are coming," said Xain. "Jordel has warned them."

"But the sellswords do not know that," said Loren. "At least, we must hope not."

"Well, these matters may concern the great and wise," said Annis. "But I am neither. We have reached the road, wizard. Now our ways part."

"You should keep south of these hills as you travel," Loren told him. "And stay wary, in case they have posted sentries on this side. But I doubt they would, for then Wellmont might spy them. You should be safe until you leave the army behind and can be on your way."

Xain's lips were pursed, and he did not answer for a moment. Then he slowly shook his head.

"I could do that, yes. But it will not solve a greater problem, one that has only just come to me—for now I see its solution. From here I travel to the High King's Seat and reclaim my son. But I cannot make that journey on foot. I will need a horse."

"So you might, but that is not our concern," said Annis, glaring. "The bargain was struck, and our side upheld. Now be on your way and we will be on ours, and may the twain never meet again."

"You may leave if you wish," said Xain carefully. "But still I cannot make my journey without a horse. And the men before us have plenty."

Loren understood his meaning at once. "You cannot think to steal a horse from this army. That is madness. They will find you and kill you. You have no gift for stealth or thievery. And I doubt your magic could withstand their whole host, even with the help of the magestones."

"I know my limits," said Xain. "I could not do it. But I wager that the Nightblade could."

Loren flushed, and was grateful Xain could not see it in the darkness. But Annis glared at the wizard in the starlight. "Do not draw us into another one of your schemes. You are worse than the Mystics, and your words grow madder the more of them you speak. Loren would never be so foolish. It is too dangerous. Our dealings are done, and not too soon if you ask me, which of course no one does."

"Too dangerous for Loren?" said Xain. "She has accomplished more, and in worse circumstances than this. The army sleeps. Only a handful patrol the tents. For Loren, such a task would come easily."

"Not easily, and you know it," said Loren. "Look there. The horses are in the middle of the army. They might not notice my approach, but they could not fail to see me leave. Or will they let a young maid walk out of their midst with one of their steeds in tow?"

But even as she spoke, a plan began to form in her mind. It would be dangerous, but she thought she might pull it off. She tried to shake the thought away, but details sprang to mind, fitting into the scheme like pieces to a puzzle.

"It is but a thin line of tents that separate the horses from freedom," pressed Xain. "You could ride out before they knew what had happened and return before sunrise."

"Loren?" Annis snorted. "She has as much skill at riding as a burlap sack, or mayhap less. And anyway, why should she do it? Your concerns are not ours to solve, nor are we beholden to you. *We* helped *you* escape the city, not the other way around. Indeed, you have brought nothing but death and danger on us since first we laid eyes on you. If not for you, the constables would never have come to my mother's caravan, and she would never have killed them. You brought Jordel into our affairs, and we have regretted it ever since. And without him, we would have had no concern with

Vivien, and I would have been happier for it. No, wizard. You draw trouble like honey draws flies, and I am sick of your sweet words."

Loren wanted desperately to agree with Annis. But for everything the girl said, Loren could think of a response in Xain's favor. Xain must have thought the same thing, for his face grew grimly amused.

"Yet without me, you would never have escaped Vivien upon the river," he said. "You would never have escaped Cabrus after your mother decided to hunt the two of you down. And if I had never met Loren . . ."

"I should still be in the Birchwood," she finished. "I would not wish for that, nor will I deny my gratitude. But still, Xain, you ask for too much."

"A weight on both scales clears the account," said Xain. "A young woman once told me that in the Birchwood, and I have not forgotten it. I failed to see her wisdom then, but it becomes clearer to me now."

"Do not think to flatter me," said Loren, though again she flushed in the darkness. "This is too great a task. You must travel on foot for now. I do not doubt you will find some place in the Greatrocks where a farmer will trade a nag for some wizardry."

"A nag will not be enough." Xain's voice grew softer, almost pleading. "Loren, you know what I pursue—but you know also what pursues me. The Mystics will not give up their hunt. And Jordel knows that I make for the Seat. He will send word to his order, hoping they can capture me there—but the arms of my enemies are long, and they will hear of it. They will be prepared for my arrival, and all hope for my success will be lost. Even the magestones will not help me then. Or I might not reach the Seat at all. Now that Jordel has found me, he will be harder to evade. I have no hope but haste. If you will not help me one last time, then break your vow of peace. Draw your dagger and slit my throat here, for it will be a quicker end than the one that will find me after."

Loren looked away. "You think to pluck at guilty strings within my heart. You helped me in the Birchwood, yes. But can you claim I did not help you as well? You cannot forget all I have done when you speak of the past."

"I do not forget it." Loren felt his hand on her shoulder. "That is why I ask this of you. Have we not traveled far enough together, daughter of the family Nelda, to earn me this final boon? Do this for me, and let us part as friends, each with some hope of achieving our desires. It is no bad thing to have a wizard in your debt."

Loren pushed his hand away and fixed him with a hard stare. "My debt, and then some," she growled. "I will expect you to conquer a city for me, if I ask it."

Annis' eyes flew wide. "You cannot mean to do as he asks!"

"One outlaw to another," said Loren. Ignoring Annis' look of horror, she held out a hand. "If I call on you, you will answer. Are we agreed?"

Without hesitation, Xain smiled and took her wrist. "One outlaw to another. I quite like that."

"On your word," said Loren, gripping his wrist and shaking hard. "Now let us see if I have yet earned my name."

THIRTY-FIVE

THEY CREPT BACK DOWN THE HILL ON ITS SOUTHERN side, where they found a narrow dell with many trees to hide them from any watchers above. There Loren told Annis and Xain to wait until she returned—hopefully with a steed.

"We shall wait," said Xain. "Only make haste, for dawn is close."

"Do not tell me to hasten my steps into danger while you wait here in safety," said Loren. "I have half a mind to bring you with me, and I would, if I did not think you would walk loudly enough to wake the whole army."

"Loren, you must not do this," pleaded Annis. "It is far too perilous, and if anything should happen to you . . . well, have you thought of what would happen to *me?* Alone here with this madman of a wizard?"

"This madman has ears," said Xain.

"I hope they burn with shame," snapped Annis, glaring at him. "I will take no sharp words from you, and you deserve to hear many more from me."

"I will not be long," said Loren. "All will be well. They will take no more notice of me than their own shadows."

"That is easily said, but harder done."

"If something should go wrong, make for the city," said Loren. "They will not turn you away, especially if you bring them word of the mercenaries. They will see no threat in you."

"Because I am only a little girl, you mean," said Annis, scowling.

Loren put a hand on her chin and tilted her face up. "It is no bad thing to seem less of a threat than you are. Remember that always. When you look at me, you see a simple woodsman's daughter. Little would you know that you match eyes with the world's greatest thief."

Annis laughed, but tears sprang into her eyes. "I do not like your talk of remembering always. It sounds too much like a last good-bye. Do not tell me what to do if you fail to return; instead, promise that you will."

Loren did not blink. "I have chosen a life of darkness and lies. I have skill in the shadows and with twisted words. But I must always have someone to whom I will speak only the truth. Without that I will go mad. That is what you are to me, Annis, and so I will make you no promise unless I know I can keep it."

Annis' tears sprang forth at last. She wrapped her arms around Loren's waist, and Loren returned the embrace, the sweet smell of the girl's hair flooding her nostrils.

"Do your best, then, or I shall walk into the sellsword camp and fetch you home myself."

"My best is all I can promise," said Loren. "And I do so willingly."

Annis turned her face and retreated into the dell. Xain studied Loren with careful eyes.

"See to her safety," said Loren. "I shall return swiftly, or not at all."

"I will," said Xain. "If anything should go wrong, I will ensure she reaches Wellmont."

"Thank you," said Loren. "Wish me luck."

"Why should I? You have never had any to begin with, and yet you seem to do well enough without it."

Loren smirked and turned from him. Her black cloak whirled around her shoulders as she slipped into the night.

As her feet whispered through the soft grass, her weariness seemed to weigh her down at once. With a shock she realized she had not slept since the morning of the Dorsean attack. Since then, she had seen enough adventure for many lifetimes of adventure, and yet now here she was, rushing headlong into her greatest peril yet.

"Still, I hope it will make a good story," she said out loud, her words swallowed by the night. "A better one if I survive, I suppose."

She had drawn near the top of the hill now, and she began to walk more carefully, neither bending the grass nor making a sound. When she crested the hill she stopped, surveying the tents below and observing the torches winding through the lines.

The mercenaries would have sentries, and she would have to find some way to slip through them. Darkness might provide enough cover, but then again it might not. There was no way to know until she saw how many there were, and how far apart.

For some while she lay in the grass, trying to pierce the darkness with her eyes. But she soon grew impatient, knowing dawn could not be far away. Her eyelids grew heavy, and once or twice her head drooped. She reached up and pinched her cheek, hard enough to make her eyes water.

"You will not fall asleep," she growled to herself. "What an inglorious end to my tale that would make: *Then she drowsed off atop the hill, and the next thing she knew a spear prodded her awake as the soldiers attacked. Her friends would have mourned her death, had they not been too busy laughing at her foolishness."*

Just as she had begun to wonder if the army had posted sentries after all, she caught a glint of starlight on metal. Her eyes shot to it, and after a moment she made out the shape of a man in a grey cloak sitting against a fallen log.

In an instant she realized her mistake, and how crafty the mercenaries had been. Their sentries on this side of the road stood in the shadows of the hills, where the moons could not shine their silver light. Only luck had given Loren a glimpse of the man as the stars caught the steel of his sword pommel. He was close to her, much closer than she would have thought possible, and her heart skipped as she imagined herself crawling ignorant down the hillside into his waiting arms.

Gone were any thoughts of sleep. Now that she knew what to look for, she crawled west along the hill-side with a sharp eye for the next sentry. This one she spotted without much trouble, not far from the first. They were close enough that she might sneak between them, but it would be a dangerous business. Even the slightest noise would give her away, and once she passed from the shadows she would not be hard to spot in the moonlight.

She would have to create a distraction. She wished for a moment that she had brought Xain, so that he could send a bolt of lightning flying. In the sentries' shock she could have slipped by. But mayhap such a plan would have been worse, for then the camp would surely be roused and her chances of emerging unscathed would diminish.

Loren thought of her dagger, but she dismissed the idea immediately. Only sheer luck had made it useful thus far, and she did not like the odds that one of these men might know and respect the Mystics who dealt with such weapons. No, she would have to draw them out, but in such a way that they would decide in the end there was nothing worth alerting the camp about.

An idea struck her. It seemed risky, but she had little time to think of anything else. South of the hills, close to the river, the grass had been lush and green. Here, beside the road, it was dry and cracked with summer's heat. Such scrub caught fire easily, and could quickly spread to an inferno. Loren had never seen a forest fire, but she had heard tales from droughts in days past, when swaths of the forest could catch ablaze at once. It was every forest dweller's greatest fear.

What were the chances that the sentries might know this? Fair, she supposed, especially if they came from lands where woods were common and grew dry in summer. A small fire, then, hardly more than wisps of smoke, might draw them out.

Quickly she went into action, pulling several dried scrub brushes and branches together. To make it look like an old campfire, she collected a few small stones and arranged them in a circle. Flint sprang to her hands from the pouch at her belt, and her hunting knife from her boot. She struck once, twice, thrice, and a few small sparks leapt to the tinder. Within a moment, a small flame licked up from the grass. Loren waited as long as she could and then stole away.

Her first instinct was to run away from the sentries while she waited for them to see the fire. But then she realized that would only put her outside their ring, and their eyes would be turned even more watchfully outward. So instead she ran halfway down the hillside towards a boulder and dropped down beside it. She pressed her face into the grass and threw her cloak overhead, and then she curled her legs up to rest beneath the hem.

It was not long before she heard a cry farther down the hill and feet running up the slope, along with the soft jingle of chainmail.

"What is it?" called a voice.

"A light!" The sentry's voice sounded as though it were right on top of Loren. "Someone has started a fire!"

Footsteps passed and receded to silence up the hillside. Then another came running by, and another. At last all fell quiet, and Loren could hear nothing but her thundering pulse.

"It looks like a campfire," said one of the men. His voice was distant, and Loren had to strain to hear the words.

"But no one is around," said another.

"That only means they are wandering about in the darkness," said the first. "Run back to camp and alert one of the officers. The men must be roused."

Loren's hopes plummeted, until a third voice spoke above the others. "Hold that order," he said. "In summer, an ember may lurk unseen for days before sparking to life. This could have been set a week ago, or more."

"Or tonight," said the first man. "We should send word."

"And risk tomorrow's march? For an old campfire, long dead? I will not risk it, for if we rouse them and find nothing, the commander's wrath will fall upon us."

"Yet if we say nothing and are attacked . . ."

"By one wanderer, mayhap lost in the darkness? It could be no greater force, for who would be so foolish as to light a fire to announce their coming? No, at worst this is some moonslight traveler who fled as soon as they saw us coming up the hill towards them."

Loren needed hear no more. She peeked under the edge of her cowl. Three figures were silhouetted against the night sky. Rising to hands and knees, she crawled around the rock before standing. Bent double to make herself small, she dashed on ahead as her eyes scanned for any other enemy. But no sentries stood near, and so in silence and shadow she crept among the tents of the sellsword camp.

THIRTY-SIX

Like a wraith she moved, her steps soft as the wind. She took no great trouble to avoid footprints—the grass here had been trampled by many hundreds of feet, and one set of boot prints looked much like another, especially in moonslight.

Her way was made more difficult by the guards patrolling with torches. Jordel could pass for a mercenary, but Loren's fine cloak and lack of armor would give her away in an instant. If she failed to avoid being seen, she would be lost.

The camp had been thrown together haphazardly, with uneven rows and no clear lanes to move through. Sometimes this was a blessing—it made it easier to slink around in a different direction and hide herself from a wandering guard. But Loren soon found that it could work against her as well. As she picked her way between two tents, she heard a rustling and a grunting inside the one on her left. She paused, afraid she had been heard. As she stood frozen, a guard with a torch stepped out from around the tent a few paces away. Loren looked at her without thinking, and the light from the torch nearly blinded her. She turned and stumbled around the tent, but tripped on one of its stakes. Her knee struck a rock as she fell, and she gasped in pain.

"What was that?"

Loren heard the hiss of steel being drawn. Blinking hard to rid herself of the white spot in her eyes, she crawled away on all fours, hampered by her knee. But the guard was faster, bootsteps pounding as she came around the tent. In a moment she would spot Loren.

"Quiet out there!" cried a voice—it came from the same tent where Loren had first heard the noise. She heard the slapping of a tent flap in the night air. "What is that bumbling about?"

"Back to your bedroll," said the guard. "I thought I heard a noise."

"So did I—when you kicked my tent."

"I did not kick your tent, I—"

"Then why are you standing by its uprooted stake?"

Loren thanked the sky above as she melted into the darkness. The quarreling voices faded behind her.

It was not long until she reached the horses. In the camp's midst they stood, though not at its center. To their south were only a few lines of tents, which she could ride through in moments.

And that is precisely what Loren planned to do—find a horse and lead it out by the reins, hiding behind its bulk in her black cloak. If she was spotted, she would have to risk climbing on the horse's back and riding for her life. But as she surveyed the line of pickets, her hopes were dashed. For around the horses stood a thin ring of guards. Though she might slip inside their watchful circle, she could not escape it with a horse in tow. Moreover, these mounts had no saddles, so her little skill at riding would be even more useless.

"Who posts guards just for horses?" Loren muttered under her breath, forgetting silence for a moment in her frustration. Mayhap Jordel would have predicted the sellswords would do so, but he was not here, and if Xain had known, he made no mention. Come to think of it, Xain had not given her any advice at all, but had only seemed eager for her to be off. She ground her teeth at the wizard's selfishness. *Send me to fetch a horse for you without helping me plan the theft, eh?* she thought. *I will have words with that man when I return.*

But now she was alone in the midst of the enemy, without any more ideas. And dawn drew ever closer.

Think, Loren told herself. *What would Mennet do?*

But that was no help. Mennet could have placed a charm of sleep upon the guards and ridden out unopposed. Or he would have mounted a horse and cloaked it in shadow, and no one would have heard him as he rode silently through the tent lines. But Loren was not Mennet, and she had none of his magic. She had only a black cloak and a dagger.

A dagger. Her fingers sank into her cloak to caress its hilt. "You have often been my salvation in danger," she muttered. "If you have any power of your own, show me now what I must do, for I fear I am lost."

Mayhap it heard her, for an idea sprang to mind. A mad scheme, to be sure, and if she could have explained it to Annis or Xain they would have called her a fool. But they were not here, and Loren was.

The horses were bound to pickets with leather ties. There was no wooden fence to constrain them. If they could be made to panic, the chaos of their stampede would provide more than ample cover for Loren's escape—and it would deal a grievous blow to the mercenary army besides.

"I suppose if Xain can do his part to alleviate the siege of Wellmont, then Nightblade can do no less," she whispered. The madness of her plan made her giddy, and she smiled in the darkness.

First, though, she would have to get past the guards. Loren crept closer until only one tent remained between her and the horses. Just before her was a man, and his nearest companions were many paces off. Loren stooped and found a small rock at her feet. From behind the tent, out of view, she reached back and flung the stone into the midst of the horses, away to the right. She heard a sharp *thunk* and a frightened whinny. Like lightning she stole from her hiding place, and as the guard turned towards the sound, she ran behind his back and vanished among the horses.

She remembered something Bracken had told her once: *Sometimes simple tricks are best.* But now she would have to be careful if she hoped to stay alive.

Unlike the sellswords' tents, the horses had been lined up neatly, and the rows were so close that even if a horse pulled free of its tether, it could not escape the press of the other mounts. Loren would have to work from the inside out.

She pressed between the beasts' heavy, sweating flanks until she was near their center, and knelt to untie a tether. But it had been worked with a well-made knot, and her fingers fumbled in the darkness.

"Very well," said Loren. She drew her dagger and slashed at the leather. The fine blade split it, and the tether fell away. The horse nickered but could hardly move, so close were the other mounts.

She did the same with the horses on either side, and then with all the ones in front and behind. In a circle she went, spiraling outward until the freed mounts outnumbered those who were still bound. Some whinnied, and a few champed at her, but they were disciplined beasts and did not try hard to move. Not yet, at any rate.

Soon she was only a few ranks from the edge of the pickets. Then she stopped and surveyed the steeds. One caught her eye: a slender but shapely beast of midnight black, the same as her cloak. The only break in its color was a star of white on its forehead, which practically shone in the moonslight.

She stepped between it and the horse beside it, a larger specimen of chestnut brown. Their tethers, each almost as long as Loren was tall, hung from their bridles. Loren tied their ends together, hoping the leather would not make the beasts collide with each other when they ran.

The black horse pressed its nose at her, and she took its muzzle into her hands. It did not bite, and she took that as a good sign. When she reached up and scratched its ears, it pressed its nose into her chest.

"If we escape from this, and I do not lose you in the flight, I will give you a name," she whispered. "But I will not risk our luck by doing so now. The world itself has ears, and it hates the prideful."

The horse nickered and stooped to pull free a mouthful of grass.

Now came the most dangerous part of the whole affair, and Loren hesitated. But she had come too far now not to go on. So again she drew her dagger, and went to the horse beside the black one she had chosen, on the other side from the chestnut.

"I am sorry," she whispered. "But it will only be a small cut."

With that she slashed the blade across the horse's flank, and in the same moment she gave a great cry. Then she whirled and seized her black horse's neck and jumped, swinging around and clinging to its back for dear life.

The horse she had cut reared in terror and gave a great whinny of fright. The moment it came down it set off into a gallop, careening into the horses around it.

The effect was immediate and tumultuous. As a panicked mass, the horses went berserk. They screamed and fought to get away from each other, bolting in every direction. Few could fall over, so the mass merely undulated in fear. But the commotion spread swiftly to the edges, and when the scent of panic reached the horses at the outside, they reared and bucked and tore at their tethers. All up and down the rows Loren saw them break free, and they galloped off into the night, many of them right into the tents.

The camp erupted in chaos. Soldiers emerged wide-eyed from their tents and dove out of the way as horses ran through the lines. Many horses ran south into the open land beyond, but some galloped into the heart of the mercenary camp. There a great cry and tumult broke out, and guards with torches fled for their lives.

But Loren's steed leapt for the south, followed by the great chestnut horse. Together they ran, keeping pace with each other as if they had been trained in a harness together, while Loren gripped her horse's neck and asked the sky above to spare her life.

They burst free as part of the stampede and ran off into the night. Horses fell away on either side, running west and east, but Loren's kept south. Into the night she vanished, leaving the mercenary camp far behind.

THIRTY-SEVEN

THE SKY HAD GROWN GREY IN THE EAST. THEY CRESTED the southern hills and came swiftly down the other side. Only then did Loren raise her head and try to regain control of her galloping mount. She reached out and seized the tether holding the horses together. But their bucking heads tore it from her grasp and nearly pitched her from the back.

She reached instead for the black horse's bridle and pulled on it. That produced some effect—the horse's head reared back, and it began to slow. Soon, the chestnut felt the tug on its tether and dropped its pace. Eventually they both came to a stop, chests heaving with deep and ragged breaths. Their flanks were lathered.

"Well done," Loren whispered, and reached up to scratch the black horse's ears. Over the hills she could still hear the screams of horses and the panicked shouting of soldiers. She hoped no one had been seriously hurt in their flight; she had not thought so many horses would charge into the mercenaries' camp.

But she had lost track of her whereabouts, and as she looked around now she saw that she was far to the west of where she had left Annis and Xain. She slid down from her horse's back, and with a slash of her dagger she parted the tethers that held the animals together. Then she climbed back up, holding onto the black horse's tether as a rein with one hand while tugging on the chestnut's so that it would follow. It was awkward, and she was unused to sitting a horse with no saddle, but somehow she got them both headed east. Their tread was slow, and Loren grew ever more nervous as sunrise drew nearer.

The sky had grown pink by the time she spotted the dell tucked between two hills. She nudged her heels into the horse's sides and rode in between the trees to the hollow space in the rocks.

At first it seemed empty, and Loren's stomach tumbled in her gut. Then she spotted a small shape in the dim light and recognized the back of Annis' new cloak. For a heart-stopping moment she feared the worst, until she saw the girl wriggling at her approach. Loren heard a few muffled grunts as she fought to roll over.

"Annis!" Loren jumped from her horse and ran to the girl's side, forgetting in her haste to hobble the steeds. She seized Annis' shoulder and rolled the girl over. Her wrists were bound, and she was gagged with cloth torn from her cloak.

Loren ripped the gag free and slashed the bonds. Annis gasped and spit in the early morning air. "Where is he?"

"You mean Xain?" said Loren. "I do not know. Who took him? What did they do to you?"

Fury lit in Annis' eye. "No one took him, Loren. He did this. The wizard trussed me up and fled almost the moment you had gone."

Loren felt as though the ground had dropped out from below her. "What? No. Why would he . . ."

Annis parted her cloak, and Loren saw her inside pocket. It lay empty. "He took the magestones. Not only his share, but all of them. That conniving, double-faced, forked-tongued . . ."

She fell silent, too angry for words. Loren sank back on her heels and sat hard on the ground. She felt lost and alone, and incredibly cold despite the summer morning. Those stones were all they had. Without them, so many dreams vanished. No longer could she give Annis and Gem a good life in the outland kingdoms. A thief she might be, but Loren did not wish to scrape a meager living robbing pennies from tradesmen. Those magestones could have let her become something more, something great.

Anger and sorrow washed through her, and then they were gone. In their place Loren felt something else—an icy burning, a raging fire that yet left her cold. Her pulse thundered, but this time not with fear.

"He cannot do this again," she said, almost to herself. "To leave me alone and unaided upon the King's road is one thing. But I will not let him steal my fortune."

"There are few words for men such as he," agreed Annis. "But at least he has left. I had hopes for those stones as well, but mayhap we are well quit of them if it means that Xain, too, is gone."

"No!" cried Loren. "I said he *cannot* do this. Those stones were not his to take. They are mine, and I will have them back."

Annis' brow furrowed. "What do you mean to do about it? He is gone and the stones with him. He is a wizard. Even if he were here, you could not hope to steal his prize."

"Indeed, he is a wizard," said Loren. "And a fool, and a poor wrestler, and a hopeless woodsman, as quiet and quick as a blind cow. He has his talents, but he is a madman if he thinks he can evade me."

Annis paled. "You cannot mean to pursue him."

"I do mean to."

"Loren, he will *kill* us! Let us return to Wellmont and flee its doom with Jordel. At least then we will be free from danger, if poorer."

"You said the same when Auntie took my dagger in Cabrus," said Loren. "My answer now is the same as it was then."

"This is not the same! Xain is mad, and far more powerful than she. He has already proven himself willing to hurt us. I do not think it will take much more for him to kill us."

"We shall see," said Loren. "Come."

"I will not!" said Annis, shooting to her feet. She stamped her foot on the ground and glared. "You will not drag me into death by the wizard's fire. Too long have I walked by his side. He is gone, and I will not seek him again."

Loren looked at her a long moment. Then she nodded. "Very well. You are right. I cannot ask this of you."

Annis looked taken aback. "What? What do you mean?"

"Just that. You have gone farther than I could expect from any friend, and with no more assurance than your faith in me. I will not ask you to take another step when I know I walk into great danger. See yourself safely to Wellmont. Take the chestnut horse."

Loren turned to her own steed. But Annis scuttled behind, lifting her skirts to keep them out of the dewy grass.

"You will go alone? That is twice as foolish. How do you even mean to find him?"

"I told you he is a poor woodsman," said Loren. "Even now I can see where his tracks lead out of the dell. I will follow them, and if I must go slowly to see his marks, still I will be mounted and he will not."

Loren grabbed a handful of mane and pulled herself onto her horse. It sidestepped, nearly unseating her, but then it calmed.

"And what do you mean to do once you find him?"

"I will make him give me the stones," said Loren. "By whatever means I can. If words will not work, I will wrestle him and twist his arm until he squeals like the pig he has shown himself to be."

"He is a *wizard!* He will set you ablaze!"

"I do not believe that. Even with all he has done. He might have killed you, rather than leave you here bound but breathing. Then you could not have told me where he was headed. But he let you live. He is not a murderer, only a stupid, stupid man." Loren pressed her heels to the mount, and it began a slow walk forwards. With a gentle tug on the tether, she guided it towards the bent grass that led off due east along the line of hills.

"Wait!" said Annis. She scrambled for the chestnut horse, which had wandered out of the dell and was now many paces away. "Wait for me!" She scrambled onto the beast's back—an impressive feat, for it stood at least a hand taller than Loren's—and kicked it forwards.

"You spoke well before," said Loren. "You should stay. This is my choice, and no one should have to share it."

"Oh, still your flapping lips," snapped Annis. "Of course I will not let you ride off into danger on your own, you sow's ear of an idiot. I did not do so when we fled my mother's caravan."

"You did not. But this is not then."

"Yet I am the same person," said Annis. "And if this is the single stupidest thing I have ever seen you do, which is an impressive claim considering our time together, still I will not let you enter such madness without someone sensible to advise you. If nothing else, I will tell you when it is time to run away."

Loren gave her a grim smile. "And I thank you for such a valuable service. But you have never seen me fight Xain. You may find him more eager to flee my company than the other way around."

Annis looked at Loren askance. "You have fought him before?"

"More often than you might believe, and every time I bested him," said Loren. "His magic might be like a bear's trap, but the body behind it is like a rusted hinge."

Annis pursed her lips and turned her eyes forwards. "I hope you are right."

In truth, Loren hoped the same. She had taught Xain a lesson or two in their time together. But the man they pursued was unlike the wizard she had met in the Birchwood. Never would she have imagined that he could betray her like this, nor harm Annis as he had.

She had one hope to cling to: that he was no murderer. But even as the thought came to her, she remembered his form crowned in light atop Wellmont's south wall. He had rained fire and lightning down upon the other side, and though she did not see the result, a tiny voice in her mind nagged at her.

What do you think he was doing? Do you not think his flame and his thunder took many lives?

That was in war, she argued with herself. *It is different. And he threw much fire at Vivien upon the Dragon's Tail, yet he did not kill her.*

He almost did. He only stopped after you argued with him.

Then I will argue with him now, until his ears catch in his own flame, thought Loren. *And that is the end of it.*

And so it seemed to be, for the voice in her mind went silent.

Xain had apparently moved in haste, for his tracks were deep and easy to spot. Loren was able to go much faster than she had hoped, and she found that her horse shifted easily beneath her despite the speed at which she drove it. The slightest tug on her tether moved the beast left or right, and she could mostly keep her eyes to the ground.

"That is a fine beast," said Annis, after some time had passed in silence. "You chose her?"

"I did. I think I shall keep her."

"She must have belonged to an officer, or someone wealthy, for she moves easily under your touch. What will you call her?"

Loren remembered her promise to the horse in the mercenaries' camp. *We are not out of danger yet.*

"I have not decided."

Once the tracks had gone east for a while, they rose up the side of the hills. Following them, Loren found they were well east of the sellswords, who were scarcely a blur in the distance. Xain's tracks went down the other side of the hills and due north, aiming for the Greatrocks that poked just above the horizon. Now on more open ground, they could move more quickly, with Loren stopping only occasionally to mark Xain's tracks. The wizard moved in a straight line, making no visible effort to mask his trail, which only made her work easier.

They came upon another line of hills, and these were wooded, forcing them to slow once more. But the sun had risen, and the ground here was softer, so Xain's movements stood out like burning flames in the greenery. At the hills they turned east and continued that way a long while.

"What course is he taking?" said Annis. "He seems aimless."

"He is not," said Loren. "Though he does not walk on the road, he is following its course. That road will go east and follow the river. After he goes that way a while he will turn north, and take the King's road until he comes again to the High King's Seat."

"And then?" said Annis.

Loren shuddered beneath her cloak as she thought of Xain arriving at the Seat for his son, his eyes glowing black from the magestones' power. "That is none of our concern. What Xain does with his share of the stones is his business. Our portion is all I care about."

The hills opened into wide plains, and they found themselves nearly on top of Xain. There he walked, a small figure in a blue coat scarcely two spans away. There were no hills in which to hide, neither rocks nor trees. He had not turned to see them, but surely he would once their hoofbeats sounded behind him.

"We are exposed," said Annis, her voice quivering. "Loren, it would be foolish to approach him like this."

My only hope is my belief in him, thought Loren. "He will not harm us. Come. Let us go and have a chat with this wizard."

She spurred her horse, and when it broke into a gallop it nearly threw her from its back. Annis rode easily, of course, and together they descended upon Xain in a thunder of hooves.

Loren's pulse quickened when he turned to face them, but he made no move to attack. Instead, she thought she saw him smile as the two of them drew near. He stood stock still, hands at his sides, and she saw no glow in his eyes.

They reined to a stop ten paces away. Loren studied the wizard in silence while thinking of what to say. But Xain spoke before she could, his voice pleasant and light on the morning air.

"Well met again, though I did not expect the pleasure. Truly, when I ask you to fetch me a horse, you are most diligent about it. I will take the chestnut, for I think the black one suits you."

"You shall have neither," said Loren. "You have betrayed me again, and for that I will not forgive you. But I will allow you to leave, if you only return our share of the magestones."

"And why should I? You cannot take them from me, and I can make better use of them than you can."

"They are *mine.* Ours," she amended, glancing at Annis. "You mean to leave us bereft and penniless. I will not let you."

"Let?" snarled Xain, eyes glittering. "Since when have you *let* me do anything, daughter of the family Nelda? You have been a burden upon my back since first we met, despite all my attempts to shake you. I would regret ever helping you escape your father, if it were not for the stones I hold in my pocket. And so I will not part from them. I will take them as payment for your caretaking."

"If you think to anger me with your insults, you may save your breath," said Loren. "With your share you can vanquish your foes and make a good life for you and your child besides. Why persist in this folly? Why not treat us fairly, so that we may part as friends the way you promised?"

"Because promises to little girls mean nothing."

Despite what she had said, Loren's blood had begun to boil. Now her anger reached the bursting point. She flung her tether to Annis and leapt from her mount, marching towards Xain with her fists clenched. She did not know what she meant to do—to strike him in the face, mayhap, or throw him to the ground and drag the magestones from his pocket by force. Jordel's words on the docks returned to her mind: gag a firemage, and he was powerless.

But Xain forced her to a stop with a flick of his wrists. Darkfire leapt into his palms, and his eyes glowed black. It was an even more terrifying sight in the light of day, and terror stilled her limbs.

"Stay your hand, wretch," said Xain, his voice thrumming again with power. "You cannot imagine the terrible things darkfire will do to flesh. But I will show you, if you are so eager to find death in my flames."

"Give me my stones, Xain," said Loren. "I will not ask you again."

"Turn around and scuttle off," said Xain. "I will not tell you again."

"Loren!" cried Annis.

Loren would not take her eyes from Xain's. Over her shoulder she said, "Be still, Annis. Or turn and leave if you must—I will not blame you."

"Oh, do not be an idiot," snapped Annis. "Look! Riders!"

Xain's fires guttered out. His eyes returned to normal as he looked past Loren in confusion.

Loren turned to follow his gaze and saw that Annis was right. Across the plain rode seven figures on horseback, thundering towards them all. And Loren felt equal parts fear and relief as she recognized the red cloaks that each of them wore, and Jordel and Vivien in the lead.

THIRTY-EIGHT

Loren drew up, and her hand dropped to her dagger. Xain muttered a curse.

"How did they find us?" said Annis.

"It must have been Jordel," said Loren. "He has some skill with tracking, and if he found our boat on the shore it would have been no great feat to follow us from there. Especially since we wasted so much time at the mercenary camp."

"And here I thought I had made a clean escape," said Xain.

"Do you jest?" said Loren. "You wander about like a drunken bear cub. I could have followed you blindfolded."

As the Mystics drew nearer, Loren saw Gem riding behind Jordel. The riders slowed as they came near. Gem slid from the saddle and ran straight for Annis to catch her in a hug. She held him for a moment, and then turned to look warily at Jordel above them.

The Mystics fanned out into a line, with Jordel and Vivien at their center. Jordel's eyes went back and forth from Loren to Xain, but Vivien looked only at the wizard. Her glare was icy, the muscles in her jaw spasming. The other five Mystics remained silent and still, faces grim. Each had a hand on their sword hilt. Loren wondered if any were wizards, or if they were mage hunters as Jordel had once been.

"I grow weary of chasing you across the nine lands, Xain," said Jordel.

"As I grow weary of running," said Xain. "It seems we would both be better served if you ceased your pursuit. Turn around and ride back to Wellmont—and you ought to go with him, Loren. I mean to leave this place and all of you behind. Nothing will sway my mind."

Jordel sighed. Loren thought she saw sadness in his eyes. "Alas, I cannot allow you to do that."

"What is this talk of allowing?" said Xain, growing angry. "You and the girl both seem to have grand ideas of what I may or may not do at your command. How exactly do you mean to stop me?"

"I would rather not have to," said Jordel. "But we will if we must. If you do not choose to aid me, you will be executed as a rogue wizard. You have attacked Vivien twice now, which is cause enough for your punishment. Mayhap you will escape us today, mayhap not—but if you refuse to join me, you will find no safety in any land where the Mystics hold sway."

"Please, though, refuse him," said Vivien. "I would happily see you destroyed."

"You would have done the same in Wellmont," said Xain. "Yet it did not work then. No matter how often I teach you the lesson, you forget that you are as powerless as a child against me. If I must dole out your punishment again, so be it."

"But you will see I am not alone," said Vivien with a smirk. "And I will happily command my companions to kill you. They have no fondness for wizards."

Jordel turned an angry look on Vivien. "You are too eager for a fight, and it ill becomes you. Keep your tongue still if you cannot keep it civil." Turning back to Xain, he spoke calmly once more. "Xain, I offer you this last chance. Honor your agreement with me. You saw the wisdom in my words when we spoke in Wellmont, and I know in my heart that your promise was no deception. If you have reconsidered since, then consider again. I know you see the purpose of joining me."

"Doubtless you think my mind will change when swayed by your threats," said Xain. "But I see no wisdom in pledging myself to a doomed cause. Mayhap you will succeed, but I think it is more likely that you and all who fight beside you will be consumed. I will not choose that fate—not while another depends on me. All I wish for is my life back, and my son. Will you deny that that is a just desire?"

"I will not," said Jordel. "Nor will I deny its fulfillment. My offer still stands, in full. Your son will be restored to you, and all your crimes against the King's law pardoned. No one else will give you better terms."

Xain did not answer for a moment. His brow furrowed; the corners of his mouth turned down in a scowl. But his eyes appeared thoughtful.

Say yes, thought Loren. *Accept Jordel's terms, and let us put this matter behind us.*

Jordel seemed to sense Xain's hesitation, for he leaned forwards earnestly. "Take the course of wisdom. You know the calamity that threatens us all. Mayhap you and your son can escape, but I do not think so. Where will you flee when darkness descends upon all the nine lands? Will you live your life in fear and flight, or will you do your part to keep that terror from others?"

The air hung silent. The hairs on Loren's arm and neck tingled as she awaited the wizard's response.

Before Xain could speak, one of the Mystics cried, "Riders!"

The air rang with drawn steel, and as one the Mystics turned their horses. All but Jordel, who kept his eyes on Xain. Loren turned to the western hills where Jordel and Vivien had emerged but a moment before.

A company of horsemen with lances and armor was riding hard and fast towards them.

THIRTY-NINE

"To arms!" cried Vivien.

"I count at least two score of them, mayhap three," reported one of the Mystics. They had formed a line, bravely facing the oncoming riders. But each of them wore only a short chainmail shirt under their red cloak. The approaching riders were bedecked in plate and mail, and their lances were long and sharp, glittering in the early sunlight.

Jordel grew exasperated as Xain still refused to answer, so he wheeled his horse around to survey the riders. "What are they doing here so far ahead of the main host? It is as though they search for something."

Annis gave Loren a pointed look, and Loren cleared her throat. "I am afraid they may be hunting me. I . . . well, you must understand our circumstances . . ."

"I have nearly run out of patience for your foolishness," said Jordel in a voice of steel. "Tell me what happened, and quickly."

"The mercenaries have suffered a catastrophe," said Loren, raising her chin in defiance. "Their horses stampeded through their camp, for their tethers were cut and they were driven to madness. I had a hand in it."

"Of course you did," said Jordel. He raised his exasperated gaze to the sky and muttered a prayer she could not hear.

"I would have had no problems if you were not here," said Loren angrily. "I could have hidden from them easily, but the seven of you in your red cloaks stick out on the landscape like roses."

"Be silent," said Vivien. The sellswords had broken into a gallop now, their horses leaping across the empty plain. "This is not the time for your prattling, for it will not stay their hands."

"I do not understand," said Jordel quietly. "Our scouts told us the mercenaries approached from the east, by the road that runs along the Dragon's Tail. Loren and I saw them ourselves. They should not be this far west."

Loren shrugged. "I saw them. They were encamped to the west, and their host has grown by many hundreds since last you and I saw them."

Jordel shot her a look. "Many hundreds? No, that is not possible. They . . ." He looked to Xain. "And where are you going, wizard?"

Loren turned to see Xain backing away slowly. At Jordel's words he stopped, glaring. "Your company seems an unhealthy place to be, at present. I would take my leave."

"We did not grant you leave," said Vivien. "There are many horsemen, and without your help they might overrun us. Then they will come after you, and you will have less help than if you lend your strength now. Even a wizard so great as you might struggle with such numbers on the open field."

Xain scowled at her. "Mind your own affairs, witch." But he came forwards, glowering. He shot Loren a dark look from beneath his brows. "This is your fault, girl."

"None of us would be in this mess if you did not try to scamper off in the darkness every chance you got," she said. "Stand for once, and act with honor."

"Says the would-be thief," muttered Gem. Loren cuffed him on the back of his head.

"I will help drive them off," said Xain. "But not at the side of Mystics. I will strike from atop that hill."

Loren caught a curious expression on his face, and she thought she understood. Thus far, the Mystics had not seen his eyes glow black from the magestones. Xain meant to separate himself from them so that that detail might remain unseen.

"Your choice is your own, but I think you go to too much trouble." Vivien swung a leg over her saddle and dropped lightly to the ground. "Three score could not trouble the both of us together."

Xain ran to the hilltop. The mercenaries were almost upon them by the time he climbed it. But once the wizards struck, the skirmish became a one-sided battle. Vivien attacked first; her fingers clutched the air as she pulled at nothing. Riders jerked from their saddles. But they did not fall backwards. Instead, Vivien pulled them forwards so they tumbled over their horses' necks. They fell to the ground and were trampled, broken and twisted bodies mashed to pulp beneath the hooves of their fellow riders' mounts. It made Loren's stomach lurch, and Gem turned his face away. Again Vivien swiped at the air, and many of the horses' legs snapped like twigs. They went down, crushing their riders and downing the horses behind as well. The air rang with the screams of beasts and soldiers.

Loren gritted her teeth at the senseless death, but it hardly felt like the right time to reprimand Vivien. She did not know what the Mystics intended to do with her.

Then Xain joined the fight. A wall of flame thirty paces long sprang up on the grassy field. It was dozens of paces ahead of the cavalry, and they had plenty of time to rein their mounts to a stop. Many of the horses bolted in fear at the heat of the flames, their riders cursing and shouting as they tried to regain control. Hardly a dozen riders still remained, trying to urge their horses through the roaring flames. But Xain waved his hand and cried aloud, and bolts of lightning struck the ground on all sides of the riders. Their last shreds of discipline vanished, and the horses screamed in terror as they bolted away. Xain let the flames die out, and the field was empty—save for the broken bodies Vivien had cast down.

Vivien growled in anger and struck again and again, pulling a few more fleeing horsemen from their saddles. But many escaped, disappearing into the hills and out of sight.

"You fool!" she cried to Xain as he came back down the hill. "Why did you let them escape? Now they will warn the host to our presence."

"Let us say I have a sympathetic heart for a runaway," said Xain.

"It matters little," said Jordel. "For we shall not be here when the Dorsean sellswords return. For the moment, Xain, we all must flee—and whether we end up in Feldemar as I wish, or the High King's Seat as you aim, east is our best choice at present. Will you at least ride with us until this danger has passed?"

Xain looked as if he might refuse, but Loren glared at him and stepped forwards. "You will, wizard, for you and I have not finished our words. And if you think I will give you a horse without your promise to come with us, you are sorely mistaken."

"Very well then, since you leave me little choice," said Xain. "Your company is harder to part with than an infestation of lice. Lead on, Mystic—for now."

Everyone mounted, Annis in front of Loren atop her black horse, and Xain on the chestnut steed. At Jordel's command, the Mystics spurred their horses, and off they rode together.

FORTY

Jordel led them south, where soon they found the empty road, and then east along it, pushing the horses as hard as they dared. Loren knew it could not be long before the outriders returned to alert the host, and then the sellswords would no doubt send their full mounted strength. How many horsemen remained after her nighttime adventure? Had the mercenaries managed to collect most of the steeds, or did they still roam free across the plains? She hoped most were lost, but something told her they would not be so lucky. If even half the horses had been recovered, they might well find hundreds of riders at their backs.

It was not long before the road turned abruptly right, heading south for Wellmont. At first Loren thought Jordel would direct them towards the city, there to hide behind the safety of its walls. Instead he reined to a stop at the crossroad, and they halted in a circle around him.

"The mercenaries will think we are scouts sent from Wellmont," said Jordel. "Or at least that is my hope. If I am right, when they come to the crossroads they will turn south to look for us, hoping to catch us before we reach the city. But we will ride east, and if we are lucky they will not follow."

Vivien kicked her horse forwards until it was next to his. "But then the army will sweep down upon the city," she said, glaring. "They will have no warning."

"They will have their walls, and that is all we can do," said Jordel in a tone that brooked no argument. "You will learn once and for all where your loyalties lie. We ride on."

"At least send one of the men to the city to give word. Send me, if you wish."

"I will not spare one warrior, you least of all," said Jordel. "Every hand will be needed ere long, and none of this would be necessary if not for your actions in Wellmont. Or do you deny that?"

Vivien's eyes met his for a long moment, and Loren saw the anger burning within her. But she dropped her gaze and nodded. "As you see fit, Captain," she said in an icy voice.

And so they rode on, dust flying from the strike of their horses' hooves on the road. Now Jordel let them take a more measured pace, for if he was right, the mercenaries would not pursue them. And if he was wrong, they might need their mounts ready for a sudden burst of speed.

Loren kept a wary eye on Xain, and often she saw him survey their surroundings. It seemed clear he planned to escape, and she regretted having brought a horse. But Jordel rode close on one side and Vivien on the other, so that he had precious little chance to dart off. The other Mystics stayed behind, their eyes watchful and their hands never far from their blades. For the time being, at least, Xain would remain with their party.

After they had left the crossroads far behind, the land rose up into sharp hills that walled the road on either side. Jordel called them to a halt and commanded his warriors to dismount. Xain followed suit. Annis began to slide from the horse's back, but Loren held her in place.

"Why do we stop?" asked Loren. "I would feel easier if there was yet more distance between us and the city."

"As might I, but halting now or in an hour will make little difference," said Jordel. "And we are all of us weary, for we stayed awake through the night.

Looking for you, as it happens. A mouthful of food will do us well for a long day's journey."

Loren felt a stab of hunger at his words, and her stomach growled as if to remind her that it was empty. So she leapt from her horse's back, patted its neck, and made a crude hobble for its legs with the end of the tether. Jordel sat by the roadside, separate from his men, while Xain sat even farther away. But Vivien's eyes were watchful upon him, and he did not try to flee. Gem and Annis sat by themselves, trading words in whispers while Annis gave Xain many dark looks. Loren went and sat across from Jordel.

"I guessed Xain had not had time to gather supplies before his flight, and you carried nothing when you went with him," said Jordel. "So I had my men fetch your sack before we rode out."

He motioned, and one of the Mystics came over with Loren's bedroll and pack. She pulled out some bread and bit down hungrily. Her stomach growled again, but this time in gratitude.

"Where did the three of you mean to go?" said Jordel. "I thought you had no wish to follow Xain to the High King's Seat."

"I do not," said Loren, speaking quietly and throwing a dark look at Xain. "The wizard proved less than faithful. He called himself my friend and asked me to steal him a horse from the mercenary camp. Once I had gone, he trussed Annis up like a chicken and struck out on his own."

Jordel frowned. "You have suffered much at his hands, and little of it has been your fault. But mayhap now you will be more cautious when dealing with wizards, and will place a bit more faith in me. But one thing is curious: why the deception? Why did he send you off alone, rather than simply leave?"

Loren's stomach turned, but she kept her face calm. Jordel was perceptive. Xain had wanted Annis alone so he could steal the magestones, but Loren knew it would be madness to confess that now—especially since Xain still had the magestones in his care. "Before he tangles with me again, the wizard will think at least twice. Every time he has given me cause to spar with him, I have sent him to the dirt. I think he wanted to make his escape with ease."

"Fighting with wizards at such a young age," said Jordel. "If you were of a different mind and temperament, mayhap you would have made a mage hunter."

Loren let herself blush. "I thank you, but I am afraid the color red suits me ill."

Jordel did not smile, but his eyes danced. Mayhap he was not as angry with her as he made out. But just then, Vivien shot to her feet. "Captain! We are found!"

Everyone rose and stared into the west. Loren saw a cloud of dust rising over the road, and the glint of sunlight on metal in the midst of it.

"Riders," said Jordel. "And far more than before."

"Curse them!" said Vivien. "How do they keep finding us?"

"Mayhap they guessed at our deception," said Jordel, but his eyes were troubled. "I do not see how they could have known. Unless . . ." He turned his gaze upwards. Loren did the same, seeing nothing but the clear blue sky.

"There!" cried Vivien. "I see it. A hawk, wheeling far above." Loren squinted and saw it—a tiny black dot, turning circles in the air.

"A weremage," said Jordel. "Likely he has watched our ride. Mayhap he even followed the three of you when you fled the camp. Eron, can you shoot it?"

One of the Mystics shook his head. "Not without a longbow." He had a bow upon his back, but Loren could see that it was far too short for such a shot.

"I cannot reach so high with my magic," said Vivien. "I can scarcely even see the thing."

"We must remove him somehow," said Jordel, "or else all hope of escape is lost. Mayhap we—"

A crackle of lightning struck in the clear sky, and a burst of feathers erupted from the hawk. It jerked and fell, plummeting towards them.

All eyes turned to Xain, but the glow had already faded from the wizard's eyes by the time they looked. He shrugged and gave them a dour grimace. "Consider him removed. Though the bolt will not kill him."

"The fall will do the job just as well," said Vivien with a cruel smile.

Loren turned her eyes skyward again and saw the hawk begin to change. It grew and grew in size, feathers sinking into its skin. Its wings grew thicker and turned into arms and fingers. The change took only a moment, and then a full-grown man fell stark naked towards the ground.

"Catch him!" Loren turned to Xain. "Please!"

His eyes met hers, and she saw he was unmoved. Slowly he shook his head. If he used air to cushion the man's fall, his eyes would turn black and he would be discovered. But no man could survive such a fall.

Jordel's voice rang out clear and strong. "Do it, Vivien. Mages are few and precious enough, and no one should wish for the death of one—least of all you."

Vivien's smile slowly faded, to be replaced with only a slight twist of the lips. Her eyes glowed, and she raised a hand. The man's descent slowed, and soon he was gently floating just above the ground. Then Vivien closed her fist, and the glow died in her eyes. The weremage fell the last few paces to land with a thud.

"Our *enemy's* life has been preserved, Captain." It was impossible to miss the bitterness in her words.

"Well done," said Jordel. "Though he was the enemy of Wellmont, not of the Mystics. Now come. Let us ride, for those horsemen will not tarry."

Indeed the cavalry had closed much of the distance already, for they had spotted the party and spurred their horses to a gallop. Still, the road was open for a long way in both directions, and they were leagues distant. The party mounted in haste and spurred their horses forwards, hampered by Xain and Loren, who were without saddles and could not move as quickly.

Loren's legs began to burn almost the moment she climbed atop her horse behind Annis. They had grown sore with riding all morning, and the brief rest had only let the pain come to the fore. Now it redoubled as they galloped. She gritted her teeth, determined to bear it as long as she had to. Annis, meanwhile, seemed entirely comfortable despite their lack of a saddle, and acted as a rock for Loren to hold.

"You ride as if born to it," said Loren. "I feel as though this horse will shake the bones from my body."

"You clutch it too tightly with your legs," Annis told her. "You must find a balance—do not hold so loose that you are shaken off, or so tightly that your body becomes taut as a bowstring."

Loren tried loosening her legs, but she almost slid backwards off the horse's rump. She held on even tighter. "I think I will have to bear it for now, else we will part company much sooner than I would wish."

After a while the land rose up and away from the river. The hills stretched higher on either side of them, and the road through them seemed to have been cut as if by a great giant with a cleaver. When they reached the top of the rise, Jordel called another halt. From their vantage point he turned, assessing the riders who chased them.

"There are more than I feared, and more than we can hope to defeat—even with our wizards. I do not understand. There are at least six hundreds of them, and mayhap more than a thousand. They could not have gained so many riders in their trek through Selvan—not even if they recruited a new company at every city along the way."

"Yet it seems they have," said Vivien. "And we have gained no ground in our flight. I think we may have lost some."

"Our only hope is to increase our speed," said Jordel. "This shelf goes on for half a league before dropping down steeply on the other side. They will have to slow their descent, and then we may make up some time."

"Why do we not strike north?" said Xain. "The wilderness might hide us, at least until they pass."

"Then they will only be ahead of us when we continue," said Jordel. "And these wildlands are unkind. You can see how steep the hills are on either side. They become no gentler farther north. After that we might find ourselves sunk in a bog or attacked by wolves, which are plentiful here. And we cannot manage a journey in the wilds across the whole of Selvan, for we have neither the supplies nor the time to waste. It would stretch our journey from weeks to months. No, our only hope now is to make speed, and to lose them after the rise."

Xain nodded, but his eyes were shifty. Loren wondered what he was plotting. She would have to keep a careful eye upon him. Until she regained her magestones, she could not let him out of her sight.

Jordel ordered them forwards, and the ground vanished beneath their horses' hooves. Loren marveled at the strength of her mount—though she carried two riders, still she kept pace with every other horse in the party. And while Loren did not enjoy riding bareback, still she felt less jostled than Xain appeared to be, bouncing clumsily on the back of his chestnut. She took an arm from around Annis' waist and reached down to pat the mare's neck.

"There is the descent!" said Jordel, shouting to be heard over the thundering hooves. "Make ready for the slope!"

The land fell away steeply before them. They reached the edge, and Loren saw what lay ahead. Her heart fell, and Annis gave a little gasp. Though Jordel issued no command, the party stopped as one, looking out over the lowlands.

The road reached level ground and then straightened again, running many leagues to the horizon far away. And upon it was an army—hundreds of horses and hundreds of men, neatly lined in rank and file, marching inexorably towards them.

FORTY-ONE

"At last I understand," said Jordel quietly, and Loren looked to him. "I knew the sellsword army could not have marched west of the city so quickly, nor grown so great in size in so short a time. That was a second force. This, the army before us, is the one Loren and I saw upon the King's road."

"A second force?" said Loren. "How? Whence did they come?"

"From Dorsea," said Jordel. "The Dorsean commander is clever. He recruited a small army of sellswords in Selvan and marched them across the kingdom, knowing they might be spotted. But they seemed a small threat, and so Wellmont would prepare itself for a mild feint from the north. But in secret, Dorsea mustered a much larger army and marched them across the Dragon's Tail at the feet of the Greatrocks. We thought the sellswords were still more than a day's march out, but the larger army can attack today, when the city will not expect it."

"Wellmont," breathed Vivien. "The city will fall." Loren could see the pain in her eyes.

"Mayhap not," said Jordel. "For it seems that a great thief single-handedly struck a mighty blow against the mercenaries' strength of horse."

"That strength rides behind us now," snarled Vivien. "And if that host is crippled, I should fear to see them at their full strength."

"My jest was ill-made," said Jordel. "But now we must think of escape."

"How?" Loren hated her voice for trembling. "They are both behind and ahead of us."

"Let us try the wildlands," said Gem. "If they are ungentle, at least they are better than being caught between hammer and anvil."

"I would not risk it unless at utmost need," muttered Jordel. "And yet it seems such need is upon us."

Looking behind them towards the pounding hooves, they saw the cavalry come into view from far down the road. As the riders caught sight of the party, they sent up a great cry and spurred their horses to even greater speed.

"Now they have seen us," cried Annis. "They will follow us over the hills and catch us!"

Xain smirked and nudged his horse to the front of the party. There he dismounted, facing the coming horsemen on foot. "Here is your only course. Climb the hills and make for the wildlands, returning to the road only when you know it is safe. I will remain here to deal with these riders."

"No, Xain," said Jordel. "You have my respect, and I do not doubt your powers, but they are too much even for you. Especially alone. If we fight, it will be together."

"I do not need your aid," said Xain. "You may trust me in this, for you have not seen the extent of my power."

"You make idle boasts," said Vivien. "I do not think you could stop a hundred riders on your own, and ten times that number now pursue us."

Gem scrambled down from Jordel's horse and ran for Loren's. "Argue if you must, until the enemy is upon us and you are all fallen. But I will not wait. Ride now, Loren! Make for the north while we still can!"

Loren seized his hand and pulled him up behind her, but she could not bring herself to spur the horse. Annis looked to her for guidance, but she did not know what to do. Only one thought occupied her mind: she could not leave without the magestones.

"Come, Xain," said Jordel. "We must try to escape. Later there may be a desperate last stand, but not yet."

"A stand I will make, but it shall not be my last." With a dark smile, Xain reached into his coat, and from an inner pocket produced a single black crystal.

Vivien sucked in a sharp breath and drew back. The other Mystics drew their swords. Jordel stared, dumbfounded.

Xain swallowed the magestone whole. His eyes glowed black. A corona of light shone around him as he raised a hand into the air. Its digits twisted and bent in ways Loren thought no human fingers should. Then he spoke dark and terrible words, loud and clear. Loren heard in his voice the power she had heard on the river in Wellmont, but ten times greater. It struck her in the chest like a hammer blow, and she gasped with the force of it. Gem cried out and gripped Loren's waist while Annis covered her ears. The Mystics recoiled at Xain's words, even Jordel.

Bolts of black fire exploded from the sky, raining down to soak the sellswords in flame.

"No," whispered Loren.

Xain struck again and again, and each time a fresh wave of horsemen caught alight. The darkfire wrapped around them, catching in their clothes, in their hair, on their skin. Men and women screamed. Their horses pitched to the ground. Some found their feet, beating at their own bodies in agony, only to be struck by the riders behind. But when they hit, the flame caught in the horses' coats. They veered left and right, and soon the flame had spread throughout the ranks. Whatever it touched caught instantly, and soon the road had become a river of fire, darker than midnight and hot as the sun.

"Stop, Xain!" cried Loren. Her voice broke, and she found there were tears in her eyes.

But Xain kept on, his cries of power growing ever louder as he sent wave upon wave of the black flames surging through the ranks. All thought of attack had gone from the cavalry; those the flames had not yet reached tried to turn and flee. But their efforts only made it worse, for they jostled and crashed into each other, and with every touch the flames continued to spread.

Darkfire rose higher and higher until Loren could feel its heat even where she stood. Then the last dying cries faded away, and the road was empty—empty, save for the mounds of blackened bodies that lay along it, human and horse both. They were dead, all of them, hundreds of them, dead, and Loren could find no words for the anguish in her soul.

"Abomination!" cried Vivien. She leapt from her horse, and her eyes glowed with magic as she raised her hands. "An eater of the black crystal. I might have known, for you defeated me too easily in our battle upon the river."

The other Mystics dismounted behind her and formed a line on either side, their blades at the ready.

Jordel, too, left his horse, but he stood apart from the others, in between Loren and Xain.

Xain laughed at Vivien, and it was a terrible sound—like some spawn of the darkness below.

"I defeated you because you are weak, and a fool besides," he said. "I could best you even without the magestones. Do not tell me you hope to win now."

"You cannot do this, Xain!" said Jordel. "You know what the crystals will do to you—what they do to you even now."

"I know dark children's stories, told to me in the Academy as a mother tells her son of wisps that lurk in the woods. But what I *feel*—that is another matter. There is greatness within me, the touch of a strength that no discipline could ever provide."

"The Mage Kings of old felt that same power," said Jordel, "and it nearly tore the nine lands asunder."

"Mayhap it should have," snarled Xain. "For then we would not suffer from the plague of redcloaks infesting us now. Tell me truly, Captain of the Mystics: were the Mage Kings outlawed because of their danger, or because they posed a threat to your precious order?"

Vivien must have thought him distracted, for in that moment she struck. Her fingers clenched, and her fist punched forwards. But if she thought to bind or strike him, she had underestimated his power. Xain swept his hand through the air, and Vivien recoiled as though slapped in the face. Then he spoke a word, held his palms outward, and sent a great wind from his fingers.

It slammed into the party. Loren's horse bucked at the impact, pitching her off. Gem and Annis fell beside her with a cry. The winds kept on, but somehow Loren could stand against them, though they threw dirt into her eyes that blinded her.

When they died at last, Vivien and Xain were locked in a mortal struggle. Vivien pushed and pulled, swiped and struck at Xain with the power of her mind, but Xain dashed aside her every attempt. One of the other Mystics tried to press the assault, but Xain batted him back with a cone of air, flinging him bodily into the hill behind. Vivien kept stepping towards him, trying to bring him within arm's reach, but Xain had learned that lesson in Wellmont. He stepped back every time she approached, and she could not reach him.

At last Vivien gave a frustrated cry, even as she kept up her barrage. "We will never stop hunting you, wizard. You will burn in a pyre for this, like the Mage Kings of old. Your name will enter the black lists in our hidden halls."

"Of course they will never stop," said Xain, calm in the face of her fury. "Once your kind find a wizard using magestones, they are relentless. It would not do to have a wizard too powerful for you to control. That would not suit the Mystics at all."

He stepped forwards and unleashed a burst of wind upon her. Vivien and all the mage hunters flew back, cast upon the ground with cries of pain. The wind swept across Loren, but once again she kept her feet as Gem and Annis were flung to the ground.

"That is why none of you can leave this place to spread the tale of me," said Xain.

"No, Xain!" cried Jordel. He had fallen near Loren, and now he scrambled to his feet. But Xain ignored him as he stretched forth his hand and unleashed a burst of white-hot flames. It swept forwards across the Mystics, consuming them. Loren cast her gaze away to avoid the sight and protect herself from the blinding glow. She cast her cloak across Gem and Annis beside her, for she feared the heat might sear their flesh.

When at last the flames had faded, Loren forced herself to look. Only blackened and twisted shapes lay on the ground where Vivien and the other Mystics had lain. Their horses, too, had burned in the fire, save one or two that had run in terror down the road.

But Jordel had escaped. The blast must have thrown him clear, for he lay on his back not far away. Much of his cloak had been burned away and hung in tatters, and he moaned with his eyes closed. She saw a deep burn across one cheek.

Xain approached the Mystic, eyes glowing black and brows drawn together in anger. No part of Loren wanted to move, but somehow she found the strength.

She jumped up and in front of the wizard, and from her belt she drew the dagger, thrusting it towards him.

The wizard stopped a few paces away and smiled at her. "Brave little thief." His deep and unnatural voice echoed in her breast. "Brought to bay saving the life of your master, who loves you no more than any of the other sad wretches he has led to death."

"Their doom does not lie on his head," cried Loren. "You alone brought it upon them. I am a fool to ever have trusted you, and I will regret it until my life's final breath. I spared you when it would have been easier to slit your throat, and a dozen times I helped you because somehow I deemed you worthy of the effort. And look what you have wrought. Now hundreds have died by your hand, when I could have let you starve on the King's road the day we met."

"Indeed, you have been foolish," said Xain. "But it seems at last you see the truth of things. This is a world of fire and swords, and sometimes a hard choice must be made."

"A hard choice?" said Loren, pointing at the blackened bodies scattered around them. "What choice did you give them?"

"I told them to leave," said Xain, growing angry. "I told you all to leave, and yet you were too foolish. I am done with idiocy. Now step aside, for it is time I ended this chase."

"No!" Loren screamed, and she stepped towards him with the dagger. "Not now, and not ever again.

You speak the truth: I have been a fool when it comes to you, but no more. I will end you if I have to, Xain, but you will not harm Jordel."

She thought to at least give the wizard pause, but she was disappointed, for he merely laughed loud and long. His eyes glowed a bottomless shade of black, and he muttered a word as he swiped his hand through the air. Loren braced herself for the impact.

Nothing happened.

Xain's face twisted in confusion, and Loren was as shocked as he. But she gave him no time to think, leaping forwards and tackling him to the ground. He twisted beneath her, but he had no skill for fighting. She wrapped an arm around his neck and rolled until he lay on his back atop her. Her hand flashed around, and the dagger came down, its tip pressed against his throat.

"Stop, Xain!" she cried. "It is over!"

But Xain would not listen, and he began to thrash in her arms. She had to lift the dagger for fear that he would press his own flesh into it with his wild twisting. Flame leapt into his hand and screamed towards her face, but it turned aside at the last moment to burst on the ground. He formed ice from the air and rained its razor shards upon her, but they melted the moment they touched her skin.

Loren did not understand it, but she had no time to wonder at the wizard's impotence. His struggles grew ever more frantic, and she felt her grip slipping. Again and again she implored him to stop, but he would not listen. He snarled at her, the sound like a wild animal.

She had no other choice. He would break free and kill her, or turn his magic on Annis and Gem, or Jordel. She had to end it. She raised her hand. The dagger flashed in the sunlight, the black designs on its blade reminding her of the midnight in Xain's eyes.

But she could not plunge it into his neck. Though half her mind willed it, the other half screamed at her to stop. Her muscles would not obey. Loren had held to only one rule since leaving the Birchwood, and she could not break it now.

Xain froze atop her and hissed between his teeth. She tightened her grip on his throat, but still he managed to mutter "The dagger."

He seized Loren's wrist, twisting it before she could react. His ferocity and her surprise made Loren drop the weapon, and it tumbled away across the grass.

Then Xain whispered, and his hands on her wrist burned with the strength of an inferno. Loren heard her own flesh sizzling, and she screamed. Her arm on his throat loosened.

Xain rolled away and quickly regained his feet. Grim and terrible he stood, looking down at Loren, the corners of his mouth twisting in a secret smile.

"The dagger," he said. "All this time—from the very day we met, you carried it with you, and yet I never suspected. But how could I? This is a magic I have not heard of."

His hand rose, and into it sprung a ball of flame. Loren could not move. Xain seemed taut as a bowstring, and any provocation might have caused him to unleash his magic.

"Still, I know it now," he went on. "And it will be one more tool in my quest. I thank you, Loren of the family Nelda, for ensuring my success. And for the last time."

His hand shot forth, flame arcing through the air towards her—but then Jordel appeared behind him. The Mystic's foot shot forth to sweep Xain's legs from beneath him, and the wizard crashed to the ground. His flame guttered out. Jordel kicked him full in the face, and Loren heard bones break. His body jerked once, and he lay still.

The air was quiet, save for the crackling of the still-burning corpses. The fight was over.

FORTY-TWO

"Is he dead?" whispered Loren.

Jordel did not answer, but then she saw Xain's chest rise beneath his coat. All the fight left her, and she fell back trembling on the grass. But the moment's peace did not last long, for Jordel strode to stand above her.

"Get up," he said, his voice like iced steel.

Loren shook at the anger in his eyes, but she forced herself to stand. He waited until she had risen before stepping close. She was reminded for a terrifying moment of her father, who had liked to place his face almost against hers so that she could look at nothing else.

"What in the sky above were you thinking?" Jordel roared loud enough to make Loren jump. "You had dealings with a wizard mad enough to use magestones? How long? How long did he use them? How long did you know of it? Tell me!"

Her knees were shaking, and she could not reply. She would not. Some part of her would not accept such harsh words from Jordel—the man who had kept from her a thousand secrets and more, who never told her anything but what he deemed her worthy to know.

Jordel did not await her reply, but instead turned and paced the grass. "Magestones. Magestones! Had I known, how much death would have been prevented? How many of our aims would have been met, and so much sooner. How much becomes clear to me now that I know."

He spun abruptly and went to Xain, who still lay senseless on the ground. For a moment Loren feared he meant to kill the wizard, but instead he stooped and withdrew the brown cloth packet from Xain's coat. He hurled it down so that the black stones scattered across the grass, and then he raised his heel.

"No!" cried Loren, but too late. Jordel stamped and stamped, until the stones were crushed into a fine black powder that scattered in the wind. Loren cried out in pain, for it felt like all her hopes were blowing away.

"What madness made you help him when he fled the city?" cried Jordel. "What madness made you pursue him out here, alone and unaided? Did you not know he was a wizard? Did you not know your own peril? And all these lives . . . I might have saved them. I might . . ."

His shoulders slumped suddenly, and the spark died in his eyes. Spent, he fell to his knees beside Xain. His head drooped. Mayhap he wept; Loren was not sure she wanted to know.

Still mute, she went for the horses. Only two had remained—Jordel's fine mount, and her own black mare. In Jordel's saddlebags she found some thin strips of white cloth. These she brought to Xain. First she tied a few around his mouth, knotting them tightly at the back of his head. Then she trussed up his feet, and his hands behind his back. Finally, she tied both knots together with a single cord so that he could not move his limbs. When she was done, Xain was trussed up like a hog.

Loren went to Gem and Annis, who still sat huddled off to the side. She knelt and looked them over. Neither seemed harmed, save for some slight singeing.

"Are you all right?" said Loren.

"What kind of question is that?" said Annis in a small voice. "Look at what has happened."

Loren had no answer, and she turned away for fear that her voice would fail her. She went back to Jordel and Xain—the Mystic and the wizard, both defeated in their own way.

Jordel rose, and Loren saw that his fury had left him. He studied her with sad eyes, and then inspected Xain. He tugged on the knots, and he must have found them to his liking, for he did not adjust them.

"I am sorry for my wrath," said Jordel quietly. "I know you had no reason to tell me of the magestones. I would guess that you knew little of their properties, but knew they were outside the King's law, and so you had many reasons *not* to tell me of them."

"That is near enough to the truth, yes," said Loren. "If I could go back, knowing what I do, I should have told you from the first—or cast them into the river as soon as I was able."

He went to his horse. Loren had left one of his saddlebags open. Idly he buttoned it shut, focusing on the motion of his fingers. Then he turned back to her, his piercing blue eyes meeting hers of deep green.

"Loren, you have proven yourself to be a woman of great resourcefulness and cunning. Those are admirable qualities, especially when joined to a kind heart and a sense of justice."

"I fear that if anything, my heart is too kind," said Loren. "I fear I must harden it if I am to have any chance at surviving this life."

"Let it remain as it is," said Jordel. "For none survive life, and a heart that is too kind may balance out those which are too evil. Do not fear mercy and compassion—fear only ignorance. It was ignorance that led you down this road of folly, not any fault in your character. You have the ability to do tremendous good—but when you leap without knowing, or strike without wisdom, you may yet be led to do evil."

"I aim to know all that I can. And if you mean what you say, then tell me. What is the dark knowledge you shared with Xain? Give me your counsel, that I may better prepare myself to weather the coming storm."

"Alas, I must prove myself false," said Jordel. "For I shared that counsel once already, to one I hoped I could trust. It proved a mistake, and one I do not intend to repeat. A great evil has awoken—but it does not know that I know of it. If our enemies were aware that I am preparing to fight them, they could undo all my efforts."

"I would never tell the secret."

"I believe that you believe that," said Jordel sadly. "Yet I have seen many terrible things. Tight lips can always be pried open by evil means, and I would not wish such a fate upon you. The truth is a burden, and I must bear it alone—for now."

He turned and leaned his forehead against the saddle for a moment, and suddenly he seemed a much smaller man. She wondered at his age, as she had before. Though his hair was so silvered as to be almost white, his face was yet free of wrinkles. His eyes shone with deep wisdom and yet with a youthful energy. So little she knew about this man, and yet so deeply her heart yearned to follow him.

The time had come for a decision, and Loren made it. She went to Jordel, and touching his shoulder she drew his eyes to hers.

"I made my choice in Wellmont. When we fought to save the city from burning. I will help you, Jordel of the family Adair. If you mean to prevent a war, a war like the one we fought in Wellmont, and which was fought here today, then I will aid you. In your service, I pledge to do whatever you ask of me—except take a life. Today I thought I might cross that bridge at last, in defense of myself and my friends. Even for that, I could not. But ask any other deed of me, and I will serve you if I can."

"You make that pledge too freely," said Jordel, "and caution is a skill you must learn. You do not know me so well, and I might ask anything of you."

"Yet I make the pledge regardless," said Loren. "It does not take me long to get the measure of a man, and I am not wrong. At least, not often." She turned her gaze sadly to Xain.

"Then I accept your service, Loren of the family Nelda," said Jordel, and he thrust his hand forwards for hers. They clasped wrists and shook.

"Excuse me," said Gem. The boy stood with eyebrows raised. "All of this grand talk is grand enough—but I feel the need to mention that another army of sellswords still marches towards us."

"You are correct, master pickpocket," said Jordel. "Though I think they will not reach this place for hours yet."

"Still, haste would serve us," said Loren. "Let us gather our things. Now that none know where we are, or our course, we can hide in the wilds until the sellswords have passed."

"That seems best," agreed Jordel. "Yet I would not say that none know of our presence, nor where we mean to go."

Loren looked at him, surprised. "What do you mean?"

"Xain struck my Mystics with his fire," said Jordel grimly, "but when the flames cleared, there were only five bodies."

"You mean that one of them escaped?" said Loren. "How?"

"My guess is that Vivien leapt on her horse in the midst of the flames," said Jordel. "Though they would have burned her terribly, her magic might yet have saved her. One of the horses that fled had a blackened figure atop it. She might live."

"That is good, I suppose," said Loren, though she was unsure she meant it.

"Not for me, I fear," said Jordel. "My actions today will not sit well with many of my masters in the order. But no matter. We must be off. Gather yourselves and your possessions."

Loren had precious few possessions left, and most of them had been carried off on the backs of the panicking horses. But she had her dagger. She went to where it lay on the grass and picked it up. But before she slid it into its sheath, she looked at it for a moment in wonder.

"When Xain struck at me with his magic, his spells turned aside. And then he said something when we struggled—something about my dagger."

Jordel looked at her carefully. "I suppose he guessed at the truth. Weapons of that kind are powerful wards, and any mage would find it hard to strike while you bear it."

"That is a wondrous enchantment," said Loren.

"It is, and one that is lost in the long years of history. The last of those weapons was crafted a long time ago. Many hundreds of years . . ." His voice trailed off, and he looked thoughtful about something.

"Can it do anything else?" said Gem eagerly, looking at Loren's dagger with renewed interest.

"It can cut tethers, or spear a bite of meat to eat," said Loren. She slid the blade into its sheath. "And that is all I require, for now."

"A magic dagger," said Gem. "The legend of the Nightblade grows."

"And will grow further still," said Jordel, roused from his musings. "But come. If any tales are to be told of this day, we must first live to recount them."

Jordel went to Xain and grabbed the wizard by his bonds, dragging him towards the horse.

"What are you doing?" said Annis, aghast. "Surely you do not mean to bring the wizard with us?"

"I do," said Jordel grimly. "Despite all, I still need him."

"But how can you think to let him live?" said Annis. "He has had too many chances to prove himself, and he has failed at every turn. How could you—how could *any* of us trust him ever again, even with the slightest task? Removing his bonds could get us all killed. What good will he be to you in your war, trussed up like a gamebird?"

"I will not trust him, nor should any of you," said Jordel. "Not for a long while yet, at least. But his doings today were not of his own mind—indeed, he has not been himself for a while. Magestones have a terrible and insidious effect upon the mind, and are poison to the flesh. Xain has clearly suffered from their influence, but now he will have to free himself. It will be a torturous affair. I do not envy him. But he will live. I am an outlaw now, at least as far as my order is concerned—but that is just as well, for in the coming months, Xain will need my aid more."

With Loren's help, he hauled Xain onto his horse and secured the wizard to the saddle's straps. The steed would be laden enough with two grown men, so Gem joined Annis and Loren on the black mare. The horse danced beneath them once they were up, but Loren found herself shifting easily with its movements.

"This is a beautiful beast," said Gem in wonder. "Stole it from the sellswords, did you? You made a fine choice."

"I think so," said Loren, reaching forwards to scratch the horse's ears. "Her name is Midnight."

She kicked her heels into Midnight's side, and Jordel did the same with his own steed. The horses climbed the steep northern hills and slid down the other side, striking out into the wide plains south of the Greatrocks. Into the wilderness they rode, while behind them an army of mercenaries continued its march on Wellmont.

Loren looked at Jordel, whose eyes were intent on the land before them. She knew that days of great danger lay ahead for all the nine kingdoms. But for the first time in longer than she could recall, Loren found that she felt safe, and her eyes joined Jordel's in looking ahead.

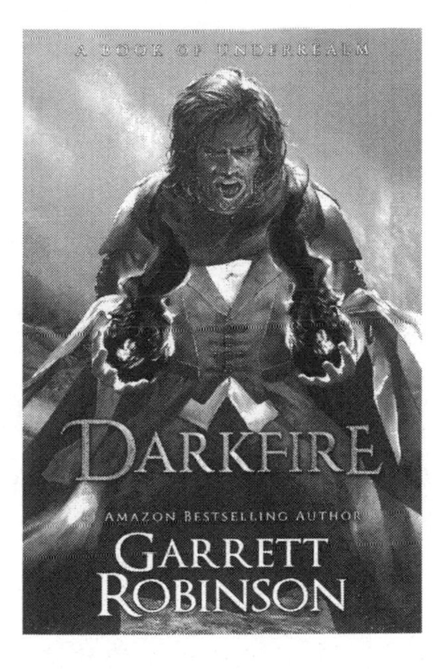

GET THE NEXT BOOK

You've finished *Mystic*, the second book in the Nightblade Epic.

Your next book is *Darkfire*. Get it here:

Underrealm.net/Darkfire

CONNECT ONLINE

FACEBOOK

Want to hang out with other fans of the Underrealm books? There's a Facebook group where you can do just that. Join the Nine Lands group on Facebook and share your favorite moments and fan theories from the books. I also post regular behind-the-scenes content, including information about the world you can't find anywhere else. Visit the link to be taken to the Facebook group:

Underrealm.net/nine-lands

YOUTUBE

Catch up with me daily (when I'm not directing a film or having a baby). You can watch my daily YouTube channel where I talk about art, science, life, my books, and the world.
But not cats.
Never cats.

GarrettBRobinson.com/yt

THE BOOKS OF UNDERREALM

THE NIGHTBLADE EPIC

NIGHTBLADE

MYSTIC

DARKFIRE

SHADEBORN

WEREMAGE

YERRIN

THE ACADEMY JOURNALS

THE ALCHEMIST'S TOUCH

THE MINDMAGE'S WRATH

THE FIREMAGE'S VENGEANCE

CHRONOLOGICAL ORDER

NIGHTBLADE

MYSTIC

DARKFIRE

SHADEBORN

THE ALCHEMIST'S TOUCH

WEREMAGE

THE MINDMAGE'S WRATH

THE FIREMAGE'S VENGEANCE

YERRIN

ABOUT THE AUTHOR

Garrett Robinson was born and raised in Los Angeles. The son of an author/painter father and a violinist/singer mother, no one was surprised when he grew up to be an artist.

After blooding himself in the independent film industry, he self-published his first book in 2012 and swiftly followed it with a stream of others, publishing more than two million words by 2014. Within months he topped numerous Amazon bestseller lists. Now he spends his time writing books and directing films.

A passionate fantasy author, his most popular books are the novels of Underrealm, including The Nightblade Epic and The Academy Journals series.

However, he has delved into many other genres. Some works are for adult audiences only, such as *Non Zombie* and *Hit Girls,* but he has also published popular books for younger readers, including The Realm Keepers series and *The Ninjabread Man*, co-authored with Z.C. Bolger.

Garrett lives in Oregon with his wife Meghan, his children Dawn, Luke, and Desmond, and his dog Chewbacca.

Garrett can be found on:

BLOG: garrettbrobinson.com/blog
EMAIL: garrett@garrettbrobinson.com
TWITTER: twitter.com/garrettauthor
FACEBOOK: facebook.com/garrettbrobinson